Delores Fossen, a *USA TODAY* bestselling author, has written over 100 novels, with millions of copies of her books in print worldwide. She's received a Booksellers' Best Award and an RT Reviewers' Choice Best Book Award. She was also a finalist for a prestigious RITA® Award. You can contact the author through her website at deloresfossen.com

Cindi Myers is the author of more than fifty novels. When she's not plotting new romance story lines, she enjoys skiing, gardening, cooking, crafting and daydreaming. A lover of small-town life, she lives with her husband and two spoiled dogs in the Colorado mountains.

Also by Delores Fossen

Her Child to Protect
Safeguarding the Surrogate
Targeting the Deputy
Pursued by the Sheriff
Safety Breach
A Threat to His Family
Settling an Old Score
His Brand of Justice
Cowboy Above the Law
Finger on the Trigger

Also by Cindi Myers

Disappearance at Dakota Ridge
Conspiracy in the Rockies
Missing at Full Moon Mine
Grizzly Creek Standoff
Investigation in Black Canyon
Mountain of Evidence
Mountain Investigation
Presumed Deadly
Ice Cold Killer
Snowbound Suspicion

Discover more at millsandboon.co.uk

SHERIFF IN THE SADDLE

DELORES FOSSEN

ALPHA TRACKER

CINDI MYERS

MILLS & BOON

First Published in Great Britain 2022
by Mills & Boon, an imprint of HarperCollins*Publishers* Ltd
1 London Bridge Street, London, SE1 9GF

www.harpercollins.co.uk

HarperCollins*Publishers*
1st Floor, Watermarque Building,
Ringsend Road, Dublin 4, Ireland

Sheriff in the Saddle © 2022 Delores Fossen
Alpha Tracker © 2022 Harlequin Enterprises ULC

Special thanks and acknowledgement are given to Cindi Myers
for her contribution to the *K-9s on Patrol* series.

ISBN: 978-0-263-30345-2

0622

MIX
Paper from
responsible sources
FSC www.fsc.org FSC™ C007454

This book is produced from independently certified FSC™
paper to ensure responsible forest management.

For more information visit: www.harpercollins.co.uk/green

Printed and Bound in Spain using 100% Renewable electricity at
CPI Black Print, Barcelona

SHERIFF IN
THE SADDLE

DELORES FOSSEN

Chapter One

There's been a murder at the Triple R Ranch.

Sheriff Leigh Mercer figured those were words no cop wanted to hear, but the dispatcher had been dead certain that was what the 911 caller had said.

Since the Triple R Ranch was in the jurisdiction of the Dark River Police Department, it was Leigh's job to check it out. But she hoped like the devil that the caller had been wrong. There hadn't been a murder in her hometown of Dark River, Texas, in nearly a decade, and for reasons other than just the obvious, Leigh wanted to keep it that way.

"You think we should call in Jeb on this?" Deputy Rocky Callaway asked her.

There was an edge to his voice, and leaning forward in the passenger's seat of the cruiser, Rocky was drumming his fingers on his holstered sidearm. The deputy was showing some nerves, and that was the only reason Leigh didn't scald him with a glance for asking that question.

Still, the question set her teeth on edge.

Jeb Mercer was her father, and before Leigh had pinned on the sheriff's badge eighteen months ago, Jeb had held that particular title for over four decades. He'd trained her. Trained Rocky, too. And even though Leigh had been duly elected after her dad's retirement, there were plenty, including Rocky, who'd always think of Jeb as the "real" sheriff.

"No, we're not bringing in Jeb," she insisted.

It was two in the morning, and she didn't need him to hold her hand at a possible crime scene. She'd already gotten Rocky out of bed since he was the deputy on call, and right now he was the only backup she intended to have.

She stepped from the cruiser, the winter wind howling and swiping at her. Mercy, it was cold, a bone-deep kind of wet cold that poked like icy fingers through her buckskin coat and boots. Leigh suspected in less than an hour, the predicted sleet would start to come down in buckets and turn the roads into skating rinks.

The wind gusts flicked away any of the usual scents that she might have picked up from the ranch, but then again, *usual* didn't apply to the Triple R. It was sprawling with its hundreds of acres of prime pastures to accommodate the hundreds of Angus cattle and prize quarter horses raised there.

The sleek white limestone house qualified as sprawling, too. Three floors that stretched out so far that it'd take a serious wide-angle lens to get it all in one photo. Lights speared out from at least a dozen of the windows.

Leigh flipped up the collar of her coat and glanced around. She hadn't been to the Triple R in fourteen years, not since she'd come to a party here when she'd been a senior in high school. She had plenty of memories of that particular event.

Memories that she hoped wouldn't get in the way if something bad had truly gone on here tonight.

Giving his own thick coat an adjustment, Rocky clamped his hand on his gun as they walked up the steps, and Leigh rang the doorbell. She automatically checked around for any signs that something was off. Nothing. And only a couple of seconds ticked by before the large double doors opened. Leigh instantly recognized the silver-haired woman who answered.

Rosa Tyree.

That was one of the advantages of living in a small town. Leigh knew most folks, and in this case, she knew that Rosa was a housekeeper at the ranch. A longtime one, having worked there for longer than Leigh had been alive. She was also well aware that Rosa didn't usually look this frazzled.

"He won't let me in the room," Rosa volunteered right away. "He said I should wait down here for you." Shivering from the cold, she frantically motioned for them to come in, and when they did, she shut the doors.

"He?" Leigh questioned though she was pretty sure she already knew what Rosa's answer would be.

"Mr. Brodie," Rosa provided, and then she added, "Mr. *Cullen* Brodie."

Yep, Leigh had been right. Cullen Brodie was the owner of the Triple R, but his brother, Nick, and their father, Bowen, visited often. Leigh had been hoping for Nick or Bowen since Cullen was a huge part of those memories that she hoped wouldn't get in the way.

"You made the 911 call?" Leigh asked the woman while she had a look around the foyer and the adjoining rooms.

Rosa nodded, followed her gaze. "The cleaning crew won't be in until morning to clear up from the party."

There was indeed some various glassware scattered on the tables in what Leigh supposed was called a great room. A room that lived up to the sprawling and plush standards of the rest of the ranch. There were also gleaming silver trays with remains of what had no doubt been tasty food. What was missing were guests, but maybe those who'd been invited to the engagement party had headed out so they could get home before the bad weather moved in.

"The, uh, body's at the back of the house," Rosa explained, fluttering her trembling fingers in that direction. "It's the big room at the end of the hall. Mr. Brodie's in there, too."

Leigh did a quick trip down memory lane and silently groaned. That was Cullen Brodie's bedroom. Or at least it had been years ago.

"Someone really got murdered here?" Rocky asked Rosa. "Who?"

"I don't know who. But that's what Mr. Brodie said, that there'd been a murder, and he told me to call 911. I didn't see the body for myself though. Please don't make me go in there," the woman quickly added. "I don't want to see a dead body."

Leigh gave her a reassuring pat on the arm. She could easily agree to Rosa's request because if this was indeed a murder, Leigh didn't want the woman anywhere on the scene.

With Rocky at her heels, Leigh made her way down the hall to the *big room*. And yep, it was big all right. The doors to the massive bedroom suite were open, and even though it'd been redecorated in the years since she'd been here, it lived up to the size in her memory.

She didn't see anything remotely resembling a dead

body, but there was a live one all right. Leigh immediately spotted Cullen.

And she felt the punch of lust.

There was no other word for it. Pure, hot lust. Of course, Cullen had that effect on plenty of women, what with his rock-star face. Not a used up, has-been rock star, either, but one in his prime who could attract just by breathing. Sizzling blue eyes, midnight-black hair and a face that, well, created those punches of pure, hot lust.

He was seated in a dark red leather chair, a glass of amber liquid in his hand. The top buttons of his rumpled white shirt were undone, and his tie was tossed on the glossy mahogany table in front of him.

His gaze slid over her, settling for a long moment on the badge she had clipped to her belt. "Sheriff," he said, and there wasn't a trace of the smirk or disapproval that some folks doled out when they mentioned her title.

"Mr. Brodie," Leigh greeted in return, and it earned her a raised eyebrow from him. Probably because the only other time she'd been in this room, they'd definitely been on a first-name basis.

Since Leigh didn't want to remember that right now or think about the lust, she got down to business. "You had Rosa call 911 to report a body?"

Cullen nodded, his gesture slow and easy. The same as his movements when he got to his feet. He definitely wasn't dressed like a rancher tonight in his black pants that had no doubt been tailored for that perfect fit.

When he got closer to her, she caught his scent. And she mentally sighed. He smelled expensive.

Leigh followed Cullen to the adjoining bath, but he didn't go in. He stepped to the side to give her a clear view of the stark white room. A view that gave Leigh a gut-jab of reactions and emotions.

Sweet merciful heaven. There was blood. And lots of it. It was spattered on the tub, the walls. Even the mirror.

There was also a body.

The woman was sprawled out on the glossy white marble floor. She was a brunette with her arms and legs flailed out as if she'd tried to break her fall and then crawl away from her attacker. Maybe she'd managed to do that, but if so, she hadn't gotten far, and it hadn't helped save her. Nothing probably could have done that, considering the back of her head had been bashed in.

"Blunt force trauma," Leigh muttered, hoping if she focused on the scene and not the body that her stomach would stop churning.

She didn't normally have this kind of reaction to blood. Or a crime scene. But then, she'd never person-ally seen one this bad. During her time at the Lubbock Police Academy, she'd stayed on the fringes of mur-der investigations. An observer there to learn. Well, she wasn't an observer tonight. She was right in the thick of it.

Leigh continued to look around. Continued to study what was right in front of her. There was no weapon that she could see, and there wasn't any blood on the sharp corners of the counters to indicate that's how the woman had been fatally injured.

"Uh, you want me to call Jeb?" Rocky asked, and the shakiness in his voice had gone up some signifi-cant notches.

"No." This time Leigh didn't manage to tamp down her glare when she glanced back at him.

Along with the shakiness, Rocky looked ready to

boot. She was pretty sure this was his first murder scene, too.

"Go ahead and call the medical examiner and the county CSI team," Leigh instructed. "We also need some deputies to do a room-to-room search and check the grounds. When you're done with that, take Rosa's statement. And the statements of anybody else who's in the house."

"No one else is here," Cullen provided. *Calmly* provided.

If she hadn't looked at Cullen, she might not have noticed the tight muscles in his jaw or the fierce set of his mouth. But she did look. Did notice. And she saw this had given him a gut-punch, too.

"But Jeb oughta be brought in on this," Rocky protested.

This time, Leigh didn't bother with words. She gave her deputy a look that could have frozen El Paso in August, and it was thankfully enough to get Rocky moving.

"I didn't kill her," Cullen said, those jaw muscles stirring again. "I found her when I came to my room after the party."

He didn't have to explain what party he was talking about. Small-town gossips had clued in everyone who'd listen or overhear about that. Cullen had hosted an engagement celebration for his friend Austin Borden and Austin's fiancée, Kali Starling.

According to the bits Leigh had heard, there'd been about a hundred guests, most from Lubbock, about a half hour away. Since Austin lived in Lubbock and it was where Cullen had his main office, that didn't surprise her. It was also no surprise that only a couple of locals had received invitations. Cullen hadn't exactly kept close ties with many in his hometown.

Including her.

Leigh gave Cullen another once-over, and this time she made sure the lust stayed out of it. "You wore those clothes to the party?"

Cullen nodded. "I didn't kill her," he repeated.

She believed him. Whoever had done this would have had blood spatter on him or her, and Leigh didn't see so much as a speck on Cullen. Of course, a smart killer would have changed his clothes before calling in the cops, but Leigh didn't think that was what happened here.

"It's Alexa," Cullen added when Leigh was about to go inside the bathroom.

That sent Leigh whirling back around to face him. "Alexa Daly?" she asked on a rise of breath.

Cullen nodded and had another gulp of his drink while he kept his eyes on the body.

Leigh swallowed hard. This just got a whole lot stickier. Because Alexa was Cullen's ex-girlfriend. There'd been plenty of rumors about that, too. Leigh didn't know how much of what she'd heard about the breakup was actually true, but just about everyone agreed that it'd been a nasty one. There'd been some public arguments and rumors of a restraining order. Later, Leigh would have to suss out how much of that was gossip and how much was fact.

"Did you touch the body?" she continued, stepping inside the room. Leigh was careful to avoid any of the blood while she surveyed the area.

"Yes. I checked for a pulse on her neck. There wasn't

one, and her body was already cold so I didn't try CPR. I called out for Rosa to dial 911."

So, there could be trace evidence from Cullen. She wished he hadn't made that a possibility, but it was instinct to make a check like that. Well, instinct for some. Others would have just panicked and run.

She stooped down to get a closer look at the body. Yes, it was Alexa all right, and even death hadn't been able to completely steal her beauty. Someone, however, had definitely stolen her life. Alexa's now blank emerald green eyes stared up at her.

"How many people had access to your bathroom?" Leigh continued her examination of the body and didn't see any self-defense wounds. No blood or tissue under Alexa's perfectly manicured nails, which had been painted bloodred.

"Anyone who came to the party, and that includes any of the catering crew who set things up. Guests don't make a habit of coming back here, but it does happen every now and then."

Leigh looked back at him again to see if that was a little jab at her. After all, she had come to his room fourteen years ago during a party. She hadn't made a habit of doing that, either. In fact, it'd been her first.

Cullen had been her first.

And that was yet something else that she nudged aside.

"I'll need a guest list along with the names of any catering staff," she told him, shifting her focus back to the dead woman. "Include the names of any of your ranch hands or hired help who might have had access."

"I'll have Rosa give it to you. Alexa's name won't be

on it," he explained. "She wasn't invited, and I didn't know she was here."

Leigh wasn't surprised that Alexa hadn't been invited, but she was wearing party clothes. A clingy silk dress the color of expensive sapphires. Her wrists, neck and ears glittered with gold and diamonds, which ruled out robbery as a possible motive. Well, unless the would-be thief had panicked after she'd hit the floor.

"Alexa had a key to the place?" Leigh asked.

Cullen shook his head. "I had the locks changed after we broke up, but the house wasn't locked tonight. She could have walked in except…" He paused.

"Except?" she pressed.

"She's not wearing a coat, and I didn't see one in here or in my bedroom. Plus, there's no vehicle unaccounted for in the driveway. I checked out the windows and didn't spot one," he told her. "I also don't see a purse."

"You're observant," Leigh muttered, not at all surprised by that.

The ranch was a huge success, and from all accounts, that was because of Cullen. He might not spend much time at the house, but he still ran it, and observation skills would come in handy for that.

"Did you notice anything unusual about any of your guests?" she went on.

"Do you mean did someone come into the great room with blood dripping off them?" He cursed, shook his head and seemed to gain control of that quick snap of temper. "No. It was a party. A celebration. And we celebrated."

Cullen turned away from her, groaned. "I don't know who'd do this."

"That's why I'll investigate." She paused, steeled herself up. "But you should know that I have to consider you a possible suspect."

With the same slow movements as he'd had before, Cullen eased back toward her. The breath he dragged in was long and weary. "Leigh," he said.

Just that. Only her name. But he'd made it sound like so much more. There was a plea in his tone, maybe a plea for her to believe he was innocent. And heaven help her, she did. It wasn't just the lack of blood on his clothes.

Or their very brief history together.

It was the whole package, even if that "package" was the assessment she'd been able to make so far. If Alexa and he had argued, if they'd had a fight that'd gotten out of hand, she didn't believe Cullen would have struck the woman from behind. Nor would he have removed the murder weapon only then to leave the body in place. This very well could be a crime of passion, but she didn't feel it in her gut that Cullen was responsible. Of course, she doubted anyone else was going to put much stock in her gut feeling.

Cullen scrubbed his hand over his face. "Will what happened between us get in the way here?"

Since she'd asked herself the same thing, Leigh didn't blister him with a look or insist that nothing would get in the way of her doing her job. She couldn't. Because, yes, their past might get in the way. It wasn't like she could go back and erase memories of her first lover. Or the tangled mess that followed.

Despite her attempts to stop them, some of those memories came now. Not a gentle blur of images but crystal clear ones of Cullen's naked body. He'd been a lot younger when they'd had sex. Just nineteen. But like the rest of him, his body had been memorable even then.

"Our past won't get in the way," she answered, hoping to reassure him, and herself, that it was true. Maybe if she said it enough, both of them would start to believe it.

Stepping around Cullen, Leigh went back into the bedroom and had another look around. No blood or signs of a struggle. It was the same for the sitting area and the adjoining office. Still, the CSIs might be able to find something.

"The bedroom door was open when you came up after the party ended?" she asked.

"Closed." Cullen moved to stand beside her and followed her gaze as it skirted around the room. "Something's missing," he said.

That got Leigh's attention. "What?"

He was already moving to the sitting area, specifically to a corner table next to a leather love seat. "A bronze horse statue. It's a replica of Lobo," he added in a murmur.

The name instantly rang a bell. In the short time that she'd been involved with Cullen, his favorite horse had been named Lobo. He had won plenty of competitions, and Leigh had heard through the grapevine that Cullen had been upset when Lobo died.

"How big was the statue?" she asked.

"About a foot high, and it was heavy." He looked back at her then, and she didn't have to ask what he was thinking. Someone had grabbed it and then used it to murder Alexa.

Leigh turned when she heard the hurried footsteps coming from the hall, and several moments later, an out-of-breath Rocky came rushing into the room. He didn't have much color in his face, and he'd drawn his weapon.

"What's wrong?" Leigh immediately asked.

Rocky's chest was heaving, and it took him a moment to speak. "On one of the side porches," he finally managed to say. "There's been another murder."

Chapter Two

Hell.

That was Cullen's first reaction, but he tamped down the string of profanity going through his head and raced up the hall with Leigh. Rocky led the way, threading them through the great room and toward the west side of the house to one of the guest suites.

Cullen saw Rosa huddled in the corner of the room. The woman had obviously followed Rocky, and her breath was gusting out, causing little white wisps of fog in the freezing room. Freezing because the glass doors leading to a patio were wide-open.

"Out there," Rocky said, pointing to the patio. The deputy didn't go closer but instead stepped to the side to make way for Leigh and Cullen. "The doors were open when I came in here so I looked out and saw him."

Leigh went straight outside, her gaze firing around the side yard before settling on the man who was in a crumpled heap on the mosaic tiles. Like with Alexa's body, there was blood. Unlike Alexa, this guy was wearing a thick coat.

"It's Jamie Wylie," Cullen blurted out the moment he got a good look at the man's face. "He's one of my ranch hands."

Cullen didn't stay put. He hurried out to Jamie even though he figured there was nothing he could do, that the man was already dead.

But Cullen soon learned he was wrong.

Jamie groaned, a weak sound of raw pain, and he moved his head from side to side.

"Call for an ambulance," Leigh shouted, taking the words right out of Cullen's mouth.

Behind them, he heard Rocky make that call, and Cullen dragged the comforter off the bed. With all the blood Jamie had already lost, it was a miracle that he was still alive, but he wouldn't stay that way if he froze.

Leigh caught onto the side of the comforter and helped Cullen cover the man. "I don't want to move him," she explained. Then she threw Rocky a quick glance over her shoulder. "Tell the EMTs to hurry."

Cullen understood the urgency. There was no way to know just how serious Jamie's injuries were, and moving him inside could end up killing him. Of course, a killer could do that, too, and that's why Cullen glanced around to make sure they weren't about to be ambushed.

Beside him, Leigh was doing the same thing.

Unfortunately, this particular part of the yard had a lot of shrubs and trees that stayed thick even in the winter. It'd been landscaped that way to create a little garden oasis for guests. Which meant there were plenty of places and shadows where someone could hide. There were no views of the front or back yards, but Cullen knew there were flagstone stepping-stones that led in both directions. Alexa's killer could have gone in either direction.

Or neither.

Whoever was responsible for Jamie and Alexa could still be on the grounds. Definitely not a settling thought.

"Rosa, find one of the portable heaters and bring it out here," Cullen told the woman.

It would maybe pull her out of the shock along with helping to keep Jamie warm until the EMTs arrived, and Cullen knew there were several of the heaters in the storage room just off the kitchen. They used them for taking the chill off the patio and porches during late-night parties.

Cullen went back into the bedroom and grabbed the spare quilt and pillows from a cedar chest at the foot of the bed, and he brought those out to Jamie, too.

"It's blunt force trauma," Cullen said, looking down at the wound. Except this wasn't to the back of the head like Alexa but rather to the man's left temple. Along with the blood, there was already a huge, ugly bruise forming on his face.

Leigh nodded. She didn't touch Jamie but did lean in so that her face was right over his. "Can you hear me, Jamie? Can you tell me who did this to you?"

Jamie managed a hoarse moan. Nothing more. His eyes stayed shut, but Cullen prayed the man would be able to answer that question soon.

"Are these patio doors usually locked?" Leigh asked, aiming that question at Cullen.

"Usually, but I had a cleaning crew in the house earlier, and they could have left them unlocked."

He'd barely gotten out that answer when Leigh fired off another question. "Any idea what Jamie would have been doing out here?"

Cullen had to shake his head. "He wasn't on duty." But then he paused. "He knew Alexa."

"Knew?" Leigh pressed, and he heard the cop's inflection of what she meant.

"Nothing sexual as far as I know," Cullen explained. "But Jamie gave her riding lessons here at the ranch."

And Cullen's mind began to play with that connection. Had Jamie brought Alexa here tonight? Cullen could see her being able to talk Jamie into doing something like that.

Maybe.

Jamie wasn't exactly a soft touch, but he was young. Barely twenty-one. And Cullen was pretty sure Jamie had been somewhat dazzled by Cullen's former girlfriend. Then again, Alexa could do lots of dazzling until you got beneath the surface and saw, well, a woman who could be obsessive and vindictive. Still, that didn't explain why Alexa was dead or why Jamie was lying there, clinging to life.

Rocky moved out onto the patio, peering down at his boss and the ranch hand. "Whoever did this musta killed the woman in the bathroom," the deputy concluded—which, of course, was stating the obvious. It was also obvious when Rocky turned an accusing gaze on Cullen.

The deputy thought he'd done this.

He doled out one of his hardest glares to Rocky, and Cullen knew for a fact that he was good at it. However, he didn't get a chance to add anything to the expression he knew would intimidate. That's because something caught Cullen's eye.

One of the small shrubs that rimmed the patio had been trampled down. He went closer, and while he didn't see any footprints, it appeared that someone had stepped on it. Maybe the someone who'd attacked Alexa and Jamie.

Leigh stood and moved closer to him, her gaze following what Cullen had spotted. "Rocky, get some photos of this with your phone. Once the EMTs arrive, they'll come rushing back here and might destroy possible evidence. Make sure you don't step on any prints."

The deputy followed her instructions just as Rosa came hurrying to the doorway. She didn't come onto the patio and didn't look at Jamie, but she did plug in the heater that she then set out on the tiles. She also handed Cullen a coat. He certainly hadn't forgotten about how cold it was, but he hadn't wanted to go inside, not with Jamie out here.

Leigh's phone rang, and because Cullen was right there next to her, he saw the name that popped up on the screen. Jeb. And he found it interesting that she hadn't listed him in her contacts as Dad but rather by his first name.

Frowning, she took the call but stepped away from Cullen. However, she continued to volley her attention between Jamie and Rocky, who was already snapping some pictures.

Cullen watched her take the cop attitude up another level and wondered if she even knew she was doing it. Probably not. It might be her go-to response when dealing with her dad. He hadn't had to hear rumors to know there was tension between Jeb and Leigh. Or at least there had been fourteen years ago when Jeb had convinced her to cut Cullen out of her life. It obviously hadn't been that hard for her to do, either, since she'd made the break and hadn't looked back.

But Cullen had.

There were times, like now, when he wondered if he should have pressed Leigh for something more. Even if that *something more* would have put even greater strain on her relationship with her father.

"Rocky shouldn't have called you," Leigh replied in response to whatever her father had just said to her. She smoothed her hand over the top of her dark brown hair that she'd pulled back into a sleek ponytail. The gesture seemed to be a way of steadying herself or maybe giving her fingers something to do other than tighten and clench. "I can handle this."

There was a long pause where Leigh was no doubt listening to Jeb's *advice*. Something that a lot of people did. Many folks still thought of Jeb Mercer as the voice of authority.

The law in Lubbock County.

It didn't matter that Jeb had been the sheriff of Dark River, a small town within the county. His lawman's reputation was legendary throughout this part of Texas.

Cullen just thought of him as a hard-nosed, bitter man who'd never gotten over his toddler son, Joe, being kidnapped twenty-seven years ago. Jeb had devoted a big chunk of his life to finding the boy, who'd now be a grown man if he was still alive. And Cullen wasn't the only one who thought that Jeb's search for his son had come at the expense of his daughter, Leigh, and his estranged son, Cash.

"I'm nowhere near ready to make an arrest," Leigh snapped a moment later, and it was definitely a snap. Judging from the quick glance she gave Cullen, he figured Jeb was already pressuring her to arrest anyone with the surname Brodie.

Hell. Old wounds and bad blood were definitely going to play into this.

"I have to go," Leigh insisted, and she hit the end call button. Cramming her phone in her pocket, she stooped back down beside Jamie and looked up at Cullen. "I'll have to bring you in for a formal interview. And not because Jeb's pressuring to do that, but because it has to be done."

Cullen stared at her, and a dozen things passed between them. Memories. Heat. The past. Yeah. The old wounds were already surfacing.

In the distance, Cullen could hear the wail of the ambulance, but he kept his attention on Leigh. "A formal interview," he repeated, following that through. "Something you'll have to do with anyone who attended the party."

She nodded. "In the meantime be thinking of who'd want Alexa dead."

At least Leigh hadn't said *Other than you, who'd want her dead?* Though Cullen was certain Jeb would be trying to put that bug in her ear. But it wasn't true. Cullen hadn't wanted his ex dead.

"Before tonight, it's been weeks since I've given Alexa a thought," Cullen admitted.

"She didn't make any threats against you?" Leigh pressed. "Or say anything about someone threatening her?"

"No," Cullen could honestly answer. She'd made threats, yes. But they'd been verbal and none were recent. Of course, that was in part because Cullen no longer took calls from her and had refused to see her.

Leigh probably would have continued to push for info if there hadn't been the sound of hurried footsteps.

She immediately rose, laying her hand on her gun. Cullen did the same to the snub-nosed .38 that he always carried in a slide holster at the back waist of his pants. But it wasn't the killer who'd come to finish off Jamie. It was two more of Leigh's deputies. Vance Pickering and Dawn Farley.

Cullen recognized both of them and had even gone to school with Vance. He didn't know Dawn as well, but one of her brothers worked on the Triple R, and he did a good job. Hardly an endorsement for his cop sister's abilities, but at least Cullen hadn't heard anything bad about her.

"We've got a DB in the master bedroom at the back of the house," Leigh explained. "Dawn, I need you to go there and secure the scene until the CSIs and ME arrive."

"Rocky told me it was Alexa Daly?" Dawn said.

Leigh spared her a confirming nod before she shifted back to Rocky. "You will not contact Jeb again about this investigation." She kept her voice low, but Cullen still heard her. He heard her warning tone, too. "Understand?"

"But—" Rocky started.

"You will not contact Jeb," Leigh interrupted. "Now, go to the front porch and direct the EMTs here." Ignoring Rocky's huff, she turned to Vance. "I need you to check the grounds. We're not sure how the DB got here so take down the license plates of any vehicle you see. Jamie lives here at the ranch?" she asked.

It took Cullen a moment to realize that tacked-on question was meant for him, and he nodded. "He lives in the bunkhouse."

Leigh shifted her attention back to Vance as Dawn

and Rocky left. "Then check there, too, and see if anyone knows what Jamie was doing on the patio."

Good question. The bunkhouse was a good quarter of a mile away from the main house, and Cullen couldn't think of a good reason why Jamie would be here in this particular spot. But he could think of a bad reason if the ranch hand had indeed helped Alexa. Help that maybe someone had objected to because Cullen doubted that Alexa had bashed Jamie on the head and then sneaked into his bedroom to have her own encounter with a killer. Then again, maybe that was exactly what'd happened.

Vance nodded at Leigh's order and stepped away, but not before giving Cullen the same kind of cop's eye that Rocky had. This time Cullen didn't even bother with a glare because his own phone rang.

Since he didn't recognize the number, Cullen started not to answer, but then he realized it could be one of the ranch hands trying to contact him. Not a hand though because it was Austin.

"It's me," Austin immediately said. "I don't have my phone so the clerk here at the gas station let me borrow his."

Normally, Cullen wouldn't have minded a call from the man he considered a close friend, but it'd been less than an hour since Austin had left the party, and Cullen wasn't in the mood for a chat.

"I figured you'd be home by now," Cullen remarked, hoping to put a quick end to this conversation.

"I was heading that way, but the roads are bad so I was going slow. I nearly ran out of gas, too, so I stopped, and I overheard the clerk talking about his girlfriend getting called out to the Triple R. He said she was a CSI."

Cullen sighed and stepped back into the bedroom to deal with this call. This was the downside to living in a small town. Gossip, especially gossip about bad news, didn't stay hush-hush for long.

"Alexa's dead," Cullen said. "And no, I didn't kill her. I don't have a clue who did."

Austin cursed. "What the hell was she doing there?"

"Don't know that, either. In fact, I don't have answers to much of anything right now." Cullen watched as the EMTs hurried toward the patio to tend to Jamie. "But we might know something soon. Did you see anyone at the party who shouldn't have been there?" Cullen asked.

Austin paused, probably giving that some thought. "No. Are you telling me that someone came into your house and killed Alexa?"

"It looks that way." Cullen dragged in a long breath. "Maybe you could ask Kali if she saw anything? Kali got here early to make sure I didn't need any help so she might have noticed something off."

Austin paused again. "Yeah, I'll call her and ask."

Cullen's forehead bunched up. "She's not with you?"

"No. After she left the party, she went back to her folks' place for the night. I think she and her mom are doing some wedding stuff first thing in the morning. But I can tell you that if Kali had seen anything off, she would have said something to me about it. She was right by my side most of the night."

That was true, but most wasn't *all.* "You stepped outside for a smoke a couple of times," Cullen reminded him. "Did you see anything then?"

"Just one smoke," Austin corrected. "And I didn't see a thing that sent up any red flags."

Cullen pushed a little harder. "Were you anywhere near the guest room patio or the patio off my bedroom?"

"No." Austin's answer was firm and fast. "Is that where you think the killer was?"

"Yeah, along with being in my bedroom. Any chance you were in the hall outside my suite at any time during the night?"

Austin cursed. "This is beginning to sound like an interrogation, but no, I didn't go anywhere near that hall. No reason for it. Ditto for staying outside very long when I went out for that smoke. It was too damn cold."

"Sorry about the interrogation," Cullen said. "But these are questions Leigh will be asking you soon enough."

"Why me?" Austin cursed again. "Does she think I'm a suspect? Because if so, she's crazy. I didn't even see Alexa tonight."

Cullen sighed. "No. You're not a suspect. But right now anyone who was at the party will no doubt be considered a potential witness." Maybe even a person of interest. But Cullen kept that last part to himself. "We just need to find out who came into my house and committed a murder."

Austin stayed quiet a couple of seconds. "And we have to stop this person from coming after anyone else. I got that," Austin said on a heavy breath. "But give me some time to think about who it could be, and I'll get back to you."

"Thanks." Cullen watched as the EMTs loaded Jamie onto a gurney. Leigh was right there, giving them instructions about keeping Jamie secure, assuring them she'd be at the hospital soon.

"That's a lot of noise for just cops," Austin remarked. "That sounds like an ambulance siren to me."

"Because it is. Someone attacked one of my ranch hands. Jamie," Cullen provided.

"Jamie?" Austin questioned. "Hell, is he dead, too?"

"No." Cullen didn't add *not yet, anyway*, because he wanted to hang on to the hope that Jamie would pull through.

"Jamie's alive?" Austin made a sound of relief. "Then, he can tell you who attacked him?"

"To be determined. I have to go. I want to be at the hospital when the doctors examine Jamie." He hoped Leigh wouldn't give him any hassles about that. Even if she did, Cullen would work his way around her.

The anger came now, shoving the shock aside and twisting his muscles into knots. Someone had come into his home and done this. Maybe had murdered and maimed to set him up. Yeah, Cullen would definitely get to the bottom of why this had happened.

"You need me there?" Austin asked, drawing Cullen's attention back to him.

"No. Bad weather's moving in, and I don't want you on the roads. But if you find out anything from Kali, let me know."

"I will," Austin assured him, "and keep me posted about Jamie. Hell, Cullen, he was just a kid."

Cullen didn't want that to eat away at him. But it did. Mercy, it did. All of this would eat away even when he found out who'd done this.

He ended the call and was about to go back on the patio with Leigh and the EMTs, who were about to move Jamie to the ambulance. But Leigh looked up, her gaze zooming past Cullen's shoulder and landing on someone behind him. Cullen turned and saw someone he definitely didn't want to deal with tonight.

His father, Bowen Brodie.

Bowen had ditched his party clothes and was wearing his usual jeans, including a rodeo buckle that gleamed out from his wide leather belt. Obviously, he'd had time to go to his house about fifteen minutes away and change before making his way back here, but then, Bowen hadn't stayed long at the party. He'd given his congrats to Austin and Kali and had then made an excuse about wanting to leave the shindig to the "young folks."

"I heard about the murder," his father said right off.

"It's the middle of the night," Cullen reminded him, and he didn't bother to take the snarl out of his tone. "Since you don't have ESP, someone must have called you."

Bowen confirmed that with a nod. "One of my assistants is dating the Dark River dispatcher. When he heard there'd been a murder at the Triple R, he called her."

Yeah, and had probably also called anyone and everyone in his contact list. Ditto for the dispatcher. This was big news.

"Normally, I would have cussed out anybody calling me at this hour, but I knew you'd have to deal with Jeb's spawn," Bowen added. "So I came straight over."

Spawn. That was a good way to start off this visit. Cullen was a thousand percent sure that Leigh felt the same way he did about not wanting to deal with his father tonight.

To say that Bowen and Leigh's father had bad blood was like saying the Pacific Ocean had a drop or two of water in it. Cullen knew it went all the way back to the kidnapping and disappearance of Jeb's son. A kidnapping and disappearance that Jeb had always thought Bowen had played a part in.

Heck, maybe he had.

Bowen might be his father, but Cullen could see the man clear enough. Along with making a game of skirting the law, Bowen could be vindictive. And that vindictiveness went back to Jeb arresting Cullen's mother for a DUI. Cullen had been five years old, barely old enough to remember, but Bowen had made an art form of keeping the incident, and what followed, alive by talking about it with anyone who'd listen. That's because Cullen's mother had died in the jail cell. Alcohol poisoning, according to the ME, but Bowen had considered it negligent homicide on Jeb's part.

And so the cycle of bad blood had begun.

A cycle fueled by Jeb's firm belief that Bowen had gotten revenge by kidnapping Jeb's little boy. Apparently, the bad blood was about to continue if his father kept using words like *spawn* and glaring at Leigh.

"You're not going to railroad my son into taking the blame for something he didn't do," Bowen snarled, and he aimed that snarl at Leigh.

Leigh looked at the EMTs, motioned for them to leave. "I'll be at the hospital in a few minutes." With that, she turned to Bowen. "I don't make a habit of railroading, and I won't be starting now."

His father made a sound of disgust. "You're a Mercer. Railroading and murder are your specialties."

Cullen groaned and stepped between them, but Leigh

obviously wasn't going to have any part of him running interference for her. She moved to Cullen's side and met his father's glare head-on.

"Someone's been murdered," Leigh stated, her voice a whole lot calmer than she probably felt. "I need to do my job."

She started to move past Bowen, but he caught onto her arm. Leigh looked at Bowen's grip, her brown cop's eyes sliding back to his father's equally flat ones.

"You'll want to let go of me," she said. Again, with a calm voice, but there was some fire in her expression.

"I will, when you hear me out. You're not going to pin a murder on my son because Cullen didn't kill anyone." Bowen's hand slid off Leigh's arm. "But I can tell you who did."

Chapter Three

Leigh had intended to walk away from Bowen and his 24-7 bad attitude, but what the man said stopped her in her tracks.

"You know who killed Alexa?" Leigh demanded, her narrowed gaze drilling into Cullen's father.

Bowen huffed, maybe because of her tone, maybe because of her glare. Then again, Bowen never had a positive reaction to her so he was often huffing and glaring around her.

"You need help, Sheriff Mercer?" Rocky asked. The deputy had obviously come back in the house and was eyeing Bowen as if he was a threat. Maybe Rocky thought she'd need some of his "manly" muscle to handle this situation.

She didn't.

"No, thanks," Leigh assured Rocky. "I was just asking Mr. Brodie a few questions."

Rocky gave Bowen a hard stare which didn't surprise Leigh. Rocky was loyal to Jeb, which meant the Brodies were the enemy. Plenty of people in Dark River felt the same way.

"It's freezing," Bowen snarled. "Let's take this inside, and I can tell you all about the kind of woman Alexa was."

Leigh didn't want to go inside. She wanted Bowen to finish with this revelation so she could get to the hospital. Besides, what he had to say might not be a revelation at all but just some ploy to throw suspicion off Cullen. Still, Leigh couldn't totally blow off something that might help with the investigation, so with the tip of her head for Bowen to follow her, she stepped through the patio doors. Rocky didn't leave, but he did step to the side so there'd be room for Bowen and Cullen.

The guest room was quiet, but it wouldn't stay that way. It'd likely be only a matter of minutes before the ME and CSIs arrived. Too bad this second crime scene had already been compromised. Rosa, Cullen and now Bowen had already been in the room. Rosa was no longer there, but, of course, Cullen was right there next to Leigh when she turned to his father.

"Make this quick," Leigh told Bowen. "I'll do a formal interview with you in the morning, but for now I want to hear about who wanted Alexa dead."

"I don't know his name," Bowen explained. "But Alexa met with him."

When he didn't add more, Leigh made a circling motion with her index finger for him to continue. That gesture earned her another huff.

"I hired a PI to follow Alexa," Bowen blurted out, his gaze shifting to Cullen. "She was threatening you, and I wanted to make sure she didn't do anything stupid."

Leigh volleyed glances at the two men, and she saw the surprise on Cullen's face, the steely resolve on Bowen's. Bowen clearly didn't think he'd done anything wrong by trying to micromanage his son's life.

"I wanted to make sure she didn't do anything stupid," Bowen repeated, the resolve also in his voice. "I didn't want Alexa to try to smear your name. Or worse. Have her try to do something violent. Hell hath no fury like a woman scorned," he added.

Leigh wasn't sure Alexa had actually been scorned, but she wanted to hear more. "I take it this PI found out something about her?"

Bowen nodded, kept his unapologetic eyes on his son. "Yesterday, Alexa had a meeting with a man in a café in Lubbock. The PI said the guy was carrying concealed, that he saw the bulge from a shoulder holster beneath his coat."

"Maybe he had a license to carry concealed," Leigh pointed out when Bowen paused again.

"Maybe," Bowen agreed. "But when the PI took a table near them, he heard Alexa and this man mention Cullen. Specifically, Alexa said she wanted the man to deal with Cullen."

"Deal with?" Leigh and Cullen repeated in unison.

"Yeah, and I don't have specific details of what she meant by that. The PI said that Alexa and this man quit talking when someone else took a table nearby, and they went outside to finish their conversation. The PI wasn't able to hear anything else they said."

Leigh looked at Cullen to see what his take on this was, but he only shook his head. "You believe Alexa was hiring this man to do something to me?" Cullen asked his father.

"Yes, I do. I think that's obvious. She wanted this guy to hurt or kill you."

Well, it wasn't obvious to Leigh. Possible, yes. But

not absolute proof of the woman's guilt. Still, Alexa was dead so this could very well be connected.

"I'll want the name of your PI," Leigh insisted.

"Thought you would." Bowen extracted a business card from his coat pocket and handed it to her.

Leigh glanced at the card only to note the PI's name, Tyson Saylor. She'd be calling him very soon.

"This should be enough for you to back off Cullen," Bowen went on. "Alexa probably had her hired goon bring her here tonight. So she could witness him killing or hurting Cullen. Then, I'm guessing something went wrong. Maybe the goon wanted more money, and when Alexa wouldn't pony up, he killed her."

Obviously, Bowen had given this some thought, but it was still just a theory. One that might not have any proof to back it up.

"I'll investigate this—" Leigh assured him.

"And you'll lay off Cullen," Bowen interrupted. "Don't you think about arresting him because of what's gone on between our families."

Leigh heard the weariness in her own sigh. "At the moment I have no plans to arrest Cullen or anyone else for that matter because there's no clear-cut evidence to point to who did this."

Bowen released the breath he appeared to have been holding, and he gave a crisp nod before turning back to Cullen. "Call me if you need anything."

So, she'd apparently appeased Bowen enough for him to get out of her face. Not Rocky though. Her deputy was aiming a questioning look at her. Probably because he believed there was indeed some *evidence to point to who did this.*

And Rocky no doubt thought the pointing should be at Cullen.

"Check with Dawn and make sure both crime scenes are secure," she instructed Rocky, not only to remind him that she was the sheriff and was therefore in charge but also because it was something that needed to be done. "I'm going to the hospital to get an update on Jamie." With some luck, she might even be able to question the ranch hand.

"I could go with you," Rocky suggested.

"I need you here," she insisted, and Leigh motioned for Cullen to follow her toward the front door. "Depending on how long I'm at the hospital or Jamie's condition, I might be able to get your statement in the next hour or two. I suspect you'll want a lawyer there for that."

Cullen had already opened his mouth, but he seemed to change his mind as to what he'd been about to say. "I'm going to the hospital, too. Jamie works for me," he added in a snap before she could protest.

She saw the weariness on his face. The worry. Not for his own situation but for Jamie. And that's why Leigh didn't tell him to stay put. Even though that would have been the smart thing to do. It'd keep Cullen out of her hair while she gathered evidence. Then again, it would keep him away from the crime scene, too. Cullen would no doubt be able to handle any flak that Rocky tried to dole out to him, but this would hopefully keep Rocky focused on his assigned duties so he wouldn't be able to take jabs at Cullen.

"You can ride in the cruiser with me," she offered, "but you'd have to find your own way back here once we're done at the hospital and my office."

Cullen didn't object to that, so Leigh reached for the

knob on the front door. However, before she could open it, Vance called out to her.

"Wait up," the deputy said, hurrying through the great room toward them. "I think I found the murder weapon." He took out his phone, showing her a picture. "I didn't touch it. Figured I'd leave it where it is for the crime scene guys to collect."

It was a bronze horse statue of Lobo.

"Where'd you find that?" Cullen demanded.

Vance waited until he got a nod from Leigh before he answered. "In some bushes on the patio off the master bedroom. I'm guessing the killer went out through the patio doors and tossed it there."

That put a knot in Leigh's stomach. Because anyone wanting to pin this on Cullen would point out that the weapon had been in Cullen's bedroom and that Cullen would be the one to most likely have access to it.

But Cullen wasn't stupid.

Only a stupid killer would have tossed the murder weapon so that it could be easily found. That meant it probably didn't have anything on it that could be linked back to who'd used it to bash in Alexa's head. Then again, maybe the killer had tossed it out of panic. Or because he or she had been in a hurry. Either way, this was going to put some pressure on her to arrest Cullen.

"If the CSIs aren't here before the sleet starts, hold an umbrella over the statue so we don't lose any prints or trace," Leigh told Vance. "Once it's been bagged and tagged, mark it priority and have a courier take it to the lab."

Vance nodded, and as Rocky had done, he gave an uneasy glance at Cullen. "You heading somewhere?"

"Cullen and I are going to the hospital."

Vance's uneasiness seemed to go up a notch. "You okay with that?"

She heard the deputy's underlying concern. That maybe she was about to get in the cruiser with a killer. It didn't sting as much coming from Vance as it had with Rocky. That's because Vance didn't have the fierce loyalty to Jeb that Rocky did. Or the equally fierce hatred of the Brodies.

"I'm okay," she assured Vance. "Call me if you find anything else. I need to know how Alexa got here tonight. And don't forget to question the other ranch hands in the bunkhouse about Jamie. We need to find out how he ended up on the patio. Rocky can help you with that."

Leigh stepped outside and could have sworn the temp had dropped even more. Worse, she heard the first pings of ice start to hit against the porch. She hoped that Vance would get the statue protected in time and considered going back in to make sure that happened. But her best bet at getting to the truth wasn't a statue that had likely been planted to frame Cullen. Her best bet was to question Jamie.

"Before you say anything," Leigh told Cullen as they headed down the steps. "I'm going to Mirandize you."

Cullen didn't curse, but the look he shot her was colder than the sleet needling against her face.

"It's necessary," she explained. "And no, it doesn't mean I've changed my mind about your guilt. It's a way of covering my butt if you happen to say something—*anything*—connected to this murder investigation that could seemingly incriminate you."

Cullen still hadn't cursed, but Leigh belted out some mental profanity. Because this was something she should have already done.

"Do you understand your rights?" she asked when she'd finished reciting the Miranda warning.

"I understand" was all he said. Or rather grumbled. And then he got in the passenger's seat of the cruiser.

Cullen was clearly insulted and riled. It was a good thing Leigh hadn't started to weave any fantasies about having a hot night with her former lover.

Except she had.

Mercy, she had. No matter how much she tried to push away this attraction, it just kept coming back.

"Do you have enemies?" she asked, pulling the cruiser out of the driveway. Leigh headed for the road that would take them into town. "Someone who'd want to cause trouble for you?"

"Of course," he readily admitted. "I'm a businessman, and I'm sure more than a few people thought they got the short end of the stick in a deal. But I don't know of anyone who'd set me up by murdering Alexa and bashing in the head of one of my ranch hands."

His voice and expression weren't so cold now. Oh, no. There was heat, and it wasn't from attraction. This was a storm of fury that Cullen was no doubt fighting to rein in. He looked formidable. And dangerous.

"Your father obviously hated Alexa," she pointed out.

"Yes, but Bowen didn't kill her," Cullen snapped before she could add anything else. "My father has bent the law too many times to count, but he wouldn't kill my ex-girlfriend in my bathroom and leave her body for me to find."

On the surface, she had to agree with Cullen about all of that. But maybe Alexa's murder hadn't been planned. Maybe it'd been an impulse kill. Ditto for the attack on Jamie. If so, that changed the rules. People didn't always make good decisions when panicked and trying to cover up a crime.

"Your father was at the party?" she asked. She mentally cursed again. This time when she tried to clear the sleet away with the windshield wipers, it left icy smears on the glass.

"He was." Cullen paused. "He left early. And no, he didn't seem upset or rattled. Maybe distracted," he added in a mumble. "Maybe because he knew he'd have to tell me about the PI he hired."

Maybe. That certainly had to be weighing on Bowen's mind. But it also gave the man a motive for murder. Cullen had no doubt come to the same conclusion.

"My advice," Cullen said a moment later, "have one of your deputies question my father. It'll go easier on both of you if you're not the one to do the interview."

Probably. But Leigh intended to do the questioning herself. When exactly that would happen though, she didn't know. Jamie came first, and then after she'd gotten everything she could from him, she'd need to contact the PI Bowen had hired. PIs often took pictures, and if he had, they might get an ID on the man Alexa had met in the café.

Because she had no choice, she turned on the wipers again and gave the windshield a spray of the cleaner that had a deicer in it. Her tires weren't shimmying on the road yet, but they soon would. Definitely not good because this was a narrow ranch road with deep ditches on each side.

Leigh saw the flash of lights to her left. But only a flash. She barely had time to process it when an SUV came barreling out from a cluster of trees.

And it slammed right into the cruiser.

Chapter Four

The collision happened fast. Too fast for Cullen to do anything to try to lessen the impact.

His shoulder and the side of his head rammed against the side airbag as it deployed. The seat belt snapped and caught, clamping like a vise over his chest and pinning him against the seat.

Probably with some help from the sleet, the cruiser went into a skid, and beside him, Leigh fought with the steering wheel. Trying to keep them on the road. She might have managed it, too, if the driver of the SUV hadn't come at them again. With the headlights on high beams, the SUV rammed them from behind, the front end of it colliding with the rear of the cruiser.

The impact slammed the cruiser headfirst into a tree.

There was the sound of metal tearing into the wood along with the swoosh of the front airbags when they punched into their faces. It knocked the breath out of Cullen for a couple of seconds, and the powder that'd surrounded the airbags flew into his eyes. Still, he forced himself to react, not to give in to the shock. Because he was certain of one thing.

Someone was trying to kill them.

The first impact could have possibly been an accident. Someone losing control as they came out of one of the trails. But the second collision had been intentional and with the purpose of causing them to crash into the tree. Which was exactly what'd happened.

Cullen glanced at Leigh to make sure she was conscious. She was, but she looked a little dazed. Still, she was already fumbling for her gun, which meant that she, too, had figured out that someone was using a vehicle to attack them.

The SUV came at them again.

This time the vehicle didn't just plow into them. Instead, the driver began to inch forward, sandwiching the cruiser between the SUV and the tree. Cullen had no idea if the front end of the SUV could actually crush the cruiser like an accordion, and he wasn't about to wait to find out.

Cullen batted away the airbag so he could take out his gun. It wasn't an easy task since there wasn't much room to move around. He finally managed it and soon saw that Leigh was still struggling to draw her own weapon.

"You need backup. I'm armed and stopping whoever's doing this," Cullen said, giving her a heads-up.

Leigh might have argued with him if she'd actually had her gun out and if this hadn't been a life-and-death situation where there hadn't been time to call for backup. Instead, Leigh just kept frantically shoving the airbag aside and battling to get her damaged door open while Cullen barreled out of the cruiser. He took aim at the windshield of the SUV, right where the driver would be.

Leigh finally got hold of her gun, and she must have given up on getting her door open because she climbed out through the passenger's side. The moment her feet landed on the ground, she lifted her body, and she pointed her gun at the SUV.

"I'm Sheriff Mercer," Leigh called out. "Stop or I'll fire."

Cullen wasn't surprised when the driver stopped. After all, the windshield probably wasn't bulletproof, and he or she had two guns aimed at him. Unfortunately, because of the high beams, the darkness and the heavily tinted windshield, Cullen couldn't see who was behind the wheel.

But it was almost certainly Alexa's killer.

That reminder had Cullen moving several steps closer, and he bracketed his right wrist with his left hand so his aim wouldn't be off.

On the other side of the cruiser, Leigh came forward, too, but she'd barely made it a step when the driver threw the SUV into Reverse and hit the accelerator. The tires fishtailed some, but he managed to keep control.

While he sped away.

Cursing, Cullen ran out onto the road, and he shot at the tires, hoping to disable the vehicle. He needed to see who was inside. Needed to see who was doing this so the snake could be put behind bars.

With her breath gusting and her gun still gripped in her hand, Leigh took aim at the SUV, too, but the driver had already disappeared around a curve. The road led back to the Triple R, but Cullen doubted that's where this clown was going. Not when there were many trails that the driver could use to turn. Trails that would lead back to the main road.

"I need to call this in," Leigh said in between those

gusts of breath, and Cullen noticed that she was limping when she went back to the cruiser.

"Are you hurt?" he asked.

"I'm fine." It was the tone of someone who didn't want to be bothered with such questions.

Cullen didn't blame her for the attitude. Not with the adrenaline and anger pumping through them. But maybe she wouldn't put up a protest about being examined by an EMT or doctor.

Behind him, Cullen heard Leigh use the radio in the cruiser to call for backup and put out an all-points bulletin on the SUV. What she couldn't give the dispatcher was the info on the license plates. That's because they were missing, and Cullen figured that was by design. A way of making sure no one ID'd the vehicle or the driver.

Cullen stayed put on the road, and he listened and kept watch just in case the SUV returned for another round. He actually hoped that would happen, and then he could put some bullets through the windshield instead of the tires.

The wind had picked up considerably, and it was whipping the ice pellets through the air. The sleet stung his face, but he stayed put, and a few seconds later, Leigh joined him on his watch.

"Vance will be here in a couple of minutes," Leigh relayed to him. "He'll look for the SUV along the way. We might get lucky," she added.

Might fell into the slim-to-none category. Unless the driver of the SUV was a complete idiot, that is. Because anyone would have been able to figure out that Leigh would have called for backup, and even if that backup had had to come from town, it wouldn't have taken long for help to arrive.

Leigh looked back at the mangled front end of the cruiser and muttered something under her breath that he didn't catch. Cullen caught the gist of it though.

"Yeah, this is connected to Alexa and Jamie," he said.

Leigh certainly didn't argue with him. "But was I the target, or were you?" she asked.

He looked at her, their gazes connecting, and in that moment it seemed as if all the bad blood between them vanished. Nearly being killed could do that. It could tear down the walls from the past and, well, connect you. Cullen certainly felt very connected to Leigh right now. Protective, too.

And guilty.

Because he could be the reason that she'd nearly just died. Cullen didn't know the specific motive of this killer. Not yet, anyway. But he soon would. He intended to give this plenty of thought and then go after the SOB who was responsible for this hellish night.

"I doubt the SUV will be back this way," Cullen said. The sleet was coming down harder now. "We should probably wait for Vance in the cruiser."

That would not only get them out of the bitter cold, it would also give him a chance to figure out just how badly Leigh was hurt. She was still limping as they made their way back to the cruiser and slid into the back seat. Cullen got in beside her to avoid the airbag debris in the front and so he could examine Leigh. It was too dark for him to see if there was any blood on her jeans, but he used the flashlight on his phone.

Yep, there was blood all right.

"You cut your leg," he pointed out.

"More like a scrape," she corrected. "When the SUV hit my door, it pushed against my knee."

Pushed wasn't the right word. More like *bashed*. But he couldn't exactly blame her for downplaying her injury. Not when they had much bigger problems to deal with. Still, he wanted her examined.

Leigh gave the back of the driver's seat a shove, but Cullen thought the gesture was from frustration rather than trying to create more legroom. Her frustration seemed to go up a notch when her phone rang, and she saw Jeb's name on the screen. She hit the decline button.

"Your father will press you to arrest me," Cullen threw out there.

She didn't look at him but made a sound of agreement. "But this might convince him that you're not responsible for Alexa's death."

"Maybe. But he might just say I hired someone to do this so I'd look innocent," Cullen pointed out. "After all, the collision was mainly on your side of the vehicle. You stood the greatest chance of being hurt."

Leigh made a quick sound of agreement to that, too, which meant she'd likely already considered it. Then she turned her head and stared at him. "You didn't do this," she said, and then she paused. "Would your father have done it?"

Cullen tried not to be insulted that Leigh had just asked if his father was a killer. A killer who wouldn't hesitate to murder his own son.

"Not with me in the cruiser. Bowen might be bull-headed and unable to let go of the past, but he wouldn't have put me at risk." Now Cullen was the one who paused. "But perhaps this goes back to the man Alexa met in that café. Maybe he was the one behind the wheel."

Leigh didn't get a chance to give an opinion on that because the approaching headlights grabbed their attention. With their guns ready, they got out of the cruiser, watching and waiting in case this was their attacker returning.

"It's Vance," she said, releasing a breath of what was almost certainly relief.

Cullen didn't relax just yet. He had no intention of standing down until he knew for sure there wasn't another threat. But this wasn't an SUV. It was a silver Ford truck, and it pulled to a stop directly in front of them.

"Are you okay?" the deputy asked the moment he got out. It was Vance all right, and while he'd drawn his gun, he didn't aim it at Leigh or Cullen.

"Fine," Leigh answered. "Any sign of the SUV that hit us?"

"None, and like you said, I made sure to look closely at the trails that lead off the road." Vance studied the cruiser and shook his head. "Man, that looks bad. You sure you're okay?"

"I'll live," she muttered. "No thanks to the driver of the SUV." She looked at Cullen. "You have a vehicle we can use? If not—"

"I have something," Cullen assured her. One that would hopefully handle better on the icy roads than her cruiser. Since there were more than two dozen cars, trucks and four-wheel drive vehicles at the ranch, there wouldn't be any trouble accessing one right away.

Leigh grabbed her purse from the cruiser, and they got in the truck with Vance to head back to the Triple R.

"I got the horse statue secured," Vance told Leigh as

he drove. He opened his mouth, probably to continue to update his boss, but then the deputy cast a wary glance at Cullen.

"It's okay," Leigh assured Vance. "Keep going. Tell me what's happening at the ranch."

The deputy gave an uncertain nod but finally continued. "I put crime scene tape around the patio and on the front door of the house and marked the area where the shrub had been trampled. There's an umbrella over the spot in case there's a print we didn't see right off."

"Good. What about Dawn and Rocky?" Leigh asked.

"Dawn's still with the body, but I told Rocky to keep on working to get statements from the ranch hands. Oh, and the CSIs are on the way, but they're having to go slow because of the weather. The roads out of Lubbock are already pretty bad."

That meant it'd be hours, maybe even days, before the CSIs were done processing his house. Cullen could go to his dad's place, but he preferred to be closer in case something broke on the investigation. He'd use either the bunkhouse or else get a room at the inn in town.

"Once you're back at the ranch, call Rocky and have him ask the hands about the SUV," Leigh instructed. "It's dark blue, has heavily tinted windows and will have some front end damage. The license plates have been removed. I don't want the driver lying in wait at the Triple R."

Cullen sure as hell didn't want that, either, and he whipped out his phone to send a text to his top hand, Mack Cuevas. He told Mack to be on the lookout for the SUV and to assist Rocky and the other deputies with whatever needed to be done.

"I'll also need the CSIs to take a look at my cruiser,"

Leigh continued as they approached the ranch. "There'll be paint transfer from the SUV."

Yeah, there would be, which meant the driver would likely ditch the vehicle as soon as possible. Of course, there was always the possibility that the driver would leave traces of himself inside the SUV. Traces that the lab could use to ID him.

"Rosa mentioned that a lot of the guests were taking pictures at the party," Vance went on, pulling to a stop in the driveway in front of the house. "She thought they were posting them on social media. Might be worth having a look at them and any other pictures on the guests' phones. If you want, I'll do that first chance I get."

"Yes, do that," Leigh agreed.

Cullen went back over the night, something he was certain he'd be doing until Alexa's killer was caught, and he did indeed remember lots of picture-taking going on. However, he was pretty sure he would have remembered if anything wasn't as it should be.

"This way to the garage," Cullen told Leigh when they stepped from Vance's truck.

They started in that direction but had only made it a few steps when Leigh's phone rang again. Judging from the huff she made, she expected it to be her father again. But it wasn't.

"It's the hospital," Leigh muttered, hurrying to answer it. She didn't put the call on speaker, but Cullen had no trouble hearing what the caller said.

"Sheriff, this is Dr. Denton. I figured you'd want to know that Jamie Wylie has regained consciousness."

Leigh released another of those hard breaths. "Is he okay?"

The doctor didn't jump to answer that. "I haven't

finished the exam, but I should know something soon. In the meantime, Jamie's insisting that he talk to Cullen and you right away. He says he needs to tell both of you about what went on with Alexa tonight."

Chapter Five

Leigh tried to ignore the adrenaline crash that was coursing through every inch of her body. Especially her head. She'd known it would happen, but she didn't have time to come down right now. She also didn't have time to process that someone had just tried to murder Cullen and her. She had to focus on talking to Jamie.

Because he might be able to ID a killer.

First though, Cullen and she had to get to the hospital, and that wasn't an easy task. As predicted, the roads were an icy mess and were giving even Cullen's huge truck some trouble. She felt the tires shimmy more than a couple of times, but Leigh consoled herself with the reminder that the road conditions might prevent the driver of that SUV from trying to come after them again. Or going after Jamie.

Leigh had beefed up security as best she could by arranging to have the hospital's lone security guard posted with Jamie. That wouldn't necessarily stop someone from coming in with guns blazing, but so far this particular killer hadn't used a gun. The bronze horse statue had been a weapon of opportunity. Maybe the SUV had, too, if the driver had stolen it. But if this guy got desperate to cover his tracks by eliminating Jamie, then there was no telling what he'd do. The security guard was armed, but she didn't know how he'd react in an actual crisis. There weren't many crisis tests at the Dark River Hospital.

There were other pieces of the investigation that she needed to put together, too. She had to get into Alexa's house and her workplace to see if the woman had left any clues as to who'd killed her. That meant Leigh would likely need warrants since she would have to access emails, phone records and such.

"Thinking?" Cullen asked, his question jarring her from her thoughts. "Or trying not to think?"

She considered that a moment. "Both, I guess. I need to go over the details of the investigation, but I'd rather not relive the SUV crashing into us." Leigh looked out the window, hoping that Cullen wouldn't see her shudder when she got a flash image of that crash.

"First time anyone's tried to kill you?" he asked.

"Yes." Leigh glanced at him. "You?"

"Second. A guy in a bar once drew a gun on me. He pulled the trigger, too, but it jammed."

He'd said it almost flippantly, as if it weren't a big deal, but the muscle that tightened in his jaw told her that it had indeed been big. Of course, she doubted anyone could ever get accustomed to having someone try to kill them.

Leigh motioned to the back waist of his pants. "Is that why you always carry a gun, even to a party? At least I'm guessing you had it at the party. Or maybe you holstered it afterward?"

The tightened jaw muscle relaxed into a quick smile. Not one of humor, either. "Always trying to get details that might or might not apply to the case. You're a cop to the bone, Leigh," he remarked.

"So many people would argue with that," she disagreed, and she wanted to kick herself for opening this particular can of worms.

"So many people would be wrong." Cullen smiled when she tossed him a scowl, and this time there was some humor in it. "No, I'm not saying that to get on your good side so you won't arrest me." He paused. "And yes, I always carry a weapon. Or two."

That last remark had a dangerous edge to it. Like the man himself. Leigh was attracted to that danger. To that edge. To the part of him that she thought might never fall into the "tame" category.

And that made her an idiot.

She needed an untamed, dangerous man about as much as she needed more criticism about her having the badge or living up to the lofty standards Jeb had set. Still, her body wasn't giving her a break when it came to Cullen. Hopefully though, once the adrenaline crash was done, her head would stay steady, and she would remember that he could complicate her life in the worst kind of way. There were people who were looking for a chance to oust her as sheriff, and those people would use Cullen as ammunition to get rid of her.

Leigh checked the hospital parking lot when Cullen pulled into it. He did the same, and she knew they were both looking for that SUV. Or any signs they were about to be attacked again. But the parking lot was practically empty. She considered that to be a small blessing but continued to keep watch as he parked right by the ER doors.

Another small blessing was the police department

was just up the street. Less than two blocks away. Three of her eight deputies were already tied up at the Triple R, but that left one, Kerry Yancy, on duty to man the police station and back up the security guard on Jamie. Still, Kerry could respond in just a couple of minutes if she needed help, and if things went from bad to worse, Leigh could call in the day-shift deputies. Most of them lived just a few miles from town.

Ducking their heads against the sleet and cold, Cullen and she hurried into the hospital, heading straight to the room where she saw the security guard. "Jamie's in there," the guard said.

Leigh knew him, of course. He was Harry Harbin, and when he'd been in his prime, he'd been one of her father's deputies. That explained the cool look he aimed at Cullen. And the dismissive one he gave her. She made a mental note to have Vance schedule a reserve deputy to do security detail. Guarding Jamie was critical, and Leigh didn't want any misplaced righteousness playing into this.

She knocked once on the door but didn't wait for a response before she entered, and she immediately spotted Jamie in the bed. He was indeed conscious, with his gaze zooming straight to Cullen and her.

"Thank you for coming," Jamie muttered, his voice hoarse and weak. He was hooked up to some machines and an IV.

Dr. Denton nodded a greeting to them. So did the nurse, Amber Murdock. Amber's silent greeting, however, warmed up considerably when her attention shifted to Cullen. Leigh didn't know if Amber had been one of Cullen's bedmates or if Amber was just hoping to become one. Women in Dark River generally fell into one of those two categories.

Sadly, Leigh was both.

Well, a confirmed former lover, whose body wanted the *former* label to switch to *current*. She was going to do everything in her power to disappoint her body about that.

"Is it true?" Jamie asked right off. "Is Alexa really dead?"

Leigh glanced at the doctor and the nurse, and it only took her one look to figure out the news of Alexa's death had come from Amber.

"It's true," Leigh verified. No need to hold back on the news since it was obviously already the talk of the town, and the hospital.

Tears filled Jamie's eyes. "Dead," he repeated. "She's really dead."

Leigh gauged his reaction. His grief and shock seemed genuine enough, but for all she knew Jamie had been the one to kill Alexa. Of course, that didn't explain how Jamie had then gotten hurt, and that's why she had plenty of questions lined up for him. Apparently though, Jamie had some for her as well.

"Who killed Alexa?" Jamie demanded. "How did she die?"

"I don't know who killed her," Leigh admitted. "I'm hoping you can help with that."

Jamie started to answer, but then he shifted his attention to the doctor. "Jamie insists on talking to the two of you alone," Dr. Denton explained, and clearly the doctor wasn't happy about that. "We have more tests that need to be done, and I don't want him getting agitated or upset."

Leigh didn't fault the doctor for wanting to do what was best for his patient. But she had a job to do as well. "I think Jamie will be less agitated and upset if I'm able to arrest the person who hurt him and killed Alexa. This chat is important," she added, purposely using *chat* instead of *interview*.

On a heavy breath and with a ton of obvious reluctance, Dr. Denton nodded, and with the tip of his head, he motioned for Amber to follow him. "Keep the visit short," the doctor insisted as he left with Amber.

Leigh shut the door and went closer to the bed. She didn't bother with greetings or niceties since Jamie did indeed look exhausted, and she figured she wouldn't have much time with him. "Who attacked you?"

"I don't know," Jamie muttered. Groaning softly, he took a moment to gather his breath. "I heard footsteps, but before I could see who it was, someone bashed me on the side of the head."

Leigh wanted to curse. Cullen probably did, too. It would have put a quick end to the investigation if Jamie had been able to give them a name. And he still might be able to do that. Sometimes witnesses and victims remembered plenty of details once they were questioned, and questioning him was exactly what Leigh planned to do.

"How did Alexa die?" Jamie pressed.

"Blunt force trauma," Leigh explained. "I think once the ME has had a chance to examine her that he'll say she had a wound similar to yours. Hers was just a lot worse."

Jamie's tears returned. "I brought Alexa to the Triple R," he blurted out and looked at Cullen. "I'm so sorry. I shouldn't have done it."

"Why did you?" Cullen asked. His voice was steady, not a trace of judgment in it, but Leigh figured he wasn't pleased about one of his hands bringing his ex to a party at the ranch.

Jamie groaned, squeezed his eyes shut a moment, and he eased his head back onto the pillow. Tears continued to slide down his cheeks. "She called me right about the time the party was starting, around seven, I guess, and said she was in town and that she wanted to know if I'd give her a ride out to the ranch. She said her car was acting up and that she didn't want to risk driving it on the country road."

"You came and got her?" Leigh pressed when Jamie didn't continue.

He groaned again, nodded. "She talked me into it. I swear, I didn't know she was gonna be killed."

Cullen came closer and sat on the edge of the bed. "How'd Alexa talk you into driving her?"

Jamie's eyes met Cullen's, and a look passed between them. Leigh supposed it was a guys' understanding thing, but she figured she got it, too.

"Alexa sweet-talked you," Leigh concluded, and it had likely involved some flirting. Maybe even the hint that she'd be interested in being with Jamie in a romantic or sexual kind of way.

"At first I told her no," Jamie went on, "that I didn't think it was a good idea for her to crash the party, but she said she wouldn't be crashing. She said she just needed a quick word with you, that she wanted you to know that she was ready to move on with her life and that she wouldn't be bothering you anymore. She insisted she wouldn't make a big scene or anything and that her chat with Cullen would be private."

"And you didn't think the party would be a bad place for her to do that?" Leigh questioned.

"Yeah, I did," Jamie readily agreed. "That's why I tried to convince her to wait, to try to see Cullen another time, but she…well, she convinced me to go get her and drive her there."

Leigh reminded herself that Jamie was very young. And if Alexa was anything like her reputation, Jamie would have been putty in her hands.

"So, you picked her up and drove her to the Triple R," Leigh summed up. "What happened next?"

His forehead bunched up. "I guess it must have been about eight o'clock by then. Some guests were still arriving so she had me drop her off at the side of the house because she said she was going to slip in and have someone on the kitchen staff go and get Cullen for her. That way, she wouldn't have to go in where the party was going on." Jamie shook his head, obviously disgusted with himself. "I know all of this sounds stupid, and I shouldn't have let Alexa talk me into taking her there."

Agreed. But Leigh had to wonder if the woman had told Jamie the truth. Had she truly just wanted to talk to Cullen? Or was there a lot more to it than that? Leigh was betting it was the latter.

"You dropped Alexa off at the side of the house where you were attacked?" Cullen asked.

Jamie nodded. "The driveway is only a couple of yards behind the trees and shrubs around the patio."

It was, and Alexa would no doubt have known the particular layout. Heck, she'd maybe even stayed in that very guest room at one time or another. At least she could have stayed there when she wasn't sharing Cullen's bed, but Leigh had heard that Alexa had started visiting the Triple R before Cullen and she had gotten involved. That was definitely something Leigh needed to question Cullen about, but according to the rumor mill, Austin's fiancée, Kali, and Alexa were close friends, and Kali had brought Alexa there often.

When Jamie reached and then fumbled for the cup of water on the table next to the bed, Cullen helped him with it. Jamie took a small sip and swallowed hard before he continued.

"After I dropped off Alexa, she told me to wait for her, that she'd only be in the house about ten minutes or so and then I could drive her back into town. She was going to get a room at the inn until she could have someone take a look at her car. She said she wouldn't be driving back to her place tonight because of the bad weather moving in."

So, Alexa hadn't planned on staying at the ranch that night. Ten minutes. Not much time for a talk to try to reassure Cullen that she wasn't going to give him any more trouble.

"Were the patio doors locked?" Leigh asked Jamie.

"No." But then Jamie stopped and shook his head. "Maybe. I didn't watch when Alexa was opening the doors so she might have had a key."

Or she could have picked the lock since Cullen had already told her that he'd changed the locks after he'd ended things with Alexa. But there was a third possibility. Someone had left the doors unlocked for Alexa. Maybe the killer. Maybe someone else she'd sweet-talked on the catering crew or the household staff. The place was so big that there was no telling how long that door had been unsecured.

"Alexa went inside the house, but she didn't come out

after ten minutes," Jamie went on. "I waited, but then I started to get worried about her." His mouth trembled, more tears came, and he kept his attention pinned to Cullen. "I thought she might be getting in a row with you. I thought you two might be arguing." His voice cracked. "But now I know she was dead."

Leigh didn't have to guess that Jamie was feeling plenty guilty about that, and he began to sob. It didn't look as if it was going to be a short cry, either. Still, she had to press him on another point.

"How long did you wait outside before you were hit over the head?" Leigh asked.

"I don't know," he answered through the sob. "Maybe twenty minutes or a half hour."

Not much time for someone to kill Alexa and then go outside to attack Jamie. And that led Leigh to another problem. How had the killer known that Jamie was on the patio waiting for Alexa?

"And you're sure you didn't see who hit you?" Cullen pushed.

Jamie shook his head again. "No. I heard the footsteps, like I said, but that was it."

"Heavy or light footsteps?" Cullen continued. "Fast or slow?"

Since Leigh had been about to ask Jamie variations of those questions, she didn't object.

Jamie's forehead bunched up again. "Fast and heavy. Like someone was running at me."

So, the killer was in a hurry to take care of Jamie. Probably because he or she hadn't wanted to be seen. That made sense. After all, Jamie was young and fit and could have probably fended off a physical attack had he gotten the chance.

But why kill Jamie at all?

Leigh figured that went back to Alexa, too. It was possible the killer thought she'd told Jamie the real reason she'd come to the house. And Leigh didn't believe that real reason was to see Cullen. Not solely, anyway. This might indeed go back to the man she'd met with in the café. Maybe she hadn't trusted him to do the job if she'd actually hired him to hurt Cullen? Or maybe she'd gone there to pay him.

"My head hurts real bad now," Jamie said. "You think you could ask the doctor to give me some meds?"

"Sure," Leigh readily agreed. "I'll be back later today to check on you." And to see if he remembered anything else. "In the meantime, there'll be a guard on your door so you'll be safe."

Jamie gave an almost absent nod to that along with wincing from the pain. She gave his hand a gentle squeeze and headed for the door.

"If you need anything, just let me know," Cullen assured Jamie, and he walked out with Leigh.

"No one other than medical staff gets near Jamie," Leigh reminded the guard.

When she only got a grunt of acknowledgment from Harry, she repeated it and stared at him until he verbally answered. "Yes, I got that."

"I can bring out a couple of my other ranch hands to do security," Cullen suggested. Clearly, he wasn't pleased with Harry's attitude, either.

"I'll ask Vance to arrange for a reserve deputy," she said, taking out her phone.

While Leigh fired off the text, she glanced around the ER to locate the doctor. There was no sign of him, but Amber was obviously waiting for them because she moved away from the reception desk and made a bee-line toward them.

"Jamie says he's in pain and needs meds," Leigh immediately relayed.

Amber nodded. "Dr. Denton will be right back and I can let him know." She shifted her attention to Cullen. "We just got a call from the Department of Transportation. The roads in and out of town are closed."

At the exact moment Amber was relaying that info, Leigh got a text giving her the same alert. She hadn't figured she'd actually make it home for hours anyway, but with the sleet projected to continue until midmorning, there was no telling when the roads would be clear enough to drive.

"I knew you'd be stuck," Amber went on, still talking to Cullen, "so I just called the inn, and they don't have any rooms."

Leigh wasn't actually surprised by that. The inn only had four guest rooms, and anyone who'd gotten stuck because of the weather would have already snapped those up.

"I could probably find you someplace to stay here in the hospital," Amber added to Cullen.

Leigh didn't smirk, but it was obvious that Amber's *interest* in him had gotten him that particular offer. An offer that Cullen apparently wasn't going to accept.

"Thanks," he said, "but Leigh and I are going to the police station."

She was indeed heading there as planned. Not only could she get started on work, but if she had to crash for a couple of hours, there was a cot and a sofa in the break room. Though Leigh hadn't counted on sharing such cramped quarters with Cullen. But she rethought that. Neither of them would likely get any sleep anyway, and this way she could go ahead and take his official statement.

"I need to bag the clothes you're wearing," Leigh said to him as they walked away from Amber.

Cullen's mouth quivered a little. "I'm guessing it's to cover all bases and not because you want me to strip down."

She frowned. Or rather tried to do that. Leigh knew she didn't quite pull it off. "Yes, to cover the bases. I can find something at the police station for you to wear."

"I've got a change of clothes in my truck. I keep a duffel bag behind the seat."

Now she did frown. "For sleepovers with admirers like Amber," Leigh muttered, cursing herself the moment the words were out of her mouth. She so didn't need to be bringing up Cullen's sexual conquests.

"Well, actually, it has more to do with horses than admirers." That sounded very tongue-in-cheek, and he let it linger a couple of moments before he added, "I've learned the hard way to have extra clothes because I often go out to other ranches to look at horses I'm considering buying. I can get pretty sweaty, and I don't like driving back when I smell worse than the livestock."

That explanation made her silently curse herself even more. Because it gave her a giddy little punch of relief to know that he didn't make a habit of sleepovers. Then again, he could, and probably did, simply have his lovers come to his place.

Once they were outside, Leigh considered just walking to the office, but the arctic blast of air had her climbing inside Cullen's truck when he opened the door for her. He started the engine and took the time for it to warm up, which thankfully wasn't long. He pulled out of the very slippery parking lot just as Leigh's phone rang.

"It's Vance," she relayed to Cullen, and she took the call, putting it on speaker. "Guess you got the alert about the roads being closed?" she asked Vance.

"I did, and Rosa was going to call Cullen to ask if it was okay if we all stayed the night here."

"Tell Rosa that's fine," Cullen spoke up.

"Thanks, I'll tell her," Vance replied. Then, he paused. "Uh, I questioned some of the ranch hands, and I might have something."

Leigh understood the subtext in Vance's tone. She might not want Cullen to hear the *something*. But Leigh figured anything that came out of the investigation would soon make it back to Cullen's ears anyway.

"What do you have?" Leigh asked Vance.

She heard Vance take a deep breath before he answered. "Wilmer Smalley is one of the ranch hands here, and he seems reliable enough."

"He is," Cullen assured them. "Did Wilmer see someone?"

"He did," Vance verified. "He said that he spotted two people outside the house when the party was going on. One was at the back of the house, right about where Cullen's bedroom is."

"No one should have been out there," Cullen provided before Leigh could ask him. "The catering staff would have come in through the kitchen entrance."

"Yeah, that's what Rosa said, too," Vance verified. "But he saw a man there. At least he's pretty sure it was a man, wearing a coat. He didn't get a good look at him."

"Height? Weight?" Leigh pushed.

"Wilmer couldn't say. He got just a glimpse of him before the person ducked out of sight. He said he didn't think anything of it at the time, that he figured Cullen had maybe stepped out for some reason. But he's obviously giving it plenty of thought right now."

Yes, he would be. But it helped that Wilmer hadn't immediately thought it was Cullen outside the bedroom. Even with just a glimpse, the hand should have known if it was the big boss.

"So far no one on the kitchen staff is owning up to being near Cullen's room," Vance went on. "And the kitchen entrance isn't near Cullen's room or the patio where Jamie was attacked." He paused again. "But Wilmer did see someone there."

Leigh jumped right on that. "Someone on the patio?"

"Yeah," Vance repeated. "And this time, Wilmer got a decent look at the guy's face. He says it was Cullen's good friend Austin."

"Austin?" Cullen said, the shock in his voice and on his face.

"Wilmer said he was positive that's who it was," Vance added.

Leigh immediately looked at Cullen. "Any idea what Austin would be doing out there on that particular patio?"

"None." Cullen pulled the truck to a stop in front of the police department and took out his phone. "But I'm about to find out."

Chapter Six

Cullen figured there wasn't enough caffeine in the entire state of Texas to get rid of the fog in his head. Or the headache that'd been throbbing at his temples for the past six hours. Still, he tried, and downed his umpteenth cup of coffee.

Leigh was drinking a Coke, her beverage of choice to keep her alert, but at the moment she didn't seem to be faring any better than he was. He saw her eyes droop more than once while she sat at her desk and typed away on her computer or sent texts to her deputies.

Apparently, the catnap she'd taken around 7:00 a.m. had been enough to at least keep her going, and she appeared to actually be getting work done. That included taking his official statement.

Cullen had managed some, too, in the chair next to her desk and while using a laptop that Leigh had lent him, but work was similar to coffee and his own catnap. No amount of either was going to block the images of Alexa's dead body.

Or the fact that Austin still hadn't returned his call.

Cullen had attempted the first call right after learning that Austin had been on the patio the night of the party. Something that Austin definitely hadn't men-

tioned in their earlier conversation. Cullen had tried
three more times to get in touch with Austin, but each
had gone straight to voice mail. He left another voice
mail on Austin's phone at work.

It was possible the winter storm had caused some
outages. Equally possible that Austin had just turned
off his phone for the night and was now sleeping in.
But Cullen needed to talk to his friend. So did Leigh.
She'd made her own attempts to contact him, and Cullen knew those attempts would continue until she could
have a conversation with him.

An official one.

Cullen didn't believe that Austin was a person of
interest in Leigh's investigation, but he could tell from
the terse voice mail messages she left for Austin that
she suspected the man was guilty of something. Maybe
the something was simply going out for a smoke. However, if Austin had used the patio for that, why hadn't
he just said so? Cullen didn't know, but he just couldn't
see how this connected to what had happened to Alexa
and Jamie. Austin could be reckless and cocky, but he
wasn't a killer.

And Cullen hoped he continued to feel that way after
he heard Austin's explanation.

He doubted Leigh's deputies would give Austin the
benefit of the doubt when it came to innocence or guilt.
Neither would plenty of others in Dark River. Folks
would want someone arrested for Alexa's murder if for
no other reason than so they could feel safe in their own
homes. Austin wasn't local, and worse, he had the dis-
advantage of being Cullen's friend. The pressure to drag
Austin in and hammer away at him would grow. Well,

it would once the deputies and anybody else actually managed to get into Leigh's office.

Right now, Leigh and he had the entire building to themselves since she'd sent the night deputy, Kerry Yancy, home several hours earlier. Kerry lived in an apartment just up the street so he hadn't had to drive to get there. Good thing, too, because the street glistened with ice in the morning sun, and it was too dangerous to be out driving. It would no doubt keep away any visitors—including Austin. But judging from the messages Leigh had left for Austin, she wanted him to do a phone interview and then another one with him in person as soon as the roads were clear enough for that to happen.

Leigh stood, stretched and motioned toward the break room, a location that Cullen had gotten very familiar with since it was where the coffee maker was located. "I'm going to grab a shower."

Cullen had already made use of the shower in the break room's bathroom when he'd changed into his jeans and work shirt. Thankfully, he'd had some toiletries in the bag, too, and had even managed to brush his teeth.

"There's stuff in the fridge if you want to nuke something for breakfast," Leigh added, yawning.

Her eyes met his, something that she'd been careful not to do throughout the hours they'd spent in her office. It was as if *out of sight, out of mind* was the way to go. It wasn't. And she no doubt got a full jolting reminder of that when her gaze collided with his.

She groaned, then sighed and shook her head. "I can't get involved with you," she muttered. But it sounded to Cullen as if she was trying to convince herself.

"So you've said." He let that hang in the air, and it

kept hanging until Leigh mumbled something he didn't catch and walked away.

He followed her to the break room to get another refill on the coffee, and he settled down on the sofa to try to get in touch with Austin again. When he had no luck reaching him, Cullen checked the time. It was barely ten in the morning, but he was tired of waiting for Austin to return his calls so he tried Kali and cursed when she didn't answer, either.

Cullen remembered Austin saying that Kali was spending the night with her folks, but he didn't have their number so he moved on to the next call he had to make. To Mack, his ranch hand. The ever-reliable Mack answered on the first ring.

"How are things there?" Cullen asked.

"Tense," Mack said after a short pause. "The hands are nervous because the deputies have questioned them."

Cullen wished he could tell them that wouldn't continue, but it would. Each and every one of them would have to make a statement. Especially Wilmer. "Did any of the others see Austin outside during the party?"

"No. And nobody saw the other man Wilmer described, the one in the coat who he got a glimpse of by your bedroom. I'm guessing it was someone at the party who stepped out?"

"Maybe. But there were a lot of vehicles coming and going, and he could have parked somewhere and walked to that spot." He decided to go ahead and lay it out for Mack. "The guy in the coat could have been the one who killed Alexa."

"Yeah," Mack said after some thought. The word *tense* applied to him, too. Cullen could hear it in his voice.

"How's Jamie?" Mack asked.

"He's doing all right." Mostly, anyway. "He texted me after they finished running tests on him. He's got a concussion but the doctor says the signs are good that he'll make a full recovery." Dr. Denton had confirmed that when he'd called Leigh earlier.

"He's lucky," Mack concluded, and Cullen had to agree.

It'd taken nearly two dozen stitches to sew up the wound, but it could have been so much worse. If Rocky hadn't found him on the patio, Jamie might have frozen to death.

"I don't know how long it'll be before I can get back to the ranch," Cullen continued. "But keep an eye on things. And if you hear anything about the investigation, let me know."

"I can let you know that Rocky believes you're guilty," Mack readily admitted.

That came as no surprise whatsoever to Cullen. And Rocky wouldn't be the only one who thought he'd killed his ex-girlfriend. That was why it was important to Cullen that the snake who'd killed Alexa be caught. He didn't give a rat what people thought of him, but this could spill back on Leigh if enough gossips thought she wasn't doing her job by not arresting him.

Cullen ended the call with Mack and sent a text to Rosa to check and see how she was doing. He also made a mental note to give her a huge bonus for everything she was having to deal with right now. When he got a quick answer that she was okay, Cullen frowned and wished he had another text or call so he wouldn't keep thinking about Leigh.

Specifically, about a naked Leigh in the shower.

Well, at least the thought of her managed to clear

out some of the cobwebs from his head. The thoughts of joining her, naked, cleared out a whole bunch more. Over the years he'd never forgotten her, but being around her like this had a way of reminding him that forgetting her was impossible.

He finally heard her turn off the water in the shower, and Cullen hoped that would quell any notion of him going in there. It didn't. Because he started to think about her dressing. Leigh had had an amazing body as a teenager, but he was betting she'd gotten even more amazing over the years.

Cullen was certain he looked guilty, and aroused, by the time Leigh came out of the bathroom. But she didn't notice, thank goodness, because she had her attention pinned to her phone.

"I got the search warrant for Alexa's home and office," she said, still focusing on the phone screen. "I'll be going through her emails, phone records, et cetera. Is there anything you'd like to tell me before I look at them?"

Cullen didn't answer right away, and he did that on purpose. He waited for Leigh to lift her gaze and look at him. "I hadn't been in touch with Alexa in months, but it's possible she kept some old emails or texts from me," he explained. "If so, there won't be any threats."

"Nothing that can be construed as a threat?" she pressed.

He gave a weary smile and went to her. "No. I don't make a habit of pouring out my heart—or my temper—in emails or texts."

She met him eye to eye. "Did you pour them out verbally?"

"Not threats. Promises," he clarified, causing her to frown.

7"I'm not a boy," Cullen stated. It was stupid, but he wanted to prove that to her. Prove it in an equally stupid way. And he did that by leaning in and brushing his mouth over hers.

It was too light of a touch to qualify as a kiss, but it sure as hell packed a wallop. He could have sworn that he felt it in every inch of his body.

He pulled back, gauging her reaction, and didn't think he was wrong in that she'd felt it, too. There was plenty of heat in her eyes, and it wasn't just anger that he'd done such a stupid thing.

She smelled good. Damn good. And her scent didn't have anything to do with the soap. No. This was her own underlying scent that added an extra kick to the effects of the kiss that hadn't been a real kiss.

"Leigh?" someone called out from the front of the building.

She backed away from Cullen as if he'd scalded her, and she groaned. Because it was her father's voice.

"Leigh?" Jeb called out again, and Cullen heard the man's footsteps heading their way.

Cullen didn't move, but Leigh sure as heck did. She put several feet of space between them and turned to face her father head-on when Jeb stepped through the open door. Cullen faced him, too, and he saw the instant sweep of Jeb's gaze. From Leigh to Cullen. Unless Jeb was an idiot, then he was no doubt picking up on the heated vibes in the room.

Cullen didn't see Jeb often, which he was sure both of them considered a good thing, and it'd been several years since he'd laid eyes on him. It seemed to Cullen that Jeb had aged considerably during that time. He looked older than his sixtysomething years, and being out in the cold hadn't helped his appearance. His face was chapped and red. His lips, brittle and cracked.

"The roads are closed. You shouldn't have come," Leigh insisted.

Cullen had to hand it to her. Her voice was solid, and she never once dodged her father's intense gaze.

"The county crews salted the roads about an hour ago so they should be opening back up soon. I used my big truck so I could come and check on you." Jeb paused. "I talked to Rocky, and he told me that Cullen and you had spent the night here."

Leigh nodded. "We were at the hospital when the roads were closed so we came here."

Jeb nodded, too, but it was obvious he was processing that. Along with likely trying to decide if his daughter had had sex with a man he considered a suspect.

"How's Jamie?" Jeb asked, walking past them and going to the coffeepot. He poured himself a cup and sipped while continuing to watch them.

"He's better," Leigh said just as Cullen answered, "Fine." It was Leigh who added, "But he wasn't able to ID the person who attacked him."

With just a flick of his gaze to Cullen, Jeb let her know that he was looking at the person he thought had done it. "Rocky said you'd had all the Triple R hands questioned, and—"

"I'm running the investigation by the book," Leigh interrupted. "It's all under control." Which was no doubt her way of saying her father should butt out.

Jeb didn't.

"If you were by the book," Jeb stated, his jaw tight and set, "we wouldn't be having this conversation in front of the man who should be on your suspect list."

"I didn't start this conversation," Leigh snapped. "You did when you came in here and started slinging around accusations and giving me *advice* that I don't need or want."

There was some serious temper in her tone, but it didn't last. Cullen could see that she reined herself right in. Probably because she'd had a lot of experience doing that over the years.

"Everything's under control," she repeated, much calmer this time.

She had a staring match with Jeb that lasted several long moments before Jeb huffed. "I'm worried about you," Jeb finally said, and he'd reined in most of his own temper as well. *Most.* "Someone tried to kill you."

"Someone tried to kill *us*," Leigh corrected, and she hiked her thumb toward Cullen. "We don't know which of us was the target."

Jeb opened his mouth but then closed it. He nodded, conceding that she had a point, and he downed a good bit of his coffee like medicine.

"I'm going across the street to the diner to see if Minnie needs anything," Jeb said.

Minnie Orr was the owner of the diner and someone that most folks classified as Jeb's *friend*. They were probably lovers and likely had been for years.

"Give Minnie my best," Leigh said, and she walked out of the break room, heading back in the direction of her office.

Jeb didn't follow her. Neither did Cullen, and he suspected that her father had a whole lot left to say to him. And he was right.

"You need to keep away from her," Jeb warned him,

his voice a growling whisper. "Leigh doesn't need your kind of *help*."

"She apparently doesn't need yours, either," Cullen threw back at him, and he didn't whisper. No way was he going to cover up for Jeb Mercer taking a dig at him.

Jeb flinched, finished off his coffee and slapped the cup on the table. "If you killed Alexa, I'll make sure you end up behind bars."

Cullen looked him straight in the eyes. He wasn't a cop, never had been, but he knew how to stare someone down. "Same goes for you."

Now Jeb did more than flinch. His eyes widened. "What the hell are you talking about?"

"You were a smart cop so follow the dots," Cullen spat out. "Someone killed my ex in my home. Someone who might have wanted to cause trouble for me. When I come up with possibilities of who'd want to cause that kind of trouble for me or my family, your name's always at the top of the list."

Oh, Jeb's temper returned. He aimed his index finger at Cullen, and the man's hand was shaking. "You—"

But that was all Jeb managed to say before his face went pasty white, and he staggered back a step. Since Jeb looked ready to pass out, Cullen hurried to him and caught onto his arm.

"I'm all right," Jeb insisted, and he tried to bat Cullen's hand away, but he held on. Jeb dragged in several short breaths, wincing with each one. "You don't say a word about this to Leigh, understand?"

Cullen ignored that and went with a question of his own. "Are you sick?"

"No. I'm just a little light-headed. I need to get something to eat at the diner." Jeb finally managed to get out of Cullen's grip, and he stepped back, making eye contact with him. "Not a word about this to Leigh," he repeated.

Cullen had no intention of agreeing to that, but if Jeb was truly sick, and Cullen thought he was, then Leigh would figure it out soon enough. An illness would explain though why Jeb had decided to retire while his approval ratings had still been sky-high. Of course, Jeb hadn't hinted at any health problems, only that he was ready to turn in his badge and take some time off to pursue the search for his missing son.

"I'm not going to hurt Leigh," Cullen told him while he had the man's attention. "I care for her. I've always cared for her, and I believe we would have ended up together had it not been for Bowen and you. And for me," Cullen added. "I was young and stupid and didn't stand up to the two of you back then. But I sure as hell will stand up now."

Jeb continued to stare at him for what felt like an eternity, but the man finally nodded, turned and walked out. Cullen stood there, watching him go, and wondering what the hell was going on.

Cullen took his time going to Leigh's office just in case she wanted to have a private word with her dad. Apparently though, she hadn't, because Jeb had already left and Leigh was on the phone.

"Rocky, I don't want you leaking any more info about the investigation," she snapped. She glanced up at Cullen, who stopped in the doorway, but she continued her conversation. Or rather the dressing-down of her deputy. "Yes, leaking details to my father or anyone else. Any info that needs to be doled out will come through me. Got that?"

Cullen couldn't hear how the deputy responded, but he doubted Rocky would like having Leigh go at him like that. But Rocky deserved it. It showed disrespect, going behind her back by talking to Jeb.

Leigh stabbed the end call button and shoved her phone back in her pocket. She groaned softly, pushed some wisps of hair from her face.

"How much grief did Jeb give you after I left?" she asked.

"I gave him grief right back," Cullen settled for saying. He went closer and tapped her badge. "Do you wear that because of Jeb or in spite of him?"

Leigh shook her head, and he thought she might be annoyed with the shift in conversation. Or maybe she was just annoyed. Period. She certainly had a right to be.

"I've wanted to be a cop for as long as I can remember. Not a cop like my dad," she emphasized. "I always disapproved of punishing enemies or playing favorites when it came to justice." Leigh stopped, gave a hollow laugh. "Which is exactly what Jeb thinks I'm doing now."

Cullen studied her a moment. "No, you're not doing that. If the evidence had pointed to me killing Alexa, I'd be in a holding cell right now."

She studied him, too. Then nodded. "You would be. The badge means something to me, and if I'd been Jeb's son instead of his daughter, he would have given me his blessing about becoming sheriff. And he'd put a stop to Rocky undermining me every chance he gets." Leigh paused. "But I'm not Jeb's son."

She didn't sound bitter about that. Just resigned. And in that moment Cullen despised Jeb even more than he already had. Damn the man and his backward way of thinking. Damn him, too, for hiding whatever health problems he had from Leigh and trying to make Cullen part of that secret.

"You were elected sheriff," Cullen reminded her.

"Barely," she muttered and then quickly waved that off.

Cullen didn't wave it off though. He took hold of her chin, lifting it so their gazes met. "You were elected sheriff," he repeated. "And what you said to Jeb wasn't lip service. You *are* handling this investigation."

She turned away from him. "If I fail at this, if I don't get reelected, I'll have to move. Dark River's my home, but I'll have to move so I can get another job in law enforcement. I couldn't just go back to being a deputy. Plus, whoever beats me in the next election wouldn't want to keep me around anyway."

Cullen understood the "home" roots. He had them. Ironic, since his life was often calmer and easier when he wasn't in Dark River. It would probably be the same for Leigh, but she was as grounded here as he was.

"We have more in common than you think," he reminded her. "That's why we became lovers in the first place."

She looked back at him, the corner of her mouth lifting into a smile. "That was hormones along with the thrill of being star-crossed lovers." Leigh made air quotes for "thrill."

No way could he pretend that the heat hadn't played into her being in his bed that night. But there was more, and Cullen was certain he wasn't the only one who'd felt it. He would have reminded her of that *more*, too, but the phone on her desk rang, and the moment was lost.

Leigh hit the answer button. The speaker function, too. "Sheriff Mercer," she said.

"Sheriff Mercer," the man repeated. "I'm Tyson Saylor."

It took Cullen a couple of seconds to remember that Saylor was the PI his father had hired to follow Alexa.

"Thank you for getting back to me," Leigh told him. "I have some questions for you."

"Well, let's hope I have the right answers," Saylor replied. "In fact, I believe I have something that's going to help with your investigation."

Chapter Seven

Leigh didn't let her hopes soar, but she truly hoped that Saylor was right and that he could help. Because heaven knew, she needed some help right now.

"As Bowen told you, he hired me to keep an eye on Alexa," Saylor continued a moment later. "He thought she might be planning on doing something to cause his son some trouble."

"And was she?" Leigh asked when she saw that was the question on Cullen's face.

"That'd be my guess, but, of course, it's all circumstantial."

Leigh sighed. "I need more than just guesses."

"I understand, and I've got a lot more than that," Saylor assured her.

She tried to manage her expectations but, mercy, that was hard, especially since none of the other evidence was falling in place just yet.

"Bowen told you that Alexa met with a man in a diner, a man who was carrying a weapon," the PI continued. "Well, it turns out that the guy is indeed a thug. I was able to ID him by asking around at the diner, and his name is James McNash."

Leigh hurried to type that into the search engine on her laptop.

"A waitress at the diner says he goes by Jimbo," Saylor explained while she typed and skimmed what popped up. "He's big, mean, and he's got a sheet for multiple assaults. He spent two years in jail on one conviction and six months on another. He's got a rep for being hired muscle."

So, a criminal with violent tendencies. That didn't mean he'd killed Alexa, but it was worth looking into. Also worth looking into why Alexa was meeting with such a man.

"What's the connection between Alexa and this Jimbo?" Leigh pressed. "How'd they know each other?"

"Don't know that, but after I did some pushing, and a little bribing, one of the waitresses finally admitted to me that Alexa and Jimbo had met more than once and that she'd overheard Alexa mention Cullen's name. The waitress also heard Alexa talk about paying Jimbo for the job. Not *a* job," he emphasized. "*The* job."

"And you think the job might have been Cullen," Leigh concluded.

She looked at Cullen, but his expression had gone icy cold. She was betting beneath all that ice, there was the heat of temper.

"I think it's a strong possibility," Saylor agreed.

So did she. But it bothered her that the waitress had offered up so much info. Yes, there'd been payment involved, but it was a lot to tell a PI. What didn't surprise Leigh was that the waitress would remember Cullen being mentioned. It wasn't a common name, and because of his wealth and power—and yes, his looks— Cullen was somewhat of a celebrity.

"I can't get into Alexa's financials, but you might be able to trace a payment to Jimbo," Saylor suggested. "And, of course, you'll want to have a talk with him for yourself. He lives on what used to be his grandfather's farm, about ten miles from Dark River."

Leigh hoped the roads were clear enough soon because she wanted to have a chat with the man today. The sooner, the better.

"I want to go with you to see him," Cullen insisted, his voice low enough that Saylor likely hadn't heard him.

Leigh sighed because she'd known that would be his reaction. She wanted to say no, but if she did, she had no doubts, none, that Cullen would just go visit Jimbo on his own. If Alexa had indeed hired a thug to hurt or kill him, then Cullen wasn't going to back off.

"We'll discuss it later," she muttered to him, holding her hand over the receiver of the phone. Then, she could try to make Cullen see that it would hurt her investigation if he was with her when she interviewed a possible suspect.

"There's more," Saylor added, getting Leigh's attention. "Over the past month, Alexa met with two other men. I don't know the identity of one of them, and she only met with him once while I had her under surveillance. I didn't get any help from any of the waitstaff on IDing the guy. Not even when I offered money. But I'm running the photo through facial recognition, and we might get lucky."

Leigh thought about that a moment. "Did Bowen see the picture? If so, he might recognize him."

Saylor made a sound of agreement. "I sent him the pictures as an attachment to emails, but Bowen's not good at opening that sort of thing. I'll call him and tell him to have a look, that it's important."

Yes, it was. "Any chance you could send me the photos so I can show Cullen?" she asked. "He might also know who he is."

"I can do that. I don't have the pictures on my phone, and my internet's down right now, but as soon as it's up and running, I'll fire them off to you." Saylor paused. "But Cullen won't need a picture for the third man who met with Alexa. I got an ID on him from some of the background data I collected on Cullen and Alexa. It's Cullen's friend Austin Borden."

Leigh's mind did a mental stutter, and the iciness vanished from Cullen's face. "Austin?" he repeated, and this time it was plenty loud enough for Saylor to hear.

"Cullen's here with me," Leigh quickly explained to the PI. "You're sure it was Austin Borden?" she pressed.

"Positive. I'm guessing he didn't mention any of those meetings to you?"

"No," Cullen said, the surprise and confusion in his voice. *"Meetings?"* he repeated. "How many of them were there?"

"Four over the past month. They met in a café once, and the other times I trailed her going into his office."

Leigh tried to figure out why Austin would have done that, and she only came up with one possibility. Well, one possibility that didn't involve anything illegal or shady. "Maybe Alexa had business with him?" Leigh suggested.

She looked at Cullen to see if that was a possibility even though she knew it'd be a slim one. Austin was a cattle broker, and Alexa didn't seem the type to need such services. Still—

Cullen shook his head in response to her silent question, and making a frustrated groan, he scrubbed his hand over his face. He also whipped out his phone, no doubt to try to call Austin again, but Leigh lifted her hand to have him hold off on that. If Austin finally answered, she wanted the first crack at him.

"I'll get those pictures to you first chance I get," the PI added a moment later. "Good luck with your investigation, Sheriff."

The moment Leigh ended the call, she turned to Cullen. He wasn't going to like her having a go at him like this, but it had to be done. "Tell me why you think Alexa would have visited Austin," she insisted. "Were they friends?"

"Friendly," Cullen answered after a long pause. He cursed. "Hell, they were all friends. Austin, Kali and Alexa. Austin and Kali are the ones who introduced me to Alexa."

Leigh tried to jump on the "no way was Austin guilty" bandwagon, but this wasn't looking good. Especially since Austin had been spotted on the patio while the party had been going on. Added to that, the man wasn't answering his phone, and the cop in her wondered if that was because he had something to hide.

"Maybe the meetings have something to do with Austin and Kali's engagement," Cullen said several moments later. He was obviously trying to make sense of this, too. "It's possible Alexa helped him pick out the ring." He paused. "It's equally possible that Alexa was working Austin so she could figure out the best way to send a thug after me."

Of those possibilities, Leigh was choosing the last option Cullen had come up with. If it'd been something as simple as ring selection, Austin probably wouldn't have kept it from Cullen. Then again, maybe Austin felt it was best not to bring up anything to Cullen about his ex. The relationship lines became a little blurred when there was a breakup of a couple in a group of friends. Austin might not have wanted it to get around that he was staying in touch with Cullen's ex.

"All right," Leigh said, "go ahead and try to call Austin again. I've already left a message insisting he contact me immediately for questioning and then to come into the station the moment the roads are clear. If you're able to reach him, let him know I want that interview to happen ASAP."

Cullen nodded, made the call and then cursed when it went to voice mail again. She hoped Austin wasn't just trying to avoid them, but if so, she'd just pay him a personal visit after she talked with Jimbo. If he continued to dodge her, she'd be forced to get a warrant to compel him to come in for questioning.

"I'll try to call Kali again," Cullen insisted. "I can leave her another voice mail, too."

However, before he could do that, Leigh's own phone rang. She answered it and immediately heard a familiar voice.

"It's me, Jamie," the ranch hand blurted out. "Someone just threatened to kill me."

Cullen must have noticed the change in her body language and expression because he hurried to her. "Jamie," she said so that Cullen would know who was on the phone. And she put the call on speaker. "Who threatened to kill you?"

"I don't know." Jamie's voice was shaky, and she figured that shakiness applied to the rest of him, too.

"I got a call from a man. It popped up on my screen as unknown, but I answered it anyway because I thought it might be somebody from the Triple R. The man's voice was muffled, but he told me if I kept talking to the cops that I'd end up like Alexa."

Sweet heaven. Leigh reined in what would have been a brusque cop tone because she knew Jamie had to be terrified. "You're still in the hospital?" she asked.

"I am, but I asked the security guard to come in the room with me. Don't tell anybody I called you. At least not until I'm out of the hospital and can fend for myself."

"I have no intention of letting you fend for yourself. The guard will stay with you and make sure you're safe. Now, tell me about this call you got." She started with an easy question. "You're sure it was a man?"

"It sure sounded like one," he answered after a pause long enough to let her know he was giving it some thought, "but like I said, his voice was muffled. You know, like someone with a bad sore throat."

The person had obviously tried to disguise his voice. Maybe because the caller had believed Jamie would recognize him.

"He threatened to kill me," Jamie repeated, and his fear had gone up another notch.

"I know. And I'm sorry. Cullen and I are just up the street. We'll be there in a few minutes and will stay with you until a deputy arrives." Leigh started putting on her coat. "I'll also need to take a look at your phone to see if we can trace the call."

"You have to trace it," Jamie insisted. "You have to stop him from killing me."

Leigh would do her best on both counts, but the

trace was a long shot since the person had likely used a burner cell.

"Jamie, did Alexa ever mention someone named Jimbo McNash?" Leigh asked.

He repeated the name several times. "No. Why? Is he the man who just threatened me?"

"I don't know. But I'll find out," she promised him. "Cullen and I will be there in a couple of minutes, and we'll talk more then."

Cullen grabbed his coat, too, putting it on as they headed to the door. Leigh hated locking up, but if anyone called in with an emergency, it would go through dispatch, who would in turn notify her. She was hoping though that there wouldn't be anything else that required her attention because she already had a full plate.

"I'm texting Kerry Yancy, the night deputy, and asking him to come in," she told Cullen, and she took care of that before they went outside.

They hurried to Cullen's truck and found the windshield scabbed with ice. Since it would take precious moments to defrost it, they headed to the hospital on foot.

And they both kept watch.

Apparently, there was no need to mention to Cullen that this could be a lure to get them out into the open so that the driver of that SUV could try to kill them again. But it was a risk she had to take. Leigh wouldn't have felt right being holed up in the office while a killer went after Jamie.

"Whoever made that call could be desperate," Leigh concluded. She lowered her head against the howling wind and tried not to think of the ache that the cold air put in her lungs. "Desperate enough to try to silence Jamie, or scare him into being silenced, anyway. I need to get out the word that he didn't see anything and can't ID his attacker. In this case, the truth might keep him safe."

"I can arrange for some of the ranch hands to stand guard in the parking lot and keep an eye on who comes and goes," Cullen suggested.

Something like that would certainly cause gossip. The wrong kind of gossip, that Cullen had his nose deep in this investigation. Still, it might prevent Jamie from being hurt again.

"You trust all your ranch hands and don't believe any one of them could have had a part in Alexa's murder?"

"I trust them," Cullen said without hesitation. "If I didn't, they wouldn't be working for me."

She considered what he said for the last block they had to walk and nodded. "Have them come out when the roads are open, but I want them to stay in the parking lot. I'll make sure security is posted inside."

And maybe none of these measures would even be necessary. It was entirely possible that the caller who'd threatened Jamie had done that as a ploy to keep the young man quiet. Thankfully, Jamie had trusted her enough to let her know about it, and Leigh wanted to make sure his trust wasn't misplaced.

They hurried into the ER, and Amber was there, waiting for them. "We've moved Jamie to another room. He was very upset so the doctor had me give him a sedative. Follow me, and I'll take you to him."

Jamie must have told Amber about the threatening call as well because the nurse was clearly shaken.

As it had been before, the hospital was still practically empty, but Leigh kept her eyes open, looking for any signs of trouble. They made their way down a hall to a room in the center of what was the patients' ward, and Cullen and she were about to go in when his phone rang.

"It's Kali," he relayed when he saw the screen. He looked at Amber when she stayed put. "I need to take this call." Cullen didn't add "in private," but Amber got the message because she strolled away, heading back to the ER.

"Kali," Cullen greeted, putting the call on speaker for Leigh. "I've been trying to get in touch with you."

"Yes." That was all Kali said for several long moments. "I got your messages, but I…well, I needed some time before I talked to you."

Oh, mercy. There was definitely something wrong, and it sounded as if the woman had been crying.

"I have to speak to Austin," Cullen continued, obviously zooming right in on what needed to be done. "Where is he?"

The next sound that Leigh heard from Kali was a sob. One that put Leigh's stomach in knots.

"What's wrong?" Cullen pressed. "What happened?"

Kali didn't answer right away. Probably because of all the crying. "I thought Austin would be with you. That's why I'm driving to Dark River now."

Cullen cursed under his breath. "Kali, it's not safe for you to be out on the roads."

"I have to see him, and he's not home. I figured he'd go to your house."

"No. If he had, someone would have called me. I'm at the hospital right now. One of my ranch hands was injured, but if Austin had shown up at the ranch, Rosa would have told me."

"Then where is he?" Kali demanded.

Apparently, Leigh wasn't the only one who wanted to know the answer to that. "I'll try to find out," Cullen tried to reassure her.

Kali didn't sound the least bit reassured though. "Did you know?" she blurted out. "Did you know about Austin?"

Because her arm was against Cullen's, Leigh felt his muscles turn to iron. "Know what?" Cullen demanded.

"That Austin was having an affair." The words rushed out, followed by another sob.

Oh, mercy. This was a new wrinkle, and Leigh already had a bad feeling about it.

"No, I didn't know about any affair. You're sure he was cheating?" Cullen pressed.

"I'm sure. I found out last night. I accidently took his phone with me."

Well, that explained why they hadn't been able to reach Austin.

"Austin's always forgetting his password so when it rang, I answered it," Kali went on. "It was just his dad wanting to make sure he got home all right after the party, but that's when I saw the texts."

"What texts?" Cullen demanded.

"God, Cullen," Kali said on a hoarse sob, "Austin's been having an affair with Alexa."

Chapter Eight

Cullen felt Kali's words land like an actual punch to his gut. Words that he had to mentally repeat a couple of times just so they'd sink in. Obviously though, Leigh wasn't having any trouble processing what Kali had said.

"Austin had an affair with Alexa?" Leigh asked.

"Who is that?" Kali demanded. "Who's listening?"

"Sheriff Leigh Mercer," she said.

Cullen could have told Leigh it was a mistake to volunteer who she was, and Kali's gasp proved it. He wasn't the least bit surprised when Kali hung up on him. On a heavy sigh, Cullen tried to call the woman back, but Kali didn't answer.

"For legal reasons, I had to identify myself," Leigh muttered. "And I didn't want her to say anything incriminating that I couldn't use because her lawyer wouldn't allow it into evidence."

Yeah, Cullen understood that, but he wished he'd been able to ask Kali if she was certain about Austin having an affair with Alexa. Then again, Leigh would almost certainly ask her when she had Kali in for questioning.

Which Leigh would do.

No way could Leigh dismiss a bombshell like that. No way could Kali dodge questioning, either, because this was a murder investigation. An investigation where Kali had just revealed a possible motive for Austin murdering Alexa. Because affairs didn't often end well. Hell, Alexa wouldn't have let it end well unless she'd been the one to call it quits.

"Let me make sure Jamie is okay," Leigh said, peering into the room. "And then we can discuss what I'm going to have to do about this situation with Austin and Alexa."

What she was going to have to do would likely include warrants. Maybe even an arrest. Yeah, this was like a punch to the gut all right.

Cullen looked in Jamie's room, too, and saw that his eyes were closed. So whatever meds Amber had given him had already taken effect. The guard, Harry Harbin, was there as well, and he actually appeared to be interested in doing his job. He was standing at the foot of the bed and had his hand on the butt of his gun.

"You need me to wake him up?" Harry asked her.

Leigh shook her head. "No. Not yet. Stay in here with him. I'll be right outside in the hall for a couple more minutes."

Harry nodded, and the moment Leigh shut the door, she turned back to Cullen. "Is Austin the type to have an affair?" she whispered. "An affair with your ex," she tacked on to her question.

"I didn't think so." Or rather Cullen didn't *want* to think so. "But obviously Kali saw something on Austin's phone to make her believe it was true. Plus, the PI said that he'd seen Alexa meet with Austin."

And there it was—the proof in a nutshell.

When he added that Austin had been spotted on the patio and that he'd kept his relationship with Alexa a secret, Cullen knew that Austin had just become Leigh's prime suspect. But Cullen could see this from one more angle.

"Even if Austin had the affair, it doesn't mean he murdered Alexa," Cullen said, thinking out loud. "But if someone found out what he was doing, they might have wanted to kill Alexa at the party to make him look guilty. That, in turn, would sling some mud on me because some would think I'd cover for him."

Cullen was thankful when Leigh didn't ask if he would have indeed covered for his friend. He wouldn't have.

"I'm guessing Austin didn't tell you about the affair," Leigh continued a moment later, "because he…what? Would have thought you'd tell Kali?"

"I wouldn't have," Cullen insisted. "But this would have put a wedge between Austin and me. Not because he was having sex with my ex but because he was cheating on Kali. I would have tried to talk him into either ending the affair or breaking things off with Kali."

Leigh groaned softly and leaned back against the wall while she studied him. "You know this gives both Kali and Austin motive for murder. Yes, Kali said she didn't learn about the affair until she saw Austin's phone, but she could have found out sooner."

Cullen tried to imagine Kali bashing in Alexa's head, and he could see it happening if she was in a rage. But what was hard for him to fathom was that Kali would clean herself up and then come back into the party as if nothing had happened. Plus, there was the problem of Jamie. Cullen hadn't kept track of Kali's whereabouts all evening, but he just couldn't see her sneaking up on his ranch hand and trying to kill him.

Then again, people did all sorts of things to cover themselves.

And Kali might have felt the need to get rid of Jamie if she'd thought he could link her back to Alexa. Maybe Alexa had even claimed to have told Jamie that she was meeting with Kali and that if anything happened to her, Jamie would know. Again, that felt like a huge stretch.

"I need to call Mack," Cullen said, shifting his thoughts. "I want to have some extra ranch hands stand guard in the parking lot."

Leigh nodded and studied him as if she was trying to figure out just how much this latest development was eating away at him. It hurt all right, but Cullen didn't hide it from her. Wasn't sure he could.

On a sigh, she touched his arm, rubbed lightly. "I'll go in and get Jamie's phone so I can get started on the possible trace."

"Thanks for that," he said, tipping his head to the arm she'd just rubbed.

Her next sigh was louder, and despite their situation, it made him smile. This attraction was really messing with both of them.

Cullen waited until she'd gone in with Jamie before he called Mack, and as expected, the ranch hand answered right away.

"I was about to call you," Mack said. He heard the man drag in a deep breath. "I took one of the horses over to the east trail. Just to have a look around. I wasn't far from the house when I found an SUV. There's damage to the front end so I bet it's the one used to ram into the sheriff's cruiser."

Yeah, that was a safe bet. "I'm guessing no one was inside it?"

"No one," Mack verified. "I didn't touch it, because I knew the CSIs would want to process it so I just let them know. They'll probably be calling the sheriff about it."

Again, that was a safe bet.

"It's one of the Triple R's vehicles," Mack added a moment later.

Hell. Of course it was. If the killer wanted to add another twist to muddy the waters even more than they already were, then it made sense to use one of Cullen's own SUVs. There were several on the ranch, along with a large number of trucks, and the vehicles were parked all around. There probably wouldn't have been keys in the ignition, but someone capable of killing could likely know how to hot-wire a car.

"Boss, if you're thinking one of the hands could have done this," Mack said, "you're wrong."

"I wasn't thinking along those lines. But it could have been someone who had been at the party. Someone who maybe stayed back when I thought they had left."

That would be something a killer would do—stay around to tie up any loose ends. Hell, for that matter the killer could have hidden in one of the rooms in the house. No one had done a head count to make sure all the guests had been accounted for.

And that led Cullen back to Austin.

Kali, too, since she and Austin hadn't left the party together. Plus, either one of them would have known where the SUVs were kept.

"If Austin or Kali show up at the ranch, let me know and then bring them straight in for questioning," Cullen instructed Mack. "Also, I need two more hands out to the hospital parking lot to stand guard. Jamie got a threatening phone call that shook him up."

"Will do." There was concern and some alarm in Mack's voice. "Look, I can get into town if you want me there with him."

"No, I'd rather you stay at the ranch and put out any fires that might pop up." Because after all, it was possible the killer was still nearby.

It was an unsettling thought that grew even stronger when Cullen saw Austin coming up the hall toward him.

"I have to go," Cullen told Mack, and he ended the call so he could give Austin the once-over.

His friend looked like hell. Dark shadows under his eyes. Scruff that went well past a fashion statement, and it looked as if he'd grabbed the jeans and T-shirt he was wearing off the floor of his room. His coat was unbuttoned and flapped against his sides with his hurried strides.

"I still haven't been able to find my phone so I accessed my office messages and found all these calls from Leigh and you," Austin said right off. "What the heck's going on?"

Cullen wasn't sure where to start, and it turned out that he didn't have to make a decision about that. Leigh must have heard Austin's voice, because she came out of Jamie's room.

"What the heck's going on?" Austin repeated to Leigh.

She glanced around and motioned for him to follow her. Leigh led Austin to a small visitors' room just a few doors down from Jamie's room. Cullen went with them since he had every intention of hearing what Austin had to say. However, he waited in the doorway so he could see if someone tried to get into Jamie's room. Leigh and Austin took seats at the small metal table.

"I'm going to read you your rights," Leigh said to Austin, and she proceeded to do just that.

Austin sat in what appeared to be stunned silence before he turned his accusing gaze on Cullen. "You believe I killed Alexa?" Austin came out and demanded.

"I have questions, and I have to make sure all the legal bases are covered," Leigh insisted before Cullen could speak. "You want to call a lawyer?"

"Do I need a lawyer?" Austin fired back, but he immediately waved that off. "Let's just clear all of this up. And I can clear it up," he insisted.

The angry fire in Austin's eyes was just as much for Cullen as it was for Leigh. Cullen didn't mind. There'd be fire in his own eyes if it turned out that Austin had indeed had any part in this.

"Let's start with your whereabouts during the party," Leigh started, and she took out her phone and put on the recorder. "Were you on the patio of the guest room at the Triple R?"

Austin opened his mouth, but it seemed to Cullen that he changed his mind as to what he'd been about to say. "Yes. I was there."

"You said you smoked on the front porch," Cullen pointed out.

"Well, I misspoke." Austin stood and poured himself a cup of what looked more like sludge than coffee. It probably tasted like sludge, too, because Austin grimaced when he took a sip. "It was on the patio. It was cold, and I left the doors open so I wouldn't freeze while I was out there."

"What time was this?" Leigh said, asking the very question that Cullen knew she would.

They didn't have a time of death on Alexa, but according to Jamie, he'd dropped her off around eight. A half hour or so later, Jamie had been attacked. So, Alexa had likely died between eight and eight thirty.

"I'm not sure." Austin's forehead bunched up. "Maybe seven thirty or a little later. It was still early, but I needed a smoke before all the toasts got started so I popped outside. It was so cold that I decided to take just a few drags off the cigarette and then get a hit with the nicotine gum I carry so I wouldn't have to stay outside."

If Austin was telling the truth, then his timing for that smoke would clear him. But Leigh probably had plenty of doubts about that "if."

"Did you see anyone else on or around the patio when you were out there?" Leigh asked, and there was some skepticism not only in her voice but also in her flat cop's eyes.

"No." Austin stopped for a moment. "Well, other than a few of the ranch hands. I saw a couple of them going to and from the barn."

"Only the ranch hands?" Leigh pressed. "No one else?" When Austin shook his head, she moved on to the next question. "Did you leave the patio doors unlocked when you came back into the house?"

Again, Austin's forehead bunched up. "Maybe. Sorry, I can't remember." He huffed. "Look, I didn't kill Alexa or hurt Jamie so all of this is unnecessary."

"This is a murder investigation," Leigh argued. "All the details are necessary. Did you see Alexa during the party?" she tacked on without even pausing.

"No." However, Austin certainly did some pausing.

"But she did text me. She wanted me to meet her, and I told her no."

Leigh jumped right on that. "Meet her where and why?"

Austin lifted his shoulder. "She didn't say."

"So, she could have wanted you to meet her in the house? In Cullen's bedroom?" Leigh continued.

"She didn't say," Austin repeated, and this time he snapped it. "And from the sound of these questions, I think I should call my lawyer after all."

"Go ahead." Leigh stood. "As soon as I get one of my deputies here for guard duty, I'll meet your lawyer and you at the police station. Deputy Yancy's already there and can show you to an interview room. He texted me when I was with Jamie," she let Cullen know.

Austin stood as well, and was no doubt about to verbally blast Leigh for treating him like the suspect that he was, but he didn't get the chance. Looking as harried as Austin had when he'd arrived, Kali came rushing in.

"The nurse said she saw the three of you come in here," Kali explained, her voice shaky and her glare already on Austin.

"Kali." Austin went to her and tried to pull her into his arms, but Kali batted him away and turned to Cullen. "You've told Austin that I know about his affair with Alexa?"

The color drained from Austin's face.

"No, I didn't tell him," Cullen admitted.

"Kali," Austin repeated, and again he reached for her. This time, Kali slapped him. Not a gentle hit, either. The sound of it cracked through the room.

Cullen stepped in, putting himself between the two while Leigh took hold of Austin and pulled him back.

"Don't you dare try to deny it," Kali spat out, aiming her venomous gaze on Austin. She held up what was almost certainly Austin's phone. "I found your texts to her."

It was hard for Cullen to believe this was the couple who'd been so happy just the night before. Or rather, they'd *appeared* happy. Obviously, appearances weren't accurate.

"I was going to break things off with Alexa," Austin pled. "I swear. I made a huge mistake by being with her, and I told her it was over, that I wanted to be with you. I want us to get married, Kali. I want a life with you."

The sound Kali made was a low, rumbling growl. "You'll never have a life with me."

She started cursing him, calling him vile names, but the fit of temper soon gave way to tears. Judging from her red eyes, these tears weren't the first of the day.

The sobs seemed to weaken her, and Kali sagged against Cullen. He helped her to the table and had her sit.

"I'm sorry," Austin said, but Leigh blocked him from going closer to Kali. "So sorry. You have to believe me when I tell you it was over with Alexa."

"I don't have to believe anything you say." Kali spoke through the wet sobs, and Cullen located a box of tissues for her.

"Please," Austin tried again. "Let me make this up to you."

But Kali didn't answer. She buried her face in her folded arms on the table and continued to cry.

"When did you break up with Alexa?" Cullen asked Austin, knowing that it was something Leigh also needed to know.

Austin cursed, groaned and squeezed his fists on the sides of his head. "Right before the party. She called me and said she wanted to have sex with me in your bed."

Cullen wanted to curse, too. Hell. That was something Alexa definitely would have done.

"She sent Austin a naked picture of herself," Kali provided, thrusting out the phone to Cullen.

That caused Austin to groan again, but he sure as heck didn't deny it. And Cullen could see how this had played out. Alexa had probably thought this was the way to get back at him.

Cullen took the phone from Kali and passed it to Leigh. "Did you see Alexa at any time during the party?" Leigh asked, scrolling past the naked photo to get to the texts.

"No, I swear," Austin insisted. "After she texted me, I told her I had no intentions of having sex with her in Cullen's bed or anywhere else for that matter, and I let her know that it was over. Then, I blocked her because I didn't want to have her texting or trying to call me during the party."

Leigh continued to scroll through Austin's phone. "You had this text conversation with her about the same time you said you were on the patio having a smoke," Leigh pointed out.

Austin was scowling when he whipped toward her. "I was having a smoke and texting her. You can see—I ended things with her. I ended things with her," he repeated, this time to Kali.

"I don't care," Kali snapped. "I never want to see you again."

"Unfortunately, you'll have to," Leigh said to Kali. "I'll need to interview both Austin and you. And take this into evidence," she added, holding up the phone. She looked at Austin. "Do I need a search warrant to examine the clothes you wore to the party last night, or will you give me permission to have them sent to the lab?"

Austin stared at her a long time. "You'll need a search warrant," he snarled. "Since I find myself without a phone, text Doug for me," he added to Cullen. "Tell him I'll meet him at the Dark River PD. I won't be saying anything else to Sheriff Mercer until he arrives, and I damn sure won't be giving her my clothes unless he says different."

Doug Franklin was a lawyer friend of theirs and had been at the party the night before. On a heavy sigh, Cullen sent him a text as Austin stormed out.

"I don't want to go to the police station right now," Kali muttered. "Let me just sit here for a little while and try to steady myself." She pulled off her engagement ring and practically shoved it into Cullen's hand. "Give that to him and tell him I hope he chokes on it."

"That should be fun," Cullen mumbled, slipping it into his pocket, and he stepped out into the hall with Leigh.

"I doubt they're flight risks," Leigh whispered to him, "but I want to go ahead and take Kali in after I get a deputy here to keep tabs on Jamie." She sent a text to arrange for a deputy to come to the hospital.

Cullen couldn't blame Leigh for wanting to get Kali in for questioning. The sooner they got answers, the better. Well, Cullen thought it would be better, anyway, and he hoped the woman he'd kissed less than an hour ago didn't have to arrest his friend for murder.

Leigh was no doubt trying to contain it, but the stress

was starting to show, and Cullen gave her one of those arm rubs she'd given him earlier.

"That shouldn't feel good," she said, her voice still a whisper. "It can't feel good," she amended with her eyes lifting to meet his. She groaned. "This is really turning into a nasty mess."

Cullen figured he was part of that mess. A complication added to the fact that Leigh now had two suspects. Or rather three since she hadn't had a chance to talk to Jimbo McNash yet. Cullen was hoping the thug would just confess to the murder and the attacks just so the investigation wouldn't be looming over them. Then, Leigh and he could…

Well, he didn't know where they'd go from there, but one thing was for certain. He needed to figure out a way to keep her in his life. Along with getting her in his bed.

Her phone rang, and she slid Austin's cell in her jeans pocket so she could answer it and put it on speaker. "This is Saylor again," the PI greeted.

"What can I do for you?" Leigh asked.

"I got your number from Deputy Yancy when I called your office. Thought you'd want to know that Bowen had a look at the rest of the surveillance photos of Alexa, and he was able to ID the other man she met with."

Cullen leaned in so that he wouldn't miss this.

"My internet's working so I just sent the photos to you," Saylor added. "But you'll recognize the man, too."

"Oh?" Leigh asked.

"Yeah," Saylor verified. "Because it's your deputy Rocky Callaway."

Chapter Nine

The sudden shock hit Leigh to the core. "Rocky?" she managed to say to the PI. "You're sure?"

"Bowen said he's positive." Saylor paused. "He also wants to talk to you about this."

Of course he did. He'd demand to know if Rocky had conspired with Alexa to cause trouble for Cullen. Maybe for her, too. And right now, Leigh didn't have the answer to that, but she soon would.

"I photographed only one meeting that Alexa had with your deputy," Saylor continued. "But it's possible there were more."

Yes, and that was something else she would ask her deputy.

"When did this meeting with Rocky take place?" Leigh asked.

"Three days ago."

So, two days before the party. Rocky definitely should have mentioned speaking to Alexa that close to the date of her murder. Especially since Leigh hadn't heard a peep about Rocky being friends or even friendly with the woman.

"Thanks for the info," Leigh told him, and she ended the call so she could access her email on her phone.

"I'm guessing Rocky didn't tell you about these meetings?" Cullen asked.

Leigh shook her head, pulled up the file with the photos, and the moment the first one loaded, she wanted to curse. It was Rocky all right, and she turned her phone so that he could see. Rocky and Alexa weren't exactly cozy-looking, the way lovers might be, but they were clearly having an intimate conversation.

"How bad does Rocky want to see you fail as sheriff?" Cullen asked.

Leigh suspected the answer to that was *very bad*. But she didn't voice that opinion because she spotted Cecile Taggart, a reserve deputy, heading her way. Cecile was in her early fifties and had plenty of experience. Better yet, she was someone Leigh trusted.

"I was already heading into town when I got your text," Cecile greeted. "Which one is Jamie's room?"

Leigh pointed to it. "The security guard's with him now, but I'd rather you be in there. The guard can stay on the door."

Cecile's eyebrow winged up. "Are you expecting big trouble?"

"Trying to avoid it," Leigh explained. "Jamie's sedated right now, but he's scared. Stay with him at all times."

"Will do. I've got my laptop with me," she added, patting the bag she had hooked over her shoulder. "If you need any help with the murder investigation, just let me know. I'll probably have some downtime while I'm with Jamie."

True, especially since Jamie was asleep and might be that way for a while. "There's a search warrant to go through Alexa's files and phone records. Get started on making that happen. I need you to earmark any communication Alexa had with Austin Borden, Kali Starling and James McNash, aka Jimbo. Also with Cullen and Bowen Brodie."

Cecile's eyebrow came up again, and she glanced at Cullen, probably to see how he felt about that. Cullen merely shrugged.

"I'm covering the bases," Leigh muttered to Cullen. But, of course, she hadn't. Because she'd left Rocky's name off that list. No doubt because Leigh didn't want Rocky to know he was under investigation. And that was probably why she also added to Cecile, "Flag anything that's connected to anyone involved in this investigation. *Anyone*," Leigh emphasized.

"Will do," Cecile repeated. "You headed home to get some shut-eye?"

Leigh shook her head. "I'll be in my office."

She waited until Cecile was in with Jamie before turning back to the visitors' room. Kali was still sitting there, but she'd stopped crying. She was staring blankly at the table.

"Would you like to walk with us to my office?" Leigh asked.

Kali shook her head. "I need a few more minutes. I'll be there soon." Now she turned and looked at Leigh. "Just make sure Austin's in a room somewhere when I get there. I meant it when I said I didn't want to see him."

Leigh gave a confirming nod, and with Cullen right beside her, they started for the exit. As she walked, she pressed Rocky's number, and he answered after several rings.

"Yo," he grumbled, sounding as if she'd woken him.

"I want you at the office right now," Leigh told him.

"But the roads—"

"Are obviously clear enough since I've got two people already waiting in Interview," Leigh interrupted.

Rocky yawned. "You want me to do the interviews?"

"I want you in the office," she repeated, a snap in her voice, and ended the call.

"Are you okay?" Cullen asked her.

No, she wasn't, and Leigh made a sound that could have meant anything so that she didn't have to verify that she was far from okay. It was possible that Rocky had withheld evidence pertinent to a murder investigation. If he had, then that would be obstruction of justice.

And possibly more.

"I'm not okay," Leigh grumbled as Cullen and she walked.

"I got that. It was a tough night, followed by a tough morning."

Yes, it had been. "Thanks for not giving me any flak about having Cecile look for correspondence between Alexa and you."

"I figured you've already got enough flak. Plus, it'll be interesting to see what she kept. Like I told you, I didn't pour out my heart in emails."

She believed him. Leigh mentally groaned because it was more than just believing him. For reasons she didn't especially want to explore, she trusted Cullen, and right now, she very much needed someone who wasn't going to stab her in the back.

Deputy Yancy was at his desk when they went into the police department, and he stood, giving a nodded greeting to Cullen.

"Austin Borden's in the interview room," Yancy volunteered. "But he said he's not saying anything else until his lawyer gets here."

"I can talk to him," Cullen suggested.

But Leigh shook her head. If Austin told Cullen he was indeed a killer, she didn't want the lawyer throwing out the confession or trying to have it suppressed. Austin's lawyer could even claim that Cullen had coerced him to admit to murdering Alexa.

"When the lawyer gets here, I want you to be the one to take Austin's statement," Leigh instructed Yancy. "He's already riled at me, and you might be able to get more out of him."

Yancy was laid-back and had more of a friendly-officer style when it came to interviews. Austin might respond better to that. Heck, he might respond better to anyone other than her. Because right now, Cullen and she were the enemy.

"Dawn and Vance finished interviewing the Triple R ranch hands and the catering staff," Yancy explained. "Nothing new so far."

Leigh figured that would be the case. Still, it was a box that had to be checked.

"You know about the blue SUV being found at the ranch, right?" Yancy asked.

She nodded. "I got a text about it. Let me know when the CSIs have it processed."

"Will do. You've also got a bunch of emails and had some phone calls," Yancy added, handing her a sheet listing the calls.

"I'll get to them," Leigh said, heading into her office. "In the meantime, I need you to start securing a warrant to search Austin's home. I specifically want to get the clothes he wore to the party last night."

Yancy's eyes went a little wide. "You think there might be blood on them?"

Leigh shrugged. "We'll see when we have the clothes. Vance and Dawn might have photos from some of the guests. They were going to try to collect them. If they've managed to do that already, we'll know what clothes to include in the warrant. Unless..." She turned to Cullen. "Do you remember?"

Cullen closed his eyes a moment as if trying to call up the image. "A black suit with a blue tie. Kali was wearing a blue dress." He opened his eyes, looked at her. "I figured you'd want to know that in case you got a warrant for her clothes, too."

"I do," Leigh confirmed, giving Yancy instructions to get the warrant for that as well. She added a search of Kali's parents' house since the woman had spent the night there. "Try to stretch the warrant to include her computer, emails and phone records." She turned back to Cullen. "And I'll have your clothes couriered to the lab this morning."

In fact, she'd already done the paperwork to get that started, and the courier would no doubt soon be on the way now that the roads were clearing. She was certain there'd be no blood on Cullen's clothes, and that might stave off those who thought he was guilty. Ironically, her own deputy Rocky was one of the ones fanning those particular "Cullen's guilty" flames, and now Leigh wanted to know if that was because Rocky had something to hide.

Because she desperately needed a caffeine hit, she went into her office to make a fresh pot. Cullen followed her, of course, and he shut the door.

"Are you going to test Rocky's clothes, too?" Cullen asked.

"If I have probable cause."

Leigh was about to continue with some legal babble to explain how she would do her job, but she cursed and gave the leg of her desk a good kick. It hurt, the pain vibrating through her boot to her toes, but she hadn't been able to hold back the frustration. No, it was more than frustration. It was a gut-punch of anger.

"Rocky will fight me every step of the way," she said on a heavy sigh. "And while he's fighting me, it'll also be a distraction from the investigation. *You're* a distraction," she added when Cullen reached for her. "You and your clothes," she grumbled.

He looked, well, amused by that, and as if she would put up no protest whatsoever—which she didn't—he pulled her into his arms and brushed a kiss on the top of her head. "My party suit or the clothes I'm wearing now?"

"The latter." She squeezed her eyes shut, and just for a moment, she let her body sag against him. "Hot cowboy clothes."

Leigh couldn't see his face, but she suspected he was smiling. After all, she'd just confessed that his well-worn jeans, faded blue work shirt and scuffed boots appealed to her more than his suit had. Then again, Cullen looked good in anything. And nothing. Especially nothing.

That, of course, only proved to her that he was a distraction.

She forced herself away from him so she could get some coffee and do some work while they waited for Rocky, Kali and Austin's lawyer. That was the plan, anyway, but the plan took a little detour when Cullen leaned in and kissed her. This was no peck like the one earlier in the break room. No. This was the full deal.

Cullen certainly hadn't lost any skills in the kissing department. He was still darn good at moving his mouth over hers. Still good at making a kiss feel as if it was full-blown foreplay. And his taste. Mercy. It was foreplay, too.

He dropped his hands to her waist, nudging her closer while also nudging her lips apart with his tongue. She remembered this. Another kick of heat. The urgency he created when he deepened the kiss.

Leigh sank into him, all the while the sane part of her yelling that she should knock this off. She listened to the sane part, knew that it was right, but she lingered a little longer, letting the kiss and Cullen's touch slide through her.

It took some willpower, but Leigh finally untangled herself from Cullen and stepped back. She didn't dodge his gaze because she needed him to see that this had to stop. Maybe she got that point across, maybe not, but either way, he didn't reach for her.

They stood there, their breaths heavy, and with the heat searing around them. She might have been tempted to go back for another round, but she was saved by the bell when her phone rang.

"It's Cash," she muttered after glancing at the name on the screen.

There was no need for her to explain that Cash was her brother, because Cullen and Cash had gone to school together. Had both been star football players. They hadn't stayed close, but then, like Cullen, Cash hadn't stayed particularly close with anyone in Dark River.

Including her.

It'd been at least six months since she'd gotten a call from him, and Leigh doubted it was a coincidence that Cash was getting in touch with her now while she was neck-deep in a murder investigation.

"Leigh," her brother greeted the moment she answered. "I just got a call from one of your deputies, Yancy. He gave me a heads-up that you'll be initiating a search warrant for Kali Starling's and her parents' residences."

Yancy worked fast, and it took Leigh several moments to realize why Cash was telling her this. Cash was the sheriff of Clay Ridge, a town about twenty miles from Dark River, and Kali and her parents lived in Clay Ridge.

"Yes," Leigh verified. "Kali was on scene at a party last night where a woman was killed."

"I heard. The dead woman was Cullen's ex. I also heard you haven't arrested Cullen." Cash paused. "How much grief is Jeb giving you over this?"

"Enough," Leigh answered honestly, knowing it was going to cause Cash to curse.

It did.

"Damn it, Leigh, you shouldn't let him run roughshod over you like that," Cash snarled.

And there was their sibling conflict in a nutshell. After doing almost daily battle with Jeb, Cash had left home and hadn't come back. Not even for her when Leigh had insisted on staying. Cash saw that as a weakness on her part, claiming that she was Jeb's doormat. But Leigh saw it as putting up with Jeb so she could be where she wanted to be and have the job she'd always wanted.

"Jeb's never going to accept you as sheriff," Cash went on. "Not really. I mean, he might say he's okay with it, but I promise you he wanted one of his sons to take over the job."

"That's probably true," she agreed. "That's why I'm focusing on the badge. You understand that," Leigh reminded him.

Cash paused for a very long time. "Yeah. I understand." She heard him drag in a long breath. "I'll help grease the way for the warrant and will have one of my deputies execute it. What exactly do you need from Kali's place?"

"Any and all blue dresses. She wore a blue dress to the party," Leigh explained when Cash made a "huh" sound. "Also, if the warrant includes it, I want a look at her computer. Specifically, her emails. Her car is here in Dark River so one of my deputies will handle that search in case the dress is in there."

"I'll see what I can do," Cash assured her just as there was a knock on her door.

The visitor didn't wait for her to invite him in. Rocky threw open the door, his narrowed gaze spearing into Leigh.

"Thanks for everything," she told her brother. "I'll call you back later."

And she turned to Rocky.

"Cullen," she said, "could you step out while I speak with my deputy?"

Cullen moved toward the door, but Rocky stepped in front of him. "What the hell have you been telling her?" He jabbed his index finger at Leigh.

"Nothing," Leigh assured him. "But I know you've met with Alexa."

The shock widened Rocky's eyes but only for a second. Then, the anger returned with a vengeance. "Nothing," Rocky repeated, and it was coated with venom. Venom that he aimed at Cullen. "You're bad-mouthing me to Leigh because you know it should be your butt that's in jail right now."

Oh, that was not the right thing to say, and it caused Cullen to send Rocky a steely, dangerous glare. "I don't have to bad-mouth you, you idiot. You did this to yourself by meeting with Alexa."

Since Cullen was apparently going to be part of this conversation, Leigh stepped around the men and shut the door. Yancy probably wouldn't repeat anything he heard, but Leigh didn't want to air this particular dirty laundry to anyone who happened to come into the police department.

"Sit down," she ordered Rocky, and yes, she made sure it sounded like an order.

Rocky tossed out some glares of his own, both to Cullen and her, but he dropped down in the seat across from her desk.

"Before you deny meeting with Alexa," Leigh continued, "you should know that Alexa was under surveillance by a PI. He took photographs. I've personally seen the photos, and I know it's you."

Part of her hadn't wanted to give Rocky a cushion like that. A part of her had wanted him to go ahead and lie so she could reprimand him. But getting to the truth was more important than any discipline she doled out. Plus, she could dole out discipline later.

"I'm going to read you your rights," Leigh told Rocky, and she proceeded to do just that. Of course, it didn't improve his mood, and he grew angrier with each word she recited.

"You're arresting me?" Rocky spat out when she'd finished. "Good luck making any bogus charges stick."

"If I arrest you, the charges won't be bogus," she assured him. "Now, tell me why you met with Alexa, and then you can explain why you withheld this information during a murder investigation. You've been a cop long enough to know that could be considered obstruction of justice."

Rocky didn't jump to answer that, and Leigh half expected him to yell for a lawyer. But he didn't. Leigh watched as Rocky seemed to make an effort to steady himself. Maybe because he remembered that how he handled this could determine if he kept his badge. Despite his attitude, Leigh knew that wearing the badge was important to Rocky.

"Alexa called me a couple of days ago and asked if I'd see her," Rocky said. "We aren't exactly friends, but I've met her a couple of times when she's been in town with Kali. Alexa told me that she had some questions about you."

It took Leigh a moment to realize the "you" was her and not Cullen.

"I had some business in Lubbock so I agreed to hook up with her at a diner," Rocky went on. "Alexa had heard some rumors and wanted to know if Cullen and you had started seeing each other again. I told her you weren't stupid so you wouldn't get involved with Cullen. Guess I was wrong about that," he added in a barely audible mutter.

Leigh didn't bother to blister him with a scathing look. She just motioned for him to continue.

"That was it," Rocky insisted. "Alexa just wanted to know if you two were sleeping together. When she figured out I didn't have any gossip to dish up to her, she paid for my lunch and left. And as for obstruction of justice, that's bull. I didn't obstruct squat because the meeting wasn't important. Hell, I'd forgotten all about it."

Leigh figured that last part was a huge lie. When he'd seen Alexa's dead body, it would have been logical for him to say something about the meeting he'd had with her just days earlier. Then again, maybe Rocky thought that might add him to the suspect list.

And it would have.

"Did you know that Alexa was going to the party at the Triple R?" Leigh pressed.

Rocky paused, shrugged. "She asked me about the party, wondered if me or any of the other deputies were doing security. You know, like Vance and Yancy sometimes do."

She did indeed know about that. Vance and Yancy had done some off-duty work like that when there'd been big events at the Triple R, but none of her deputies had been tapped for the engagement party.

"In hindsight, I guess Alexa asked me about that because maybe she thought I could get her into the party, but I didn't think of that until later. I didn't think of a lot of things." Rocky looked at Cullen. "I got the feeling that Alexa would do anything to get back at you."

"Well, she didn't kill herself," Leigh pointed out.

"No," Rocky quietly agreed. "But I think she was trying to stir up some kind of trouble."

"Something specific?" Cullen asked when Rocky paused.

"I'm not sure, but I figure she planned on doing

something at the party. I mean, why else would she want to make sure she got in?"

If Austin was telling the truth, then Alexa had indeed planned on doing *something*, and that was getting into Cullen's bed with Austin. But Leigh figured Alexa intended to do more than just that. Maybe the woman had intended for Cullen to walk in on Austin and her.

"Why didn't you tell me about this sooner?" Leigh pressed.

"Because like I said, I'd forgotten all about it. See?" Rocky added, and some of his usual cockiness was back in his voice. "No obstruction of justice. No withholding evidence. I simply had lunch with a woman who might or might not have tried to manipulate me. Either way, I didn't have anything to do with Alexa getting into the party or being murdered, and you don't have any evidence to say otherwise."

She didn't. Leigh would give him a written reprimand for not volunteering the meeting with Alexa, but Rocky would no doubt believe it was petty. That the reprimand was because he was Jeb's ally and that he actually hadn't broken the law.

"Can I go now, *Sheriff*?" Rocky snarled, getting to his feet before she could nix that or agree. Of course, he used a mocking tone on her title. "I'm way past my normal shift hours and need some shut-eye."

Leigh nodded and watched as Rocky breezed out of her office. She battled with her temper, tamping it down—and trying not to kick the trash can again.

Rocky walked out to the dispatch desk, where Yancy was sitting, and struck up a conversation with his fellow deputy. All the while keeping an eye on Leigh. Of course, she was keeping an eye on him as well.

"Rocky could have been the one who came after us in the SUV," Cullen pointed out.

She nodded again. Heck, Rocky could have killed Alexa, hurt Jamie and then tried to kill Cullen and her—and all because he hated her and wanted her job. Then again, it was indeed possible that Rocky had done nothing wrong other than forgetting a meeting with a dead woman.

Her phone rang, and with her attention still on Rocky, Leigh pressed Answer. However, her attention wasn't on Rocky for long because the deputy gave Yancy a pat on the back and then headed out the front door.

"This is Jimbo McNash," the caller greeted Leigh. His voice was like gravel. "You left me a couple of messages, said it was real important that I call you back."

That got her attention firmly focused on the "thug" who Alexa had met at the diner. "Yes, it is important," she verified. "I have some questions for you."

"Cops," he grumbled in the same tone as Rocky had said *sheriff*. "Got a call from Cullen Brodie, too. Now, he's somebody I'd be interested in having another chat with."

Leigh didn't know that Cullen had tried to get in touch with the man, and she hit the speaker function on her phone so he could hear the rest of the conversation.

"You said Cullen Brodie called you?" she pressed.

"Yep. This morning."

Cullen shook his head. *I didn't call him*, he mouthed.

"What exactly did Cullen say to you?" Leigh asked McNash.

"He said he'd heard I'd been meeting with his woman. His ex-woman," McNash emphasized. "And he said he'd be willing to pay me to hear anything his ex told me."

"And you agreed to that?" Leigh continued.

"Sure did. So, when you come out to see me, make sure you bring Cullen and his money with you," Mc-Nash snapped right before he ended the call.

Chapter Ten

"I didn't call McNash," Cullen repeated as Leigh put her phone back in her pocket.

She nodded. "I believe you. And that means some-one wanted either McNash or me to believe you'd called him."

Yeah, and Cullen had a good idea of who'd done that. "The killer or someone the killer hired."

Which, of course, didn't rule out Kali. Both Austin and she had had ample opportunity to contact McNash. Rocky had, too. But that led Cullen to another question.

"How would the killer have known about Alexa's meetings with McNash?" Cullen threw out there, but the moment the question was out of his mouth, he came up with possible answers. "Alexa told the killer. Or else McNash was the one who killed her." He paused, huffed. "Am I going to have to convince you to take me along on this visit to McNash's place?"

"No." She didn't hesitate, either. "If money's his mo-tive, I'm counting on him telling you exactly what Alexa and he discussed. Then, if he presses you for payment, I'll arrest him for extortion." Leigh took a deep breath. "For now though, I need to find out why Kali hasn't gotten here yet."

However, Leigh didn't get a chance to do that because her phone dinged with a text.

"It's from Vance," she relayed. "The ME's finally taken Alexa's body to the morgue. We should have a verified time of death soon."

Cullen figured the TOD wasn't going to vary much from the 8:00 to 8:30 p.m. range that Jamie's timeline had already given them. Still, it was something Leigh needed to know. It was possible she'd be able to use the timeline and the photos from the guests to determine who was in the great room and who wasn't when Alexa had been murdered.

"You have Kali's number?" she asked, firing off a response to Vance's text.

Cullen took out his phone, pulled up Kali's contact, and Leigh called the woman. She put the call on speaker just as Kali answered.

"This is Sheriff Mercer. You're on your way to the police station." Leigh definitely didn't make that a question.

"No." And Cullen heard Kali sobbing again. "I'm on my way home. I need to try to settle my nerves. I'm not running away or anything," Kali quickly added. "I just have to get myself together before you start asking me a bunch of questions."

Leigh huffed. "You should have come here."

"I know." Kali continued to sob. "But I didn't want to risk having Austin see me like this. I don't want him to know that he's crushed me. I'll be there in a couple of hours, I swear, and I'll tell you whatever I can. Promise."

Leigh's scowl deepened, and she checked the time. It was almost noon. "All right. I should be back from another interview in about three hours, and you can come in then." She paused a heartbeat. "Kali, just so you know. This interview isn't optional. If you don't show, I'll have to send a couple of my deputies over to escort you here."

"That's not necessary. I'll be there."

Leigh ended the call and glanced down at the torn knee of her jeans. And at the dried blood. It was a reminder that she hadn't gotten any medical attention. Maybe she didn't need it, but Cullen made a mental note to give her a push in that direction the next time they visited Jamie.

"I'll need to stop by my house and change my clothes," she muttered, reaching for her coat. She was still putting it on when Yancy came to the door.

"There's a problem with Austin Borden's lawyer," Yancy said. "The roads still aren't clear between here and his office in Ransom Ridge, and he can't come until later this afternoon."

"Great," Leigh muttered, and Cullen understood her frustration. Not only did she want answers from Austin, she probably also didn't want Kali and Austin squaring off when they were in the building together. "You confirmed that it's true about the roads not being clear?"

"I did," Yancy verified. "The work crews are just now salting the roads so there's still plenty of ice."

Leigh nodded. "All right. Cut Austin loose for a while. Tell him to be back here by four o'clock. Since you haven't gotten much sleep, Vance or Dawn can interview Austin and Kali. They should be back here once they're able to get away from the Triple R."

"I'm okay," Yancy assured. "I can do at least one of the interviews."

She seemed to consider that a moment and then nodded again. "All right. Make sure you do it by the book. I'm going to visit Jimbo McNash."

"I just saw that name on a preliminary report from Cecile," Yancy explained. "She sent it to you and all the deputies."

"Did Cecile see Jimbo's name in any of Alexa's emails?" Leigh quickly asked.

"Not that she said. I don't think she's had time to go through them yet. This was just a quick report to say that she'd be looking for that particular connection." Yancy paused. "You think this guy had something to do with Alexa's murder?"

"That's what I intend to find out. I intend to question him after I've made a quick stop at my house for a change of clothes."

"Then you should probably take backup," Yancy said, the concern in his voice.

Leigh slid a glance to Cullen, maybe deciding that he could play backup if necessary. Maybe also calculating how long it would delay this visit if she had to wait for one of the other deputies to arrive.

"I have a license to carry," Cullen simply reminded her. "And you know I'm carrying." Though the reminder wasn't necessary since she'd seen him fire at the SUV that had attacked them.

"All right, I can legally deputize you," Leigh said after a short pause. "Temporarily deputize you," she emphasized.

Cullen didn't smile. Or curse. But he wasn't sure how he felt about being a cop. Even a temporary one. Still, this was about protecting Leigh and getting answers, so he'd handle the deputy label for the next couple of hours.

Leigh started toward the door but then stopped and looked at Yancy. "If possible, arrange the interviews so that Kali and Austin aren't in here at the same time."

Yancy assured her that he would, and Cullen and she headed out, only to have Leigh stop again when she glanced around the parking lot. "My cruiser's wrecked," she muttered.

"We can take my truck," Cullen offered.

She didn't turn him down, though Cullen suspected she would have preferred to use an official vehicle for this visit with a suspect. Especially since she might have to arrest the man. But if that happened, Cullen's truck did have a narrow back seat they could use to transport him back to the police station.

Cullen deiced the windshield, noting that there were more people out and about now. People who noticed Leigh in the truck with him, and he wondered how much gossip and grief that was going to cause her.

"I'm muddying your reputation," Cullen joked, hoping to get a smile out of her.

No such luck. She looked at him with a slew of emotions crossing her face. Two of those emotions might have been frustration and regret, but there was also the heat.

"I would kiss you here and now just because I'm riled enough at the people who love picking my every move apart." Leigh took in a deep breath. "But that'd be using you."

Now he smiled. "If you kissed me, I'm positive that I'd feel plenty of things, but *used* isn't one of them."

She smiled, too, while shaking her head. Much to his disappointment though, she didn't kiss him.

Cullen drove to her place on the edge of town. Her

one-story white limestone house sat in the center of four acres surrounded by white fence. A small red barn was behind the house, and he spotted a couple of bay mares inside. He'd known that Leigh was a horse lover, which wasn't a surprise since she'd been raised on a ranch.

He pulled up in front of her house, and both of them glanced around, looking for any signs of trouble, before she used her phone to disengage her security system. As they got out, Cullen pushed open the side of his jacket in case he had to go for his gun, but when Leigh unlocked the door and they went in, nothing seemed to be out of place.

"I won't be long," she said, leaving him in the foyer. But she only made it a couple of steps before she turned back, caught onto him.

And she kissed him.

Cullen didn't even care that she'd chosen to do this behind closed doors. What he cared about was the instant slam of heat and need. The feel of her mouth. The pressure of her body against his. She didn't linger long, just enough to assure him that this attraction wasn't going away anytime soon.

Mumbling something he didn't catch, she pushed away from him and headed for the hall. "Help yourself to whatever you find in the fridge."

He wasn't the least bit interested in her fridge and considered going after her and seeing how far he could take things. Of course, he already knew that would just lead them to bed, and they couldn't take the time for that now. The sooner they got to Jimbo, the sooner they might have the answers they needed.

Forcing himself to go anywhere but to her bedroom, Cullen strolled into the living room. No fuss and frills here. There was a comfortable leather sofa the color of caramel, and from the looks of the way things were arranged, Leigh spent time in here reading, watching TV and working on a laptop that was open on a rustic coffee table.

He went to the fireplace to have a closer look at the single framed photograph on the mantel. A family shot of Cash, Leigh, their mother and their missing brother, Joe. It'd been taken when Leigh had been about five. That would have meant Cash was about seven and Joe three and a half. They were all smiling, and Cash was holding up a fish that he'd likely just caught.

It was a happy photo of a happy family, taken on a sunny summer day. There probably hadn't been many happy days after that because by Cullen's estimation, Joe had gone missing shortly afterward. A year later, Helen Mercer had died in a car accident that many had considered suicide. Losing her mother when she'd been so young was something they had in common.

"It used to hurt when I'd see that picture," Leigh said from behind him.

Cullen looked back at her, at the clean pair of jeans she was wearing. She'd also freed her hair from the ponytail, and it fell loose just below her shoulders.

"But now it gives me, well, comfort," she added. "Jeb took the picture. That's why he's not in it."

She probably didn't know that there was a tinge of bitterness in her tone when she said her father's name, and Cullen doubted that photo would be there for a daily reminder had Jeb actually been a visual part of the "happy" scene.

"You remember your mom?" he asked.

"Some. I have good memories, then the memories

of her crying after Joe was taken." Leigh motioned for him to go with her to the door. "What about you? Do you remember your mother?"

"Some," he said, echoing her answer. And like Leigh, there were some good memories, but there'd been plenty of times when his mother had had way too much to drink. Something she'd done the night she died. As a child he couldn't see it. Now he knew she'd been an alcoholic. A mostly out-of-control one who'd made a habit of drinking and driving.

"You blame Bowen for her death?" Leigh asked.

"No." That was the truth. "But I love my father. Most of the time, anyway. So it's not something I talk about with him. Mostly though, I just blame my mother for not getting the help she obviously needed. Then again, I should put some of that blame on my dad, too, because he had to have known that the drinking had gotten way out of hand."

Leigh made a sound of agreement and added a genuine sounding "I'm sorry" as they went to his truck, and she reset the security system with her phone. She then gave him Jimbo's address so he could put it in the GPS.

"How much grief would your father give you…" But Leigh stopped and waved that off.

"How much grief would he give me if I started seeing you again?" Cullen finished for her. "Plenty," he readily admitted, "but that won't stop me. At this point, I doubt there's much of anything that'd stop us."

She didn't disagree with that, but the long breath she took let him know that she'd be getting plenty of grief as well.

"Your father approved of Alexa?" she asked.

Cullen nearly laughed when he recalled the many

arguments Bowen and Alexa had had. "No. Not one little bit. He thought she had too much flash, too much temper."

Which was true, but Cullen had been attracted to her. That attraction was a drop in the bucket though compared to what he felt for Leigh. And he knew it was best to keep that to himself. He could coax Leigh into having an affair with him, but she wouldn't want to know how deep his feelings for her ran.

Cullen wasn't sure *he* wanted to know.

It had crushed him all the way to the bone, or rather the heart, the last time Leigh walked out of his life and he didn't want another round of that. Still, he was going to have to take the risk.

The roads were mostly clear and there was almost no traffic, but Cullen kept watch as they made their way out of Dark River and to the farm road that led to Jimbo's place. With each passing mile, Cullen's concerns grew, and he forced his mind off Leigh and back on the danger hanging over them.

"If Jimbo killed Alexa and was the one driving that SUV, he might try to finish us off," Cullen reminded her.

"Yes." She said it so fast that it'd obviously been on her mind. "I think the best way for us to do this is for me to call Jimbo when we get to his house. I'll insist that he come out so I can check him for weapons."

That was a good start, but Cullen wanted to go one step further. "You could question him while we're in the truck. That way, you're not out in the open in case he has a partner in crime."

She stayed quiet a moment. "Jimbo might not go for standing out in the cold while I talk to him."

"He might if he thinks this could lead to a payoff," Cullen quickly fired back.

Cullen gave her some time to work that around in her mind. Leigh finally nodded and took out her phone. She didn't press Jimbo's number though until Cullen took the final turn toward the farm.

And that's when Cullen saw the smoke.

There were dark coils of it rising into the sky, but the winter wind was whipping away at it, scattering it almost as soon as it rose. Since it was way too much smoke for an ordinary fireplace, Cullen got a very bad feeling in his gut.

"Jimbo's not answering," Leigh said, her attention focused on the smoke.

It was less than thirty seconds before they reached the house. Or rather what was left of it. The structure was engulfed in flames.

THE SIGHT OF those flames sent Leigh's stomach to her knees. In that instant, she knew the chances were very high that this wasn't an accidental fire.

And that Jimbo might be dead.

Because she doubted the man had set this fire. Then again, maybe he had if he'd thought he was about to be arrested for murder. There was a problem with that theory because of the truck parked in front of the house, and she was betting the truck belonged to Jimbo. Still, she wanted to hold out hope that he'd caught a ride with someone and torched his house to conceal any evidence inside.

Even though she didn't like the idea of a prime suspect being in the wind, it was better than the alternative of the man being dead. Dead men couldn't give her answers about those meetings with Alexa.

Since Leigh already had her phone in her hand, she called 911 to get the fire department out to Jimbo's house. But she could already see that they wouldn't get there in time to save the place.

She glanced around the yard, at the rusted-out farm equipment, overgrown trees and piles of junk. No Jimbo. In fact, no sign of anyone, but if he'd been attacked, then maybe he'd managed to make it outside before he would have been overcome by the smoke and fire.

"I'm keeping watch," Cullen assured her.

Leigh was already doing the same thing. Because even if Jimbo had been the one to set the fire, it was possible he'd stayed around to try to ambush them. That possibility, however, bit the dust when she saw Jimbo stagger out the front door.

The man's head and chest were bleeding, and he was clearly dazed. Added to that, his shirt was on fire.

Cullen and she threw open their doors at the same time. They also drew their guns as one. Cullen sprinted across the yard toward Jimbo, catching onto him to take his weight and slapping out the fire with the sleeve of his coat. Leigh went to help, but she also looked all around the yard to make sure there was no other threat.

Jimbo mumbled something she couldn't understand and collapsed. If Cullen hadn't had hold of him, he would have fallen face-first to the ground. Cullen grabbed the man's arms, dragging him away from the house.

In the nick of time.

Because a chunk of the roof came crashing down and

sent out a cloud of smoke, ash and cinders. When some of those cinders landed on Cullen, she had to use her own sleeve to stop them from igniting into full flames.

From the corner of her eye, she caught some movement to the right, but the wind shifted, sending the thick smoke right at them. She couldn't see her hand in front of her face much less someone who could be yards away. But the good news about that was the person might not be able to see them, either.

Leigh heard the sharp cracking sound, and for a split second she thought the rest of the house was collapsing. But then she knew what it was.

Gunfire.

Someone had just taken a shot at them, and the bullet tore into the ground just a few feet from where they were dragging Jimbo.

Cullen cursed, and he tried to shove Leigh behind him. "Get down," he snapped.

No way would Leigh do that. Not with someone shooting at them. She moved to take Jimbo's other arm to help Cullen drag him to the side of the truck so they'd have cover.

"Did you see the shooter?" Leigh asked Cullen. "I think he was running up from the right."

"I didn't see anyone," he said. His words rushed together with his heavy breath, and he peered over the front end of his truck. The shot came right away, skimming across the metal hood and slamming into a tree behind him. Cursing him, Leigh grabbed Cullen and forced him back down.

What he'd just done was way past being dangerous, but it'd helped pinpoint the direction of the shooter. He was in or near that area with the old farm equipment. Equipment that was plenty large enough to conceal whomever it was she'd glimpsed from the corner of her eye.

It had to be the killer.

But why hadn't he been in place to shoot them when they'd arrived? It would have been the perfect time since their attention was mostly focused on the burning house. Later, she'd give that some thought, but for now she needed to work on how to get them out of this.

They couldn't stay put. They were too close to the house, and it would collapse. No doubts about that. And when it went, some of those fiery chunks of wood could land on them. Plus, Jimbo was bleeding and needed medical attention ASAP. Leigh sent a quick text for an ambulance and backup.

More shots came, all of them slamming into the truck, but some of the bullets seemed to have come from different angles. The gunman could be on the move, maybe making his way to them so he could shoot them the moment he rounded the truck.

"Watch the front. I'll keep an eye on the rear," Leigh told Cullen.

Cullen dropped down on the ground next to Jimbo so he could look out underneath the truck. "He's coming this way," he snarled, and he shifted his gun to take aim.

Cullen fired.

The pain shot through Leigh's ears. It'd been necessary though. With the angle of his shot, Cullen would have likely only managed to wound the gunman in the leg, but that might be enough to stop him.

Cullen cursed again. "Smoke," he snapped.

That was the only warning Leigh got before another cloud of smoke came at them. It was thick and smothering, and it must have gotten to the gunman as well because she heard someone cough. And then she heard something else. More of the house collapsed, and the blazing debris landed between them and the shooter.

"I'm dying," Jimbo muttered, drawing her attention back to him. Unlike Cullen and her, he wasn't coughing, and the man seemed to be on his last breath.

Leigh needed him alive, and the only chance they had was to get him to a hospital fast. She reached up, fumbling for the door, and opened it as wide as she could manage.

"Get in and stay down," Cullen told her through his coughs.

"You do the same," she insisted.

She took hold of Jimbo's arm, and while Cullen and she both tried to keep watch, they hauled the man into the center of the seat. Cullen quickly followed, getting behind the wheel. He threw the truck into Reverse and gunned the engine.

Leigh braced herself for the hail of gunfire.

But it didn't come.

Still, she kept her gun ready while Cullen sped out of the driveway. Once they were out of the cloud of smoke, she looked around, trying to pick through the yard to spot the person who'd just tried to kill them.

Nothing.

The shooter was nowhere in sight.

Chapter Eleven

Cullen could feel the exhaustion all the way to his bones, and he figured it was the same for Leigh. They were both dragging when they walked into her house, nearly ten hours after they'd left to do the interview with Jimbo. What was supposed to have been a short trip had turned into a grueling ordeal. One that could have ended with Leigh and him dead.

Like Jimbo.

Despite their efforts to save him, Jimbo had died shortly after they'd arrived at the hospital. He hadn't been able to tell anyone who'd put the two bullets in his chest that'd killed him. And with his house a total loss, his killer hadn't left any evidence behind. In fact, he'd left nothing behind. The local cops hadn't been able to find him or a vehicle he'd used to get to Jimbo's. It was as if the guy had vanished like the smoke from the fire.

At least during the ten hours, Leigh's deputies had done the interviews with Austin and Kali. According to the updates Leigh had gotten, neither had given any new info, but the interviews ticked off some necessary legal boxes. So had the searches of both Kali's and her parents' houses. Some blue dresses had been collected at both and had been sent to the lab.

"The bathroom's there," Leigh said, motioning toward the hall. "The guest room's right next to it." She glanced at his jeans and shirt that were stained with Jimbo's blood. "I'll see if I can find you something to wear while you wash those. The laundry room's just off the kitchen."

Cullen wasn't sure if he wanted to think about why she'd have men's clothes in her house, and he sure as heck wasn't going to press on getting something from the Triple R. According to Mack, the ranch was still being processed as a crime scene, and the CSIs didn't want anything removed until they were finished.

Leigh glanced down at her own clothes, at the blood there, and she groaned softly. It didn't matter that Jimbo had been a thug with a long criminal history. A man was dead, and he'd almost certainly died because Alexa's killer had wanted to tie up any loose ends.

But how had the killer known to go after Jimbo?

That was a question that'd been circling in Cullen's mind. No doubt circling in Leigh's, too.

"Help yourself to anything in the kitchen," she added. "Once you're done with your shower, let me know, and I'll take one."

Neither of them moved, and exhaustion was only part of the reason why. Cullen could practically feel the guilt coming off her.

"You couldn't have saved Jimbo," Cullen insisted.

"I could have if I'd realized the killer would go after him." She muttered some profanity and then groaned. "I should have realized it. I should have asked the locals to provide him protection until I could get out to his place."

He could have reminded her that she'd been embroiled in a murder investigation and that she was functioning on very little sleep. But she'd see that as part of the job so he saved his breath. Instead, he went to her and pulled her into his arms. Maybe it was the exhaustion playing into this again, but she didn't resist. She went body to body with him and dropped her head on his shoulder.

Cullen knew she was allowing this because she needed some comfort, and there weren't exactly a lot of people in Dark River who could offer her that. Heck, he needed what she was giving as well. It'd been a damn long day, and it felt good to stand there with her like this.

"Don't kiss me," she said. "I don't have the willpower to do anything about it."

Cullen managed to laugh. "That's probably not something you should tell me."

"Yes, it is," Leigh argued. "Because underneath all that bad boy, you're a decent guy."

Well, hell. How could he kiss her after she'd said that? And yes, he had indeed been thinking about a kiss or two. Nothing more though. When they ended up having sex again, he wanted them to have enough energy to enjoy it. Still, Cullen settled for brushing a kiss on her forehead because there was indeed some bad boy beneath the decency.

The kiss caused her to chuckle a little, and she stepped back to meet his gaze. Mercy, she was beautiful even now with those tired eyes.

"You're not thinking about sex, are you?" he asked, hoping that she'd managed to get a second wind.

"No." The corner of her mouth lifted in a smile. A smile that quickly faded. "I was thinking about how the killer knew to go after Jimbo."

So, her mind had indeed been toying with that.

"Let me change my clothes," she added a moment later, "and then I'd like to hear your theories on how that could have happened." She went into her bedroom but didn't close the door all the way. "I'm thinking Alexa could have told her killer about Jimbo. Maybe she did that in passing, and then the killer might have decided that Alexa could have told Jimbo about him or her."

Cullen could see that happening with Austin or Kali. Austin because he was having an affair with Alexa, and Kali because Alexa was her friend. He'd heard Leigh talking on the phone with Yancy, and the deputy had taken both Austin's and Kali's statements, and it'd be interesting to see if there was any connection to Jimbo.

When the killer was finally identified and locked up, Cullen knew he was also going to have to deal with the impact of his best friend having a relationship with his ex. Even though Cullen had no longer loved Alexa, the affair still felt like a betrayal. One that he'd need to process. Process and then hopefully put aside since he had a lot of things to deal with. That included his feelings for Leigh.

"Or maybe Jimbo had a partner," Leigh added a moment later, "and the partner killed him rather than risk Jimbo tying him or her to a murder."

Despite the seriousness of the conversation, it took Cullen a moment to focus on something other than remembering Leigh and her beautiful, tired eyes from moments ago. "Either of those are possible," he said, leaning against the wall outside her door. "But Rocky would have gotten the preliminary report that your other deputy sent out. He knew you'd be earmarking any emails or texts between Alexa and Jimbo."

He had no trouble hearing her quick sound of agreement which meant that had already occurred to her.

"This rules out your father," Leigh went on. "He knew about Jimbo before Alexa's murder, and if he was a killer, he probably wouldn't have waited hours to eliminate someone who could have incriminated him."

"Bowen will be pleased to hear that." And yeah, he added a little tongue and cheek to that comment.

"Jeb won't be pleased." Leigh had a tongue-in-cheek tone, too.

At the mention of her father's name, Cullen recalled what'd happened in the break room when Jeb had had the dizzy spell. Or whatever the heck it'd been. He nearly brought it up now, but Leigh continued before he could say anything.

"But I'd prefer to arrest the person responsible rather than the person I want it to be," she said, and he heard her sigh.

"You want it to be Rocky," he concluded. "He's withheld evidence and backbites you any chance he gets."

"And that's why I'm being very careful about how I'm dealing with him. I don't want to project something on him that might not be there. He might not be more than just a backbiter."

She opened the door, and he saw that she was wearing a white terry cloth bathrobe. It wasn't clinging, low-cut or anything else provocative, but it still got his attention.

Before he could give in to the temptation of sliding his hand inside that robe, she thrust out a pair of black pj bottoms.

"Sorry," she said. "It's the best I can do. Cash stayed here about six years ago when his house was being painted, and he left them behind. Just the bottoms," Leigh clarified. "So, you'll have to do the bare-chest thing while your clothes are being washed."

He was about to joke and ask her if she'd be watching for that, but her doorbell rang. Leigh whirled around, scooping up her holster. At the same time, Cullen also drew his gun.

"I doubt the killer would ring the doorbell," he said, trying to steady her nerves. But Cullen didn't plan on putting his gun away until he was sure who was at the door.

Cullen went to one of the side windows. Leigh went to the other. And they both groaned when they spotted Austin on her porch.

"I have to talk to you," Austin called out, ringing the bell again.

"I'll get rid of him," Cullen offered, and he didn't wait for Leigh to object.

He held on to his gun as he opened the door and faced his friend. That would be *former* friend since one look at Austin and Cullen knew Austin was still riled. Heck, Cullen was, too.

"Where's Leigh?" Austin demanded.

With just those two words, Cullen got a whiff of Austin's breath. He'd clearly been drinking.

"What do you want?" Leigh asked, moving in front of Cullen to face Austin head-on.

"Kali thinks I murdered Alexa," Austin blurted out, pointing his index finger at Leigh. "You made her believe that."

Hell. This was not what Leigh needed to be dealing with after the day they'd already had. "Leigh was doing her job," Cullen quickly pointed out. "And you didn't exactly volunteer information about your affair with Alexa."

Austin's rage-filled eyes slashed to Cullen. "Because it was my personal business. My mistake. There was no reason for me to tell a cop."

"No," Leigh disagreed. "There's no such thing as personal business in a murder investigation."

"Have you tried to ruin Cullen the way you're ruining me?" Austin fired back. Then, he smirked. "No, you haven't because you're sleeping with him again." He gave a hollow laugh. "Alexa was right about that."

Cullen stared at Austin. "What do you mean by that?"

Austin continued the smirk. "Alexa saw you looking at an old picture of the two of you. The one taken at a party when Leigh was still in high school."

The party where Leigh had lost her virginity to him. Cullen did indeed have a picture, but he didn't remember looking at it while Alexa was around.

"Alexa was so jealous of you," Austin continued, his comment aimed at Leigh. "And she had a vindictive streak and wouldn't have wanted Cullen and you to be together. I could have sent her after you like that." He snapped his fingers. "Too bad I didn't. If I had, you wouldn't have ruined my life."

Enough was enough. Cullen stepped in front of Leigh again. "You ruined your own life," Cullen snarled. "By not keeping your jeans zipped when you were around your fiancée's best friend. If you want to put the blame on someone, just look in the mirror."

Austin clearly didn't care much for that, and he reached out as if he might try to clamp onto Leigh's arm. Cullen didn't let that happen. The punch he landed on Austin's jaw was hard and fast. Austin staggered back, the blood already oozing from his mouth, and he glared at Cullen.

"You two deserve each other," Austin snarled, and weaving, he started off the porch and toward his truck in the driveway.

Leigh sighed, took out her phone. "You've been drinking," she called out to Austin, "and you're not getting behind the wheel. We have a couple of people in town doing Uber, and I'll get you a ride."

"I don't want a ride," he insisted, although he didn't get in his truck. He started walking back toward town. Cullen was about to go after him, but he saw the truck approaching the house.

"Great," Leigh muttered. "It's Jeb."

Cullen hadn't thought this day could get any worse, but he'd apparently been wrong. Jeb stopped his truck next to Austin and lowered the window. Cullen couldn't hear what they said, but they had a very short conversation before Austin got in the passenger's seat.

Jeb drove to the house, got out and was sporting a serious scowl as he walked to the porch. "I'll see that Austin gets to the inn. There should be rooms open by now."

"Thanks," Cullen said, and he was glad Jeb was seeing to this. Austin was in no shape to drive or walk in the cold.

Jeb didn't acknowledge Cullen's thanks. In fact, he didn't acknowledge Cullen at all. He stared at his daughter.

"I came to give you a heads-up," Jeb said. "Rocky's asked the town council to have a meeting tomorrow. You'll need to be there."

"And why would I need to do that?" Leigh asked.

Jeb swore under his breath and scrubbed his hand over his face. "Because Rocky's going to present what he says is evidence to have you removed as sheriff."

LEIGH READ THROUGH the CSI and ME reports and tried to stay focused. Hard to do because she'd had yet another night with little sleep.

Cullen probably hadn't fared much better in the sleep department, and he looked as tired as she was as he worked on a laptop in her living room. She wanted to tell him to take a break, especially since she'd have to be heading into her office soon, but he was going through the photos that the deputies had collected from the party guests. Those photos might end up holding some clues as to what had happened that night.

She desperately needed answers. Desperately needed the attacks to stop before anyone else died. She could still feel Jimbo's blood on her hands. Could still hear the sound of gunfire.

She pushed back what would have been a shudder, drank her coffee and kept reading. Basically, there was no news in either report that she could use to make an arrest, but the ME had concluded that Alexa had recently had sex. That didn't necessarily mean that sex had been with Austin, but Leigh would need to take another look at Cullen's friend. Before she did that though, she wanted the lab results on the clothes that'd been taken from Austin's house. There was no telling when those would be processed, but she'd give the lab a call and try to hurry them.

If she had a job, that is.

She tried not to think that she could lose her badge today. It could happen though. She doubted that Rocky had any actual evidence to present to the town council, but he could use her connection with Cullen. That was a darn good reason for her to put some distance between Cullen and her. But if she did that, it would be for all the wrong reasons—because she'd been pressured into it.

There were right reasons for distancing herself. A possible broken heart and butting heads with Bowen. However, one look at Cullen, and Leigh knew she didn't exactly have a choice about her feelings for him.

"Problem?" Cullen asked, and that was when Leigh realized he'd caught her staring at him.

She waved that off just as her phone rang. "Jeb," she muttered and hit the decline button. Leigh wasn't in the mood for a lecture or advice.

Cullen stood, facing her, and he crammed his hands in the pockets of his jeans. It seemed to her that he was having a debate about what he wanted to say. "Is your father okay?" he asked.

Of all the things Leigh had thought Cullen might say, that wasn't one of them. And his tone only added to her surprise. He seemed concerned, and that didn't mesh with his usual feelings about Jeb.

"Why do you ask?" she countered, and she hoped this wasn't about to turn into a discussion of whether or not Jeb could have killed Alexa and Jimbo.

Again, Cullen hesitated. He shook his head, then huffed. "Jeb wanted me to swear not to tell you, but he had a dizzy spell yesterday in the break room. It happened shortly after you left for your office."

Everything inside Leigh went still while she tried to wrap her mind around that. "A dizzy spell?"

Cullen nodded. "He went pale and staggered back before I caught him. If he hadn't told me to keep it from you, I might have dismissed it as nothing. But it feels like something," he added.

Yes, it did, and Leigh tried to wrap her mind around that, too. Was Jeb sick? Or was it worse than that? Either way, she could see him wanting to keep it from her. Maybe because he didn't want her thinking he was weak. Or perhaps because it was just something he wanted to keep to himself. Neither of those excuses would work on her. Jeb and she might not be close, but she wanted to know if he was having health problems.

Leigh pressed Jeb's number, and since he'd just tried to call her, she expected him to answer. He didn't. In fact, it went to voice mail, but before she could leave him a message, she got an incoming call from the reserve deputy Cecile Taggart.

"Is everything okay with Jamie?" Leigh immediately asked.

"He's fine. In fact, the doctor might let him go home late today or tomorrow."

Leigh released the breath she was holding. That was good news. No one had tried to kill Jamie again, but his release would pose a few new problems. She'd need to get with Cullen on that and see how they could protect him while he was on the Triple R.

"I was calling about those emails and phone records you wanted me to check," Cecile continued a moment later. "Alexa's emails and phone records," she explained. "I've been going through them, and I think I found something."

"I'm listening," Leigh assured her, and she was. So was Cullen, who'd moved closer to her. Leigh put the call on speaker so he'd be able to hear.

"Well, it might be nothing, but there's a text from

Alexa to Kali Starling where Alexa confesses that she's having an affair with Kali's fiancé."

Leigh was reasonably sure this wasn't *nothing*. "When did Alexa send that?"

"About four hours before the start of the party," Cecile quickly answered. "It appears Alexa deleted some other texts from her sent folder but not this one."

"Did Kali respond to the text?"

"Not with a text, but there's a record of an incoming call from Kali shortly after she would have gotten the text."

Leigh groaned. It would have been better to have that particular conversation in writing, but maybe Kali could fill in the blanks. "I want you to forward me that text," Leigh instructed.

"Will do, but there's more. Vance and Dawn have been going through the pictures of the guests at the party. I don't think it's my imagination that Kali looks pretty upset in several of them. In one, she looks sort of disheveled. Windblown, I guess you'd say. Her hair is a little messy, and she looks as if she's been crying."

Interesting, and Leigh very much wanted to know what Kali had to say about that. She ended the call with Cecile and immediately contacted Kali. Leigh almost expected the woman to dodge her, but she answered.

"Kali, one of my deputies just went through Alexa's texts," Leigh said, going right to the heart of the matter. "Anything you want to tell me that you left out of your interview?"

"W-what?" Kali answered, slurring the word.

"Alexa's texts," Leigh repeated.

Kali moaned softly. "Uh, I can't think right now." That was slurred, too.

"Kali, are you all right?" Leigh demanded.

There were more moans. "Sleeping now. I took something to help me sleep." And with that, the woman ended the call.

Leigh cursed and immediately contacted dispatch. "I need someone to go to Kali Starling's residence and do a welfare check. Make it fast," she told the dispatcher. "It's possible the woman has overdosed on sleeping pills."

If she had, hopefully help wouldn't be late in getting there.

"Would Kali try to kill herself?" Leigh asked Cullen.

He lifted his shoulder. "I don't know. But if you think it'll be a while before someone can get to her place, I'll go."

Leigh considered it, then shook her head. "If Kali's the killer, this could be a trap." And that was something Leigh relayed to the dispatcher when she called him back.

She'd just put her phone away when there was a knock at her door. Heck, what now? Frustrated, she went to the side window, looked out and spotted Jeb. He must have known she would peer out like that because his gaze zoomed right to hers.

"I need to see you," he said.

Leigh looked at him, studying his face to see if there were any signs of the paleness and staggering that Cullen had described. Nothing out of the ordinary except his eyes were tired. Then again, her eyes were probably tired, too.

She went to the door and opened it. "I'm not up to a long visit," she said, "but I do have questions for you."

With his mouth tightening, Jeb shifted his attention

to Cullen. "If something's wrong with you, Leigh should know," Cullen told him.

"No time for that," Jeb insisted, turning back to Leigh. "The mayor just called, and he's assembled the town council. You're about to get a call from him, and he'll tell you that they want you there right now."

Chapter Twelve

Cullen thought the mood in the town hall felt like a witch hunt. And he was pretty sure that at least some of the council considered Leigh to be the witch. But Cullen hoped that Rocky hadn't been able to turn all of them against the woman the majority of residents had elected sheriff.

"If the town council votes to start the process to oust you," Jeb explained as they paused outside the door of the meeting room, "it wouldn't be immediate."

Leigh nodded. "They'd have to initiate a recall." Her jaw was tight. Eyes, narrowed. "The voters would have to decide if I should stay or go."

Cullen couldn't blame her for being riled to the core. He knew how much the badge meant to her, and how devastated she'd be if it was taken away.

Leigh stepped ahead of them and opened the door. She didn't hesitate but instead walked into the room and went straight to the front. The mayor, Noble Henning, was there at the center of the rectangular table, and part of his mayoral duties was to head the council. He was flanked by the five other members who made up the town council. Those other members were business owners or prominent citizens—which explained why Jeb was on it. He took his seat at the far end of the table.

Noble was a huge man with an equally huge belly. Since he was a rancher, Cullen had done business with him and had found him fair enough. Right now though, nothing felt fair, and Cullen cursed Noble, Rocky and everyone at the council table for putting Leigh through this.

Rocky was there in the front row, and he made a point of staring at Leigh as she stood in front of the people who could decide her fate. Word of the meeting apparently hadn't gotten out because other than the mayor and the members of the council, Rocky was the only other person there.

Cullen stayed at the back of the room, but Leigh went all the way to the table to face the council along with giving Rocky a cold, hard glance that was effective enough to cause him to look away.

Noble cleared his throat and also had some trouble looking Leigh in the eye. Instead, he read from his notes. "Sheriff Mercer, there have been complaints and concerns about you being negligent in carrying out your duties in the murders you're currently investigating. Deputy Rocky Callaway claims you've shown preferential treatment to a suspect and have failed to arrest that suspect because you're having a sexual relationship with him."

That got Cullen moving forward, but Leigh spoke before he could say anything.

"I'm assuming that my deputy is referring to Cullen Brodie." Leigh's voice was calm, but Cullen suspected there was no calmness beneath the surface.

Noble nodded just as Rocky blurted out, "You should have arrested Cullen instead of sleeping with him."

"There was no evidence to make that arrest," Leigh countered, turning her attention back to the mayor. "Cullen's clothes were taken to the lab and there was no blood on them. The CSIs used a UV light on other clothes in his closet and didn't detect any blood. According to the assessment of the crime scene, the killer would have gotten some blood spatter on themselves."

"Cullen was alone with the body—" Rocky started, but the mayor motioned for him to hush.

"The lab is still testing the clothing of others who attended the party," Leigh continued without missing a beat, "and once I have those results I might be able to make an arrest if the evidence warrants that. There are several people who have means, motive and opportunity, and some, including Deputy Callaway, weren't forthcoming with information about the victim."

Rocky practically jumped to his feet. "I wasn't forthcoming because it wasn't relevant."

"I decide what's relevant in a murder investigation." Leigh tapped her badge. "And you failed to tell me about a meeting you had with the victim."

Noble made another motion for Rocky to sit back down. The deputy did after several snail-crawling moments. Then, Noble's gaze shifted to Cullen.

"I'm guessing you've got something you want to say to the council?" Noble asked.

Cullen was certain his body language conveyed that, yes, he did have something to say. He wanted to tell them all to go to hell and take the backstabbing Rocky with them. But that venom wouldn't help Leigh.

"I'm not especially happy that any one of you would

think I'd need to sleep with the sheriff in order to keep myself out of jail," Cullen snarled. "It especially pisses me off that you'd think Leigh would sleep with someone she believes could bash in a woman's head."

"Are you saying you haven't shared the sheriff's bed?" Noble asked.

"I'm saying it's none of your business," he snapped at the same time Leigh said, "Cullen's not a suspect so you don't have cause to ask that question."

Rocky smirked, obviously pleased because he probably thought Leigh was digging herself into a huge hole.

The door practically flew open, and Vance, Dawn and Yancy all came rushing in. They glanced around the room as if assessing the situation and then went to the front to stand by Leigh.

"Sorry," Vance said, "but we just got the word that the sheriff was having some trouble here. We didn't want her facing that trouble alone."

Leigh made eye contact with all three of them and nodded her appreciation. "Thank you," she said plenty loud enough for everyone in the room to hear.

"The *trouble* is," Noble spoke up, emphasizing the word, "the sheriff doesn't seem to be close to arresting anybody for murder."

"She's had less than two days," Cullen argued and got sounds and mumbles of agreement from the three deputies standing with her. "You want her to arrest the wrong person just so you'll have someone behind bars? I don't think you want that kind of justice doled out here."

"No, I don't want the wrong person arrested," Noble countered, "but I want the threat gone. I want people to know they're safe in their own homes."

"This might help," Vance said, and he handed Leigh a piece of paper.

She read through what was written on it, and while she didn't smile, Cullen thought he saw some relief. "The SUV that rammed into my cruiser was sent to the lab for processing," Leigh relayed to the council. "The steering wheel had been wiped, but they found a partial print. The lab's going to try to match it."

Noble blew out what Cullen thought might be a breath of relief. "Good," he said. "Then, we'll postpone this meeting until you've had a chance to get the match."

It didn't seem nearly enough. More postponing the witch hunt rather than giving Leigh the credit she was due.

Jeb stood as if he might say something for, or against, his daughter, but Leigh's attention wasn't on her father. Or anyone else on the council. It was on her phone as it rang.

"It's Austin," she relayed in a whisper to Cullen and her three standing deputies. While Noble officially ended the meeting, Leigh stepped to the side of the room to take the call. Cullen went with her.

"Something's happened to Kali," he heard Austin blurt out.

Cullen thought of the part of the phone conversation he'd heard when Leigh had been talking to Kali. Leigh had been concerned enough to send someone out to check on the woman.

"What's wrong?" Leigh demanded.

"I came to her house to check on her, but she's not here." Austin groaned. "And there's blood on her back porch. Leigh, you need to come right away."

LEIGH HAD PLENTY on her mind as Cullen and she hurried out of the town hall toward his truck. She still had plenty of anger about the town council meeting that Rocky had been able to wrangle. Plenty of anger directed at Rocky, too. But right now, her focus was on Kali.

She certainly hadn't forgotten about her brief conversation with Kali, and Leigh had suspected then that the woman was in some kind of trouble. Not the kind of trouble that would cause blood to be on her porch though. No. However, Leigh knew this could have turned out to be an overdose, either accidental or intentional.

"Where are you now?" Leigh asked Austin.

"I'm trying to figure out a way inside Kali's house. She must have changed the locks because my key doesn't work, and all the windows are locked up."

It didn't surprise her that Kali would change the locks. The woman had been very upset over Austin's cheating. But that led Leigh to another question. "Why call me and not the locals?"

"Uh, I don't know the locals," Austin answered. "I know you."

Yes, and it was a huge understatement to say he didn't much care for her. Still, it was possible this wasn't a trap and had nothing to do with his feelings about her. Maybe Austin was truly panicked about Kali, and he would have had her phone number right there in his contacts.

"Call an ambulance," Leigh instructed Austin, "but don't go in." Because if this wasn't an overdose, it could be another murder. The killer could still be inside. "There should be someone from Clay Ridge PD arriving soon. Tell him or her what you just told me."

She ended the call and instructed her own deputies—Vance, Yancy and Dawn—to go back to whatever needed to be done, that she would handle things with Kali. Then, Leigh called her brother, and she was thankful when Cash answered right away.

"One of my deputies, Karen Wheatly, should be at Kali's house soon," Cash said without any kind of greeting. "I'm guessing that's why you're calling?"

"I am," Leigh confirmed. The moment they'd buckled up, Cullen took off, heading out of town. "Her former fiancé is there now, and he says there's blood on the porch."

Cash cursed. "The dispatcher didn't say there were any signs of foul play or danger so I didn't send any backup with Karen."

"I just now found out about the blood, and Cullen and I are on the way there now," Leigh assured him. "Call your deputy and tell her to approach with caution. The same person who killed Jimbo could have gone after Kali."

Cash belted out some more profanity. "I'm in Lubbock right now and won't be able to get there for at least thirty minutes. You'll be backing up my deputy?"

"I will. I'll keep you posted," she added and ended the call. Leigh immediately started glancing around, no doubt to make sure they weren't about to be attacked.

"Are you okay?" Cullen asked, but he, too, kept watch.

It took Leigh a couple of seconds to shift gears from her conversation with Cash, but she knew what Cullen was really asking. He wanted to know how she was handling what had just happened in the town hall.

"If I don't make an arrest soon, the mayor could press for a recall and have me ousted from office," she said. "Rocky might have been the one to set everything in motion, but Noble will get pressure, and he just might cave."

Still, Noble wouldn't be able to start the recall process to get rid of her by himself. It would take a majority vote from the council. Leigh had no idea just how many, or how few, votes would swing her way. Heck, she couldn't even count on getting Jeb's support. But that wouldn't stop her from doing her job for as long as she held the badge.

"I know you won't want it, but Bowen could put some pressure on Noble," Cullen offered.

She gave him a thin smile. "You're right. I don't want it." She paused. "But thanks. Right now, you and the three deputies who showed up are my biggest supporters."

The sound of agreement that Cullen made let her know that he was more than that. Yes, he was. Even though they weren't lovers, Leigh knew that would soon change. She'd land in bed with him, but she needed to keep her heart and the heat in check until after she'd finished this murder investigation.

Thankfully, the temps had warmed up enough that most of the ice was gone so the trip to Clay Ridge didn't take that long. Good thing, too, because Kali didn't live in town as Leigh had expected. According to the background data Leigh pulled up on her phone, Kali's house was situated on ten acres where she had horses. And it wasn't a sprawling, expensive place, either. The white frame house looked simple and cozy.

When Cullen pulled into the driveway, she spotted the cruiser and the lanky female deputy who was in the front yard with Austin. Leigh immediately looked to see if he was armed. He didn't have a gun in his hand, but that didn't mean he wasn't carrying one beneath his bulky coat.

"The blood's back here," Austin said the moment Leigh and Cullen were out of his truck. He motioned for them to follow him. But Leigh took a moment to introduce herself and Cullen to Deputy Karen Wheatly.

"I haven't been here long," Karen explained, "but Mr. Borden's right about the blood. There are some drops on the back porch."

"Drops," Leigh repeated. That was better than a huge amount, but it was still troublesome. "You haven't been inside?"

"I was about to do that now. I've knocked on the door, and Kali hasn't responded so that and the blood gives me probable cause to break the lock."

It did indeed, but before Leigh could ask if the deputy had a crowbar with her, Cullen pulled out a utility knife from his pocket. "I can get us in."

He didn't wait for permission, either. With Austin right on his heels and telling him to hurry, Cullen went to the front door. He had the lock open within a matter of seconds.

"Nick," Cullen said as an explanation.

Since his brother, Nick, was an ATF agent, Leigh figured that he'd taught Cullen how to get through locks. She was glad Noble or Rocky hadn't been around to see him use those skills or they probably would have considered it more reason for her to arrest him.

They stepped into the house, and Leigh noted that no security alarm went off. Maybe Kali had disengaged it. It wasn't a large place, but all the furniture appeared to be high-end. There also didn't seem to be anything out of place. Definitely no signs of a struggle.

"Kali?" Austin called out, and he would have bolted toward the hall had Cullen not took hold of him.

"It might not be safe," Cullen warned him.

"But Kali could be hurt," Austin insisted.

He slung off Cullen's grip. However, he waited, going with Karen, Leigh and Cullen as they went through the place room by room. Like the other parts of the house, there was nothing to indicate there'd been a problem.

Until they reached the kitchen.

There were what appeared to be drops of blood on the floor. Again, it wasn't a large amount and there was no spatter on the walls or counters to indicate blunt force trauma.

"The back door's locked," Karen pointed out.

Yes, and that was puzzling. The blood clearly led toward the door so if Kali had been attacked or hurt, why would she or her attacker take the time to lock up behind them?

Karen unlocked the door, and stepping around the blood, they went onto the back porch. More drops here, and these would have been the ones that Austin and Karen had already spotted. Leigh hoped that Austin hadn't compromised the scene by touching anything. As it was, he was going to be a suspect if anything had happened to Kali, and it'd be worse for him if he'd left traces of himself behind.

Leigh went down the steps, spotting a few more blood drops on the brown winter grass. She continued a few more feet, but when Leigh didn't see any more blood, she stopped and glanced around.

Kali's place was a lot like Leigh's. There was a small barn, what appeared to be a storage shed and plenty of fenced pastures. There was a heavily treed area to the right and a creek on the left. Leigh felt her stomach tighten because she didn't want Kali to have ended up in the icy water. Austin must have had that same thought because he started to run in that direction.

"I'll go with him," Karen insisted. "Why don't you two have a look around the barn?"

Leigh nodded, but before she moved, she spoke to Karen in a whisper. "I'm not sure I can trust Austin so watch your back."

Karen's eyes widened a little when she glanced at Austin. "Thanks." She slid her hand over the butt of her weapon and went after him.

Leigh continued to keep an eye on Austin until Cullen and she made it to the barn. Both drew their guns and stepped inside. She went still, listening, but didn't hear anything. She also didn't see any signs of blood.

"This doesn't make sense," Leigh muttered. She was hoping if she spoke her thoughts aloud that Cullen could help her understand what'd gone on here. "If Kali was taken, why would her kidnapper have brought her out through the back door? Why wouldn't he have just put her in his vehicle?"

They stepped out of the barn, and Cullen tipped his head to the woods. "There are probably trails out there where the kidnapper could have left his vehicle." He stopped and shook his head. "But it's a long way to take an injured woman. Especially since none of her neighbors are close enough to see if he'd taken her out through the front."

True, and that left Leigh with an unsettling theory. "If Kali tried to kill herself, she could have maybe staggered out of the house and collapsed somewhere." In this bitter cold, she wouldn't last long.

"The shed." Cullen motioned toward it, and that's when Leigh noticed the door was slightly ajar.

Mercy. Was Kali in there? Hurt and maybe hiding?

"Kali?" Leigh called out. "It's Sheriff Mercer. Cullen's with me. Do you need help?"

When Leigh got no answer, Cullen and she started in that direction. But they didn't get far. Only a couple of steps. Before they heard the scream. Not coming from the shed but rather from the woods.

"Kali," Leigh said on a rise of breath, and they began running toward the scream.

The shot rang out before they even made it past the shed.

Leigh was already moving to take cover, but Cullen hurried that along. He took hold of her, dragging her back behind the shed. Just as another shot blasted through the air.

Her adrenaline kicked in. So did the memories of the shooting just the day before. A shooting where Cullen and she had come close to dying. Hard to not let that play into this now, but Leigh battled the fear and forced herself to focus.

"The shot came from the woods," she said.

"Yeah, and it sounded like a rifle," Cullen agreed. "I'm pretty sure it came from the same area as the scream."

Leigh believed that, too, and it could mean that Kali

had just been shot. Or worse. Killed. Her instincts were to go after Kali, to try to save her. But that would be suicide, and it could get Cullen killed, too, because there was no way he'd let her go out there alone.

"Kali?" Leigh called out again.

Her voice would give away their position, but the shooter probably already knew their exact location. She got confirmation of that when more shots came, and all of them smacked into the storage shed.

Cullen cursed and dragged Leigh to the ground, until they were practically on their bellies. Leigh only hoped that Karen and Austin were also taking cover.

"Kali?" Leigh tried again, not expecting the woman to answer.

And that's why it surprised Leigh when she did.

"I'm here!" Kali shouted. She was definitely in the woods. "Someone's trying to kill me."

Welcome to the club. Since the shots all seemed to be coming right at the shed, maybe that meant the gunman wasn't actually firing at Kali. Then again, if the shooter had injured her and taken her into the woods, it was possible Kali was the target and the guy was just missing.

But Leigh didn't believe that.

No. The bullets were coming too close for them not to be in the crosshairs of this snake.

"Help me!" Kali shouted.

"Get down!" Leigh yelled back. "Take cover."

"I'll create a diversion," Cullen said. "I'll get the shooter to focus on me."

Leigh didn't even get the chance to say no to that because Cullen got up and hurried to the back end of the shed. He kept low, but Leigh knew it wouldn't be nearly low enough for the bullets that were still coming their way.

"Don't do this," Leigh snapped.

He didn't listen. Cullen peeled off his jacket, and he thrust it out from cover. It drew immediate gunfire and sent Leigh's heart into a tailspin. Mercy. He was making himself a target, and if the shots went just a little to the left, they'd hit Cullen.

Hurrying, she crawled to him, took hold of his leg and jerked him back down. Cullen didn't go easily. He was obviously still hell-bent on saving Kali because he tossed out his jacket, probably with the idea of drawing gunfire while Kali managed to take cover.

But the shots stopped.

Suddenly, it was quiet, and the only sounds were their ragged breaths and her pulse throbbing in her ears.

"He's getting away again," Leigh murmured.

She groaned and punched the shed with the side of her fist. The frustration and anger washed over her. Catching the shooter was the only way to stop these attacks. The only way to stop him from killing again. But part of her was relieved, too. If the shots stopped, then Cullen wouldn't be gunned down.

"Don't ever do anything like that again," she snapped. At least she'd intended to snap, but her voice was too breathy and her words too broken.

Cullen looked at her. But he didn't nod or make any sounds of agreement. Instead, he kissed her. It was hard, fast and like another punch of adrenaline.

"Sheriff Mercer?" Karen called out. "Are you both okay?"

"Yes." Leigh had to steady herself to add more. "What about Austin and you?"

"I'm fine. Not sure about Austin. He got away from me before I could even get to the creek. I don't know where he went."

Cullen's gaze met hers, and in his eyes, Leigh could see the same emotions that were no doubt in hers. Damn. This wasn't good. Leigh hated to think the worst about the man, but it was possible Austin had planted a rifle before Cullen, the deputy or she arrived, and he could have been the one to fire the shots.

"Any signs of the shooter?" Leigh asked the deputy.

"No. And none of the shots came my way."

"Good. Stay put until we're sure it's clear."

But the words had barely left her mouth when Leigh heard Austin. "I found her," he shouted. "I found Kali."

Chapter Thirteen

Cullen steeled himself, preparing for the worst when he saw Kali. But she was nowhere in the "worst" category.

He saw that right away when Kali came running out of the woods.

Leigh, Karen and he all started toward her. Kali's hair was disheveled, and there were smudges of dirt on her face, but he couldn't see any injuries that would have left those blood drops.

"Kali, wait!" Austin called out to her.

But Kali kept running, and she practically collapsed into Cullen's arms when he caught her. "I don't want Austin here."

In the grand scheme of things, that seemed small compared to everything else that had just happened. And to everything that could still happen. The shooter could still be out there, ready to fire off more shots, and that's why Cullen led Kali to the side of the shed so they'd have some cover.

"Are you hurt?" Leigh asked her.

With her breath gusting, Kali nodded. Then shook her head. She lifted her hand, to show them the gash on her palm. "I cut myself in the kitchen." It was deep enough that she'd need stitches, but it wasn't life-threatening. Unlike those shots.

"What happened?" Leigh pressed, still glancing around and no doubt keeping an eye out for the gunman. "Why were you in the woods?"

Kali sobbed, throwing herself against Cullen again. Her face landed against his shoulder. "Someone was breaking in through the front door so I ran out the back."

"But the back door was locked when we got here," Cullen pointed out.

"It locks automatically unless you adjust the thumb turn. And I didn't. I just ran and kept running so I could hide in the trees, but I didn't have my phone with me so I couldn't call anybody."

"Kali, are you all right?" Austin tried again.

"Make him leave," Kali snapped.

Cullen gave Austin a hard stare, hoping that he wouldn't give them any trouble about this.

"She needs to go to the hospital," Austin insisted, but he turned and headed toward the house.

"I'll have to question you later," Karen called out to him. "And question you, too," she added to Kali. "But Austin's right about you needing to go to the hospital. You should have someone take a look at that cut."

Kali turned not to Karen but to Leigh. "But what if the killer comes back?"

Leigh met her eye to eye. "You saw the killer?"

"No, but he shot at me." Kali paused, then shook her head again. "At least I think he was shooting at me. I didn't see him though."

Hell. Cullen had hoped Kali had at least gotten a glimpse of him. That could have put an end to the danger if they'd gotten an ID. But maybe the CSIs would be able to find something.

Karen stepped to the side to call in the shooting. It didn't take long, and when she was finished, she looked at Leigh. "Two other deputies are on the way here now so they can search the woods." Glancing up at the sun that would be setting in the next hour or so, she added, "A thorough search might have to wait until morning though."

That meant valuable trace could be lost, and it would sure as heck give the shooter plenty of time to get away.

"I'll go ahead and take Kali into the ER and get her statement," Karen continued a moment later. "I'll send you a copy. Cash will also need statements from Cullen and you."

"I'll make sure he gets them," Leigh told her. "I'd also like to see reports on any evidence the CSIs collect."

"Will do," Karen assured her, and she led Kali away while she kept watch around them.

Cullen and Leigh kept watch as well, but they didn't speak until they were in his truck. "Austin could have been the one to fire those shots," Leigh said.

Since Cullen had already considered the same thing, he nodded. "Or Kali could have."

Leigh's sound of agreement was fast and firm, causing Cullen to curse. Not because he was upset with her but because Kali and Austin had been his friends, and now he wasn't sure if one of them was a killer.

"Rocky could have gotten out here, too. I didn't see anyone following us, but it's possible he overheard us at the town hall."

Definitely possible, and he could have arrived after

them and slipped into the woods. He would have had plenty of time to set up a shooting while Leigh and he had been searching inside Kali's house.

But Rocky couldn't have been responsible for the blood drops on the porch.

No. Not enough time for that so maybe Rocky had an accomplice.

Leigh took out her phone, probably to start the calls and texts that a sheriff needed to make when she'd just been under attack, but she stared at the screen a moment and put it away. That's when Cullen noticed that her hands were trembling a little.

"I don't want to go back to the office," she murmured. "I don't want my deputies to see me like this."

It didn't surprise him that she'd held things together while she'd been talking to Kali. That was the job for Leigh. But with the pressure she had coming at her from all sides, she wouldn't want anyone to think she was weak. And Leigh would definitely see trembling hands as weak.

Since his own house still hadn't been cleared by the CSIs, Cullen drove her home, and he hoped like the devil that they wouldn't have any visitors. Leigh didn't need another round with Austin, Rocky or Jeb tonight. Didn't need to tangle with him, either, and that's why he'd give her some space so that maybe she'd be able to get some sleep.

Leigh kept her eyes open, still watching for the gunman, but she lay her head back against the seat. Not relaxing. No. She'd balled her trembling hands into fists, and she was no doubt reliving each and every one of the bullets that'd come at them.

"Rocky's not that good of a shot," she said, getting

his attention. "He barely qualifies at the shooting range when he has to take his annual test. What about Austin? Is he into guns?"

Cullen sighed, wishing that she'd been able to turn off her mind at least for this short drive but apparently not. Besides, it was a darn good question.

"Austin collects guns," Cullen explained. "I've never seen him fire one, but people who collect usually know how to use them. That doesn't mean that he's a good shot though."

She made a sound of agreement. "And Kali? I didn't see any guns in her house."

"Don't have a clue if she can shoot or not. But her father is a rancher so she's probably been around firearms." He paused. "Will your brother have Kali and Austin tested for gunshot residue?"

"Probably, but GSR doesn't always show up. And these shots likely came from a rifle so there might not be any GSR on their clothes."

So, it could be another dead end, but at this point any and all evidence could fall into that category.

Cullen pulled to a stop in front of Leigh's house, and he was pleased when exterior security lights flared on. It made it much easier for them to see that her yard was empty. Still, Cullen didn't take any chances.

When they went inside, they both shed their coats and checked to make sure no one had gotten in. The place was just as they'd left it to go to the meeting at the town hall.

Leigh used her phone to reset the security system, and then she just stood there in the hall. She did the same when her phone rang. She stared at the screen as if debating if she should answer it. Groaning softly, she finally hit the answer button and put the call on speaker.

"Jeb," she said. "What do you want?"

"I want to make sure you're okay and that you're not alone."

She took a couple of moments before she responded. "Cullen's here. He's staying the night again."

Cullen figured that would earn her a lecture from Jeb, but it didn't. "Good," Jeb said. "Because it's not a good idea for you not to have some backup."

"Backup," she repeated. There was both weariness and a little surprise in her tone. "So, you no longer believe I should be arresting him?"

"No." Jeb paused, sighed. "I heard about the shooting. Heard, too, that Cullen was with you again. If he was behind these attacks, he wouldn't keep putting himself in the line of fire like that."

Leigh sighed as well. "He's not behind the attacks nor the murders. You might have put him in the same tainted light as Bowen, but Cullen's not—"

"I did do that," Jeb admitted. "And I'm sorry."

Leigh pulled back her shoulders. Cullen had a similar reaction because Jeb was not the sort of man to admit a mistake. Worse, this conversation was starting to sound like a last-ditch effort to mend the rift between Leigh and him.

"What's wrong?" Leigh demanded. "Are you sick?"

Jeb's laugh was quick and dry. "I don't have to be sick to tell you that you were right about Cullen. Right about the way you've handled the investigation. Right about a lot of things," he added in a mutter.

"Am I right about you being sick?" she asked.

Jeb's silence confirmed that she was. "I'm waiting

on test results, but the docs think it's my heart. Might need bypass. Might need something more. I won't know for a couple more days, and I hadn't planned on telling you until I knew for sure."

Leigh drew in a long, slow breath. "Does Cash know?"

"No. He doesn't take my calls. And before you say anything, I know he's got reasons for that. So do you. But thanks for hearing me out. If you want, I'll tell you the test results when I have them."

"I want that," she assured him.

It seemed to Cullen that Jeb blew out a sigh of relief. "Good night, Leigh," he added and ended the call.

Once again, Leigh just stood there, but she looked even more exhausted than she had been before Jeb's call.

"I'm sorry," Cullen told her.

She nodded, put her phone away and then turned to him. Their eyes met. Held.

"Don't sleep in the guest room tonight," she whispered, taking hold of his hand. "Come to bed with me."

LEIGH FIGURED SHE should just tell Cullen this was a mistake. Maybe then he'd do the right thing and back away from her.

She knew for a fact that she wouldn't be doing the backing away.

This was despite the lecture she'd given herself about waiting until after the investigation to get involved with him. She should wait. But the fear and emotions were crushing her like an avalanche, and Cullen was the one person who could make that stop. For a little while, anyway.

"The timing for this isn't good," Cullen said. "You want to talk about Jeb?"

Leigh didn't have to take time to consider her answer. "No. I don't want to talk about anything at all. It doesn't have to be sex tonight…" She groaned, pushed her hair from her face and kept her gaze nailed to his. "Yes, it does."

The corner of his mouth lifted, and she got a flash of that hot smile that had no doubt lured many women to his bed. But tonight she was doing the luring. Leigh rethought that though when Cullen pulled her to him and kissed her.

His kiss was exactly what she needed. She sank into it. Sank into his arms, too. Because, mercy, she needed this.

She needed him.

The years they'd been apart vanished, and it felt as if they'd always been together like this. Always *should* be together. But now wasn't the time for Cullen to hear that or for her to realize it.

Cullen picked up on her need for him by her deepening the kiss, and he didn't waste any time backing her into her bedroom. They moved together without breaking the kiss or the arms she'd locked around him.

"I should give you a chance to reconsider," he said, getting off her boots before easing her back on the bed. He looked down at her. "Don't reconsider."

Now it was her turn to smile, and Leigh pulled him down on top of her. All in all, it was a great place for him to be. The weight of his body on hers only fueled this ache she had for him. The kisses did as well when Cullen took his mouth to her neck.

She remembered this part. The foreplay and fire.

The urgent heat that started to build inside her. Cullen was very good at the building. At making her need him more than her next breath.

He did something about her breath. He made it vanish when he lowered the kisses to her stomach. He shoved up her top, his mouth teasing her bare skin and kicking up the urgency even more.

Leigh reached for his shirt, but he pinned her hands to the bed and kept on kissing her. Going lower until he reached the zipper of her jeans. With his own hands locked with hers, he simply used his mouth. And his breath. Cullen kissed her through the denim and kept kissing her until Leigh could take no more.

She rolled with him, reversing their positions so she could go after his shirt. She wanted her mouth on his chest. Wanted to touch him. And she did both. She took a moment to admire the view—the man was built—but she couldn't stave off Cullen.

Once she had his shirt off, he did another flip, straddling her so he could rid her of her shirt. He flicked open her front-hook bra and gave her a quick reminder that breast kisses were hot spots for her. He fanned the heat even higher, managing to kiss one breast, then the other, before he moved lower to shimmy her out of her jeans and panties. He kicked off his own boots as well.

Then, he kept kissing her.

Leigh had no choice but to hang on and enjoy the ride. She fisted her hands on the quilt, anchoring herself, but she knew that if he kept up those clever flicks of his tongue that she'd climax too fast.

"We do this together," she insisted.

She maneuvered away from him so that she could tackle his jeans. And finally his boxers. Yes, the man was built, and the past decade had only improved everything about him.

"Condom," he ground out when she ran her hand the long length of him. "In my wallet."

Since she wanted that long length inside her, Leigh rummaged through his jeans, located the wallet, then the condom.

Cullen did some more maneuvering, flipping their positions again so that he was on top of her. Thankfully, it didn't take him long to get the condom on, and with their gazes locked, he slipped inside her.

The pleasure speared through her, and the sound she made was a long, slow moan. It felt as if she'd been waiting for this for way too long.

Cullen made his own sound of pleasure, and he began to move inside her. Building the fire with each maddening stroke. Making everything pinpoint to the need to finish this. And that's what he did.

He finished it.

Leigh held on to Cullen and let him finish her.

Chapter Fourteen

Cullen sipped his coffee while he stared out Leigh's kitchen window. It was a good view of the frost-covered pastures, the barn and the horses.

Leigh had set up automatic feed dispensers, probably because of the long hours she often worked, and he'd heard talk that she had part-time help for the chores that came with running a small horse ranch. But for this morning, they had the place to themselves.

That's why he'd found it damn hard to leave her bed.

However, Cullen had forced himself away from her and into the shower. Then, into the kitchen so he could give her some thinking time. He fully expected when she came to her senses that she'd tell him they'd made a huge mistake by having sex. And maybe they had. But at the moment it felt like something he wanted to continue doing beyond just this time together. First though, they had to find a killer and stop him or her from coming after them again.

He continued to sip coffee, and then saw Leigh. Not in the house but headed toward the pasture. Since she hadn't come through the kitchen, she'd likely gone out through the patio doors off her bedroom.

Wearing a bulky buckskin work coat, she stopped at

the pasture fence, and a bay mare immediately came to her. Leigh ran her hand over the horse and murmured something. Even though Cullen couldn't hear what she said, he smiled. Obviously, they had common ground when it came to their love of horses.

His smile faded though when he remembered that it wasn't a good idea for her to be out in the open like that. Not with a killer on the loose. A killer who favored taking shots at them. Cullen grabbed his coat and went to join her.

The sun was out, making everything look as if it'd been doused with diamond dust, but the cold air still had a sting to it. His boots crunched on the ice-crusted grass, and it was that sound that likely alerted her, because with her hand still stroking the mare, Leigh turned to look at him.

"I know," she said before he could speak. "I shouldn't be out here. But being around the horses helps me clear my mind."

He smiled again. Yeah, they had common ground all right.

"This is Buttercup," Leigh said, introducing him to the mare. "And that's Smoky and Honey." She tipped her head to two other horses, who were also heading their way. "If they'd caught a stranger's scent, they would let me know about it. Like now." All three horses were snorting and whinnying.

Well, they weren't as good as guard dogs in sending up an alarm, but it was better than nothing.

Because he wanted the taste of her, Cullen moved closer and brushed his mouth over hers. That also got him some attention from the mare, who gave his arm

a nudge. He gave her a quick rub, then lingered a moment longer on the kiss with Leigh.

Leigh eased back, her eyes partly closed and a
dreamy look on her face. Obviously, the kiss had been
just as potent for her as it was for him. But potency
aside, being out here was too dangerous. Cullen hooked
his arm around Leigh to lead her back to the house. He
considered trying to coax her to bed, but they'd barely
made it inside the kitchen when her phone rang.

"It's Vance," she said, answering and putting the
call on speaker.

Since this almost certainly had something to do with
the investigation, Cullen was very interested in what
the deputy had to say.

"Just got off the phone with the crime lab," Vance
explained. "It's not good news. The fingerprint on the
SUV is too smudged for them to get a match."

Leigh didn't groan, probably because she'd already
considered that might be the outcome. She shucked off
her coat and put it on the peg by the door. Cullen did
the same.

"I want you to put out the word that the print isn't
smudged and that the crime lab believes they'll be able
to get a match from the database," she told Vance after
a short pause. "Tell everyone you know because I want
word to get back to the killer. But also alert the lab so
they've got full security in place in case the killer tries
to eliminate the evidence."

"Will do," Vance assured her.

Cullen could help with that, too, and he fired off a
quick text to Austin. He told Austin that it was good
news, that the killer might soon be ID'd. If Austin was
guilty and did indeed try to destroy evidence against

him, then he'd be caught. That still felt like a heavy-weight's punch, but it was better than having Austin come after Leigh.

"I'll be in the office soon," Leigh added to Vance a moment later. She ended the call, but before she could put her phone away, it rang again.

"Cash," she said, glancing at the screen. The muscles stirred in her jaw. "I'm not going to tell him about Jeb. Not over the phone. I'll pay him a visit to give him the news."

That made sense, and her tone let Cullen know that her father's illness was weighing on her. Despite the rift between them, she almost certainly still loved him.

As she'd done with Vance, Leigh put the call on speaker while she helped herself to a cup of coffee. "Please tell me you found the shooter," Leigh greeted her brother.

"No," Cash answered after a huff. "And I'm about to add another complication to your murder investigation."

"What happened?" Leigh demanded.

"I'd better start with what didn't happen," Cash explained. "Kali didn't have a break-in, and she didn't run into the woods because she was afraid. During the interview, she broke down and admitted that it was all staged. She claimed she knew Austin was coming over because he'd texted her and said he was. So, she told me that she set up her injury to leave the blood drops, and then she ran and hid so it'd make him sick with worry."

Leigh groaned and set her coffee aside so she could scrub her hands over her face. "And what about the shooter?"

"Kali insists she doesn't have a clue about that. Says

she didn't see anyone in the woods before or after the shots started."

"You believe her?" Leigh pressed.

This time Cash wasn't so fast to answer. "Not sure. Plenty of people are good liars, and I don't know if she's one of them. But if she fired those shots, then the rifle is probably still somewhere in the woods, and the CSIs are out looking for it now."

Leigh gathered her breath before she spoke again. "Did Kali agree to let you test for GSR?"

"She did. Nada. Then again, the EMTs had their hands all over her clothes when they examined her. She had a panic attack in the ambulance, and they had to restrain her."

Cullen didn't even bother to curse. Leigh had already known that the GSR would be a long shot.

"Unless I can prove Kali's the shooter," Cash went on, "I can't charge her with anything other than a misdemeanor for wasting law enforcement resources. She didn't make a false 911 call, and she admitted the ruse once I got her in interview. I can't arrest her for wanting to worry her ex-boyfriend."

No, but it did show how desperate and hurt Kali was. So desperate and so hurt that she might have killed Alexa. Especially if Alexa had taunted Kali about her affair with Austin.

Leigh finished her call with her brother, gulped down some more coffee and gave her shoulder harness an adjustment. "You should be able to go back to the Triple R sometime this morning," she said, her gaze lifting to meet his. "But you're welcome to stay here."

That was an invitation Cullen had no intention of turning down. Not just because he wanted to be with

Leigh but also because he wasn't about to leave her alone as long as the killer was still gunning for them. Cullen would have told her that, too, but they got another call. This time, it was his phone.

"It's Jamie," he said, answering right away. He also put it on speaker. "Are you okay?" Cullen immediately asked him.

Jamie, however, didn't give him an immediate answer. "I'm getting out of the hospital. Deputy Cecile Taggart is still here, and she's going to drive me to the bunkhouse."

Cullen was thankful Jamie would still have police protection, but something was wrong. He didn't think he was mistaken about the worry he'd heard in Jamie's voice.

"Did something happen?" Cullen came out and asked.

"Yeah. And that's why I need to talk to the sheriff and you." Again, Jamie hesitated, and he lowered his voice to a whisper. "The killer called me again."

LEIGH RESISTED SNATCHING the phone right out of Cullen's hand, but she did hurry to get closer so that Jamie would have no trouble hearing her. "What did the killer say to you?" she demanded.

"I don't want to get into it here over the phone," Jamie said, still hesitating, still whispering. "Deputy Taggart and I will be at your house soon. I need to talk to you about going into protective custody or something. I can't go on like this."

Jamie hung up before she could demand again that he tell her about the phone call he'd gotten from the killer.

"I should go to the hospital," Leigh grumbled.

"You could end up passing him and Cecile on the road," Cullen quickly pointed out.

His voice was calm and reasonable. Too bad she wasn't feeling either at the moment. She wanted to know about the killer, and Jamie might have key information. Information that could possibly stop another attack.

"Witness protection," she repeated like profanity. "I'm guessing that means the killer threatened him again." And that reminder sent some fresh alarm through her. "I should send Cecile backup."

She whipped out her phone and called the deputy, and Cecile must have been expecting her call, because she answered on the first ring.

"Jamie's fine," Cecile said right off. "He's just scared. We're heading out of the hospital right now, and then I'll drive him straight to your place."

"Why is he scared? What did the killer tell him?" Leigh pressed.

"I don't know. I didn't hear any of the actual call, but he's insisting on talking to you about it. I called your office and they said you were still home so I figured that's where I'd bring him. I had Dawn come here to the hospital, too, so she'll ride along with us."

Some of the tightness eased in Leigh's chest. She had good cops working for her, and this was proof of it. Cecile had arranged for backup on her own. Maybe it wouldn't be necessary, but taking precautions was the right call.

"Come straight here," Leigh instructed. "If we end up doing protective custody, I've got contacts with the marshals that I can bring in. That way, they could meet with Jamie here so he doesn't have to go back out again."

"Will do," Cecile assured her. "We're getting in the cruiser right now and will be there in just a couple of minutes," she added before she ended the call.

"I can arrange for security at the ranch, too, if Jamie wants to go back to the bunkhouse," Cullen offered. "Or if he wants to go to his folks' place, I can send men there with him."

Leigh gave his arm a gentle squeeze. "Thank you." She took a deep breath. "I just wish I knew if Jamie was in actual danger or if the killer is just trying to intimidate him. Either way, he needs protection," she added in a mumble.

"Nick might be able to help," Cullen suggested.

It'd been a while since she'd seen his brother, but since Nick was an ATF agent, it was highly likely that he had other contacts in law enforcement. Nick might be able to streamline the process for Jamie.

When she heard the sound of an engine approaching the house, Cullen and she hurried to the front window. But it wasn't a police cruiser. It was a big silver four-by-four truck that maneuvered over the dirt and gravel like a bulldozer, and it pulled to a stop behind Cullen's truck.

Cullen groaned. "It's Bowen."

Leigh wanted to groan as well. She didn't have time for a visit from a man who was likely there to give her grief.

She disarmed the security system so Cullen could open the front door, and Leigh went onto the porch with him when he faced down his father. Bowen stepped from his truck, leaving the engine running and door open as he started toward them. He sighed in obvious disapproval when he saw them.

"It's true, then," Bowen said to Cullen. He stopped at the bottom porch step and stared up at them. A stare from narrowed eyes. "You're staying here with Leigh."

Yep, she'd been right about the grief-giving, and apparently Bowen was going to dole some of it out to Cullen as well as her.

"Last I heard I didn't have to check with you about my sleeping arrangements," Cullen fired back.

"Well, you should because you know Jeb will use this to try to lock you up." Bowen flung his index finger at Leigh. "And she might not be able to save you. They're trying to kick her out of office."

"Yes," Cullen agreed, "and they're trying that because she won't give in to the gossip that I killed Alexa." He put his hands on his hips, shook his head. "You and Jeb are a lot alike, you know. He was at the station and had the same complaint."

"Of course he did," Bowen snarled. "He'd rather see you dead than with his daughter."

That might be true, but Leigh didn't believe Jeb would do anything to cause Cullen's demise. However, Jeb might indeed want to rid her of her badge so she couldn't tarnish the reputation he had in the county.

"I'm pretty sure I'm in love with Leigh," Cullen said, stunning his father.

However, Bowen's reaction was a drop in the bucket compared to Leigh's. "What?" she managed to say.

Cullen had likely tossed that out in anger. Something to get his father off his back. But one look at him, and Leigh thought it might be true.

Well, heck.

This wasn't good. Not now, anyway. She didn't have the focus or time to sort out how she felt about that announcement. Or how she felt about Cullen for that matter. Yes, she had feelings for him. Deep ones. Always had. But love?

It was something she had to push to the back of her mind though because the cruiser pulled into the driveway. Dawn was behind the wheel, and she pulled up in front of Bowen's truck.

"This conversation isn't over," Bowen said like a warning. "I'll come back after you've dealt with business."

"Just stay put a couple more seconds," Leigh instructed, keeping her attention on the cruiser. "You can leave after Jamie's inside the house."

"Jamie?" Bowen asked, and there seemed to be genuine concern in his voice. "What's he doing here?'"

"Business," Leigh said, using Bowen's own choice of words.

The young ranch hand got out from the back seat of the cruiser. There was a white bandage on his head, and he looked more than a little pale and wobbly. The unsteadiness was probably why Cecile rushed around the cruiser to take hold of Jamie's arm. Leigh went into the yard, too, with Cullen right behind her. Something Leigh appreciated. If Jamie was about to collapse, they might need Cullen's muscle to get him into the house.

Leigh intended to call the doctor as soon as Jamie was safe. No way did he look ready to have been released from the hospital. Then again, maybe Jamie had pushed for his release because he'd been afraid the killer would get to him.

With Cullen on one side of Jamie and Cecile on the other, they started toward the house.

"Is the boy all right?" Bowen asked.

Leigh was asking herself the same thing. But she didn't get a chance to answer Bowen.

Before someone fired a shot.

CULLEN MOVED FAST when he heard the gunshot. He hooked his arm around Leigh's waist and pulled her to the ground next to some shrubs and landscape boulders. Cecile did the same with Jamie. But the deputy wasn't fast enough.

The bullet slammed into her shoulder.

"Cecile," Leigh said on a gasp, and she pulled away from Cullen so she could go to her deputy.

Apparently, Dawn was trying to do the same thing. Cullen heard the cruiser door open. Heard the shot that followed. And because he was on the ground, he could see Dawn fall on the other side of the cruiser.

Hell.

There were two deputies down.

Cecile was alive. Cullen could see that. But he could also see the blood that was already spreading across the front of her coat. Cecile was also writhing in pain. Pain that would get a whole lot worse if the shooter managed to put another bullet in her.

Cullen couldn't see Dawn well enough to know if she was alive, but she wasn't moving. Definitely not a good sign.

"Oh, God," Jamie muttered, and he kept repeating it.

Another shot came, this one slamming into the ground between them and Bowen.

"Get down!" Cullen yelled to his father, and he drew his gun.

But there really wasn't any cover where he was. Ditto for Leigh, Jamie, Cecile and him. They were all literally out in the open in the yard with two injured cops and a ranch hand who looked on the verge of a full-out panic attack.

While Leigh applied pressure to Cecile's wound, Cullen made a quick call to the police station to get them some backup. It wouldn't take long for the other deputies to arrive, but a gunman could take them all out in just a matter of seconds.

Cullen had to do something about that. He couldn't just let Dawn and Cecile bleed out. He glanced around, looking for a way to get everyone to safety. The cruiser was a good fifteen feet away. It was the same for Bowen's truck. They'd be easy targets if they tried to get to them.

Another bullet cracked through the air, and because he'd been waiting for it, Cullen used the sound to pinpoint the location. The shooter was to the right of Leigh's yard, probably in the thick cluster of oak and pecan trees.

"Get flat on the ground next to those bushes and try to crawl to the left side of the house," he told Bowen, but his father was already scrambling to do that.

More shots came, and none seemed to be aimed at Bowen. They all came toward Leigh. Even though Cullen knew she wasn't going to like it, he climbed over her, took aim in the direction of the shooter, and he fired. It didn't faze the shooter one bit because he sent more bullets their way.

Making a sound of outrage, Leigh levered herself up, and she, too, fired at the gunman. Cullen figured the chances of either of them hitting the guy were slim to none, but they needed a lull in the gunfire so they could get to the side of the house where Bowen was.

"I'll get to Bowen's truck," Cullen told Leigh, and he made sure it sounded like a plan of action and not a suggestion. "I'll bring it here so we can get Jamie and Cecile inside."

Leigh was already shaking her head before he finished. "He'll shoot you before you can get to it."

Maybe. *Probably*, Cullen silently amended. "You can try to take him out when his attention's focused on me."

She was still shaking her head when they heard the sound of more gunfire. But this hadn't come from the direction of the shooter. No. This was coming from the far right, behind Leigh's house. And it wasn't aimed at Leigh and him but rather at the shooter.

"Bowen," Leigh said, glancing in the direction where Cullen had last seen his father. Bowen was no longer there. Since his father always carried a gun, he'd probably gone around the back of the house so he could try to stop the gunman.

And it worked.

Well, it worked in distracting the gunman, anyway, because the shots began to go in Bowen's direction. Cullen knew Bowen was taking a huge risk. One that Cullen hoped didn't cost him his life. But maybe it would be enough of a diversion for him to get Leigh, Jamie and Cecile behind cover.

"Jamie, you need to stay down and move," Cullen told him, and he hoisted Cecile over his shoulder in a fireman's carry. The deputy moaned in pain, but she was still conscious.

Leigh's eyes met Cullen's. It was just a split-second glance, but a lot of things passed between them. The fear. And the hope. This was their chance, and they had to take it.

"We need to get to the left side of the house," Leigh added.

Cullen was right there with her, and once he was sure Jamie was in a crouching position, Cullen got them moving. Leigh turned, covering their backs as they hurried across the stretch of yard.

It didn't take long for the bullets to come their way.

They smacked into the ground, tearing up the grass and dirt. But Bowen didn't let up. He continued to fire shots at the gunman, and Cullen figured that slowed the guy down at least a little.

Each inch across the yard seemed to take an eternity, and with each step, Cullen's heart pounded even harder. His fears skyrocketed. Not for himself. But for Leigh. She was putting herself between them and the shooter. Not only that, she was almost certainly the primary target.

The moment Cullen reached the left side of the house, he caught onto Jamie, dragging him to the ground and handing him Cecile. Thankfully, Jamie took the injured deputy and that freed up Cullen to lean out and give Leigh and Bowen some help. He fired at the gunman until Leigh was able to scramble next to him.

"I need to get some help for Dawn," Leigh immediately said, taking out her phone.

She called dispatch to request medical assistance, but Cullen tuned her out when he heard the hurried footsteps coming from the back of the house. He pivoted in that direction, bringing up his gun, but it wasn't the threat his body had braced for.

It was Bowen.

His father wasn't hurt, which was somewhat of a miracle, and with his gun still drawn, he hurried toward them.

"Who's trying to kill us?" Bowen snarled.

Cullen shook his head and turned back to the front yard so he could keep watch. He didn't see the gunman, but he saw something else. Dawn. The deputy was crawling to the front of the cruiser. Like Cecile, she was bleeding, but at least she was alive. She might not be that way for long though if they couldn't get an ambulance out here.

"I can try to make a run for my truck," Bowen said, causing Cullen to glance back at him.

There were times his father's stubbornness could irritate the heck out of him, but Bowen was no coward. He would indeed go out there just as he'd drawn fire so that the rest of them could get to cover.

"There's an ATV in the barn," Leigh said when she finished her call. "One of us could use it to get Cecile to the trail at the back of my property. The trail leads out to the road. She needs to get to the hospital ASAP," she added, looking directly at Cullen.

Cullen had no doubts that Leigh meant for him to be getting Cecile out of there. He wouldn't have minded doing just that if it didn't mean leaving Leigh behind. Where he knew for a fact that she would take huge risks to try to get to Dawn.

"And what about Dawn?" Cullen asked her.

"I can go through the back door into my house. One of the windows on that side should make it easier to take out the shooter."

It would. And Leigh would have the added advantage of having some cover.

"You'll take Cecile to the ATV in the barn?" Cullen asked his father.

Bowen hesitated, but that was probably because he, too, was thinking of the danger to those who stayed behind. His father finally nodded and hoisted Cecile as Cullen had done. "But, damn it, don't do anything stupid."

Cullen didn't make him any promises. Couldn't. Because he'd definitely do something stupid if it meant keeping Leigh safe. Unfortunately, she probably had the same thing in mind when it came to him.

"I'll be in the house with Leigh," Cullen explained, still keeping watch of the front and back yards. He didn't want the shooter sneaking up on them from behind.

"I can help Mr. Brodie with Cecile," Jamie volunteered. "Then, I can wait in the barn until it's okay to come out."

Leigh nodded. "Let's go."

As she'd done in the yard, Leigh took the back position, and Cullen jogged ahead so he could make sure the gunman wasn't lying in wait for them. He didn't see anyone so he gave Bowen and Jamie the go-ahead to get to the barn. They were only about halfway there when Cullen heard something he definitely hadn't wanted to hear.

Not a gunshot.

But an engine.

It was Bowen's massive truck, and when the driver hit the accelerator, the truck barreled right toward them.

Chapter Fifteen

Leigh got a quick flash of images from when the SUV had rammed into her cruiser. Those had been some terrifying moments, but at least she and Cullen had been in the vehicle. There'd been some protection.

Not now though.

They were out in the open, where they could be mowed down and killed.

"Run!" she shouted.

That order wasn't just to Cullen but to Bowen and Jamie. They weren't in the barn yet, and they were out in the open, too, where they'd be easy targets. Especially since Bowen was carrying Cecile and Jamie obviously wasn't in any shape to outrun a truck with a driver hell-bent on killing them.

Leigh didn't dare take the time to look back to see how close the truck was to them. Every second counted now, and the moment she reached the back porch, she cursed the railing. It was too high to vault over, and if she tried to climb it, she could be sideswiped. That meant going around and up the steps.

But she didn't get a chance to do that.

From the corner of her eye, she saw Jamie fall, but it was just a blur of motion because she was moving.

Or rather Cullen was moving her. He caught onto her arm, jerking her away from the porch.

And it wasn't a second too soon.

Because the truck rammed into the exact spot where she'd just been.

Neither Cullen nor she had had time to fire at the driver, but Cullen's momentum got them away from the impact. They fell, but immediately scrambled to get up. However, Jamie wasn't doing the same. He was still down, and Bowen must not have even noticed because he was still barreling toward the barn with Cecile in tow.

The railing on the porch gave way. So did part of the porch. However, the truck didn't seem damaged at all. The driver spun it around, taking aim at Cullen and her again.

Leigh had to make a quick decision. If Cullen and she ran toward Jamie, they might not be able to get him up in time to stop him from being run over. Obviously, Cullen had the same concern because he took hold of her arm and started running toward the front of the house.

Where the cruiser was.

And Dawn.

The truck would almost certainly follow them, but if they could get the deputy into the cruiser, then they stood a chance of protecting her. Then, they could drive back around to the barn to help Jamie and Bowen.

Leigh braced herself in case someone fired shots at them. After all, the driver could be working with a partner. But the only threat came from the truck itself. The driver managed to get it turned around and came at Cullen and her again when they reached the front yard. Because the windshield was so heavily tinted, they couldn't see who was trying to kill them.

Once again, Cullen and she had to dive out of the way of the speeding truck. It whipped right past them, so close that Leigh could feel the heat of the engine. They fell again. Hard. Leigh rammed into some rocks, causing the pain to shoot through her. The impact also knocked the breath out of her, and she lost critical moments of time fighting for air. No way could she stand when she couldn't breathe.

Cullen helped with that though. He got to his feet, hauling her up and practically dragging her out of the way. Good thing, too. Because the driver threw the truck into Reverse and came at them again.

Leigh was thankful that Cullen still had hold of her because he got them out of the way again, this time diving behind some landscape boulders. Still, they'd just come close to dying, and it was obvious the driver wasn't finished. He did a doughnut in the yard, the tires slinging up dirt and rocks. Obviously, taking aim at them again.

But he didn't hit the accelerator.

He just sat there, revving the engine. Waiting. But for what? Maybe he thought it would shred the tires if he hit the boulders. And it might. But the two-foot-high rocks wouldn't give them enough protection if he started shooting. That's why Leigh had to try to stop him from doing that. She still had hold of her gun so she pointed it at the windshield.

And she fired.

Just as the driver sped forward. Her bullet tore through the safety glass, and she cursed when she realized her shot had been off. Not directly at the driver but a little to the left. She might have injured him, but it likely hadn't been a headshot. Right now, she figured killing him was the only way for the rest of them to survive. If this killer managed to take out Cullen and her, he'd take out the rest. No way would he want to leave witnesses behind.

Cullen pulled her to her feet again, and they darted to the left. But not far. The driver would have to at least clip the boulders to get to them. That would certainly slow him down.

However, he didn't come at them again.

The driver spun around, speeding not toward them but rather in the direction of the barn. Leigh's stomach went to her knees because she was pretty sure she knew what he was doing. He was going after Jamie, Bowen and Cecile.

"No!" Leigh shouted, hoping to draw the driver's attention.

But she didn't. The truck kept going, past the house and into the backyard. Straight to Jamie. He was still on the ground, but he was conscious, because he was struggling to get up and out of the way.

With the howl of police and ambulance sirens just up the road, Cullen and she started running. Hoping to stop the driver from killing the ranch hand. However, there was a lot of distance between Jamie and them.

The driver slammed on the brakes, but Leigh couldn't tell if he'd hit Jamie or not. She couldn't tell if Jamie was still alive. Worse, she couldn't see the driver. But she heard what she thought was the passenger's-side door opening.

"He's grabbing Jamie," Cullen said, pulling up so he could take aim.

Leigh immediately understood why he'd do that. The killer had to know backup was on the way, and he could use Jamie to escape. But there was a possibility that was much worse. Maybe he was about to kill Jamie so he could eliminate him as a loose end.

"I can't risk shooting," Cullen snarled like profanity.

No, he couldn't. Because he might hit Jamie instead. The windshield wouldn't help with that, either. There was a gaping hole from her own shot, but the rest of the glass had cracked and webbed. It was as effective as putting a mask on the killer.

She heard the door slam, and the driver quickly turned the truck around. So that it was facing Cullen and her again. It came at them. Slowly this time. Like a predator stalking its prey. Since that slow pace could mean the driver was preparing to fire at them, Cullen and she moved back behind the boulders. Even if they were belly-down, it wouldn't stop them from being shot, but it was better than standing out in the open with a killer bearing down on them.

"Be ready to jump out of the way," Leigh warned Cullen.

The driver held the snail-crawling pace until he stopped just a few yards away from them. Leigh saw some movement behind the damaged glass, and a moment later, Jamie peered through the fist-sized hole in the windshield. She could only see part of his face, but it was enough for her to know he was terrified.

"Me for you," Jamie said, his voice trembling with fear. He aimed those fear-filled eyes at Leigh. "That's the deal I'm supposed to tell you. If you don't trade places with me, I'll die."

HELL. THAT WAS the one word that kept going through Cullen's mind.

It was bad enough that Leigh and he had to face down a killer, but now Jamie was in the middle of it.

Cullen seriously doubted that Jamie was in any shape to fight off the killer, especially since he was almost certainly being held at gunpoint. Being told what to say, too. The killer had no doubt told Jamie word for word what he was supposed to say to Leigh and him.

He made a quick glance at the road and spotted a cruiser and an ambulance. They'd turned off their sirens, but their lights were still flaring. Leigh obviously saw them, too, and she fired off a text. "I told Vance to try to get Dawn out of here and take her to the EMTs," she relayed to Cullen. "I don't want him or the ambulance coming any closer."

That was a wise decision. If the cruiser came speeding in, it might help Leigh and him by giving them some cover, but it could be a deadly move for Jamie. If the killer didn't shoot him on the spot, he might try to flee with him. Then, the snake could just murder Jamie once he was in the clear.

But Cullen wanted to make sure this SOB didn't get away.

"Me for you," Jamie repeated.

"And how do I know you won't gun all three of us down if we make this trade?" Leigh called out to the driver.

There was a short silence, probably for Jamie to get his instructions, and he finally said, "You don't know. It's a risk you'll have to take if you want to keep me alive." Jamie's voice trembled. Then, it broke. "Don't take the risk," he blurted out. "Don't trade yourselves for me."

Cullen could see enough of Jamie to spot the barrel of a gun as it jammed into the ranch hand's temple.

"All of this is to cover up you murdering Alexa," Leigh called out. "And it's stupid. Backup's already arrived, and you won't be able to get out of here. Just toss down your weapon, let Jamie go, and I'll see what kind of deal I can work out."

Jamie winced when the gun dug even harder into his head, but he didn't say anything for several seconds. "You're lying. There'll be no deal," he said, obviously repeating what the killer had told him.

The killer was right about that. No way would he get a reduced sentence when he'd murdered at least two people and attempted to murder others, including cops. Still, maybe there was a way to bargain with him.

Or her.

Cullen couldn't rule out that it was Kali behind the wheel. It wouldn't have taken much muscle to force Jamie into the truck at gunpoint.

"If your plan is to get away, you'll need money," Cullen called out to the killer. "You could consider it a ransom. I'll pay you to release Jamie."

"Money won't fix this," Jamie said, repeating his instructions. "But Leigh and you will. This is your last chance," Jamie added. "Me for you."

"Any chance you have a shot?" Leigh asked him.

Cullen studied the distorted images behind the heavily tinted glass. "Maybe. I figure the killer is still behind the wheel. Maybe keeping low. But I could keep the shot to the side so that it won't hit Jamie."

Well, maybe it wouldn't. Cullen doubted the driver

had Jamie fully in front of him like a human shield—there wouldn't be enough room for that—but any shot would be a risk. If Cullen didn't kill the driver, then he or she could turn the gun on Jamie. Of course, the odds of that happening were already sky-high.

That's why they had to go for it.

"I'll take the shot," Cullen told her.

She nodded, her breath mixing with the cold air and creating a wispy fog between them. "On the count of three, you fire, and I'll run to the side of the house. That might buy Jamie some time."

Yeah, it would. Because the killer would turn the gun on Leigh.

"No." Cullen couldn't say that fast enough. "You're not running out there."

Leigh looked him straight in the eyes. "Neither one of us can crouch here and let Jamie die. It's what has to be done."

Cullen cursed, ready to argue with her, but then he spotted something he definitely hadn't wanted to see.

Bowen.

Crouched down, his father had come out of the barn, and it was obvious he was trying to sneak up on the driver of the truck. Not directly behind it. But rather to the side. It'd be a damn good way for Bowen to get himself killed.

"What the heck is he doing?" Leigh snarled. "Text him. Tell him to get down right now."

Even if Bowen read the text, he wouldn't just get down. His father's stubborn streak wasn't reserved just for Jeb and members of his family. However, Cullen had to try, and he motioned for Bowen to drop.

He didn't.

Bowen took aim at the back tires of the truck, and he started firing. Not one shot but a barrage of them that would almost certainly flatten the tires and prevent a quick escape. But it wasn't escape that Cullen was immediately worried about. It was Bowen and Jamie.

The driver's-side door flew open, and Cullen saw Jamie being dragged out of the vehicle. Now he was a human shield, and that position prevented Cullen from seeing who was holding him, especially since his captor was hunkering down.

"Keep that up, and I die," Jamie yelled.

Again, it was the words the killer wanted him to say, and Cullen was thankful he could actually say them. Because it meant he was still alive. The killer hadn't panicked and just taken him out.

Not yet, anyway.

However, the fact that Jamie was being forced to do all the talking meant the killer didn't want Cullen or Leigh to hear his or her voice because they would recognize who it was.

Bowen did stop firing, and he had the sense to drop down on the ground. That, and the fact that he was on the other side of the truck from the killer, might prevent him from being shot.

Leigh levered herself up a little and took aim. Cullen had to resist the need to push her back down. To give her that small margin of cover. But she was a cop, and no way would she put her safety over Jamie's.

"Bring the cruiser around to the back," Jamie said.

So, the killer wasn't panicking or giving up. He could use the cruiser to escape, and if he managed that, then Leigh wouldn't be safe. This snake would just keep coming after her.

"I'm going to take that shot now," Cullen whispered to Leigh. "I'll aim for their legs. If I miss and shoot Jamie, he'll drop down. That'll give you a clearer shot at the killer."

She pulled her gaze from the truck for just a second, and in that quick flash of time, he could see her trying to work out whether or not that was the right thing to do. It might or might not be. Cullen knew that. And so did she. But they had to do something before this escalated even more.

"The cruiser now," Jamie shouted. "You've got one minute."

Leigh nodded. "Take the shot," she told Cullen.

She got into a crouch, and he knew what she had in mind. She was going to make that run to the side of her house to create a distraction. And to get herself in a better position to take a kill shot. Again, he had to do battle with his instincts to try to keep her safe. Instead, he brushed a quick kiss on her mouth and took aim.

"Now," Cullen said.

And Leigh took off running.

Cullen kept the shot low, going for the edge of the boot that he saw behind Jamie's, and he pulled the trigger. The shot blasted through the air. So did the howl of pain.

A man's howl.

Bowen lifted his head and his gun, trying to take aim. The killer shifted, staggering a little. Enough to let Cullen know that he'd hit his target. But the killer quickly recovered. At the exact moment Leigh reached the side of her house, the killer pivoted, hooking his arm around Jamie's neck and dragging his human shield back in front of him.

"Big mistake," the killer yelled. "Now Jamie dies."

The words were like fists, but Cullen now knew exactly who they were dealing with because he had no trouble recognizing the voice.

Rocky was the killer.

LEIGH HAD KNOWN that it could be Rocky behind the wheel of the truck. But it still brought on an avalanche of emotions. Anger, betrayal, shock. He'd worked side by side with her, and until the last twenty-four hours, she hadn't seen any signs that he was a killer.

But she was seeing them now.

Rocky had a gun to Jamie's head, and Leigh knew with absolute certainty that he'd kill Jamie. In fact, the only reason Rocky hadn't already pulled the trigger was because he needed a shield, and the terrified Jamie was it. However, it wasn't Jamie Rocky wanted.

No.

He wanted her. Probably Cullen, too, but Leigh wasn't sure she knew the reason for that.

"Have you always wanted me dead?" Leigh called out to him. "Or were you worried I'd prove that you're the one who murdered Alexa and McNash?"

"You don't deserve the badge," Rocky spat out.

His response surprised her. Not because of his obvious venom, but because he'd answered her at all. Leigh had figured he'd just spout out his demand for the cruiser so he could make his escape.

Something she wanted to make sure didn't happen.

That's why Leigh glanced around to try to figure out how to stop him. Rocky was going to pay for the murders—which he hadn't denied. Pay for the attacks against Cullen and her, too. And he was especially going to pay for the hell he was putting Jamie through.

From the angle she had now, she could no longer see Bowen, but it was possible he'd try to sneak up on Rocky. Which wouldn't be a good thing. It could cause Rocky to have a knee-jerk reaction and pull the trigger. Especially since Rocky was already hurt. There was blood on his leg just above his boot.

Cullen was still on the ground, using the boulders for cover, but he also had his gun aimed and ready. If he got a shot, she could count on him to take it—and not miss.

She didn't know where Vance was but suspected the text she'd just gotten was from him. Probably asking for instructions on what he should do. Without taking her attention, or her aim, off Rocky, Leigh motioned toward the last spot where she'd seen Dawn. If Vance hadn't gotten to her already, then maybe he'd do that now.

The one person Leigh didn't want to look at was Jamie. She could practically feel the fear coming off him in hot, slick waves, and she couldn't let her worry for him get in the way. He could help best by diffusing this mess.

"So, you wanted me dead because I'm the sheriff," Leigh called out to Rocky.

"You're sleeping with Cullen Brodie," Rocky snapped. "Now, quit yapping and get me that cruiser." He peppered that *request* with a lot of crude profanity.

Again, she wasn't surprised that Rocky was enraged about her relationship with Cullen. With a Brodie. Jeb's anger toward Bowen might not have erupted into violence, but it had spilled over to Rocky. Still, she wasn't putting a drop of the blame on Jeb. This was Rocky's deal, and she was betting at the core that it had less to do with his feelings about Cullen than it did about him trying to cover up Alexa's murder.

And she'd try to use that.

"You killed Alexa in the heat of the moment," Leigh said, trying to keep her voice calm. "That's second-degree murder. Maybe even manslaughter."

Rocky gave a hollow laugh. "You expect me to believe you'd offer me a deal! Don't insult me. I'm a cop. A better cop than you'll ever be."

She could have pointed out that he was a killer and had also committed numerous other felonies, but that wouldn't help diffuse this. Maybe nothing would help, but she had to try for Jamie's sake.

"Maybe you are a better cop," she said. "Because I can't figure out why you'd kill Alexa."

"No more yapping," he yelled. "Get me that cruiser now."

"It'll take a couple of minutes. Vance used it to get Dawn to the ambulance. She's hurt, Rocky, and she needs the EMTs so she won't bleed out."

Rocky cursed. "She got in the way. She got herself shot. Like Alexa."

Wincing, Rocky staggered back a step. Obviously, the gunshot wound was giving him some pain, and pain didn't go well with logical thought.

"The cruiser," Rocky shouted. "Get it now, or I'll start putting bullets in Jamie. While I'm at it, I'll send some shots at Cullen and you. I might get real lucky and finish you both off."

Even with Rocky's stagger, Cullen still didn't have a shot so Leigh sent a quick text to Vance to have him bring the cruiser around. She had no intention of letting Rocky get in with Jamie, but with all the maneuvering around that would take, it would increase their chances of one of them getting that clean shot.

She heard the movement behind her and thought it was Vance. Still, she pivoted in case Rocky was working with a partner. So did Cullen. And they saw Jeb walking toward them.

"Get back," Leigh warned him.

But Jeb kept on walking, and he wasn't using anything for cover. He was out in the open, and he had his hands lifted, maybe in surrender, maybe to show Rocky he wasn't armed.

"You don't want to do this, Rocky," Jeb said, his voice as calm as a lake. "You're scaring the boy. Let Jamie go, and we can talk this out."

"I got no choice," Rocky argued. "You understand that." There was nothing calm about his voice. Every word had a sharp, raw edge to it.

Leigh wanted to curse her father for doing this. For putting himself in the direct line of fire. But if she went into the yard to drag him back, it could get them both killed.

"I understand. But you've got choices," Jeb argued back. "You can drop your gun and let Jamie go."

"No!" Rocky shouted, and he volleyed wild-eyed glances from Jeb to her to Cullen. "I can't go to jail." He tapped the badge he still had clipped to the waist of his jeans. "You know what they do to cops in jail."

Jeb nodded. "I know, but you could be placed in solitary confinement—"

"I don't want to talk to you," Rocky interrupted, and this time the edges were even sharper. The man was losing it. "Leigh's the one who messed this up. She shouldn't be the sheriff. I should be."

But he stopped, and he didn't say anything else. She wondered if what he'd said had just sunk in. He was a killer, and there was no way he should be sheriff. He'd broken the very laws he'd sworn to uphold. Yes, the first—Alexa's murder—had no doubt been committed in the heat of the moment, but everything else since had been calculated.

So was what Leigh was about to do.

It was a risk, but she didn't want Rocky killing Jeb because he didn't want to hear what her father had to say. Leigh stepped out, took aim at Rocky.

"You have no right to wear that badge," she said, staring him right in the eyes.

With his gun trained on Rocky, Cullen stood, too, moving to Jeb's other side. Leigh wanted to yell at him for doing that. Especially since she figured that Rocky would indeed try to kill Cullen. But she knew he was feeling the same thing she was. Neither of them wanted the other to die. She could include Jeb in that, too.

"Don't you dare take a bullet for me," she snapped, aiming that at both Jeb and Cullen.

She might as well have been talking to the air though because she knew both of them would. Because they loved her.

Leigh stared at Rocky. "Put down your gun now."

Again, Rocky staggered back just a little, and Jamie made a strangled sound. Maybe because he thought this was all about to come to a head and that he'd die. And he might. Leigh couldn't make any guarantees that any of them would make it out of this alive.

"Do the right thing, Rocky," Jeb said.

Just as all hell broke loose.

The gunshot tore through the air. And also tore right

into Rocky's leg. It took Leigh a moment to figure out where the shot had come from, but then she spotted Bowen. He was belly-down on the ground behind the truck, and he'd been the one to put another bullet in Rocky.

Rocky howled in pain, cursed and shoved Jamie forward. In the same motion, he brought up his gun.

Taking aim at Leigh.

Chapter Sixteen

Cullen didn't think. He just pulled the trigger, double-tapping it and sending two shots into Rocky's chest.

The moment seemed to freeze with the sound of the bullets echoing through the icy air. Rocky just stood there, his face masked with shock, and the blood already spreading across the front of his coat. Finally, he crumpled, dropping first to his knees before collapsing to the ground.

With Leigh right beside him, Cullen ran toward him. And behind them, he heard Jeb shout for the EMTs to come to the backyard. Rocky still had hold of his gun, and Cullen didn't want him having a chance to try to kill Leigh. They reached Rocky at the same time, and Leigh ripped the gun from his hand. She also frisked him for other weapons and found a backup gun and a knife in his boot holsters.

"Where's Cecile?" Leigh asked, aiming her question at Bowen.

"I used the ATV to take her to the ambulance. I left her with the EMTs while I came back to try to help."

Leigh released the breath she seemed to have been holding. "Thank you. You did help. Thank you for that, too."

Cullen doubted this would be the end of the bad blood between their families, but it was a good start. It was too bad that it'd nearly taken them all being killed before it happened.

Jamie pushed himself away from the truck and staggered toward Bowen, who caught him in his arms. "You okay?" Bowen asked him.

Jamie nodded, but Cullen thought the ranch hand was far from okay. He'd likely have to be admitted to the hospital again. But at least this time, there wouldn't be the threat of danger.

Well, maybe.

Rocky probably didn't have much time left. He was bleeding out fast, and even the EMTs likely wouldn't be able to keep him alive. That's why Cullen had to press him for answers now. If not, Leigh and Jamie might never have peace of mind.

Cullen got right in Rocky's face. "You said Alexa got herself killed? How?"

Clamming up, Rocky laid his head back on the frozen ground and looked up at the sky. Leigh didn't stay quiet though. She read Rocky his rights. That was the smart thing to do in case Rocky survived.

"You really want to take all of this to the grave?" Cullen shrugged and shifted as if to get up. "Suit yourself. You'll be remembered for being an idiot and a coward."

"I'm neither of those things," Rocky snapped. He coughed, grimaced and then gathered his breath again. "Alexa got herself killed because she hated your guts. That's why. And she wanted me to help her set you up because she knew I could. She knew I was just that good." He was actually bragging now, puffing up his bloody chest. "Alexa was going to bruise up her face some and get me to say I'd witnessed you assaulting her."

Cullen felt his jaw tighten. Hell. If Alexa and Rocky had done that, it would have definitely caused him some trouble. Leigh might have had to arrest him after all. Especially with Alexa and Rocky pushing her to do just that.

"You were going to help Alexa frame Cullen?" Leigh demanded.

Rocky narrowed his eyes and gave her a defiant glare. "Yeah. But when I met her in Cullen's bathroom the night of the party, she said she'd changed her mind, that she was giving up on Cullen and wanted Austin instead."

Cullen gave that a moment to sink in. Yeah, he could see Alexa moving on to her next mark, and she might have enjoyed trying to twist up Austin and Kali.

"I told Alexa no, that I wasn't going to let you off the hook," Rocky snarled, and he aimed all that anger at Cullen. "I told her that if she didn't go through with it, then I'd go to Leigh and rat her out."

"I'm guessing Alexa didn't care much for that?" Leigh prompted.

"She didn't," Rocky verified in a snarl. "That's when Alexa called me, well, a lot of names. She shoved me, told me to get lost. Nobody talks to me that way. *Nobody.* I got the horse statue and bashed her on her idiot head."

Cullen could see all of that playing out. See it playing out with Jamie, too. He was betting that Alexa had mentioned Jamie bringing her to the Triple R. Rocky had probably wanted to make sure Alexa hadn't told

Jamie that she was there to meet him. It would have been something similar with McNash. Rocky couldn't risk that Alexa had told the thug about her hiring Rocky.

And that left Kali and Austin.

With everything Rocky had just spelled out for them, Cullen doubted Austin and Kali had had any part in the attacks. Austin had lied and cheated, and Kali had set up the ruse to get back at Austin, but if Rocky could have put some of this blame on them, he would have.

The EMTs came closer, but Rocky waved them off. "Nobody touches me. You think I want to live behind bars for the rest of my life? I don't," he said, answering his own question. He shifted his gaze to Leigh, who was staring down at him. "I want to say my piece. I want both of you to know how much I hate your guts."

The hatred was obvious, but it didn't enrage Cullen nearly as much as Rocky using that hatred to try to kill Leigh. He darn near succeeded, too. Any one of those fired shots could have left her dead.

"You're the one who called me," Jamie said. "Threatened me. You told me you'd kill me if I went to the cops."

Cullen glanced at his ranch hand, who was now being treated by the EMTs. Jamie was still plenty shaky. With good reason. He'd just come close to dying again. But there was some steel in Jamie's eyes, too. Ditto for Bowen's. His father moved away from Jamie to come closer to Rocky and them.

"So what if I threatened you?" Rocky snapped, dismissing Jamie with a split-second glance. "I didn't want you remembering that I was the one who nearly bashed in your brains. I figured the calls would make you shut up."

"I didn't know it was you," Jamie fired back. "Not for sure, anyway. But I'd got to thinking that it could be you and that's why I wanted to talk to Leigh and Cullen after I got out of the hospital. I wouldn't have had any proof it was you if you hadn't kidnapped me."

"Oh, boo-hoo," Rocky taunted. "You whiner. Go home to your mommy."

"Oops," Bowen said, his voice dripping with sarcasm. He stepped on Rocky's leg. Right in the spot where Bowen had shot him minutes earlier.

Rocky gave a feral howl of pain. But nobody felt sorry for him. And nobody did anything to stop Bowen from adding even more pressure before he finally stepped back.

Leigh stooped down, and she waited until Rocky tore his narrowed gaze from Bowen and moved it back to her. "Who helped you with McNash's murder and the attacks against Cullen and me?" Leigh demanded. She didn't sound hateful or filled with anger. She sounded like a cop.

"Nobody," Rocky spat out. "I didn't need any help. I'm the one who fired those shots in the woods by Kali's house." He paused, winced and dragged in a ragged breath.

"Austin and Kali didn't work with you?" Leigh pressed.

Despite the obvious pain, Rocky managed a dry, nearly soundless laugh. "No, I didn't need them. Both of them are stupid. Austin was cheating with Alexa, and Kali was too blind to see what was right in front of her face. Alexa was a viper, ready to ruin anyone who got in her path." He looked at Cullen. "You were stupid, too, to ever get involved with her."

"It wasn't my finest moment," Cullen admitted. "But

you've had some damn un-fine moments yourself. You wanted to kill Leigh because she beat you in the election. Because the majority of people in Dark River wanted her and not you for their sheriff. Considering what you've done, that was a seriously good decision on their part."

The light might have been dwindling from Rocky's eyes, but there was still plenty of bitterness and hatred in them. He looked past them at Jeb. "She shouldn't have the badge, Jeb. You shouldn't have the right to call her your daughter. She betrayed you with Cullen."

"*You* betrayed me," Jeb said, his voice hard and mean. "I'll be damned if you'll die wearing this." He reached down, tore off Rocky's badge and handed it to Leigh. "Now, go to hell, where you belong."

Jeb stepped back, letting the EMTs move in to start treating Rocky. Leigh stepped away, too, heading to Vance, who was making his way to them.

"How are Dawn and Cecile?" she immediately asked.

"They'll be okay. I had another ambulance come, and they're both on the way to the hospital."

Cullen knew Leigh would be checking on her deputies as soon as she could wrap up everything with Rocky. Leigh would also have to deal with some guilt for their injuries, and it wouldn't matter that it wasn't her fault. She'd still feel responsible that she hadn't been able to stop Rocky before he did so much damage.

"We also found a truck near Leigh's house," Vance added. "It's probably the vehicle Rocky used to get here." He glanced at Rocky. "He tried to kill you?"

Leigh nodded. "And he succeeded in killing Alexa and McNash. He just confessed."

Vance shook his head, muttered some profanity. "I'm sorry, Leigh," he said. "So sorry."

Cullen figured there was some guilt playing into that apology as well. Vance was a good cop, and he'd be kicking himself for not seeing that he'd been working with a dirty one.

"Is Rocky going to live?" Vance asked a moment later.

But the moment the question was out of his mouth, one of the EMTs stood and checked his watch. "Time of death is 9:35. You want me to go ahead and call the ME?"

She gave a weary nod, sighed and closed her eyes for a moment. Steadying herself. Cullen tried to help with that. He went to her, and despite the fact that they had an audience, he pulled her into his arms. Judging from the way she leaned into him, she needed the hug as much as he did.

While Vance dealt with the EMTs and the body, Cullen led Leigh up the back porch steps and into her kitchen. He left the door open though so they could still keep watch of what was going on.

"I'm not going to ask you if you're okay," Cullen whispered.

"Good. I won't ask you, either." But she did look up at him as if trying to see just how much this had shaken him.

He was shaken all right and could still hear the roar of the truck engine bearing down on them. But flashbacks and bad memories weren't going to overshadow the good feelings he had about Leigh. That was why he brushed a quick kiss over her mouth. It packed a punch despite being barely more than a peck.

"Should I have seen that Rocky was dirty?" she asked.

Cullen didn't even have to think about this. "No. Rocky hid the depth of his hatred. Well, until the end when he knew he was caught."

She stared at him, obviously considering that, and nodded. That nod was a victory and the start of her accepting that what Rocky had done was beyond her control.

Leigh moved out of the hug when Jeb came to the doorway, but she stayed close. Arm to arm with Cullen. And because they were still touching, he felt Leigh tense up a little. Probably because she didn't know what she was about to face with her father. Jeb obviously hadn't condoned Rocky's actions, but then, he might not condone her kissing Cullen, either.

"The town council won't have a leg to stand on if they try to dismiss you," Jeb said. His voice, like the rest of him, was coated in weariness. A man who'd seen way too much. Maybe there was some guilt, too, because he hadn't seen the dirty cop who'd worshiped him. "You held your ground and didn't arrest an innocent man."

"But I didn't arrest the guilty one before he could kill again," she muttered.

Jeb lifted his shoulder. "The town council, including me, gave Rocky the green light to go after you. We'll be eating that particular dish of crow for a while." He met her eye to eye. "Nobody's going to challenge you... Sheriff."

Leigh's arm tightened again when Jeb stuck out his hand for her to shake. It was hardly a tender family gesture, but coming from Jeb, it was practically a blessing of his support. Maybe his love, too.

Leigh shook his hand. Then relaxed. "Thank you. You taught me well."

Again, not especially tender, but Jeb blinked hard as if trying to keep his eyes dry. "What will you two do now?" he asked.

The timing was lousy, but Cullen decided to go ahead and declare his intentions. All of them. "I'm going to ask Leigh on a date. If she says yes, then I'll ask her on a second date. Then, a third. Then, a—"

"Yes," Leigh interrupted. And even though the timing was just as lousy for her, she smiled a little. "That's yes to the first, second and third."

"What about a fourth?" Cullen pressed.

She looked up at him. "Yes to that, too."

Cullen smiled as well, and he would have kissed her long and hard if Jeb hadn't cleared his throat.

"I'll be going," Jeb muttered. He turned to leave, then stopped, his gaze going to Leigh's. "You probably don't want my opinion, but I think yes is the right answer. You should go on those dates with Cullen."

"She should," Bowen said.

Cullen hadn't realized his father was close enough to have heard their conversation, but obviously he had been.

"My son's in love with your daughter," Bowen added, sparing Jeb the briefest of glances.

Jeb nodded. "And she's in love with him." He lifted his hand in farewell and walked away.

Leigh stood there. Her eyes wide. Her body still.

"You look stunned," Cullen said.

"I am," she admitted.

"Because you didn't know you were in love with me?" Cullen clarified, sliding his arm back around her.

"No, because our fathers didn't take swipes at each other." She looked up at him. "I'd already figured out I was in love with you."

Now Cullen did kiss her, and he didn't give a rat that his father and everybody else was watching.

"I know you're about to get busy with reports and such, but I'll want to hear more about how you figured out you were in love with me," he said with his mouth against hers.

"We can get into that on our fifth date," Leigh whispered, and she kissed him right back.

* * * * *

ALPHA TRACKER

CINDI MYERS

For Carol and Podrick

Chapter One

If Roslyn Kern had been the superstitious type, she might have taken the ominous clouds of smoke gathering in the distance beyond Jasper, Idaho, as a bad omen. But she wasn't superstitious, she reminded herself, only nervous and uncertain what the outcome of this visit to Jasper might be. She didn't want to be here, but part of being an adult meant doing things that scared you. She had been doing a lot of that lately.

"Next!" The young woman behind the counter at Millard's Diner summoned her forward. The diner at the corner of Main and Second was busy with both table and counter service on this Friday before the Fourth of July, but everyone around Roslyn seemed in a good mood. "What can I get you?" the clerk asked.

Roslyn looked longingly at the latte the previous customer was carrying away, then ordered an herbal tea. "Would you like a blueberry muffin to go with that?" the woman asked. "They're fresh out of the oven."

Roslyn's stomach rumbled. "Yes, please," she said.

The clerk rang up her sale and accepted Roslyn's debit card. "Are you here for the holiday weekend?" the clerk asked as they waited for the card machine to process the charge.

"Yes," Roslyn said. "Do you think the fire is going to head this way?" The smell of smoke lingered in the air, though maybe Roslyn was more sensitive to the odor than most.

"I know it looks close, but the fire is a long way away," the woman said. She returned Roslyn's card. "There's a ridge between us and the blaze, though if the wind shifts..." She shrugged. "The firefighters are keeping an eye on things. I'm not too worried."

Roslyn nodded and moved on to accept her muffin and tea from another server. She spotted a small table against the side wall and headed for it. She had arrived in town late last night from Chicago and hadn't had much time to formulate a plan. She needed to find Dillon, but wasn't certain where to begin. Should she start with the police? She shook her head. No, not unless there was no other way. The first time she saw him, she wanted a situation that was more private.

She tore a piece from the muffin and popped it into her mouth, savoring the sweet cake surrounding a single juicy berry. She would have to stop in again tomorrow for another muffin. It almost made the tea bearable. She gazed out the window at the town of Jasper. She had visited the Chamber of Commerce website before she planned her trip, but the photos there of broad streets framed by Western-style buildings with wooden false fronts and Victorian brickwork hadn't captured the flavor of the bustling town. The sidewalks were filled with people, most of whom appeared to be vacationers enjoying the sunny July day in spite of the distant smoke clouds. Barrels of pink and white and purple petunias dotted the sidewalks, and hanging baskets of red verbena and blue lobelia hung from every light post. Red, white and blue bunting draped storefronts and a banner over the street welcomed everyone to the annual Independence Day celebration.

A flyer in the bed-and-breakfast where she was staying had advertised a dance, a parade, a rodeo and fireworks as part of the weekend's festivities. Roslyn wondered if she would be in any mood to celebrate once she had accomplished what she had come here to do.

She realized she was searching the crowd for Dillon's handsome face. Her heart beat a little faster at the idea that he might be close by. She had such a clear picture of him in her mind—tall, broad-shouldered, with olive skin, sculpted cheekbones and close-cropped brown hair. He had captivated her from the moment they rode a lift chair together at the nearby Brundage Mountain Resort. He had been so easy to talk to and they had ended up skiing the rest of the day together, having dinner together, then going back to her hotel room.

They had spent the whole weekend in a magical bubble. She had come to the ski resort in McCall feeling broken and fragile, only a few weeks past a humiliating public breakup with her fiancé and the loss of a job she had loved. Thanks to a wonderful two days and nights with Dillon, she'd left feeling stronger than she had in weeks. He had been just what she needed during an awful time in her life. Saying goodbye to him had been hard, but the short time she'd spent with him had given her the strength she needed to go back to Chicago and clean up the mess she had left behind. She would always be grateful to him for that.

She had delayed coming here to find him because she wanted to keep that beautiful memory unspoiled, but life had a way of interfering with the best of plans.

She needed to talk to him, and she couldn't put it off much longer. Jasper was a small town, so she had thought finding him wouldn't be that difficult. But now that she was here, she wasn't so sure. Maybe if she sat here long enough, he would walk through the café door, and give her that smile that warmed her clear to her toes, his hazel green eyes sparking with delight. She turned toward the doorway, almost expecting to see him there. Instead, she was startled to see another familiar face.

"Roslyn? Oh my gosh—what are you doing here?" Cheri Benton, one of Roslyn's best friends, rushed forward to greet her, followed by her boyfriend, Buck, and another couple.

"Amber and Wes, this is Roslyn," Cheri made the introductions.

Roslyn stood and shook hands with everyone. "We're staying in McCall for the weekend and came over here to hike," Cheri explained. "Kind of a last-minute trip to get out of the city, you know?"

"You made such a big deal about how much you enjoyed your visit to the area this winter that we wanted to check it out," added Buck.

"It's a last-minute trip for me, too." Roslyn latched on to this convenient explanation for her presence here. "I had some time free, so I figured, why not?"

"Yeah, you'd better relax while you can, right?"

"Where are you planning to hike?" Roslyn asked, anxious to steer the conversation away from herself. Not that Cheri and Buck weren't good friends, but they didn't know everything about her life, and she didn't want them to know the real reason she was in Jasper. Not yet.

"There's a trailhead not far from here that leads up into the mountains," Buck said. "The Williams Gap

Trail. There's supposed to be a lot of wildflowers this time of year."

"You should come with us," Cheri said. "You're up for it, right?"

"Of course," Roslyn said. She had hiking boots and a water bottle in her car. "If you're not going too far."

"Not far at all," Cheri said. "You should definitely come."

"Come on," Buck agreed. "It will give us a chance to catch up."

It had only been a couple of weeks since Roslyn had been to Cheri and Buck's apartment for dinner, but she appreciated his warm invitation. "I would like to come with you," she said.

"Great," Cheri said. "We'll grab some coffees to go and head out. You can ride with us."

While they waited for coffee, Roslyn gathered her belongings. The hike wouldn't take long—not more than a couple of hours. Maybe in that time she could come up with a plan for finding and approaching Dillon. What she had to say to him would be a shock. He probably wouldn't like it. She needed the extra time to prepare herself for what would probably be another rejection. It wouldn't be the first time a man had turned his back on her. She straightened her spine and smoothed her loose tunic. She shouldn't anticipate trouble. Whatever happened with Dillon, she would deal with it. She'd been getting very good at looking after herself lately—the one good thing that had come out of the disaster she had made of her life so far.

SERGEANT DILLON DIAZ guided his pickup into one of the last open parking slots in front of Daniels Canine Academy. Even from here he could see half a dozen people moving among the kennels and around the main building that housed the dog training facility. Why all the activity on a Friday morning of a holiday weekend?

He opened the truck door. "Come on, Bentley," he called.

Bentley, a four-year-old black-and-white Australian shepherd, leaped to the ground and danced a circle around Dillon, tongue hanging out in an excited doggy grin. "You know where you are, don't you, boy?" Dillon asked, and bent to pat the dog's side. Bentley had spent many hours training at the academy for his work as a search and rescue canine. "We're just stopping in to say hello today."

Bentley trotted beside Dillon up the gravel path toward the DCA office, ears pricked to take in the excited barking of dogs and the murmur of human voices that filled the air. Dillon pushed open the door to the office and administrator Barbara Macy looked up. A pleasant, middle-aged woman with long brown hair, Barbara kept everything at DCA running smoothly. Her frown transformed into a smile as she recognized him. "Hey, Dillon," she called. "And hello, Bentley."

Bentley wagged his plumed tail and trotted toward the desk. "What's all the commotion?" Dillon asked, closing the door behind him.

"We're prepping kennels to take in dogs from people who might have to evacuate for the fire," Barbara said. "We got word this morning that there are some neighborhoods on the periphery of the national forest that authorities would like to clear out just in case the wind shifts suddenly. What can I do for you?"

"I was hoping to speak with Emma," he said. "But it's not urgent. I can come back another time."

Barbara stood. "Let me get her. I know she'll want to see you." She disappeared through a door at the back of the office.

The door to the outside opened and Piper Lambert, Emma's chief assistant in training the dogs, bustled in. She wore her long red hair in a braid trailing down her back, and a harried expression on her face. "Has anyone seen the extra folding kennels? They're supposed to be in the barn but we can't find them." She looked around the room, frowning, until her gaze came to rest on Dillon. "Hello, Dillon. What are you doing here? And where is everybody else?"

"Barbara went to fetch Emma. I stopped by with a question for her, but I didn't expect you to be so busy."

"It's a bit chaotic this morning, but nothing new about that," Piper said. "Any news about the fire? I've been too busy to keep up."

Dillon pulled out his phone and checked the latest fire report. The InciWeb site, which tracked wildfires on public lands, listed the blaze as the Gem Creek fire. "InciWeb says the fire grew overnight to just under ten thousand acres, but it's still well west of Jasper, confined to national forest land."

"That's still too close for comfort to some of those neighborhoods to the north," Piper said. "I expect we'll be getting a lot of evacuees."

"Probably." People around here had learned to be cautious and prepare for the worst, even while putting faith in wildland firefighting crews to keep the flames away from houses and towns.

The door at the back of the room opened and Barbara

returned, followed by Emma Daniels, whose light brown hair was pulled back in a ponytail. The founder of Daniels Canine Academy, Emma had established a reputation as one of the finest dog trainers in the West, as well as a generous and giving member of the community. "Hello, Bentley." In typical fashion, Emma greeted the dog first, then looked up to smile at Dillon. "Hello, stranger. What brings you here?"

Piper had already turned to ask Barbara about the missing kennels. The two of them left to check the storage shed where Barbara thought they had been moved, leaving Emma and Dillon alone. "I didn't mean to interrupt when you're so busy," Dillon said.

"When are we not busy?" Emma asked. "What can I do for you?"

"I wanted to see if you knew anything about wilderness tracking training for Bentley," Dillon said. "He's been great for search and rescue work, but I was thinking the wilderness training would be useful in some of the places we have to search."

Emma nodded. "Those courses focus on the kind of rough country we have here." She walked over to a filing cabinet and opened a drawer. "I'm sure I have some information here somewhere."

"Don't bother with it now," Dillon said. "I can get the information later. Barbara told me you're going to be taking in evacuees."

"We're part of the county's emergency management plan," she said. "The fairgrounds over in McCall take horses and other livestock. We try to take as many dogs as possible, to free up the animal shelter in town for cats and birds and other small animals. There isn't enough room in the evacuation centers for people and their pets, had felt the same strong connection between them that had stunned him, but then she had simply disappeared.

There was also the big chance that Rosie had something to hide. As a cop, he had had plenty of experience trying to track down missing persons, but so far she had eluded him. She had said she was single—recently split from someone. But maybe she and her former boyfriend had gotten back together. Maybe she was even married now, with a new name. That would explain some of his difficulty locating her.

He started the truck and looked over his shoulder at Bentley, whose harness was fastened securely in the back seat. "I don't like unanswered questions," he said. The dog pricked his ears, focused intently on Dillon.

Dillon faced forward again, checked the backing camera and pulled out of the parking spot. A need to solve puzzles made him a good cop, but it also made it impossible for him to let things go. He had unfinished business with Rosie Kenley, and he wouldn't rest easy until it was settled.

. . . .

Chapter Two

"This is so gorgeous!" Cheri swept her arm wide to indicate the field of wildflowers spread out before them. Magenta paintbrushes, purple lupines, scarlet gilia, golden sunflowers and more painted a tapestry against a backdrop of dark green conifers and granite peaks. Even the clouds of smoke rising in the distance didn't detract from the beauty of the scene.

"It's amazing." Roslyn studied the flowers through her camera lens. "I'm so glad you invited me to come with you. I might have missed this."

She loved to hike—why hadn't she done more of it in the past year?

The answer to that was easy enough. Her former fiancé, Matt, hated to hike. They had gone together exactly once. He had huffed and puffed after her on a fairly moderate trail in Starved Rock State Park. "What about this, exactly, is supposed to be fun?" he'd gasped out when he reached the top of the hill where she was waiting.

"Check out this view." She'd gestured to the fall scenery spread out before them.

"I bet there are hundreds of pictures of this online," he'd said. "Even videos. All of which I could see without having to make that climb." He'd pulled a bottle of water from his pack, unscrewed the top and drunk deeply.

"You just need to get in better shape," she'd said, poking at his stomach, which had developed a bit of a paunch lately.

"Hey!" He'd drawn back. "I thought you liked my shape."

"I was just teasing," she'd said. "Of course I like your shape."

He had calmed down after that but had still made it clear he hadn't enjoyed the day, and they had never gone again. One more reason things probably would never have worked out for them.

"Hey, Roslyn, come on!"

She looked up to find the others a hundred feet ahead of her down the trail. "Coming!" she called, and started out after them. But she hadn't gone far before she veered off to take photos of a group of brilliant red paintbrushes. Everywhere she looked she spotted something else she wanted to capture.

Cheri trotted back to join her. "I don't mean to hold you up," Roslyn said. "I just keep seeing more flowers I want to photograph. I'm thinking I could frame a bunch of these photos for a gallery wall in my dining area."

"That would look great," Cheri said. "I never think of things like that."

"Cheri! Roz! We need to head back!"

Both women turned to see Buck waving from a couple hundred yards down the trail. Wes and Amber stood with him. Cheri returned the wave. "We're on our way!" she shouted. She glanced over her shoulder and frowned at the column of smoke rising over the ridge in front of them. "The smoke does look worse," she said. "I guess Buck's right and we'd better go."

"I'll catch up in just a minute," Roslyn said. "There's a thick patch of paintbrush up the slope a little that I want to get a shot of."

"I can wait for you," Cheri said.

"Don't be silly. I'll get the picture and catch up in no time. Go on."

"Cheri!" Buck shouted.

"Don't be too long," Cheri said, then turned and started back toward Buck and the others.

Smiling to herself, Roslyn hugged the camera to her chest and headed up the trail a little farther. The clump of flowers she wanted to photograph was just at the top of a rise to her left. The muted light from the smoke-filled skies really made the colors pop. She left the trail and picked her way through the thick grass and scattered rocks toward the blooms. At the top of the rise near the flowers she stopped to catch her breath. She definitely wasn't as nimble as she used to be. While she waited for her breathing to return to normal, she scanned the landscape before her. Not far from here the meadow ended at a rock outcropping shadowed by a thick growth of trees. Movement in the shadows attracted her attention and she shaded her eyes with one hand and squinted, hoping to spot an elk or other wild animal. She probably couldn't get a good photograph from here, but if she waited and it stepped into the light…

She shook her head and dropped her hand to her side. She didn't have time to wait for an animal to move into the perfect position for a photograph. She needed to get back to Cheri and the others. She turned toward the flowers and crouched to get a better shot. She took several photos, then shifted to focus on a butterfly perfectly positioned on a sunflower. The light was perfect, the smoke in the air softening the harshness of the sun and lending depth to the colors.

While she was crouched down like this, she aimed her camera up the hill, toward the contrast of blue sky and dark smoke rising above the deep green trees and variegated gray of the rocks. With the right cropping, she might end up with a really moody landscape.

A sudden noise, like someone—or something—scrambling over the rocks, startled her. She gasped and tried to stand, but she lost her balance and fell sideways, her feet sliding out from under her. She swore as a sharp pain lanced through her, bringing tears to her eyes. She managed to keep hold of the camera and rolled over into a sitting position, then stared down at her now-throbbing ankle. She tried to flex her foot and was rewarded with another sharp pain. "Ouch!" she cried out loud, and sat back once more.

She scowled at her foot, then leaned forward and gingerly untied her hiking boot and felt her ankle. It was definitely swelling. Not broken, she hoped, but too sprained to go far. "Cheri!" she shouted, putting as much energy behind the cry as she could. "Buck! Help!"

She waited, holding her breath, but heard no answer. The wind had picked up and was blowing toward her, carrying her voice in the wrong direction.

She shifted again to remove her day pack. She stowed the camera inside the pack and slipped her cell phone from the side pocket. A message in the top left corner read No Service. If she could climb up on those rocks, she might be able to find a signal. She considered the challenge for a moment. If she was very careful, maybe she could walk. She moved forward, onto her knees, and tried to stand.

"Owww!" She howled in pain and crumpled as her foot refused to support her weight. Tears stinging her eyes, she eased into a sitting position again and considered her situation. Cheri and Buck would be worried when she didn't join them soon. They'd come back to find her, and they could help her limp down the trail. All she had to do was wait.

And hope that whatever she had heard up there in those rocks didn't decide to come down and investigate. An elk would probably leave her alone, but there were bears and mountain lions in the area. Maybe one of them had been displaced by the fire and was looking for a new place to live. And a meal.

She pushed the thought away and tried to focus on the beauty around her. She would be all right. All she had to do was wait for help. Patience wasn't exactly her strongest quality, but she had learned these last few months that there were plenty of things in life that you just couldn't rush.

DILLON WASTED THE rest of the morning on a fruitless internet search for Rosie. Plenty of people had advised him to let go of what was clearly becoming an obsession with the woman, but he couldn't get past this need to know why she had disappeared. If she really didn't want to see him again, he needed to hear it from her own lips.

He stared out the window of his home office, at the expanse of woodland in front of the home he had purchased the year before. Immediately after the weekend he and Rosie had spent together, he had imagined bringing her here. Would she see the same possibilities here, to make a home and a family? Or would she run away as fast as she could when she realized the direction his thoughts were taking? Even he didn't understand why he felt this way about her. He had been happy so far to date casually and have women as friends. No one had ever affected him the way Rosie had.

"What makes you happy?" she had asked. They had been lying in bed, drowsy and content after making love. She was good at asking questions that required more than one-word answers. Not nosy questions, exactly, but queries that made him think. And she seemed truly interested in his answers.

"My work makes me happy," he'd said. "I enjoy my coworkers, but I also feel like I'm doing something important. I'm helping people."

"Police are supposed to help people, so that's good," she'd said. "What else? What else makes you happy?"

"My family makes me happy. They're good people. Fun to be with. And when we're together, I know they love me and will always love me, no matter what. It's what I want one day, with my own family."

"That's nice." She snuggled closer to him, so warm and soft. He couldn't remember being more comfortable and content.

"Your turn," he said. "What makes you happy?"

"Right now I'm happy," she said. "Just being here with you, in this perfect moment."

"What else?" he asked.

"That's enough." She kissed his shoulders, her lips soft, sending a tingle of awareness through him. "That's all I need."

The moment had been perfect, in a way. But he wanted more moments like that. More moments with her.

He straightened in his chair and picked up his phone. One more call, one he had been reluctant to make because it meant using his badge for what was, after all, a personal search. But he was getting desperate.

"Brundage Mountain Resort Grand Lodge. This is Susan. How may I help you?"

He introduced himself and explained that he was looking for a guest who had registered there five months before. She had introduced herself to him as Rosie Kenley. "But she might be going by another name. What I need from you is a list of all the female guests who stayed with you between February thirteenth and fifteenth of this year."

A long silence followed, so long he wondered if they had been disconnected. "Sir," Susan finally said. "You do know it's a holiday weekend, right? I'm here by myself and I've got a line of guests checking in. I can't possibly find that information for you now. I wouldn't even know how to find someone who stayed here five months ago. If you call back next Tuesday maybe somebody from our IT department can help you."

Dillon thanked her and ended the call. It had been a long shot, but he'd had to try. Bentley rose from his bed beside the desk and whined. "I know," Dillon said. "Time to quit sitting here and get moving. Want to go for a hike?"

Bentley let out an excited bark and trotted toward the mudroom, and the hook that held his leash. Dillon sat on a bench by the door and was lacing up his hiking boots when his phone rang again. This time the call was from Lieutenant Brady Nichols with Jasper Police. Was he calling to tell Dillon his day off was cut short?

"What's up, Brady?" Dillon answered the call.

"Corb Lund is playing in McCall next weekend. Cassie and I plan to go and wanted to see if you'd come along."

"I doubt if your girlfriend wants a third wheel on your date," Dillon said.

"You wouldn't be a third wheel. Cassie has a friend who wants to meet you, or you could invite someone."

"Thanks, but I'll pass," Dillon said. Ever since Brady had found the woman of his dreams in Cassie Whitaker, he'd been trying to help Dillon find his own happily-ever-after. It wasn't that Dillon was opposed to the idea of settling down—not at all. But he preferred to find his own women.

"Come on," Brady said. "It'll be fun."

Dillon's phone buzzed with an incoming text. He glanced down at the message: Lost hiker. We need you and Bentley at the Williams Gap Trailhead.

"I have go to, Brady," Dillon said. "I just got a text from Andrea. They need me to help find a lost hiker." Andrea Wayne, Mountaintop Search and Rescue Commander, would expect a prompt response to her summons.

"Good luck," Brady said. "But think about next weekend. It would be good for you to get out."

Yeah, he wouldn't mind going out next weekend, but with the right woman. One who captivated him as much as Rosie Kenley had. That was proving very hard to find. He stuffed the phone back in his pocket and grabbed Bentley's leash. "Change of plans," he said. "Are you ready to do some work?"

Half an hour later, Dillon and Bentley found Andrea and half a dozen other search and rescue volunteers gathered in front of the signboard for the trailhead, with two worried-looking couples. "Our friend, Roslyn Kern, was taking photographs of wildflowers," one of the young men, who introduced himself as Buck Teller, said. "She told us to go on and she would catch up. When she didn't show up after fifteen minutes, we went back to look for her but we couldn't find her."

"She couldn't just vanish, could she?" the young woman beside him asked. "Roslyn is so smart, and she's an experienced hiker."

"Even experienced hikers can get disoriented," Andrea said. "Do you have a photograph of Roslyn?"

Buck turned to the woman. "Cheri?"

Cheri paled. "I left my phone on the charger back at the hotel."

"Never mind," Andrea said. "Give us a description. How far up the trail did you last see her?"

"About two miles?" Buck said. "Something like that."

"Roslyn is about my height," Cheri said. "Five-six. With blond hair and green eyes. She's wearing jeans, a blue tunic top with lace, hiking boots, and she has a small day pack."

Andrea turned to Dillon. "This is Sergeant Dillon Diaz from the Jasper Police Department. He and his search dog, Bentley, are going to help look for your friend."

"Don't you need an item of clothing or something that belongs to Roslyn to do that?" Cheri asked. "I don't have anything like that."

"Bentley is trained to focus on the scent of any person in the area and follow the scent trail to that person," Dillon said. "It would be helpful if you could tell us where you became separated from her."

"It was about two miles up the trail, I think," Buck said. "I know it was this kind of open area."

"She stayed back to take pictures of this big clump of flowers up the hill from the trail," Cheri said.

Dillon nodded. "That's helpful to know. It will give us a place to focus on."

Buck looked down at Bentley. "Doesn't he get confused, with so many people around?" he asked.

"Not usually." Dillon looked down at Bentley, who stared up at them with intelligent, alert eyes. It was difficult to explain to people who hadn't worked with dogs before just how good they could be at their jobs. "Bentley is young, but he's had good success so far. I can't guarantee we'll find your friend, but you did the right thing, not waiting to report her missing."

"The fire looks like it's getting worse." Cheri looked back toward the smoke that filled the sky behind them. "I'm worried she'll get caught in it."

"We're going to head out now," Dillon said. He shared Cheri's worries about the fire. In the last half hour the wind had shifted, pushing the flames—and a lot of smoke—in this direction.

"We'll have other groups of searchers farther back on the trail," Andrea said. "Radio if you determine a direction Ms. Kern is headed in."

"Roger that." Dillon started up the trail, moving quickly, Bentley on a leash at his side. When they were away from the crowd at the trailhead, he unclipped Bentley's leash. "Ok, boy," he said. "Find."

Bentley pricked his ears and lifted his nose into the air, then trotted forward, tail waving, ears alert. Dillon moved on, setting a brisk pace. He didn't expect the dog to zero in on any one scent until they were closer to the place where Cheri and Buck said they had separated from Roslyn. A hot wind hit him in the face, bringing the strong scent of wood smoke. For a human, the mixture of aromas might be distracting, but Bentley had been trained to zero in on the scent of people.

As part of Dillon's search and rescue training he had taken a class that discussed the ways people tended to behave when lost in the wilderness. The patterns varied depending on a person's age, background and location but shared many similarities. The majority of people, even those with experience in the backcountry, tried to walk out on their own. Roslyn's friends probably hadn't found her because she had left the trail. In this country, with rapidly changing elevations, stretches of open land interspersed with woods, and barriers to travel such as rock outcroppings and cliffs, it was easy for someone to disappear from sight even a few feet from an established trail.

His phone buzzed with a new text. Before long, he would be out of reach of a cell signal, but for now he still had enough bars for reception. This one was from Andrea: This is who you're looking for.

Dillon clicked on the attached photo and his heart stumbled in its rhythm. Smiling up at him was a photo of Rosie Kenley—the woman he had been searching for for months.

He stared, heart racing, then his gaze shifted to the caption beneath the photo, which was from the website of a Chicago newspaper. "Rockin' Roz Kern greets fans at the annual WZPR Christmas bash."

Rockin' Roz? He scrolled further and found nothing. He tried a search on the name, but his signal was too weak. Bentley returned to his side and whined, the dog equivalent of "What's up? I thought we were looking for someone."

Dillon stuffed the phone back in his pocket. "Come on," he said to the dog. "Find Roslyn."

He moved faster now, the knowledge of who he was really looking for lending urgency to his steps. At the same time, he dreaded what he might find. Anger warred with longing. What did she mean, running out on him the way she had? What was up with the fake name? Had everything she had told him that weekend at Brundage been a lie? What was she doing here in Jasper?

And where was she now? Was she merely lost, or was she hurt? The idea made his stomach clench. "Roslyn!" he shouted, but the name only echoed back at him.

"Rrruff!" A bark from Bentley drew Dillon's attention. The dog stood, looking intently off trail. He glanced back at Dillon, tail wagging, and as soon as he saw that the man was following, the dog took off. He was running now, nose twitching and tail wagging. Ten yards up the trail, he veered off into the grass and picked up speed. Dillon jogged to keep up. "Roslyn!" he called again. "Roslyn Kern!" The name felt wrong on his tongue. His brain wanted to shout "Rosie!"

"Here I am! Over here!"

Dillon stopped and scanned the wildflower-strewn landscape for the source of the voice, but Bentley was already bounding up the hill. Dillon followed. He had to crest the ridge before he saw her, sitting almost hidden behind a tall clump of sunflowers. No wonder her friends hadn't spotted her. And they must never have gotten close enough for her to hear them calling for her.

Heart in his throat, he ran toward her. She was his Rosie all right—the same softly curved cheek and wavy golden hair. He couldn't see her eyes behind the sunglasses she wore, but he heard her gasp as he drew near.

"Dillon!" she cried—though he couldn't tell if she was delighted to see him or merely shocked. She pushed up her sunglasses, as if to see him more clearly. "What are you doing here?"

"I'm looking for a lost hiker," he said. "You."

Bentley had stopped and sat beside her, tail thumping the ground. "Good boy!" Dillon said and scratched the dog's ears, then fished a chicken treat from his pocket and fed it to him.

"Is this Bentley?" Rosie—Roslyn—patted the dog. "I remember you talking about him, though I never thought he'd have to find me." She looked up and her eyes met his—a deep, clear green, and full of a mixture of emotions that mirrored his own—regret, curiosity and more than a little longing. "I'm sorry," she said. "I meant to get in touch with you before this, but things were so complicated when I got back to Chicago." She spread her hands wide in a gesture of surrender or helplessness—though he couldn't think of Rosie as helpless. One of the things that had drawn him to her was an impression of strength. She had been grieving the end of a relationship when they met, but she had been determined to get on with her life. He'd liked that about her.

"Never mind that now," he said. "Are you okay?"

She grimaced and looked down. For the first time he noticed she had taken off one of her hiking boots. "I think I sprained my ankle," she said. "A noise on the rocks up there startled me and I moved too fast and I guess I lost my balance." She sighed. "I figured the best thing to do was to stay here and wait for help. I thought my friends would come back to find me, but they must've been already too far ahead when they realized I wasn't going to be joining them."

"They did come back to look for you, but you some-how missed each other. They called 911 as soon as they were within cell phone range." He slipped off his pack and dropped it on the grass beside her, then knelt to ex-amine her ankle.

"I'm really glad you came along when you did," she said. "The fire is looking a lot worse, and I wasn't sure how much longer I should stay here."

He glanced up at the sky, which had darkened with more smoke. "Let me take a look at that ankle," he said. He was grateful for something to do. Tending her injury would give him time to settle his emotions and figure out what to say to her.

She flinched when he took her foot in hand, but made no sound. He felt a shiver of desire as he stroked his hand across her instep and up to her ankle, and shoved aside the emotion. He was touching her in a professional capac-ity now, not as the lover he had been. "It's not too bad," he said. "I think if I wrap it tightly you could probably get your boot back on and I'll help you walk out. Or I could radio for a crew with a litter to carry you out."

"No! I'll walk! I hate to be so much trouble." She shifted as if prepared to stand up right then, but he laid a hand on her arm.

"Let me get this wrapped up first."

He fished first aid supplies from his pack, then radi-oed the commander. "I've found Roslyn," he said. "She has a sprained ankle, but it's not too bad. I think we can walk out, though you might send a couple of folks up the trail to meet us."

"Roger," Andrea said. "Hurry every chance you get. The wind is up and the fire is getting squirrelly."

"Understood. Ten-four." He stowed the radio once

more and checked the sky. The wind was blowing smoke in their direction and Roslyn coughed, pulling his attention back to her. He took a bottle of water from his pack and handed it to her. "Drink this."

She took the bottle and twisted off the cap while he wrapped the foot in an elastic bandage. She said nothing, but he could feel her gaze on him, and his every nerve vibrated with awareness of her. All the times he had imagined them meeting again, he had never pictured a scenario like this, with her needing his help, forcing them into such intimacy.

He replaced her sock and helped her into her boot. She made a small noise of pain and he jerked his head up. "Are you okay?" he asked.

She relaxed her grimace. "I'm fine." She leaned forward and began to tie the laces of the boot. "I just want to get out of here." Their eyes met and she held his gaze. "Then you and I need to talk."

They had a lot of things they could talk about—but Dillon had no idea what he would say to her. His earlier anger had been overshadowed by his concern for her and the physical memory of how good they had been together. She finished lacing the boot and he bent to take her arm. "Lean on me all you want to," he said.

She nodded, and he pulled her to her feet and she leaned against him, pressed to his side. She felt different. Rounder. He glanced down and what he saw shook him, though he remained steady on his feet, still supporting her. She put a protective hand on her rounded belly. "That's what we need to talk about," she said. "I'm pregnant, and the baby is definitely yours."

Chapter Three

"Listen up, everyone." Jasper Chief of Police Doug Walters stood in the doorway of the department's squad room, a broad-shouldered man in his early sixties, with both the build and demeanor of a bulldog. He addressed the three officers gathered there: rookie Jason Wright, Lieutenant Brady Nichols and Officer Ava Callan. Brady, who had been texting with his girlfriend, Cassie, straightened and looked up at the chief, as did the others, including Ava's canine partner, a two-year-old German shepherd dog named Lacey.

"We've got a couple of urgent updates," Walters said in a voice that commanded attention. The chief had a no-nonsense approach to policing that could come across as gruff, but everyone under his command knew he had their backs. "The Gem Creek fire blew up in the last hour and headed east, toward Evans Ranch and the Skyline subdivision. We need every available officer out there going door-to-door to evacuate people and animals. The way the fire is headed, it could cut off the exit routes from those areas. Fire crews have requested we close Skyline Drive, County Road 16 and County Road 14 to all but local residents to clear the way for their personnel to get in and work on establishing fire breaks."

Adrenaline spiked through Brady as he imagined the scene near the fire. Though smoke-filled skies and heightened fire danger were a reality of summer in the West, having a big blaze practically in their backyard set everyone on edge. That kind of tension didn't bring out the best in some people.

"The Williams Gap Trailhead is on County Road 14," Ava said. "It's a pretty popular spot." A transplant from Chicago, Ava had been spending a lot of her off hours exploring local hiking trails with Lacey.

"If you see anyone there, tell them to leave," the chief said. "Otherwise, leave a notice on any vehicles parked there. We don't have time to look for hikers."

"Search and Rescue is already up there," Brady said. "I was talking to Dillon when he got the call to go out with Bentley to look for a lost hiker." He'd been hoping his invitation to hear some live music and meet Cassie's friend would get Dillon's mind off the mysterious Rosie, the weekend fling Dillon seemed obsessed with, but his friend hadn't seemed interested.

"He may have to call off the search if he's going to get out of there ahead of the fire," the chief said. "Focus on the homes in the area. Remind people that Daniels Canine Academy will take their dogs, and the animal shelter is open for other pets. They can move livestock to the fairgrounds in McCall."

"We've got better things to do than round up puppy dogs and horses," Captain Arthur Rutledge spoke from the doorway behind the chief. With thick, dark hair, brilliant blue eyes and a movie-star smile, the captain struck some people as being handsome and charming, but his coworkers in the police department weren't similarly impressed. Rutledge shouldered into the room, his expression grim. "This just came in from McCall PD." He handed the chief a piece of paper, then addressed the others. "Kent Anderson escaped from the South Boise Prison complex sometime last night. The PD in McCall contacted us because they received what they believe is a credible tip that Anderson was headed this way. He's apparently spent some time in the area and may have a hideout here."

Chief Walters looked up from the printout. "There's not much information to go on," he said. "Any idea who this 'credible tip' is from?"

Rutledge's suspiciously smooth forehead didn't crease, but the expression around his eyes tightened. "McCall PD thinks it's credible. That's enough for me. Anderson is a convicted mass murderer who's a danger to society. We should have every available officer out hunting for him."

"Hunt for him where, exactly?" Walters asked. "It's a big county and we don't have any information as to where he might be." He glanced at the others. "Everyone keep an eye out for anything suspicious while you're out and about. If you see anyone you think is Anderson, don't engage. Call for backup."

"Is Kent Anderson the guy who was convicted of the shooting on the Idaho State campus year before last?" Jason asked. The rookie had an eager energy that made Brady feel jaded sometimes.

"That's him," Captain Rutledge said. "He killed two prison guards when he escaped. I'm not going to give him a chance to get the jump on me."

"That's enough, Arthur," the chief said.

The captain faced the chief. "Instead of worrying about people who ought to have sense enough to evacu-

ate without being told, we should be out hunting this fugitive," he said.

Nothing new here. The captain and the chief often
disagreed about the best approach to policing. Their dis-
agreements had only escalated since the chief announced
his intention to retire soon. Rutledge, who as the most
senior member of the force was the natural successor
to Walters, seemed to believe he was already in charge.

"When we have a location, or even an area, to search,
we'll do so," the chief said. "Until then, we have a duty
to help our local citizens. Now get out there and do your
job." He turned and left the room, leaving Rutledge staring after him.

The others stood and began gathering items, ready to
head out. Rutledge glared at them a moment, then left.
Moments later, the others followed.

Jason fell into step beside Brady. The young officer
had grown up in the area and fit in well with the department. His recent engagement to his long-time girlfriend,
veterinary assistant Tashya Pratt, had given him a new
maturity. "What do we do if someone refuses to evacuate?" Jason asked as they headed down the hall toward
the exit.

"We can't make them leave," Brady said. "Just remind
them if the road gets cut off by the fire, no one will be
able to come in and save them. If someone is adamant
they don't want to go, ask about other family members
or pets. Do they want to endanger them, too? Sometimes
that works."

"And if it doesn't, they're on their own," Ava said as
she and Lacey caught up with the two men at the employee entrance of the Jasper Police Department head-

quarters. "We do everything we can to help, but in the end, they're entitled to make their own decisions."

"I wonder if there's really anything to that tip about Kent Anderson being in the area," Brady said. "I never heard anything about him having a connection to Jasper. If he had, this place would have been crawling with reporters. The media was all over that story for months."

They exited into the parking lot and stood for a moment, continuing the conversation. "I was still in Chicago when the shooting at Idaho State went down," Ava said. "I didn't pay much attention to the details."

"Anderson was a graduate student at ISU," Brady said. "He had been removed from a teaching assistant position because of what university officials said was 'erratic behavior'. One April day he walked into his former class and shot and killed six people, including the professor."

"I remember," Jason said. "Didn't his defense team claim he had snapped because of the stress of exams?"

"They did," Brady said. "But the jury didn't buy it."

"Maybe the captain is right," Ava said. "And we should be focused on hunting him."

"Without more to go on than a tip that he was seen 'somewhere' near here, where would we even start?" Brady shook his head. "I'm all for going after the guy, but with the town full of tourists and a wildfire threatening, we're already spreading ourselves pretty thin."

"And Dillon is off trying to track down one of those tourists," Ava said. "Is it an adult or a kid?"

"An adult, I'm pretty sure," Brady said. "He said the text from the commander said a lost hiker, not a lost child. I think Andrea would have differentiated." A child at risk always added urgency to any mission.

"I've got to admit, I'm a little envious," Ava said. "I'd

rather be out there working with my dog than knocking on doors telling people they need to leave their homes." She smiled down at Lacey, who returned the fond look and wagged her tail.

"If I hadn't been on duty today, Winnie and I would be out there," Brady said. The yellow lab loved nothing better than time in the woods, using that incredible nose of hers to find someone in trouble. She and Dillon's dog, Bentley, had trained together. It was one of the things that had brought the two men closer.

"Let's hope Dillon and Bentley find whoever they're looking for and get back before the fire cuts them off." Ava glanced at the dark clouds of smoke in the distance. "In the city all I had to deal with were gangs and the occasional riot. When Mother Nature goes rogue, all you can do is get out of the way. Can't say I like that much."

"It's one of the trade-offs for living in such a beautiful place," Brady said. "When you're skiing on a blue-sky day in the backcountry this winter, you'll know it's worth it."

"Right." They moved farther into the parking lot and Ava opened the door of her cruiser. Lacey hopped into the back seat, graceful in spite of her ninety-pound bulk. "I'm going to stop at the trailhead on my way over to Skyline," Ava said. "If I see Dillon I'll give him a hard time about being off today and missing out on all the fun."

Brady shook his head and slid into the passenger seat of his own cruiser. The smell of smoke was stronger now, and a gust of wind sent ash drifting onto the hood of his vehicle. The fire was still some distance away, but things could change so quickly. Mother Nature was definitely going rogue. He'd feel better when his friend was back with them, dealing with more controllable things like unruly tourists or even fugitive killers.

STILL LEANING AGAINST DILLON, Roslyn studied his face, trying to gauge his reaction to her announcement about her pregnancy. She had hoped to work up to the subject more gradually, but this close together, there was no hiding her condition, so she'd blurted it out. His normally bronzed skin had blanched a shade paler and his hazel green eyes had widened, then he looked away, even as his arm around her tightened. "Come on," he said. "Let's see if you can walk."

She wanted to protest that they should stay and talk, but given the thickening smoke, that wouldn't be smart. And maybe the walk out would give him more time to digest this big upheaval in his life—and give her a little more space to think of what to say. She had so much to apologize for, and so much she needed to explain.

Gingerly, she eased her weight onto the wrapped ankle. A twinge of pain shot through her but soon subsided to a dull ache. "The bandage really helps," she said. She took a step forward, then eased her arm from around him. "I think I'm good. At least enough to get back to the trailhead."

"How are you feeling besides your ankle?" he asked. "I should have asked before."

"I'm fine." She glanced back at him. His gaze was focused on her midsection, so no sense avoiding talking about the baby altogether. "Now that I'm past my first trimester, I'm actually feeling great. My doctor says I have nothing to worry about."

"Hold up a minute." He put a hand on her arm, then took off his pack and dug in it. "I should have thought of this before." He held out a packaged mask. "All this smoke can't be good for you or the baby. This will help."

"Thanks." She opened the mask and slipped it on, then met his eyes once more.

"Why didn't you tell me about the baby before now?" he asked. "Were you planning to keep it a secret forever?"

She tried not to flinch at the anger behind his words. He had a right to be upset with her. But how could she explain that she had been reluctant to tell him about the baby because she feared the worst—another rejection from a man she had grown to care about? After all, she and Dillon had spent a single weekend together. Why should he welcome her turning his whole world upside down? "No! I came to Jasper this weekend specifically to find you and tell you." She smoothed her tunic over her belly, a habit she had developed of late, as if to reassure herself the baby was still there. Still all right. "As for why I didn't tell you before, it's complicated."

He moved up beside her on the trail. "We've got a long walk ahead of us," he said. "Why don't you start at the beginning?"

So much for waiting. Apparently, he didn't think he needed more time. But she felt far from ready. How many times in the last months had she anticipated this conversation? She had rehearsed what she would say to him, and formulated defenses and explanations based on the various reactions she had imagined he might have. But now that she was here, with him so close she could smell the scent of his shampoo and feel the heat of his body beside her, all those planned words vanished. She glanced up at him, his jaw set in a firm line, his gaze directed outward. She sensed the hurt behind that stony expression and felt ashamed.

"I'm sorry," she said again. "I know I've messed this up. I was just…" She shook her head. No excuses. She had been dealing with a lot, but that didn't make up for the way she had treated a man who had been nothing but kind to her.

"Start with why you told me your name was Rosie Kenley," he said.

She nodded. "I told you the truth about why I came to Brundage Mountain that weekend," she said. "I broke up with my fiancé and lost my job and needed to get away and regroup. What I didn't tell you was that the man I was engaged to and I were the top-rated morning drive-time team on Chicago Radio. It was a very public breakup and a huge scandal. The local media wouldn't let up about it. The pressure was really getting to me."

"Rockin' Roz," Dillon said.

She stared at him. "You knew?" Come to think of it, he had addressed her by her real name when they had first met today. Had he known her identity all along and hadn't bothered to contact her?

"Not until today. The picture the search and rescue team received of you was from a newspaper in Chicago. The caption identified you as Rockin' Roz."

The hurt in his eyes wounded her. "I didn't use my real name when I checked into the resort because I didn't want the Chicago media tracking me down. I can't even describe the way they hounded me." A clip of her fiancé, DJ Matt Judson, talking about their breakup had gone viral and for weeks she had dealt with reporters camped out in front of her condo building and photographers following her when she went to buy groceries or work out at the gym. It didn't help that within a few weeks of their split, Matt had started a new relationship with the woman who had replaced Roslyn on-air. He was quick to portray Roslyn as the cruel woman who had broken his heart, while his new love was the sweetheart who was going to heal his wounds.

"When I met you it seemed like a good idea to keep up the pretense," she said. "I didn't know you that well, after all. By the time we became closer, there was never a good time to reveal my real identity." Being someone else for a weekend had been such a relief—an escape from the mess she had made of her life.

"When did you find out you were pregnant?" he asked.

"Three months ago. I was shocked." She had burst into tears in the doctor's office, not her proudest moment. "I knew I had to tell you, I just needed time to figure out how. I didn't want to just call out of the blue. And I didn't have your number, anyway. I thought this was something that needed to be revealed in person, but I didn't know where you lived, only that you were an officer with the Jasper Police."

"You could have come looking for me three months ago," he said.

"Maybe I should have, but I was too scared."

He stopped, and she stopped, too. "You were scared of me?" He looked incredulous.

"I'd already been rejected, in front of hundreds of thousands of people, by the man I thought I would marry," she said. "I lost the job I loved." One day, she was on top of the world, the next it felt as if she had lost everything. How could she make Dillon understand the devastation of that experience? The baby had felt like one more obstacle to try to manage. She had had to pull herself together and find a way to not only support herself, but a child. She had to rebuild her reputation and her self-esteem. The idea of facing Dillon before she had pulled herself together had been too much. "Matt had made a big deal out of not wanting children," she added. "And he wasn't the first man I'd dated who talked about not wanting to be a father. What if you felt the same way? Maybe I'm a coward, but I couldn't face that." She hugged her arms across her stomach.

Some of the stiffness went out of his shoulders. "It's a lot to take in. I can understand that." He raked a hand through his short hair. "But you don't ever have to be afraid of me."

She blinked back sudden tears. Surely part of her had known that, or she might never have come to Jasper. The truth was, she had wanted to see Dillon again, to see if he was really as special as she remembered.

"The smoke is getting a lot worse," he said.

She started to answer, but a cough cut off her words. She looked around them, and was surprised to see that in the short time they had been walking and talking, the sky had darkened even more, with dense gray clouds boiling up over the mountain peaks. Her eyes stung from the smoke and as she gazed up at a ridge to their left, orange tongues of flame leaped up amid the black clouds. Fear lanced through her, and she gripped his arm more tightly. She wanted to ask him if they were in danger, but she couldn't form the words.

Dillon started to say something else, but his radio crackled. He unsnapped it from his belt and keyed it to receive. "What's your twenty?" a woman's voice asked.

"We've walked about half a mile on the trail, toward the trailhead," he said.

"The fire has crossed the trail near the base of Wilder Mesa." The woman's voice was pinched with agitation.

"You'll need to cut across to the Cow Creek Loop and come back that way."

Dillon's forehead creased in a scowl. "Cow Creek Loop adds at least nine miles," he said. "Is there another route we can take?"

"Negative," the woman said. "The whole area under the mesa is active fire right now. The wind is blowing away from Williams Ridge and the loop follows Cow Creek for several miles, so that's an extra buffer."

"Ten-four," Dillon said and snapped the radio back into its holder. He turned to meet Roslyn's worried gaze. "You heard?"

"Yes."

"How's your ankle?"

They both looked down at her bandaged foot.

"It's okay," she said. Throbbing a little, but she could deal with that. After all she had overcome in the last months, she wasn't going to let a wildfire defeat her. She drew in a deep breath, straightened her shoulders and looked him in the eye. "I guess we'd better start walking."

Chapter Four

The normally quiet grounds of Daniels Canine Academy resembled a cross between a dog show and a circus when Brady pulled up in his cruiser late Friday afternoon. Vehicles occupied every spot in the gravel lot and lined the driveway, and people and dogs milled about in every direction, agitated barks and excited shouts filling the air with sound.

Brady maneuvered his cruiser into a tight spot between a camper van and a one-ton pickup and turned to his passengers. "You two are going to behave for me, right?"

Two dogs—a "may have been a Lab" black mutt and a long-haired dachshund—panted at him, ears drawn back with anxiety. Brady leaned back and snapped on the leashes the owners had supplied, then went around to the back and retrieved the dogs. They jumped out and the black one—Billy—immediately lifted his leg on the back tire of the cruiser. The dachshund—Dolly—sniffed the ground with interest.

"Come on." Brady tugged on the leashes. "Let's see what Emma has set up."

He passed half a dozen people walking dogs on leashes as he made his way around to the kennel entrance. Some of them he recognized—others he didn't know. A few waved, and some of the dogs barked. Dolly let out a low growl, while Billy gamboled at the end of the leash like a kid on an outing to the zoo.

Brady pushed open the door to the kennels and was assaulted by even more noise and the mingled odors of dog hair, urine and kibble. People and dogs were lined up along the walls. At her desk, Barbara talked into the phone tucked between her shoulder and cheek and typed into the computer while a man in jeans and a Western shirt leaned over her desk, a pug cradled in his arms.

The man glanced at Brady and inched to the side. "Hello, Officer," he said.

"Hello, Tom." He recognized Tom Fletcher, from the feedstore in town. "Who do you have there?" He nodded to the pug.

"This is Denny." He shifted to give a better view of the dog. "I was in town when we got the word we needed to evacuate. My wife didn't know what to do, so she let one of the deputies take Denny to bring him here. Soon as I found out I came here to get him. We'll drive over to Riggins to stay with my sister until this is past, and she's got plenty of room to take Denny, too." He rubbed the dog's ears. "I'm grateful to Emma for taking in people's pets, but Denny will be happier with us."

"And you'll be happier, too," Brady said.

"That, too," Tom agreed.

Barbara set down the phone and looked up at them. "Thanks for waiting, Tom. Just sign here that you took charge of Denny and you can be on your way." She slid a clipboard toward him, then leaned over to look past Brady to the two dogs at his feet. "Who do you have for us, Brady?"

"This is Billy and Dolly. Their owner, Darlene Zapata, is taking her four kids to stay with her brother in McCall, but they needed a safe place for the dogs."

"Billy and Dolly Zapata," Barbara said as she typed, eyes on the computer screen. "Address and phone?"

Brady gave her the information and Kyle, one of the boys who worked for Emma, came to take the leashes. "I'll put them in a kennel together," he said. "They'll be okay."

"Thanks." Brady turned back to Barbara. "Looks like you've got a full house."

"And then some," she said. "But we're making room for everybody. Emma even has some of the smaller dogs up at her house. I'm making sure we keep track of everyone."

"Have you heard anything from Dillon?" Brady asked.

"No. Is he helping with evacuation?"

"No. He's off today. He and Bentley got called out to look for a lost hiker. I was hoping he was done and had stopped by here."

"He was here for a few minutes this morning, but I haven't heard from him since. Sorry." She looked over his shoulder. "Can I help you?"

"The officer we talked to said we could bring Samson to stay while we're at the shelter," a woman said.

Brady turned and stifled a gasp as he faced one of the largest dogs he had ever seen. The petite brunette—she couldn't have weighed more than ninety pounds fully clothed—who was holding on to the leash smiled. "Samson is an English mastiff. He's big, but he's really a big baby."

Samson panted, tongue lolling, and regarded Brady with liquid brown eyes.

"Ma'am, can I get a shot of you and that humongous dog?" Both Brady and the woman turned to face a man with a shoulder-mounted video camera. "Officer, move over beside her, would you?"

A trim redhead in a purple sleeveless dress and low heels stepped out from behind the man and thrust a microphone toward Brady. "Officer, could you tell us how local law enforcement is handling the crisis brought on by the wildfire?"

Brady pushed the microphone aside. "Who are you?"

"Belle Fontaine, KBOI TV, Boise." She flashed a smile full of dazzling white teeth. "How are you dealing with the twin emergencies of an out-of-control wildfire and an escaped murderer in your charming, but tiny, town?"

Brady wanted to point out that the fire was not out-of-control, and demand to know how she had learned of the supposed sighting of Kent Anderson in Jasper, but his training held firm. "No comment," he said and turned away.

"I thought I told you people you need to leave. Now!" Emma had emerged from her office and made a beeline for Ms. Fontaine and her cameraman. "This is private property and you are not welcome here."

Belle Fontaine's smile never faded. "I'm sure our viewers will be very interested in the work you are doing to help local people and their pets," she said. "They'll probably be inspired to donate money to help Daniels Canine Academy with the important work I'm sure you do."

"I don't need your viewers' donations," Emma said. Her cheeks were flushed red, though the rest of her was pale. Brady had the impression of an overheated kettle about to blow. "I need you to leave."

Brady stepped forward. "You need to leave now, ma'am," he said. "This is private property and you're trespassing."

"I'm just trying to do my job," Belle protested. Her cameraman was already headed toward the door.

"So is Ms. Daniels," Brady said. "You need to leave her to do it."

He ushered her toward the door, then followed her and her cameraman all the way to their van. "What are you doing here?" Belle asked. "Why aren't you hunting for Kent Anderson?"

"How did you learn about Anderson?" Brady asked.

She sniffed. "I'm not obligated to reveal my sources."

And I'm not obligated to answer your questions, Brady thought but remained silent.

"We have a right to report this story," she said.

"Or course you do," Brady agreed. "As long as you stay on public property."

He waited until they had driven away, before he returned to the kennels, where he found Emma with the brunette and her dog. "Aren't you gorgeous?" Emma cooed to Samson.

"They're gone," Brady said. "Though I can't promise they won't come back after I leave."

"Thanks," Emma said. "And it's not that I have anything against press coverage of DCA, but it's just too crowded right now to have anyone here who isn't necessary."

"I'll take that as my cue to leave," Brady said.

"Thanks again," Emma said. "And thanks for helping people with their pets."

He waved and turned away. "I've got just the place for

this boy," he heard Emma say as he left. "Do you know if he likes horses?"

"He loves horses. We have two of them," the woman said.

"Then he can have a kennel in the barn with my two." Emma waved at Brady and led Samson and the brunette away.

He threaded his way once more through the mass of people and dogs, back to his cruiser. At the vehicle, he tried Dillon's phone. No answer. Then he called the PD. Teresa, the department secretary, answered. "Hello, Brady," she said. "I don't even have to ask where you are—I can hear the barking."

"Just checking to see if there's anything else for me before I call it a day," Brady said. "Any more news about Kent Anderson?"

"The chief was able to get a little more information from McCall. They received a report that Anderson hitched a ride from a man who dropped him off just north of the town limits," Teresa said. "That part checks out, but if anyone has seen him since, they haven't told us."

"Any word on that missing hiker Search and Rescue was looking for?" Brady asked.

"I believe she was found. But I don't know any more. My other line is ringing. Anything else?"

"No. That's it."

"Then get some rest. I imagine you'll be even busier tomorrow. We've got overflow crowds on the street and no telling what the fire will do overnight. It's guaranteed to be an exciting weekend, though whether the excitement is the good kind or the bad kind, it's too soon to tell."

Brady ended the call, then pulled up Dillon's number again. Where are you? he texted. You can't hide from the tourists forever.

DILLON WALKED BEHIND ROSLYN, back the way they had come. From behind, he couldn't even tell she was pregnant. With that loose top she was wearing, it hadn't been obvious when she was sitting down, either. Only when she had stood and leaned against him had he realized what he had missed before. Her announcement floated on the surface of his thoughts, refusing to sink in. A baby. *His* baby. He was going to be a father? He couldn't believe it.

He was still hurt that she hadn't confided in him sooner, but the anger he had nursed for months was quickly melting away. The distress in her voice when she had described her humiliating breakup and the harassment from the press afterward had cut through his own annoyance. And as much as he wished she had told him all of that in the beginning, she was right when she said they hadn't known each other that well. Yes, they had grown close in a very short time, but he could understand her feeling cautious about trusting another man again.

And now she was going to have a baby. His baby. His mom was going to be over the moon about this news. Colleen Diaz had made no secret of the fact that she thought she was overdue to be a grandmother. "Bentley is a wonderful dog, but he's no substitute for a grandchild," she had told him only last week. "I know you don't have any trouble attracting women. Can't you find one to settle down with? Someone who will make you happy and give me beautiful babies to spoil?"

He should probably hold off telling his mom about Roslyn for a while. Colleen was warm and generous, but she could be a bit of a steamroller sometimes.

He shifted his attention to Roslyn once more and noticed she was favoring her injured ankle. "Hold on a minute," he said and hurried up to take her arm. "Let's find someplace to sit and rest a minute."

"But the fire." She looked around them, at the smoky skies.

"We're headed away from the fire," he said. "See, the wind is blowing away from us. The smoke isn't as heavy here as it was only a few minutes ago. We'll be okay."

He led her to a cluster of boulders beside the trail and settled her against one. "Sit here and let me check your ankle. It's hurting you, isn't it?"

"Just a little." Bentley hopped up to sit beside her.

Dillon had noticed how quick the dog was to not only find people, but to comfort them when they were upset. "He's a natural for search and rescue work," Emma had said during their initial training. "He would be a great therapy dog, too. Just naturally empathetic."

Roslyn smoothed her hand over the dog's black-and-white coat. "You sure are a sweetie," she said. He knew she was talking to the dog, but he felt the words in his gut, an echo of things they had said to each other so many months ago. He pushed the memories aside and knelt and unlaced her boot, then cupped his hand around her ankle.

"It's pretty swollen," he said. "It would be better if you could elevate and ice it."

"That will have to wait." Bentley hopped down and she slipped off her pack and her mask and took out a water bottle and drank.

"At least your boot comes up high enough to offer some good support." He replaced the hiking boot and tied the laces, then moved to sit beside her. Bentley sniffed through the grass nearby. "You should eat something," he said. He should have thought of that before. She would need a lot of calories to keep going.

"I've got a protein bar in here somewhere," she said, digging in the pack.

"Take this." He retrieved an energy gel from his pack, something search and rescue teams routinely carried to provide quick fuel to rescuers and the rescued alike.

Roslyn accepted the packet and looked at it doubtfully. "It's okay," he assured her. "It tastes pretty good, and it's an easy to digest source of calories."

"Okay. Thanks." She opened the packet and squeezed some into her mouth. "Not bad." Then she frowned. "You're not having anything?"

"I ate right before I set out." Only a small lie, but he wasn't very hungry, and he wanted to save as much food as he could for her. And the baby. If he kept reminding himself, maybe the child would become more real to him.

"How long is it going to take us to get back to town?" she asked.

"With this detour I don't think we can get back there before dark." Nine miles was a lot to hike in a single afternoon for a determined athlete who wasn't dealing with an injured ankle and a pregnancy. "We'll need to spend the night."

He watched her closely and saw the flicker of panic in her eyes, though she quickly pushed it aside. "That doesn't sound very comfortable," she said after a moment.

"It probably won't be, but we'll find some kind of shelter. I can filter water and I've got enough food that we won't starve, though it won't be the best meal you ever ate." He smiled, hoping to lighten the mood. While he was sure he could keep her safe, he wished he could do more to make her comfortable. And he would feel a lot better once a doctor had checked her out and reassured them both that she and the baby were okay.

"If I wasn't moving so slowly we could get back to town sooner," she said. "I'll try to walk faster."

"No. It's more important that you take care of yourself."

She looked amused. "I'm pregnant, not ill."

"You're pregnant and you have a sprained ankle and this is really rough terrain. How far along are you?" She had said, but he had been so stunned that the information hadn't registered.

She laughed. "Do the math, Dillon."

Right. They had been together five months ago. Four months until he would be a father. He broke out in a cold sweat at the thought.

She laughed again. "What's so funny?" he asked.

"You. The tough, charming cop thrown for a loop." Her expression sobered and she laid a hand on his arm. "I'm sorry. I know you didn't ask for this, and the way I sprung it on you was a little rough. I understand if you don't want to be involved."

"No." He grabbed her hand and held it when she tried to pull away. "I mean, yes, it's a surprise, but I'm not going to bail on my own kid. I just… I need a little time to wrap my head around this."

"I understand," she said. "I was pretty stunned when I first found out, too. I mean, I thought we were being careful."

"We were. Most of the time. But there was that one early morning…" They'd just awakened, warm in each other's arms, moving together still half asleep but so drawn to each other. No talking, only touching. Enjoying. Both knowing they wouldn't have much longer together.

Her cheeks flushed, and he thought she was probably remembering those moments also. She brought their still linked hands to rest on the small mound of her belly. "Do you feel that?" she whispered.

"Feel what?" But then the sensation of movement beneath their clasped hands startled him. He freed his fingers from hers and laid his palm flat against her, a rush of wonder going through him. "Is that the baby?"

"Yes." Their eyes met and hers were shiny with tears, though she was smiling.

A storm of emotion threatened to undo him—awe, fear and a rush of incredible tenderness. His palm still resting on her belly, he brought his free hand up to cradle the side of her face and brought his lips to hers. She stilled, and he started to pull away, then she leaned in, her mouth moving against his, the velvet brush of her lips reawakening old memories and kindling new passion. She angled her body toward his, and he slid his hand down the line of her neck and across her shoulders. How many nights since February had he dreamed of her in his arms again? Those dreams had kept him searching for her, long after a more sensible man would have accepted that she had rejected him.

This didn't feel like a rejection now.

"Ruff!"

Bentley's sharp bark jolted them apart. Dillon turned his head to see the dog at attention, body stiff, ears forward, staring intently toward a cluster of trees a hundred feet off the trail.

"What is it?" Roslyn asked. "Why is he acting like that?"

"I think someone is out there." He stood. "Maybe someone is following us."

Chapter Five

In a flash, Dillon had transformed from tender lover to this colder, harder version of himself. Like his dog, he was completely focused on whatever was in the woods out there, automatically positioning himself between her and possible harm, every nerve alert to danger. "Why would someone be following us?" she asked, the words pinched off and strained.

"I don't know." He checked the dog again. Bentley remained rigid, leaning toward whatever had caught his attention.

"Maybe it's an animal," Roslyn said. "They're probably trying to get away from the fire, too."

He didn't take his eyes off that line of trees. "Bentley tends to be pretty cautious around dangerous animals such as mountain lions or bears," he said. "The few times we've come across something like that while we're out hiking, he's stayed quiet and right by my side. This alert is more like when he finds someone he's been tracking—but different, too." He frowned.

"Different how?" she asked.

"More cautious."

His words sent a shiver up her spine. "As if whatever out there is dangerous," she said, her voice just above a whisper. She squinted, trying to make out anything in the shadows, but she saw nothing.

"Hello!" Dillon shouted. "Is anyone there?"

She held her breath, waiting, but only ringing silence answered.

"Bentley, find," Dillon commanded.

The dog looked up, eyes questioning, then sniffed the air and took a few tentative steps forward. He sniffed again, moved forward a few more steps, then stopped and sat. He looked back at Dillon, clearly asking what he should do next.

Dillon glanced toward the woods once more. "Whatever was out there must have moved on," he said.

"Do you really think someone is following us?" she asked.

"You were probably right about it being an animal."

She was about to point out that he had already told her Bentley wasn't reacting the way he did to an animal, but Dillon slipped on his pack and fastened the chest strap. "Are you ready to go?" he asked.

"Of course." She stood and settled her own pack. As far as she was concerned, the sooner they moved on, the better.

Dillon was staring at the line of trees again. "I want to walk up there and see if I spot anything," he said. "You can wait here."

"I'll go with you." The idea of being separated from him—especially if someone really was after them—unsettled her.

They started out across open ground toward the woods. They hadn't traveled far on the uneven ground before her ankle began to throb again. She focused on Dillon's back, determined to ignore the discomfort. She would have plenty of time to rest once they were safe. And Dillon was freaked out enough about her pregnancy without her adding to his fears. He did a pretty good job of masking his emotions regarding the baby, but she recognized the panic behind his surprise and awe.

She had felt that same awe when she had stared at the results of that first pregnancy test. She had even taken two more tests, sure that the first one must have been wrong. Even when she saw her doctor and he confirmed that she was indeed pregnant, it had been days before it felt real to her. She had even forgotten about the baby a few times until she began to feel him or her inside her. Though her doctor had offered the opportunity to learn the gender of the baby, she had declined. Everything about this baby had been a surprise, so why not one more?

Dillon moved much faster than she could up the slight slope toward the trees, the dog trotting in front of him. He made a striking figure, tall and muscular, long strides easily conquering the terrain. She had noticed him in the lift line that day at Brundage even before they loaded onto the same chair, but his easy charm and sense of humor had captivated her. Add intelligence and an all-around sexy vibe, and he had been the perfect distraction to take her mind off her troubles.

But she apparently wasn't cut out for the kind of fling she could easily walk away from. Even before she had discovered she was pregnant, she had thought longingly of Dillon Diaz. She had daydreamed about going to Jasper and looking for him, to see if they could manage a long-distance relationship. But trying to juggle that along with rebuilding her career and regaining her confidence had been too daunting.

Now that she was here, though, and he wasn't running in the other direction from her and the baby, her old daydreams of being with him were quickly resurfacing. And that kiss…it had been unexpected, but definitely not unwelcome. Did it mean he was interested in something more, too? She hadn't dared to allow herself the fantasy of the two of them raising their baby together, but obviously that hope had been in the back of her mind all along, since it came rushing up to fill her thoughts now.

They reached the wooded area and Bentley raced around, barking and tail wagging. "That's the way he acted when he found me," she said.

Dillon didn't answer, his attention focused on the loose duff beneath the trees. "Do you see anything?" she asked, when she could stand the silence no longer.

"No." He turned back toward the trail. "Let's go. We need to find a safe place to spend the night."

They had been so close for a few moments there, but now he felt distant again. Was it because of this mysterious, unknown intruder, or because of something else? She searched for some topic of conversation to bring him back to her. "What have you been up to since February?" she asked. "Are you still with the police department?"

He straightened his shoulders and turned toward her. Not as open as he had been in the moments before he kissed her, but making an effort to be warmer. "I am," he said. "And I was pretty busy with search and rescue this past winter and spring. And I've been working with Bentley. I'm thinking of training him for wilderness rescue."

"How is that different from what you already do?" she asked. This was the wilderness, wasn't it?

"Right now, Bentley is trained as a tracking dog," Dillon said. At the sound of his name, Bentley looked over his shoulder at them. "He finds people by following

their scent in the air. He's able to follow the scent someone leaves as he or she moves across an area and distinguish that aroma from smoke or plants or animals. He
can follow the trail for miles. Wilderness tracking takes
that talent for scent detection and hones it for rougher
terrain and longer distances. That kind of work also requires more endurance, to travel over rougher terrain in
varying conditions."

She nodded. It was interesting, but not what she most
wanted to know right now. "Are you dating anyone?"
she asked. Did he have a girlfriend? A fiancée? Someone who would definitely complicate any attempt to have
a relationship that extended beyond their shared child?

"No."

Just—no. Without elaboration. She bit her tongue,
sensing she shouldn't probe further. But what was this
gorgeous, smart, gainfully employed and genuinely nice
guy doing single? He clearly liked women and probably
had half the women in town drooling over him. Was she
really, really lucky, or was he really, really good at avoiding commitment?

"What about you?" he asked. "Did you get a job with
another radio station?"

"No." She had put out a few tentative feelers, but after
a couple of hints that she was too "controversial," followed by advice that she wait for the scandal to die down
before she submitted any more applications, she had been
fearful of ever being on-air again. "I started my own
business," she said. "I do voice-overs for commercials
and television. And I record audiobooks." She had spent
years training for radio work and reasoned those skills
would translate well to other voice work. Plus, she had
experience doing commercials as part of her radio gig.

"Do you like the work?"

"I do. It's very different from what I did before, but I really like it. And I can set my own schedule, which will work well after the baby is born."

"Do you know if you're having a boy or a girl?" he asked.

"Not yet. I thought it might be nice to be surprised. But I'm scheduled for an ultrasound when I get back to Chicago. The doctor says I should be able to find out then, if I've changed my mind, though I don't think I will." She started to tell him he was welcome to attend the test with her, but that seemed like too much, too soon. Would he think she was pressuring him to be more involved than he wanted to be? He had a job and a life here in Jasper. She had no right to pull him out of that.

"How's the ankle?" he asked.

The change in topic made her wonder if talk of the baby was making him uncomfortable. She reminded herself once more that he hadn't had as much time to get used to the idea as she had. "It's okay." She was almost accustomed to the pain. "It's not getting any worse. I'll be fine." She looked around them. The trail had climbed and was following the top of a ridge now. As Dillon had promised, they had moved away from much of the smoke, though dark clouds on the horizon cast the landscape in twilight hues until it resembled a charcoal drawing. "Do you have any idea where we'll spend the night?" she asked.

"There are some caves a couple of miles ahead. They'll make a good shelter. We can make a fire, spread some pine boughs to sleep on." He looked back at her. "It won't be a posh hotel, but it won't be so bad."

Was he thinking of the very nice hotel where they had

spent the weekend together all those months ago? That time seemed so long ago now, but in many ways like only last week. He was easy to be with, though she still didn't feel she knew him well. She would have to trust him, though. He was her best chance of getting herself and her baby to safety.

BRADY WAS ON his way back to his cabin when dispatch radioed for him to report to the station. He arrived to find the station crowded with officers, the assistant fire chief, and the search and rescue commander. "What's going on?" he asked Lieutenant Cal Hoover, who stood in the doorway of the squad room.

Cal's normally affable, dark face was creased with worry, making him look older than his forty-nine years. "I think we have a situation," he said. "The chief will fill in the details."

Brady followed him into the squad room and stood along the back wall, next to Jason. "I saw a television news van in town this afternoon," Jason said. "Think this has anything to do with them?"

"Maybe," Brady said. "A reporter and cameraman were out at DCA, trying to interview Emma."

"I bet that went over big," Jason said.

"She sent them packing. I told them they were free to do their job as long as they did it on public property."

"Are they here because of the fire, or because of Kent Anderson?" Jason asked.

"Both, I think," Brady said.

They fell silent as the chief entered the room, followed by Rich Newcomb, assistant fire chief, and SAR Commander Andrea Wayne. "Some of you already know that Sergeant Dillon Diaz isn't here because he and his search dog, Bentley, were called out this afternoon to look for a lost hiker," Chief Walters said. "I called you all here to fill you in on the newest development with that situation."

Brady's stomach dropped, and he exchanged anxious looks with several others around him. Had something happened to Dillon?

"Dillon and Bentley located the missing hiker, Roslyn Kern," Andrea said. "But before they could make their way back to the trailhead, the fire shifted and crossed the trail ahead of them. Thick smoke made visibility difficult, and the trail being blocked led me to direct the two of them to backtrack and head farther north and west to stay out of danger. Unfortunately, that put them out of cell phone and radio range, though we have no reason to believe they're in any trouble. During our last communication, Dillon reported that Ms. Kern had a sprained ankle but was capable of walking with his assistance. The friends who were hiking with Ms. Kern and reported her missing are fine, but apparently they've been talking to the reporters in town." Andrea looked to the chief, who took up the story.

"Roslyn Kern is from Chicago," Walters said. "Where, apparently, she was a very popular radio disc jockey and was involved in some kind of scandal. Among other things, she's pregnant. About five months, according to her friends."

"They should have mentioned her pregnancy when they first reported her missing," Ava said.

"Apparently, they were trying to honor her wishes to keep the pregnancy private," Walters said. "In any case, when the reporters heard Kern's name, and that she was trapped by the fire—their words, not mine—they latched on to the story and ran with it. National news picked it up and media is descending on the town, searching for every angle they can find about the fire and Ms. Kern. Not to mention Kent Anderson."

"If they can find a way to link those three things, I guarantee they will," Captain Rutledge said.

Walters nodded. "Reporters have learned that Ms. Kern is with Sergeant Diaz, and they're playing that up in their stories as well. As you're carrying out your duties this weekend, you're probably going to be asked about Dillon, the fire, Kent Anderson, or all of the above. This is your official notice that your only reply is 'No comment.'"

"Have there been any more sightings of Anderson?" Cal asked.

"This afternoon I interviewed the driver who gave a ride to a man who fits Anderson's description," Rutledge said. "He seemed credible, though we can't know for sure. He said the man he later realized might be Anderson told him he was meeting friends in the area, and he seemed jumpy."

"How does he know the guy was Anderson?" Lieutenant Margaret Avery asked.

"He said he saw a news bulletin about Anderson's escape and recognized him."

"Where did he drop off this hitchhiker?" Jason asked.

"He says the guy asked to be let out at the intersection of County Road 14 and North Maple. The guy told him friends would pick him up there. The man he let out was wearing khaki trousers and a faded black T-shirt advertising a landscape service in McCall. McCall police think those items of clothing might have been taken from a clothesline in a backyard in town."

"That intersection isn't far from the Williams Gap Trailhead," Brady said.

"That information is definitely not to be shared with the media," Walters said.

"We didn't see anyone else up there when we were looking for Ms. Kern," Andrea said. "And her friends said they hadn't seen anyone else on the trail, either."

"We don't know for sure this hitchhiker was Anderson," Margaret said.

"We have to operate on the assumption that it was," Walters said. He turned to Newcomb. "Now I'd like the chief to update us on the latest situation with the Gem Creek fire."

Newcomb, a muscular man in his forties with a blond buzz cut, stepped forward and turned toward the map of the area that was tacked to the wall behind him. "This afternoon the fire grew to twelve thousand acres," he said. "To the east of Jasper, primarily on public land, though the Lazy H ranch lost a corral and a couple of outbuildings. Fire crews are establishing a line of defense that runs from here to here." He indicated two points on the map. "That's directly behind the Skyline development. Those homes have been evacuated as a precaution, and we have crews patrolling that area for any fire activity. The wind has decreased somewhat this afternoon, allowing us to gain some ground. Overnight, temperatures should cool, which should allow for more containment, and the forecast is calling for cloudy conditions in the morning, though whether or not that pans out we don't know. We're calling it twenty percent contained at this point."

Brady studied the map and tried to picture the location of the trail Dillon and Ms. Kern would follow to get back to town. It looked like they were away from the immediate path of the fire.

"As you all should know, wildfires are unpredictable," Newcomb continued. "There's a lot of fuel in the national forest around us. But we have at least one slurry bomber dedicated to this blaze, and a crew of smoke jumpers from Pinedale arrived this afternoon, so we're optimistic we can bring this under control. We're asking for your help keeping unauthorized persons out of the evacuation areas, or areas with active fire. Depending on how things play out, we may need to evacuate more houses."

"What about Dillon?" Ava asked. "Is there anything we can do to help him?"

"We're hopeful he'll move back into radio or cell phone range before long," Andrea said. "Given that Ms. Kern is injured and probably traveling slowly, I don't expect them to make it back to town before sometime tomorrow. I've asked the pilots of the spotter planes who are regularly surveying the burn area to keep an eye out for them. Right now, that's all we can do."

"Are the spotters looking for Kent Anderson, too?" Rutledge asked.

"They are," Walters answered. "They look for anyone down there who shouldn't be."

"What happens if they spot someone?" Cal asked. "Can we go in after them?"

"That depends on where they are and what they're doing," Walters said.

"We haven't had reports of any campers or hikers in the area who are unaccounted for," Newcomb said. "Though there's always the possibility of a lone backpacker or hiker who didn't register at the trailhead. If someone is in distress, we try to help them, but we can't put our volunteers in danger to do so."

"The trails in that area are well-marked," Walters said. "If they can get to a trail, they should be able to follow it out."

"Unless they don't want to leave," Rutledge said.

"Why wouldn't they want to leave?" Jason asked.

"I can't think of a better place to hide than the national forest," Rutledge said. "Especially if a wildfire is keeping authorities from getting to you. Anderson is supposedly familiar with the area. He may intend to travel deeper into the wilderness, where he could make his way down to Boise. Or he could head north, toward Canada."

"That's taking a big risk," Ava said.

"He's doing a life sentence," Rutledge said. "Maybe he feels he has nothing to lose."

"Any more questions?" Walters asked.

There were none, so he dismissed them. Brady pulled out his phone. Still no answer from Dillon. He texted Cassie to let her know he was on his way home, then for the second time that day emerged into a crowd of people, only this time without the dogs. "Officer, what can you tell us about the search for Roz Kern?" A tall man in a white shirt and blue tie thrust a microphone into his face.

"What can you tell us about Sergeant Diaz?" a woman, also with a microphone, asked.

"No comment," Brady said. He put his head down and headed toward his vehicle, which, unfortunately, was parked at the far end of the lot.

"Have you heard from Sergeant Diaz?" someone else asked—Brady didn't look up to see who. "Are he and Ms. Kern in danger from the fire?"

"How badly is Ms. Kern injured?"

"Do they know Kent Anderson is in the same area? Are they aware he could be stalking them?"

Brady did look up then, and zeroed in on the older man with heavy jowls who had asked the question. "What makes you think Anderson is stalking anyone?" he asked.

The reporter looked smug. "Anderson made it clear at his trial that he doesn't like lawmen. He swore to kill as many cops as he could. If he spots your friend out there alone with no backup, he probably won't pass up the chance to take him out."

Brady bit back a reply. Dillon wasn't in uniform, so how would Anderson know he was a cop? People said other cops and people who had spent a lot of time around law enforcement—like criminals—could always tell, but was that true? And the chance of Dillon and Anderson crossing paths seemed pretty remote. Still, the reporter's questions, and his attitude, angered Brady. Which he supposed was the point. He took a deep breath and looked the man in the eyes. "No comment," he said and continued toward his truck. To think he had who knew how many more days of dealing with this. *Hurry back anytime you can, Dillon,* he thought.

Chapter Six

As they continued along the trail, Dillon kept a watchful eye for signs that someone was following them. He hadn't said anything to Roslyn, but he knew Bentley wouldn't have alerted that way if someone hadn't been there. He had worked with the dog long enough that Dillon trusted him to be right. And hadn't Roslyn mentioned that she had sprained her ankle when she had been startled by the sound of someone in the woods? It might have been an animal, or even the wind in the trees, but what if it wasn't?

The shadows had lengthened and the sun wasn't as intense as it had been earlier in the day. They'd be out of light as soon as it dropped below the ridge to the west. Roslyn was sinking too; her shoulders slumped and her limp was more pronounced. She hadn't complained, but he knew she needed rest. The first aid course he had taken as part of his search and rescue training hadn't said much about special precautions for pregnant women, but he couldn't help thinking Roslyn's condition made her more vulnerable.

"The caves are just a little farther," he said.

"That's good." They were climbing and she sounded out of breath.

"Do you want to stop and rest a minute?" he asked.

"No. I'll rest when we get to wherever we're going to spend the night. When I stop, I don't plan to get up for a while."

That was Roslyn, quick-witted and cheerful whether faced with a long lift line or a night in the wilderness. He was sure she had her moments of despair—he hadn't missed the sadness in her voice when she had talked about her breakup and her job loss. But she was the type of person who worked to get past any setbacks and move forward with a positive attitude. That took a special strength he couldn't help but admire.

They entered a grove of aspens, the temperature dropping perceptively in the shade, the smell of damp leaf mold cutting through the faint tinge of smoke that clung to their clothing and hair. Their footsteps echoed as they crossed a footbridge over a small creek. "The caves are up here, overlooking the creek," he said and moved ahead of her to lead the way. The creek itself had slowed to a trickle in these dry months, but there were still a couple of pools where he could collect water to filter.

He hadn't hiked this trail in a couple of years, but the route was well-worn and easy to follow. The caves were a series of shallow openings carved into the rock over centuries. He led the way to the deepest one, which provided a space about eight feet deep and a little over five feet tall. Roslyn could stand upright, but he had to duck. A fire ring, the coals long grown cold, was arranged just inside the opening to the shelter. "This looks like a popular place," Roslyn said, looking around at the smooth stone walls and several large logs arranged as seating around the fire ring.

"Backpackers use this as an overnight spot sometimes," he said. The wildfire had probably sent everyone out of the area, so they had the campsite to themselves. "It's not deluxe, but we'll have shelter here." He touched her shoulder and she turned toward him. He could read the fatigue in her eyes and was glad they had stopped before dark. "I'm going to get some water and firewood. Will you be okay here by yourself?"

"Of course." She slipped off the mask and lowered herself to one of the log seats. If her smile was forced, at least she was making an effort. "I'll be fine."

He didn't like to leave her alone, but Bentley hadn't alerted to anyone near them since they had reached the ridge top, and it would be difficult for someone to sneak up on her as long as she stayed in the cave. He could have asked Bentley to stay with her, but the dog had already set out ahead of him. Dillon retraced their footsteps along the trail, but instead of heading down toward the creek, he first climbed up to a point that gave him a view of the surrounding area. Bentley turned and followed him, and sat by Dillon's side as he scanned the treed area along the creek, as well as the more open fields beyond. He saw nothing amiss. No other people, or any sign that anyone had passed this way in a while. The wind continued to blow away from them, clearing most of the smoke, though the valley below was still hazy. He watched a long time but saw no movement.

He tried his radio but raised only static. No surprise—they were a long way from a tower or a repeater. He didn't expect any better result from his phone, but when he took it out he was surprised to see a single bar of signal, flickering in and out. It wasn't enough to make a call, but he might be able to send a text. And at some point in their journey he had passed through an area where he was able to receive a text from Brady. You can't hide from the tourists forever, Brady had written.

Dillon hit the reply button. We stopped for the night at the caves above Cow Creek. Hold down the fort until we make it back tomorrow. He paused, his finger hovering over the screen. Part of him wanted to share the news that he had found the elusive Rosie—and that he was going to be a father in about four months. But the information still felt too raw and precious to expose to the public, even someone as nonjudgmental as Brady.

He hit Send, waited to make sure the message went through, then shut off the phone to conserve the battery, which had already drained to 40 percent. Then he headed back down to the creek to filter a couple of bottles of water. He would gather some firewood to boil water for hot drinks and to cook the freeze-dried meals that were part of his emergency rations. He could cut some pine boughs, too. He had never actually slept on pine boughs before, but he had a vague memory of reading about wilderness explorers sleeping on them, and they sounded more comfortable than the hard rock floor of the cave. Tomorrow he and Roslyn would walk out to safety, but for now his goal was to get through the night with as little trauma as possible.

Roslyn FELT GUILTY sitting while Dillon worked, so after a while she shoved to her feet. She found a broken tree branch and used it to sweep the dirt floor of the cave, sending dried leaves, loose rock and coals from long-ago campfires over the edge toward the creek below. She straightened the arrangement of logs around the firepit, then looked for anything else to do. There was nothing, so she settled onto a log once more to wait.

Hunger gnawed at her like a wild animal. This sudden desperate need to eat was only one of the many things that surprised her about her pregnancy. She dug in her pack for the protein bar and ate it quickly. She felt only a little guilty about not waiting for Dillon. He was probably hungry, too. He hadn't eaten all day. But he had said he had plenty of provisions in his pack.

She washed the bar down with the last of the water in her bottle, then inventoried the rest of the contents of the day pack. She had one of those foil blankets that were supposed to keep you warm by reflecting body heat. That would probably come in handy tonight. Another protein bar, and some water purification tablets in a small brown bottle. A first aid kit that contained bandages, ibuprofen and antibiotic ointment, a roll of gauze, some tape and a pair of tweezers. A tin of matches. A whistle. A small mirror for signaling. All the things a person was supposed to carry hiking, though they hadn't helped her much today.

She took out the camera and turned it on to scroll through the photos on the memory card—not the pictures she had taken today, but photos from her weekend with Dillon in February. A shot of him next to her on the chairlift, only his grin recognizable beneath the helmet and goggles. A selfie of the two of them at the top of the mountain, goggles pushed up on top of their helmets, leaning in close with shoulders touching, a snow-covered peak rising behind them. Another photo of Dillon, this time seated across from her at dinner, freshly showered and shaved and wearing a black sweater, so handsome he had taken her breath away when they met up at the restaurant.

She had more images of him in her mind—walking

arm in arm across the snowy parking lot to her hotel room, naked beside her in bed, sleepy-eyed with the shadow of a beard on his jaw as he sat across the breakfast table from her the next morning. Those pictures had occupied her more than she cared to admit in the months since she and Dillon had been together.

She had told herself she was so attracted to him then because he was such a change from Matt. Dillon had no expectations that she behave a certain way. Matt had choreographed every aspect of their relationship from the very beginning, as if writing a script for an on-air skit. She hadn't seen it that way at the time, of course. When he suggested she say a certain thing on air or wear a certain outfit when they appeared together, he had somehow made it seem as if they were brainstorming ideas together. Except the only ideas that ever developed into reality were his.

Dillon listened more than he spoke, and he didn't argue when her ideas or beliefs didn't match up with his. He seemed interested in what she had to say and trusted her to make her own decisions. In these last few hours she had spent with him she had felt the old attraction all over again but intensified. Maybe she was drawn to him not because he wasn't Matt, but because of what he was. The kind of man worth knowing better.

The sound of something approaching on the path made her heart beat faster. She stood in time to see him climbing up the trail with an armload of firewood. He dumped the wood beside the fire ring, then left again and returned shortly, dragging in a pile of pine branches. "Bedding," he said by way of explanation. He slipped off his pack and set two bottles of water beside the firewood, then unzipped a pocket and took out a packet she recognized as a foil emergency blanket.

"I have one of those in my pack," she said.

"Great. I'm thinking we can spread them over the boughs and maybe it will be better than sleeping on the ground."

She nodded. She had been dreading trying to get any rest on the hard rock. As it was, so much of her body ached she didn't think the few ibuprofen in her pack were going to do much good. And her doctor had recommended she avoid painkillers if possible.

Dillon shook out the blanket and let it drift down over the pile of branches, then regarded it critically. "It looks kind of lumpy," he said. "Want to try it out?"

She had her doubts but knelt and crawled onto the makeshift bed, the blanket crackling beneath her. She lay back, then squirmed until she settled into an almost comfortable position. "It's better than I thought it would be," she said. A little noisy. She sniffed. "And it smells good." Fresh and woodsy. Much better than the musky cave.

"That's about the best we can do," he said. He settled onto one of the logs and pulled his pack over. "You must be starving," he said. "I am."

"I ate a protein bar." She sat beside him, the pack between them. "Sorry, but I couldn't wait."

"It's okay." He pulled out a couple of foil pouches. "I've got chicken and noodles or lasagna," he said.

"The chicken." She didn't want to think about the heartburn the lasagna was liable to give her.

"There's hot chocolate and instant coffee, too. And some tea. Don't know what kind." He held up a handful of packets.

"Chocolate, please. You come well prepared."

"We never know how long we're going to be out on a search and rescue mission, or who we might need to feed in addition to ourselves, so we always carry some basics." He pulled out a small pot, unfolded handles from the side and poured water from one of the bottles into it. He set this aside, then leaned forward and began arranging wood in the fire circle. "I take it you didn't plan on being out very long today?"

"You mean because of the little pack I was carrying?" she asked.

"Your boots look pretty broken in," he said. "And I remember we talked about hiking in the area back in February, so I figured you would be better prepared for a long hike."

"This was kind of a last-minute outing," she said. "I ran into my friends Cheri and Buck in a café in town this morning. They're from Chicago, too, and came out for the holiday weekend. They were with another couple I didn't know, but they asked me to go hiking with them. Everyone had assured us there was no immediate danger from the wildfire, so I figured, why not? It was a beautiful day and I hoped I could get some good photographs of the wildflowers."

"I remember you took a lot of photographs at the ski resort," he said. "Is photography a passion of yours?"

"Sort of. I'm trying to improve. I've taken a few classes, but nothing serious. It's a good creative outlet. Anyway, I was taking photos of flowers when I got separated from my friends, and then I hurt my ankle."

"I'm sorry you were hurt, but I'm not sorry I found you."

She leaned forward and added a stick to the small fire he had kindled. "I promise, I was going to look for you as soon as we got back from the hike." She glanced at him. "You saved me a lot of trouble, walking right up to me like that."

"I never stopped looking for you," he said. "But I wasn't having much luck. The name thing threw me."

She winced. "I'm so—"

"No. I understand why you did it. But why Rosie Kenley?"

"My grandpa always called me Rosie, and Kenley was my mother's maiden name." She shrugged. "I didn't want to make things too complicated."

"It felt a little strange, thinking of you as Roslyn at first, but I like it. It suits you."

"Thanks." She would always have fond memories of him calling her Rosie, but better to put that behind her.

"Did you use your real name when you registered at the hotel?" he asked.

"I had to. That's the name on my ID and my credit card. But I told the desk clerks I was hiding from a stalker and to not tell anyone I was there. They were very sympathetic and helpful." She frowned. "It wasn't a lie, either. The press really had been stalking me for weeks at that point."

"You were a big celebrity in Chicago?"

"It was that slow a news period." She added another twig to the fire. "I think a lot of it was because the station had played up my romance with Matt so much. And I went right along with it. I was angry with Matt for being so ambitious and putting his career ahead of everything, but I was just as driven. I never objected to any of the ways he and the station manager suggested for us to promote ourselves. I believed it would benefit my career, too."

"It sounds like you really needed a getaway by the time you came to Brundage."

"It was Valentine's weekend, remember?" She smiled ruefully. "The radio station was doing a big promo for the holiday and everywhere I turned I saw another billboard or ad. I was determined to get far away until the holiday was over."

"I'm glad you did," he said. "It was one of the best Valentine's Days I've had."

Me, too, she thought, but she couldn't say it. Not yet. She had been too free with such declarations in the past and her words had come back to wound her.

"How did you get into being a DJ?" He added a large piece of wood to the fire. "It sounds like interesting work."

"It is. I love music and originally wanted to be on the production side, but there aren't a lot of jobs in that field, and it's still a very male-dominated profession. I started DJing when I was still in college and worked for several small stations around Chicago before I got a break at WZPR." Her voice trailed away. How to explain what had happened there without sounding self-pitying?

"You don't have to talk about it if you don't want to," he said.

"No. I want to tell you." She shifted, trying to get more comfortable. "It was like any new job at first," she said. "I started at the bottom—working in the middle of the night. But listeners liked me, and I gradually worked my way up to midmorning. I was aiming for morning drive time, but I wasn't allowed to carry a prime time slot on my own. Finally, I was paired with Mad Matt Judson!— always written with an exclamation point after his name in all the promos. He'd been working with another man for a couple of years, but that person moved on to a bigger market. I was excited about having a chance to show what I could do." She paused for a breath. "Later on, Matt told me he was upset that the station wouldn't let him be a solo act. I think we initially bonded over our frustration with station management."

"So the two of you hit it off right away?"

"We did. He was charming, or so I thought. He paid a lot of attention to me and flirted a lot—on and off the air. The listeners loved it, but I wasn't so sure. It was fun, but I didn't want to date him because I didn't think getting involved with a coworker would be okay. I kept turning him down when he asked me out, but one day the station manager pulled me aside and said the attraction between us was obvious and it was okay with the station if we pursued a relationship."

"That seems a little weird," Dillon said.

"In hindsight, it does. At the time, I was so naive I thought it meant they cared about me and wanted me to be happy. Matt and I started dating and I wanted to keep things quiet, but he insisted we didn't have anything to hide and made a point of telling everyone about us on-air. I was upset about that, but he said it was no big deal. The first of many warning signs I failed to heed."

Dillon balanced the pot of water on the fire. "Why did you split up?" he asked. "Or is that none of my business?"

She had told so few people about that time. It felt good to pour out the whole story to someone who cared, yet was objective. Dillon didn't know the people involved, except her. And she felt he wouldn't judge her, at least not as harshly as she had already judged herself. "We got engaged," she said. "Matt popped the question on-air. It was a very big deal. The station made a huge production of the whole thing. I was embarrassed, but also, well, who doesn't like to be made a fuss over? Part of me thought we were rushing things. It was too soon. But I felt backed into a corner. And after a while, I could see that our ratings were climbing. Management kept telling us this was great for our careers. And Matt wasn't the only one who was ambitious. I let my aspirations over-rule any qualms I had." She sighed. "At first it was all good. Matt was attentive and romantic. But he refused to talk about a wedding or plans. He said we should milk the engagement hype—our ratings were skyrocketing." She smoothed her hands over the baby bump. "I tried to talk to him about having a family and he was adamant he didn't want children."

"So that was the beginning of the end."

"Not really." She sighed again. "I was still blissfully naive. And I thought I could change his mind about chil-dren. Then one day I overheard Matt talking to another DJ. The guy told him it looked like he might actually have to marry me. Matt told him that wasn't the plan—he was going to milk the engagement hype long enough to get picked up by a bigger market. Once that was done, it was bye-bye Roz."

"That must have been devastating." Dillon spoke softly, but the steel in his voice sent a shiver through her.

"I was a mess," she said. "I tried really hard to remain professional, but I was also so angry. Matt had proposed on-air, so I thought about breaking up with him on-air, too, but I knew that would be risking my job. So instead, I gave him back the ring when we were alone one eve-ning. Then I went to management, told them we were no longer engaged and that I needed to be moved to another time slot. Matt could handle the morning slot by himself. I even said I was sure the listeners would love it."

"What did management say?" Dillon asked.

"They told me if I wouldn't work with Matt, I couldn't work for them. And just like that—I had no fiancé and no job. And then Matt went on-air the next morning and played the jilted lover card and everything blew up. I went from Chicago's darling to the most hated woman in town. People yelled terrible things at me from passing cars when I walked down the street. Photographers stalked me, newspapers and television covered the story. It was ridiculous. Looking back, I realize the station was probably feeding the frenzy in order to up ratings for Matt's show, but at the time I just felt like I was drowning and couldn't catch my breath."

"You should sue the station," Dillon said.

She nodded. "I thought about it, but in the end I just wanted to put the whole experience behind me. Coming to Brundage Mountain on vacation was the first step in making a fresh start. Meeting you—spending that weekend with you—I felt like I started healing then. You helped me more than you could know."

He put his arm around her and pulled her close. Just held her, his warmth encircling her, his strength pushing back some of the weariness and pain. "I understand better now why you didn't tell me the truth about who you were. Maybe in your position I would have done the same thing."

"When I met you, I really didn't want to be that person anymore," she said. "It was nice to be Rosie—a woman who attracted the attention of a fabulous, handsome man. Not Roslyn, who had screwed up everything."

"What happened wasn't your fault," he said.

"In some ways, it was. I ignored my own misgivings about the situation. I told myself I needed to go along with everything in order to make it in my chosen career." She let out a deep breath. "If nothing else, this whole experience has taught me to be more discerning."

"I'm glad you told me now," he said. "Though maybe it's just as well I didn't know about all of this back in February. I would have been tempted to follow you back to Chicago and teach a lesson to a certain DJ. Not to mention his bosses."

She laughed. "One look at you and I think they would have been shaking in their shoes." Dillon's dark good looks, not to mention muscular build, would be enough to make anyone think twice about arguing with him. And Matt had never impressed her as being particularly brave. He took the easiest path through life, including going along with a fake engagement in order to improve ratings.

Dillon opened both packets of food, then added hot water from the pot and sealed them again. "Five minutes to dinner," he said. "I'm going to feed Bentley, then I'll make chocolate."

He poured kibble he had stowed in his pack into Bentley's portable bowl and the dog crunched it down while Dillon made hot chocolate to accompany their meal.

Roslyn struggled not to wolf down the food. "It's not gourmet, but it's not bad," Dillon said.

"I'm so hungry I could eat almost anything," she said. "Though I'm glad I didn't have to."

"When we're done, I want to take a look at your ankle," he said.

"All right."

They finished the meal in silence, then he rinsed the cups and forks and returned them, along with the trash, to his pack. "Now let's see that ankle." He patted his leg, motioning for her to rest her ankle on his thigh.

She removed her boot and sock, then lifted her bound foot into his lap. He carefully unwound the bandage, his fingers warm and deft. "It's still pretty swollen," he said. "Does it hurt?"

"Not as much now that I've had a chance to rest it."

"The water in the creek is pretty cold. If you could hike down there, you could soak it."

"I'm too tired to go anywhere else tonight," she said.

He probed gently at her ankle, then began to massage her foot. She closed her eyes and bit back a moan. "I'll give you ten hours and twenty minutes to stop that," she said.

He slid his hands up to her calf and began gently kneading there. This time she did moan. "That feels amazing," she said.

"It feels pretty good from this side, too."

She opened her eyes and met his gaze, then he looked away and took his hands from her also. "I'll let you get some rest," he said. "We've got a long day ahead of us tomorrow."

Her body needed that rest, she knew. But her mind insisted on thinking about all the other things they could be doing together, here alone in this cave, with only the soft glow of the firelight. His touch had awakened a lot of pleasant memories in her body. Memories she very much would like to repeat. She had told him she was smarter about relationships now, but was that really true? She was ready to jump back into Dillon's arms after five months apart when she still knew very little about him. Her instincts told her he was a good man, but those instincts had proved her wrong before.

DILLON LAY ON his back in the dark, the bed of pine boughs offering limited cushioning from the rock floor of the cave. He closed his eyes and told himself he needed to sleep, but he was too aware of Roslyn, only a few inches away from him in the dark. He imagined he could feel the heat of her body and smell the floral-and-vanilla scent of her perfume. The space blanket crackled with every shift of her body as she tried to get comfortable.

He'd gotten a little carried away, massaging her leg, the feel of her in his hands awakening memories of how wonderful it had felt to make love to her. She had been so responsive, and they had been so in sync with each other…

He had forced himself to move away from her. The last thing she needed right now was for him to come on too strong. She had made it clear what he had been to her—a weekend break from her troubled life back in Chicago. A way to jump-start her healing. She was willing for him to have a part in their child's life, though how much of a part she hadn't said, but she gave no indication she wanted anything else from him.

If she really had feelings for him—the kind of feelings he was beginning to have for her—she wouldn't have waited five months to contact him. For all he was ready to forgive her for concealing her true identity, he couldn't get over the fact that she had waited so long to let him know about the baby.

He rolled onto his side, blanket and branches crackling, and focused on his breathing. In on four counts. Hold four counts. Out four counts. Roslyn seemed to have settled down. He thought she might even be asleep.

Don't think about her, he reminded himself. *Don't think about anything.*

Breathe in four counts. Hold four counts. *What was that noise?* He held his breath, listening. Yes, a faint scraping noise. Like a footstep on the path outside the cave. Carefully, he pushed the blanket away and sat, wincing as it crackled beneath him. He waited long minutes and heard nothing.

Maybe he had imagined the sound. Or it was a small animal scurrying, or dried leaves stirring in the wind?

Then he heard it again, and adrenaline surged through him. Something was out there. Maybe just an animal.

He looked toward Roslyn. She lay on her side with her back to him, a dark silhouette in the fading firelight. Dillon rose, shoved his bare feet into his boots and tightened the laces. Bentley appeared at his side, watching him intently, ears forward, tail wagging slowly from side to side. Dillon patted the dog's side, then crept toward the cave opening. He moved outside, the dog at his side, intent on finding out if he was imagining a threat, or if they were really in danger.

Chapter Seven

Emma did not have time Friday evening to stop by the Jasper Police Department, but she was going to make time. Some things could be overlooked, but not this. She pushed her way through the television crews and spectators on the sidewalk outside the police station and into the front lobby. Department secretary Teresa Norwood moved to intercept her as she headed toward the doors leading to the heart of the station. "Emma, you look upset," Teresa said. Her warm, motherly manner betrayed a keen perceptiveness, but Emma supposed there wasn't anything subtle about her obvious anger.

"I need to speak to Captain Rutledge," Emma said. "And to the chief, if he's here."

"I've been telling the chief for the last hour that he needs to call it a day, but you know how stubborn he can be."

"As stubborn as you, since you're still here." The chief joined the two women. "What do you need, Emma?"

Emma glanced at Teresa, who had moved to her desk and was pretending to sort papers, but was as alert as any retriever on the hunt. "Let's discuss this in your office," she said.

Walters escorted her to his office. Emma glanced into

the office across from him and spotted Captain Rutledge. She leaned in to address him. "Lucy Green told me what happened at her place this afternoon," she said. "You scared her and her son half to death. You could have killed someone."

Rutledge rose from behind his desk. "That mutt of hers attacked me. I had every right to defend myself."

The chief moved past Emma into Rutledge's office. "Close the door, Emma, and let's discuss this," he said. Always the calm voice in a storm, she thought. They were all going to miss him when he retired.

"That dog—" Rutledge began, but Walters held up a hand to silence him. "Emma, you go first. What did Lucy Green tell you that has you so upset?"

"First of all, Captain Rutledge told her she couldn't take her dog with her when she evacuated this afternoon. That was a lie and completely uncalled for."

"The dog was racing around, barking like a maniac," Rutledge said. "It wouldn't come when Mrs. Green called and I didn't have all day to wait around. We'd had a report that the fire was near the exit road. If it jumped the ditch and crossed the road, we'd all be trapped. She needed to forget about the dog and leave."

"Peaches was upset, but instead of trying to calm everyone down, the captain escalated the situation," Emma said. "Lucy came to me crying. I told her to file a formal complaint, but after what happened, she was too afraid."

"That dog attacked me," Rutledge said. "I had every right to defend myself."

She turned on him, all her fury unleashed. "That dog was a fifteen-pound, ten-year-old toy poodle. He doesn't even have most of his teeth. You were never in any danger." She turned back to Walters. "Lucy said Captain Rutledge drew his gun and threatened to shoot Peaches. Her seven-year-old son, Carter, rushed between Rutledge and the dog to protect it. If that gun had gone off, he could have been killed."

The lines on the chief's face were deeper than ever. "Arthur, is this true?"

Rutledge's face flushed crimson. "I was trying to help the woman with her dog, which wouldn't stop barking and refused to cooperate. I was going to pick it up and put it in her car for her and it tried to bite me."

"If an angry giant started yelling and grabbed you by the neck, you'd try to defend yourself, too," Emma said. "I know Lucy and I know her dog. I've worked with Peaches. He was a puppy mill dog and was abused. I'm sure he was terrified and defended himself the only way he knew how." She glared at Rutledge. "Pulling a gun was out of line."

"I want a full report on my desk by tomorrow morning," Walters said. When Rutledge started to protest, the chief added, "You drew your service weapon in a situation with civilians. That requires a full report. You know that. I could suspend you, effective immediately."

"I was defending myself. And the kid rushed in out of nowhere."

"I'm taking into consideration that you truly believe that, but don't let it happen again. And there will be a disciplinary review." He turned back to Emma. "Do you want to file a complaint?"

She stood up straighter, a little calmer now that she had gotten the story out in the open. "No. I want to offer Captain Rutledge a free training session at Daniels Canine Academy," she said. "I want him to learn how to properly interact with dogs."

"That's ridiculous," Rutledge protested. "A complete waste of my time."

"You're going to have plenty of free time if you don't watch yourself," Walters said. "What exactly are you talking about, Emma?"

"I've been thinking for some time that it would be a good idea for first responders to have training on how to interact safely with dogs. At many of the calls they respond to, they're confronted with family pets who may be upset and protective. Dogs are very sensitive and they pick up on the tension around them. Knowing how to de-escalate that tension in the dogs as well as the people could make it easier for police, firefighters and EMTs to do their jobs and could prevent injury to both animals and people." She turned to Rutledge. "You can be my first student, and help me iron out any wrinkles in the program."

"I don't—" Rutledge began.

But Walters interrupted him. "What Emma is describing sounds like an excellent program. It wouldn't be a bad idea for all our officers to go through similar training. You can be the first."

"I can't possibly take time out from my duties for that now," Rutledge said. "Not with this fire, and a killer to track down."

"You can schedule the class later," the chief said. "But I'm making it a requirement."

Rutledge wanted to argue, she could see, but he clamped his mouth shut. She and the chief moved out of his office, back toward the lobby. "Thank you," she said. "And I'm sorry I stormed in here so upset."

"I think your anger was justified, and I think the

course you're designing is a good way to address the problem. So thank you."

She started to say goodbye but hung back. Something else Rutledge had said was nagging at her. "What's this about a killer?" she asked.

"You haven't seen the story on the news?"

"I haven't had time to listen to the news. I've had my hands more than full with my own dogs and the evacuees' pets, not to mention the press."

"The press have been bothering you?"

"They're looking for human-interest stories related to the wildfire. I understand, and I know the publicity could be good for DCA, but I don't have the bandwidth to deal with them right now. Brady helped escort the last bunch off the property this afternoon."

"Don't hesitate to call if they show up again. I'll send an officer to clear them out."

"Thanks. I hope I don't need that. But what about this killer?"

"I don't think he's anything for you to worry about. The Idaho State University killer, Kent Anderson, escaped the South Boise Prison complex a couple of days ago and is supposedly headed here. We haven't had a definite sighting since a tourist claimed to have dropped him off on the north side of town. But keep an eye out for anyone suspicious hanging around."

"One thing about having dozens of dogs on the premises," she said. "No one sneaks up on us." Another worry intruded. "Any word about Dillon? Someone told me he and Bentley went out to search for a lost hiker and were cut off by the fire."

"Nothing to report there, though they would have had to get pretty far off track to be in an active burn area.

We think they're having to take a circuitous route back to town and are out of phone range."

"I hope they're okay." She had a soft spot for the handsome cop, not to mention his dog.

"Anything else I can do for you?" Walters asked.

"Just keep Captain Rutledge away from dogs."

AT HOME FRIDAY EVENING, Ava changed into leggings and a sweatshirt and switched on the TV while she puttered around the house. Lacey had made herself comfortable on the sofa. Eli was working late tonight, so Ava heated leftovers for dinner and settled on the sofa beside the dog. "You can't take up all the room," she said as she scooted Lacey over to make a place for herself.

"Two searches with very different aims continue tonight outside Jasper, Idaho, as authorities hunt for escaped mass murderer Kent Anderson, who is reported to be at large in the area of the Gem Creek fire. The wildfire has consumed over twelve thousand acres of public land in the area, but threatens several neighborhoods. Also missing in the vicinity is former Chicago DJ Roz Kern, who disappeared while hiking with friends shortly before the trail she was on was closed by authorities due to the fire danger."

Ava leaned forward and punched the remote to up the volume on the television as a sandy-haired woman with large glasses appeared on the left half of the split screen. White block letters beneath her identified her as "Rockin' Roz's Best Friend." "With us this evening we have Cheri Benton," the female news anchor, a Latinx woman with short dark hair and large gold hoop earrings, said. "Cheri, you were hiking with Roz this morning, is that correct?"

"Um, yes, that's right."

"And how did Roz seem to you this morning?" the anchor asked.

"She likes to be called Roslyn now." Cheri tucked a strand of hair behind one ear and shifted in her chair. "She was fine. Looking at the scenery and taking pictures and stuff."

The anchor's image was replaced by a picture of a slight woman with shoulder-length blond hair and a harried expression. Obviously a candid shot taken on a city street, this was a far cry from the glamorous woman in the publicity shot that the police department had received when Roslyn first disappeared.

"Roz—Roslyn—Kern was a top-rated disc jockey for Chicago rock station WZPR until January of this year, when she abruptly broke her engagement with morning drive-time partner, Matthew 'Mad Matt' Judson, and left the radio station. Since this, Ms. Kern has avoided the public eye and refused to answer questions about her erratic behavior."

"Maybe she didn't think she owed anyone an explanation for her private decision," Ava said.

The anchor's image replaced the photo of Roslyn. "Cheri, I understand your friend is pregnant."

"Yes." Cheri looked uncomfortable.

"Who is the baby's father?" the anchor—Ava thought her name was Val—asked.

"I don't know," Cheri said. "Roslyn never said and I respected her privacy."

"We spoke with Matt Judson and he denies being the father of Roz's child."

"Oh, Matt definitely isn't the father," Cheri said. "I know that much."

"Why did Roz come to Idaho?" Val asked. "Does she know someone here?"

"No. She just came on vacation. Like we did. We ran into each other in the coffee shop in Jasper this morning and all decided to go hiking together." Cheri's voice broke. "I should have stayed with her when she told me to go ahead. I could have waited while she took her pictures and we could have walked back together. If I'd done that, she would be here now."

"Perhaps Roz wanted you to leave her," Val said. "Maybe she came to Idaho intending to disappear."

Cheri shook her head, eyes wide. "No. She wouldn't do that."

"Does Roz know Kent Anderson?" Val asked.

Cheri frowned. "Who is that?"

Another photo appeared on the screen, this one a mug shot of a man with thinning brown hair, a sharp nose and a grim expression. "In May of last year, Kent Anderson, a former teaching assistant at Idaho State University, entered a classroom carrying a semiautomatic rifle and shot and killed six people, including a professor. He was sentenced to life in prison last month and was awaiting transfer to the supermax facility in Florence, Colorado, when he escaped and headed straight for Jasper, Idaho, where he vanished in the same location where Roslyn Kern disappeared."

"Roslyn didn't know him," Cheri protested. "How could she?"

"Thank you for talking with us, Cheri," Val said. Cheri's image disappeared and the shot widened to show Val and a U-shaped desk with a handsome older man with swept-back silvering hair.

"That's quite a coincidence," the man said. "Two people disappearing on the same day in the same remote area."

"Roz Kern and Kent Anderson are about the same age," Val said. "His trial was just beginning when she dumped her fiancé and left her job at the radio station."

"Why would a young woman with a stellar career and a devoted fiancé leave everything and disappear into obscurity, only to turn up pregnant a few months later, refusing to talk about the father of her unborn child, then abruptly head to Idaho and drop off the map?" The male anchor shook his head, his expression somewhere between concern and scolding. "It's a mystery you can be sure we'll be following closely."

Ava switched off the television. Considering Kent Anderson had been under lock and key for the better part of the last two years, the idea that he might be the father of the baby being carried by a young woman in Chicago was ludicrous. But plenty of people would latch on to the idea. Heaven help Roslyn Kern when she did surface again.

She picked at her meal but finally gave up and hugged a pillow to her chest. Everything about the news report had unsettled her, from the nervous, on-the-spot friend, to the snide innuendo of the anchors. Maybe it was because she and Roslyn Kern were close to the same age, and she had been a single woman on her own in Chicago.

She leaned over and hugged Lacey. "Dillon and Bentley will find Roslyn Kern," she said. "But I'd just as soon Kent Anderson stayed far away."

A QUICK RECONNAISSANCE of the path on either side of the cave showed no one and nothing disturbed that Dillon could see. Bentley sniffed the ground and whined, a faint, low sound that Dillon took to be a question as to why they were even out here at this time of night, instead of sleeping. He stood for a moment outside the cave, breathing in the air that still carried a faint hint of smoke, the utter silence of the moment surrounding him. Some of the tension eased from his shoulders. The noise he had heard was probably only a pack rat, or the wind. Finding Roslyn again, learning about the baby, detouring because of the fire—the tensions of the day were getting to him. Time to relax and get some sleep.

He turned to walk back toward the cave as a woman's scream cut through the air, stopping his heart, then sending him running.

Bentley was faster, barking furiously at the figure that emerged from the cave, running in the opposite direction. Man and dog gave chase, Bentley sounding the alarm and speeding forward. The figure left the path, crashing through the brush as it leaped toward the creek, like an elk bounding through the forest. But this was no elk. "Stop! Police!" Dillon called, but the fleeing man kept going. Dillon ran until his sides ached. Bentley had stopped barking, and though the thick underbrush slowed him, he kept powering through, until Dillon called him back. "Bentley, come!" he commanded, and the dog obediently wheeled around and headed back to him.

He stared into the darkness, though he could no longer see whoever he had been pursuing. This must have been the person Bentley had alerted them about earlier today. Who was he and what was he doing, following them?

He bent over, trying to catch his breath, waiting for Bentley to reach him, then he remembered the scream. Roslyn! He turned and pounded back down the trail. "Roslyn!" he called as he neared the cave. "Roslyn, are you all right?"

"I'm fine." Her voice was strong and steady. She met him at the entrance to the cave. "Who was that?" she asked. "I woke up and someone was right by me. At first I thought it was you, then I realized it wasn't. That's when I screamed."

He shook his head and ushered her back inside. He sat beside the fire and stirred the coals, and began feeding in small pieces of tinder to get the blaze going again. He wanted the light and heat the fire would give. She settled onto the log beside him. "Was someone really there?"

"Someone was there," he said. "Bentley and I chased after him, but he got away."

She hugged herself. "Do you think it was the same person Bentley sensed was following us on the trail?"

"I don't know. You go on back to sleep. I'm going to stay up in case whoever it was comes back."

"No way could I sleep now," she said. "Let's have some tea." She turned and reached back for the packs they had piled behind the logs, then froze. "Dillon? Where's my pack?"

"It's not with mine?" He turned to look.

"No." She looked around. "Do you think whoever was here took it?"

He slipped a flashlight from his pack and shone it around the cave. They found the pack on the floor near the cave entrance, the contents spilling from it. Roslyn's camera bag was a few feet closer to the entrance. She picked up the bag and opened it. "The camera is still here," she said.

"He was probably trying to steal the pack when your scream startled him," Dillon said.

"The whole pack, or just the camera?" She removed

the camera from the pack and switched it on. "It doesn't seem damaged."

Dillon came to stand beside her. "Why would a thief want your camera? Especially here in the middle of nowhere?"

She shook her head. "It's worth some money but not out here." She started to switch it off, but he covered her hand with his, stopping her. "What did you photograph today?" he asked.

"Wildflowers. Some shots of the fire and scenery."

"Let me see."

She handed him the camera and showed him how to scroll through the photos. He scanned close-ups of brilliantly colored wildflowers and wider shots of the scenery, smoke clouds making for dramatic skies as a backdrop to mountain peaks and wildflower-filled meadows. He stopped on a photo that showed rocks in the distance, and a figure standing against the rocks. "Who is this?" he asked.

She leaned over his shoulder to look. "I don't know," she said. "I was focused on that patch of paintbrush and sunflowers, not the background."

"Could it be one of the friends you were hiking with?"

She took the camera from him, pressed a few buttons, then studied the screen again. She had enlarged the photo and zoomed in on the figure in the background. The image wasn't clear, but it was clearly a man with very short dark hair and pale skin, dressed in a black T-shirt and khaki trousers. "It's not anyone I know," she said. She looked up, her green eyes troubled. "Do you think it's the person who's been following us?"

"Maybe." He studied the photograph for a long moment, then switched off the camera. "Maybe he knew you took that photo of him and he doesn't like the idea. He followed us and waited until he thought we were asleep, then tried to steal the camera."

"The idea gives me the creeps." She replaced the camera in its case, and stuffed it into her pack and returned the pack to rest next to Dillon's.

"I should have kept after him," Dillon said. "Maybe Bentley and I could have caught up with him."

She slipped her arm into his and leaned close. "I'm glad you didn't leave me here by myself," she said. "I feel safer with you around." She stretched up and kissed him, a gentle pressure from her lips, her arms moving around him, urging him closer.

His earlier restraint fell away in the warmth of that kiss. If she wanted this, then he definitely wasn't going to argue. "I've missed you," she murmured as her lips traced a trail down his throat.

"I missed you, too." He shaped his hand to her breast, reveling in the new fullness.

She arched against him, the baby bump pressing into his stomach, the sensation new, but somehow thrilling. "Maybe now isn't the best time or place," she said. "But I really want to make love with you."

"Yeah. I want that, too." It was crazy—they hadn't seen each other in five months, and he had spent so much of that time angry and confused over his feelings about her. But now that they were here all he could feel was how much he wanted her. Not Rosie Kenley, but Roslyn Kern. The beautiful, bewitching woman who was going to have his baby.

He stood and pulled her to her feet beside him, then traced his hands down her sides and over the hard round curve of her abdomen. "Sexy, huh?" she teased.

"Yes." He crushed his lips to hers, letting her know just how sexy he found her. They moved together, kissing and caressing, a dance without music, until finally she led him to the bed of pine boughs. Before they lay down, he reached down and flicked away the space blanket. "I draw the line at making love on a bed of aluminum foil," he said.

She laughed, the sound sending a new rush of heat through him. "I agree, but I don't really want pine needles poking me in the back."

"Wait just a minute." He returned to their packs and pulled out the extra jackets they both carried. He spread these over the pine needles, then eased down and pulled her on top of him. Not bad. And when she straddled him and began kissing him again, it wouldn't have mattered if he had lain directly on the ground. All he felt was her against him, stirring a need that had never really abated since they had parted five months ago.

She started undressing and he lay back, wishing the light was better, though on second thought, the play of flickering firelight across her breasts, her bare shoulders and her face was an erotic show he didn't think he would ever tire of watching. Her breasts were fuller now, her body more rounded and sensual. When she was naked, she knelt beside him, the sexiest sight he had ever seen. "Now it's your turn," she said and reached to unbutton his jeans.

Chapter Eight

Roslyn remembered what Dillon had been like in bed before—so confident, sure of himself, clearly practiced in pleasing a woman. He enjoyed sex and made sure she enjoyed it, too. They had had fun together, something she had needed so badly just then.

The man who was stripping off his clothing in front of her now was the same, and different, too. Being with him now felt more intense. Urgent. They had a history together now. They had made the child she carried inside her, and that added to the moment an excitement she hadn't known before.

He lay back on their makeshift bed and beckoned her. "I think it will be more comfortable for you on top," he said. His gaze swept over her body and a grin spread across his face. "And I get to enjoy such a great view."

She had been self-conscious about undressing in front of him, but had made herself get it over with, telling herself he wouldn't see that much in the firelight. But what he saw obviously pleased him, and the desire in his eyes made her own need for him more urgent.

She straddled him, his erection hot at her entrance, but she made him wait, moving in a sensuous dance against him, tracing her fingers over his chest and stomach, rubbing against him until they were both panting with need. His fingers grasped her hips. "You're driving me wild," he said. Then he slid one hand around to touch her and she moaned.

Hands flat on his chest, she pushed herself up and slid over him, the sensation of him filling her stealing her breath for a moment. She had missed this so much. She had missed him.

With his hands, he coaxed her to move, and with his mouth he caressed her face and then her breasts. She trembled with her need for him and tried to hold back, to make the moment last, but he wouldn't let her. He knew just how to touch her to bring her to completion and she didn't have the will to resist. She didn't want to resist, and before long her climax shuddered through her, with an intensity she didn't remember from before.

He grew still, holding her, and she stared down at him, dazed and unable to stop smiling. Then he began to move again, and her with him. She stroked the side of his face and his chest, and moved with care to give him pleasure. She was rewarded when he cried out and arched upward. She rode the wave of his climax, then collapsed onto him, his arms tight around her, her body cradled between his legs.

It was a long time before either of them spoke. She slid off him and lay by his side, her head in the hollow of his shoulder, his arm still around her. "We should probably check if the packs are still here," she said after a while. "I think anyone could have come in while we were busy and I wouldn't have noticed."

"Bentley would have let us know," Dillon said.

At the sound of his name the dog, who lay by the fire with his back to them, as if to give them privacy, raised his head and gave a single thump of his tail. "Good boy," Dillon said, and Bentley lay down again, silent.

"I wish I knew who the man was in that picture," she said.

But Dillon didn't answer. He breathed deeply and evenly beside her, already asleep.

Trapped By Wildfire
Rockin' Roz Risks All on Wilderness Hike

Former Chicago DJ Roslyn "Rockin' Roz" Kern took what began as an innocent hike while on vacation in Jasper, Idaho, last Friday. But the pleasant outing with friends turned into a dangerous one as Roz ended up lost in the wilderness, her path back to civilization cut off by an out-of-control wildfire.

Many residents of the Windy City know Roz from her top-rated morning drive-time show with fellow DJ—and former fiancé—Matthew "Mad Matt" Judson. Roz abruptly left the station in January, following a breakup with Mad Matt that had the airwaves buzzing. Though she has kept a low profile since then, this paper recently learned that Roz is expecting a baby. Is the father Mad Matt? And was Roz's hike really so innocent? Despairing about her broken engagement and future as an unemployed single mom, did Roz deliberately leave her friends, searching for another way to end her dilemma?

Authorities in Jasper are supposedly searching for Roz, but the wildfire is hampering their efforts. Several neighborhoods in the area have been evacuated and local residents are worried about their safety as the fire nears the small town.

"THIS SO-CALLED REPORTER must be making things up as he goes along." Brady tossed aside the printout from a website that Teresa had handed out to the gathered officers. "She talks like the fire is racing toward town unchecked. Jasper isn't in any danger, and those neighborhoods were evacuated as a precaution, not because anyone was in immediate danger."

"This one is worse." Ava passed over another printout, this one from a Chicago tabloid. "Rockin' Roz pursued by deadly killer while fleeing wilderness fire," she read. She tossed the paper aside. "I saw a television story last night where the anchors tried to insinuate that Roslyn Kern came here and ditched her friends so she could meet up with Kent Anderson. They even tried to insinuate that Anderson might be the father of Kern's unborn child. Never mind that he's been in jail for two years."

"Stranger things have happened," Brady said.

"Oh, please," Ava said. "We have no idea where Roslyn Kern or Kent Anderson are, but there's no reason to believe they're close to each other."

"What about Roslyn being pregnant?" Jason asked. "Did Dillon say anything about that in his message to you?"

Brady shook his head. "All the text says is that he found Roslyn and they planned to spend the night in those caves above Cow Creek and head back on the trail today." He leaned back in his chair. "I sent a reply asking if he needed anything, or wanted someone to hike out to meet them, but I never heard back."

"From what I remember, cell reception is terrible there around the creek," Ava said.

The door opened and the chief entered and everyone sat up straighter. Even Lacey, Ava's police K-9, grew more alert, focused on the podium at the front of the room. The bags under Chief Walters's eyes were fuller, the lines around his mouth and across his forehead deeper. Brady suspected he had worked late and come in early. Behind him, Captain Rutledge looked fresh and crisp, a commander straight out of Central Casting, except he didn't have the character to go with the image.

After a brief pause, two more men entered. Captain Eli Thorne from the McCall, Idaho, police department was familiar to them from a case they had worked recently, involving a disgruntled employee setting bombs around town. He and Ava had become involved during that investigation and seemed pretty serious about each other now. But what was he doing here this morning?

Behind Eli was a fifty-something man with the lean build of a runner and close-cropped salt-and-pepper hair. He wore a suit, but everything about him, from his erect posture to the hard look in his eyes as he scanned the room, screamed law enforcement. "Looks like a Fed," Ava whispered next to him.

"Brady, do you have any more messages from Dillon?" the chief asked.

"No, sir," Brady said.

"Anyone else heard from Dillon?" Walters asked.

Everyone shook their heads.

Walters looked down at the papers in front of him. "As you can see from the articles and online postings Teresa printed for us, there's a lot of interest from the press in this Roslyn Kern. Apparently, she's something of a celebrity in Chicago."

"A pregnant celebrity lost in an out-of-control wildfire, pursued by a dangerous killer," Ava said, her voice carrying plenty of snark.

Walters's scowl showed what he thought of that assessment. "I spoke with the incident commander this morning and he estimates the Gem Creek fire is thirty-five percent contained. There's still activity near Skyline Road, so we're going to keep that area closed for another day. The slurry bomber will be working in there this morning. Spotters overnight pinpointed areas hotshot crews will focus on."

"Did the spotters see any sign of Dillon and Roslyn Kern?" Cal Hoover asked.

"Not of them," Walters said.

"If they were in the caves by Cow Creek, they wouldn't have been visible from the air," Brady said.

"You said 'not of them,'" Lieutenant Margaret Avery said. A veteran of Jasper PD, Margaret had a reputation as an excellent detective. "Did the spotters see someone else?"

Walters plucked a sheet of paper from the pile in front of him. "A spotter plane flying over Williams Park saw a campfire, with a single camper visible, at approximately eleven fourteen p.m."

"How can he be sure it was a campfire, and not a remnant of the wildfire?" Rutledge asked.

"Apparently, they use infrared cameras that allow them to differentiate the heat generated by humans and animals from that of the fire," Walters said. "They were sure this was a person by a campfire."

"No one has reported any campers missing, and there are no cars at the trailhead," Jason said.

"I doubt that's a camper," Rutledge said. "We know Kent Anderson was last seen not far from the Williams Gap Trailhead."

"But what would he be doing way out there?" Ava asked.

"Deputy Rand from the US Marshals is here to address that."

Deputy Rand moved to the microphone. "The US Marshals Service is in charge of the pursuit and apprehension of Kent Anderson. Following his escape from custody outside Kuna, Idaho, which resulted in the death of two law enforcement officers, we have tracked him to McCall, Idaho." He glanced over his shoulder. "Captain Thorne has more information about that."

Eli took Rand's place at the microphone. "We've received new information about Kent Anderson I wanted to share with you," he said. "We've tracked down his connection to this area—a woman named Deena Marquette. She's Anderson's cousin and they apparently grew up together. She and her boyfriend, Sean Tyson, moved to Jasper eight months ago. She and Anderson exchanged letters while he was in prison and apparently used a childhood code to pass messages that looked innocuous on the surface, but are now believed to have included plans for Anderson's escape. Prison authorities reviewed all of his correspondence after the escape and they think they've figured out the code. Marquette and Tyson agreed to place a cache of supplies for Anderson near the Williams Gap Trail—a backpack, food and water, and other equipment he could use to travel cross-country. Apparently, he planned to travel through backcountry all the way to Alaska."

"That could take months," Rutledge said.

"Anderson was willing to take the time," Thorne said. "Though Marquette and Tyson aren't admitting any part in the plan, she did say Anderson had a lot of experience camping and backpacking and liked being out of doors.

He probably thought the fire would make good cover for his getaway."

"Do you think he's the lone camper the spotter saw?" Ava asked.

Eli started to answer, but Rand interrupted. "We don't think the camper spotted in the fire zone is Kent Anderson," he said. He nodded to Eli, a clear dismissal, and Eli yielded the podium. "We also interviewed Marquette and Tyson, as well as a friend of Anderson's, a man named Donald Aldeen, who lives in Yellow Pine, Idaho, and is purported to have been friends with Anderson since the third grade. He was very cooperative and says Anderson's plan is to head west to Nevada. We believe Marquette and Tyson made up the story about Alaska to deliberately mislead us. I'm here today to thank you all for your assistance with the search so far, but we'll be moving the pursuit to the west as of this morning."

"Have there been other reliable sightings of Anderson in the west?" Ava asked. Leave it to Ava to question the Feds while everyone else remained silent.

"We are not releasing any further information at this time," Rand said. "All you need to know is you don't have anything to worry about."

"What about all these stories in the news?" Captain Rutledge asked. "The media is needlessly frightening people by focusing on Anderson's supposed presence here."

"We don't have time to waste contradicting the media," Rand said. "Besides, it's to our benefit to have Anderson believe the search is still focused here." He stepped back and Walters moved to the microphone again.

"Thank you, Deputy Rand," he said. "I know you're very busy with this search, so we won't keep you any longer."

"Thank you, Chief." Rand nodded to the other man at the front of the room, then left.

Everyone waited a long beat until they were sure Rand was gone. "If that camper the spotters saw in the fire area isn't Anderson, who is it?" Lieutenant Cal Hoover asked. Tall and taciturn, Cal was an experienced officer and others listened when he spoke.

"It could be Dillon and Ms. Kern," Rutledge said.

"I have the coordinates where the camper was spotted," Walters said. He turned to the map behind him, consulted the paper in his hand, then positioned a red pin. "About here. About twenty yards off the Williams Gap trail, on the edge of that big open area known as Williams Park."

"Less than a mile from the Cow Creek caves," Brady said.

"We don't know for sure Dillon and Roslyn made it all the way to Cow Creek," Rutledge said. "The campfire could have been theirs."

"The report from the spotter says their equipment only picked up one person," Walters said.

"Do you know what other information the marshals have that makes them so sure Anderson isn't here?" Margaret asked.

"They seem to put a lot of stock in the information they gleaned from Anderson's friend," Brady said. "Do we know anything about him? How likely is it that he's telling the truth?"

"You heard Deputy Rand," Rutledge said. "This isn't our concern."

"Except if they're wrong and that is Anderson out there, and Dillon is close to him, it is our concern," Ava said.

They all looked to the chief, waiting for his answer.

"We have an unknown person in an area that is closed to the public," Walters said. "It makes sense to keep an eye on the situation and learn what we can about this person, as our schedule allows. But we have plenty of real crime to keep us busy here."

Chairs creaked as bodies shifted. "If the Feds are wrong and that is Anderson, does he know Dillon and Roslyn are on the same trail?" Brady asked.

"If he does, wouldn't he be moving away from them?" Jason asked.

"Most likely, yes," Thorne said. "Unless he's learned that Dillon is a law enforcement officer. He's made several public declarations, at his trial and in interviews he has given since his conviction, that he intends to kill any law enforcement officers who cross his path. He's attacked several officers in his time in prison, resulting in him spending much of his sentence in administrative segregation."

Solitary confinement, Brady translated. "How did he ever escape?" he asked.

"Ahead of his transfer to the federal supermax prison in Florence, Colorado," Thorne said. "An accomplice, one of the prison trustees, secreted a weapon in the transport van and Anderson used it to kill both his guards. He unlocked his restraints, stole some clothing, and hitchhiked to Jasper."

"He wouldn't know Dillon was an officer," Cal said. "He was on that trail as a search and rescue volunteer."

"The spotters are doing regular flyovers of the fire and we've asked them to keep an eye out for anyone," Walters said.

"Why not set a helicopter down in the area and send a

team after this mysterious camper?" Rutledge asked. "If it does turn out to be Anderson, we'd be heroes."

"We don't have the budget to send a helicopter after someone who might not even be a threat," Walters said. "Thought I doubt we'd find a pilot who would agree to go in there. The terrain is very rough in that area, and visibility is poor because of the smoke, and most of the available aircraft are helping to fight the fire."

"If this is Anderson, depending on his position, he might spot a group of officers headed toward him," Eli said. "The letters he exchanged with his cousin indicate they agreed to supply him with guns and ammunition, and he had sworn to kill cops on sight."

"In any case, that decision is out of our hands," Walters said. "We can do some low-key investigating to try to learn the identity of the lone camper, but federal marshals are in charge of the pursuit of Anderson. Local forces are on call to assist."

"Someone should warn Dillon," Ava said. "A couple of us could hike up the trail to meet him."

"I've spoken to Search and Rescue about doing just that," Walters said. "I would send a couple of officers with them. But Commander Wayne says they're stretched to the max dealing with the usual demands of a holiday weekend. They've had three calls in the last two days, in addition to the search for Roslyn Kern. Another lost hiker, an ATV accident, and a white water rafting accident. Andrea pointed out that Dillon is an experienced rescue volunteer who is well equipped to spend a night out and he hasn't indicated he and Ms. Kern are in any kind of trouble."

"Roslyn Kern is pregnant," Jason said.

"That is a concern," Walters said. "I asked about get-

ting a rescue helicopter to her — provided we could locate her and Dillon. But all air resources in the area are
focused on fighting the wildfire. We'll keep trying to
reach out to Dillon and searching for Anderson. In all
probability, the marshals are right and Anderson is on
his way to Nevada. Dillon and Ms. Kern are on their way
back to Jasper, and Anderson is moving away from town
as quickly as he can." He turned to Rutledge. "Captain,
what do we have on the docket for today?"

Rutledge stepped forward and began reading off a
list of the usual problems that accompanied a busy holiday weekend—illegal fireworks, minor traffic accidents,
shoplifting, noise complaints and angry exchanges fueled
by overindulgence in alcohol. "We also have the media
harassing everyone in town," Rutledge concluded.

"The press is allowed to be here as long as they don't
trespass on private property," Walters said.

"They are," Rutledge agreed. "But I think it would
help calm the situation, and possibly quell some of the
rumors that are spreading around, if we held a press conference to talk about the search for Anderson and for Dillon and Roz Kern."

"No," Walters said. "I don't have time to deal with
the press."

"I could speak to them," Rutledge said. He smoothed
back his hair. "I'm used to dealing with the media."

"No," Walters repeated. He scanned the room, his gaze
sharp. "Any questions?" No one spoke up.

"Dismissed. Do a good job today."

Chairs scraped back and voices rose as everyone collected their belongings and filed out of the room. Thorne
met Ava and Brady at the door. The McCall police captain had an imposing presence, but his stern face relaxed

into a smile as Lacey leaned against him, tail wagging. "Sorry I can't stay longer," he told Ava as he rubbed the dog's ears. "McCall is even more crowded with visitors this weekend than Jasper. I'll call you later."

"Let us know if you hear anything more about Anderson," Ava said. "If I wasn't on duty today, I'd take Lacey for a hike out that way, just to have a look around."

"The trailhead is closed to the public," Brady said.

"Lacey and I aren't public," she said. "We're sworn law enforcement officers."

"Woof," Lacey barked, as if in agreement.

"One more reason for you both to stay far away from anyone who might be Anderson." Thorne kissed her cheek. "I'll see you later."

"See you." Ava watched him go, then turned to Brady. "Have you tried texting Dillon again? He needs to know about the other person who's out there near him. Even if it isn't Anderson, the person might be up to no good."

"I've tried calling and texting, but I'm not getting through."

She sighed. "At least he has Bentley with him."

"Bentley isn't a police dog—he's a search dog, like Winnie," Brady said. His dog, Winnie, a yellow Lab, was terrific at finding people, but her biggest asset was her friendly, gentle demeanor. "Search dogs aren't supposed to be threatening." Lacey didn't look particularly threatening at the moment, either, but the German shepherd was trained to take down criminals.

"Any dog would smell or hear someone approaching a long time before Dillon would know they were there," Ava said. "He can warn Dillon if they're being followed."

"I figure Dillon will need all the help he can get," Brady said. "He probably has his hands full with this

Roslyn Kern—celebrity DJ who couldn't find her way on a marked hiking trail."

"You don't know what happened out there," Ava said. "It's easy to get turned around if you're not familiar with the area, and with the fire and everything, anyone could get lost."

"You're right," Brady admitted. "I'm just worried about Dillon. I'll feel better when he's back home."

"We all will." She looked down at Lacey. "Come on, girl. Let's go distract the reporters." She grinned at Brady. "The cameras always zero in on Lacey."

"Jasper's finest," he said. He waited until they were gone and pulled out his phone and sent yet another text to Dillon. There's someone else out there with you— lone man. Could be escaped fugitive Kent Anderson or someone else, he wrote. Watch your six.

Chapter Nine

Dillon woke as soon as Roslyn got out of their makeshift bed. It wasn't noise that woke him, but the absence of her weight and warmth beside him. He opened his eyes to thin, gray light. "Is everything okay?" he asked.

"I'm fine." She retrieved her clothing from the cave floor and began to dress. "I just need to, um, use the bushes."

"Don't go too far." He told himself he should look away as she raised her arms to slide her tunic over her head or bent to pull on her jeans, but her body fascinated him—the lusher curves, and the swelling abdomen. Their baby. He tore his gaze away and found her watching him.

"I look a lot different now, I know," she said.

"You're beautiful." He sat up and reached for her. "If we were somewhere besides a cave in the middle of nowhere, I'd take you back to bed right now."

Heat flashed in her eyes. "I'll take a rain check on that offer." Her trained contralto voice made even an offhand comment like this sound sexy. She tugged her hand away from his. "Now, I really do have to go."

She finished dressing and slipped from the cave. He thought of the man he had chased away last night and rose to follow her to the entrance to the cave, where he stood and kept watch. But he saw no one, and heard nothing but birds beginning their morning chorus.

When he heard her returning, he moved to the fire ring and began coaxing a blaze from last night's coals. "Do you have more coffee?" she asked.

"Yes." He filled the pot with water and set it to heat.

She sank onto a log across from him. "I don't drink much caffeine these days but I really need a cup this morning." She rubbed at her ankle.

"Is the ankle bothering you?" he asked.

"Not much," she said, but her frown told him she was probably lying.

"Let me see." He moved over beside her and she shifted to allow him to remove her boot and sock. He probed at the puffy flesh around her anklebone. "I don't think it's as swollen as yesterday," he said.

"How many miles do we have to hike today?" she asked.

"About six." A long way over sometimes rough terrain on a painful ankle. "We'll take it slow."

She laughed. "I'm glad to hear it, since that's the only speed I'm capable of right now."

"How's the baby?" he asked.

She shaped both hands to the bump. "He, or she, is awake and raring to go."

He started to touch her, then hesitated. "Can I?" he asked.

"Of course." She smiled, the knowing grin of someone sharing a wonderful secret.

He placed his hand over the bump, fingers spread, and felt the flutter of movement beneath. That tiny sensation made him feel momentarily weightless.

"I know," she said, apparently interpreting the look on his face. "I'm still in awe."

His hand still on her, he met her gaze. "How did you feel when you found out?" he asked. "You can tell me the truth. This changed your whole life."

"I was shocked," she said. "And a little afraid. Raising a child—another human being—is such a big responsibility. And to do it alone…"

"You won't be alone," he said. Would she think he was presuming too much? "I want to be a part of my child's life," he added. Though he was beginning to hope he could be a part of her life, too.

"I want that, too," she said. "But when I first found out, I didn't know how you would feel. Some men feel blindsided by something like this. Resentful." She looked away. "It was one of the things Matt and I argued about, even before I found out our engagement was just a stunt to grab ratings."

He was beginning to really despise Mad Matt. "What do you mean?" he asked.

"He and I were talking, the way you do. I asked him how many children he thought we should have. He said none. He was very firm about it, too. No kids. He said it was a deal breaker for him. I was shocked. I told myself that he loved me and he would change his mind, but looking back on it now, I think we would have split up over that even if I hadn't learned what was really going on." She smoothed her shirt over her belly. "Maybe he even told me that so he would have a good excuse to break things off when the time came."

"Does that mean you're okay with having a baby now?"

"I'm more than okay. I'm excited and happy." Her

smile was genuine. Radiant. "Once the shock wore off and the reality set in, I realized that I was in as good a place as I could be to add a child to my life. I had a new career with a flexible schedule. I didn't have to answer to anyone but myself."

And now he was in the picture. Did she see that as a good thing—a partner to help raise this child—or as someone who would interfere? They had so many things to figure out, and only a few months to do so.

She bent forward and began pulling on her sock once more. "Don't worry about me today," she said. "I can be pretty stubborn when I set my mind to do something."

So could he, though he didn't say so. She would learn soon enough that he had made up his mind to look after her and the baby. After so many months of searching, he wasn't going to let her go again.

VALENTINE'S DAY AT Brundage Mountain Resort had attracted a crowd. When Dillon had set out for the resort that morning, he hadn't even thought about the date, but it didn't take long to notice the heart decorations everywhere, and the abundance of couples in the lift lines, sliding forward two by two.

Which was one reason the woman in the black ski pants and silver puffy jacket stood out in the crowd. She had a good figure and wore a black helmet with blond hair curling at the nape of her neck. Their eyes met across the line and she smiled at him and for a moment he didn't breathe. He was used to pretty women smiling at him but no one had ever stopped his breath before. Not because she was beautiful—though she was—but because it was as if she knew him, though he swore they had never met before.

He continued to watch her as the line inched forward. She had an air of separateness about her—not sadness, just something that was holding her apart from everyone else. The idea intrigued him, and he determined to try to find out more about her.

He had to do a little maneuvering to make sure he ended up on a chair with her, just a matter of letting another couple go ahead of him. He waited until the last second to slide up beside her, then waited until the lift was in the air before he turned to her and smiled. "Hi," he said. "My name's Dillon. It's a gorgeous day for skiing, isn't it?" Not the most original introduction in the world, but he didn't want to come on too strong.

"It is." She hesitated, then returned his smile. "I'm Rosie. I'm visiting from Chicago."

"Nice to meet you, Rosie from Chicago. Are you here with friends?"

"I'm by myself for the moment."

Smart woman, not revealing everything to an inquisitive stranger. "What about you?" she asked.

"I'm by myself, too." He looked around, toward the sign on the large pink and white banner draped across the midmountain restaurant, which proclaimed Brundage Is for Lovers. "I'd forgotten what day it was when I decided to come up this morning."

"I kind of feel like a unicorn on the ark," she said, but her smile took the sting out of the words.

"Hey, nothing wrong with being single," he said. He thought about adding that he was surprised someone as pretty as her was by herself, but that felt like such a line. And he had heard variations of the same often enough from his friends. As if good looks and commitment naturally went together.

"Are you from around here?" she asked.

"I live in Jasper, just north of here," he said.

"What do you do in Jasper?"

"I'm a cop." Better to get it out there—it would either relieve her fears that he was a serial killer shopping for his next victim or send her skiing off in the opposite direction as soon as possible. He had learned that not everyone was a fan of law enforcement.

Some of the tension went out of her and she angled toward him a little. "That must be interesting work."

"Jasper is a small town, so not usually that interesting." He had been involved in some exciting cases, but he wasn't one of those cops who felt the need to try to impress the people around him with his exploits. "What do you do in Chicago?"

"Nothing that interesting." She looked out at the expanse of groomed ski runs. "What's your favorite run here?"

He followed her lead into a conversation about the various skiing options. The more they talked, the more intrigued he became. Rosie had a low, contralto voice that was one of the sexiest things he had ever heard, and she was an experienced enough skier that when he suggested they try a more difficult blue run that led off from the top of the lift, she didn't hesitate.

"See you at the bottom," she said and took off, forcing him to pursue, which he didn't really mind since it afforded him a view of her skiing gracefully in front of him.

He passed her halfway down the run, but she caught up with him when they were almost to the bottom, and skied to a stop in a spray of snow, laughing. "That was wonderful," she said. "What other runs should we try?"

The smile she sent him warmed him through, in spite

of temperatures in the teens. "Tell me the last book you read that you enjoyed," she said on the way up, and there followed a discussion of novels—she enjoyed historical fiction, while he confessed a preference for detective novels, which made her laugh.

"Don't authors get things wrong and ruin the book for you?" she asked.

"Not in the really good novels," he said. "Besides, I'm always hoping I'll learn something."

"Do you solve many murders in Jasper?" she asked.

"There's a first time for everything."

At noon they stopped midmountain and ate beneath the Brundage Is for Lovers banner. She removed her helmet and goggles to reveal blond waves, and eyes a deeper shade of green than his own, with long lashes. Neither of them said anything when the server wished them a Happy Valentine's Day. "It is a good day," she said when the server had gone. "Even if I'm not celebrating Saint Valentine."

He toasted her with his water glass and silently thanked whatever fates had put them in the same lift line this morning. Though he never minded skiing alone, spending the day with her was an unexpected gift.

"Do you have a last name, Rosie?" he asked over bowls of chili smothered in cheese.

"Rosie Kenley."

He set down his spoon and extended his hand. "Pleased to meet you, Rosie Kenley. I'm Dillon Diaz."

"So what is a guy like you doing alone on a day like this?" she asked. "I'd have to be blind not to notice how every woman in the place looks at you. And you seem like the type who'd have plenty of friends."

He unwrapped a packet of crackers. "I'm not involved

with anyone at the moment and sometimes I prefer to ski alone."

"I'm sorry I ruined that for you," she said.

"I'm not." He spooned up chili, watching her as she ate also. "As long as we're asking nosy questions, what are you doing alone?" he hazarded after a few moments. "There are plenty of men here watching you, too."

She covered her mouth with her hand and choked back a laugh, glee dancing in her eyes. She sipped water, then sat back. "I guess I deserved that one. All right, I'll confess. I just split up with someone and the thought of staying in the city for Valentine's Day was just too much. Getting away and doing something active seemed like just the thing."

"Your ex must have been an idiot," he said.

"He is. But so was I." Her smile had faded and there was real pain behind her words, so he didn't ask for details, and she didn't volunteer any. "Do you want to keep skiing together this afternoon?" she asked. "I'll understand if you want to be alone."

"Now that I've met you, I don't want to be alone at all," he said. They spent the rest of the day together, attraction building, and when the lifts began to shut down, he was reluctant to leave her. "Do you want to have dinner?" he asked.

"Yes. I'd love that."

At dinner, she took a camera from her backpack and took a photo of him, then they took a selfie together. She leaned close to him and he put his arm around him. The perfume of her hair enveloped him as her breast pressed against his arm. "I could get used to this," he said in a low voice, and he saw the same desire he felt reflected back at him.

"I'm staying at the Grand Lodge," she said after they had battled over the check and she had reluctantly allowed him to pay. "Would you like to come back with me?"

"Yes."

They were barely though the door before they came together with a hunger that surprised him. She kissed him fiercely and he felt her need, which only made him want her more. Whoever that jerk was who broke up with her, Dillon was going to make sure she forgot about him tonight. He swept her into his arms and carried her into the bedroom. She threw back her head and laughed. "Too much of a cliché?" he asked as he stood by the bed.

She shook her head, then pulled his mouth down to hers. He fell with her onto the mattress, and together they swept half a dozen pillows from the spread and tore at each other's clothing. They weren't gentle or graceful or the least bit tentative, but oh, was it wonderful. Dillon didn't really believe in perfection, but that evening had been close to it. They had no past baggage or outside concerns to interrupt their focus on each other. Their lovemaking had been intense, intimate and magical. He had awakened beside her the next morning a little dazed— grateful and awed and unnerved by the intensity of his feelings. But he had long ago learned not to run from fear, but to ride with it and through it.

She rolled over and curled against him, her head on his shoulder. "What do you want to do today?" she asked.

"You came to ski," he said.

"I came to forget." She kissed his cheek. "You're helping with that."

They made love again, sleepily, tenderly, thoroughly. That must have been when it happened—one lucky sperm making its way to her egg because in their haste they forgot the condom. So strange to think in that moment they hadn't known what was to come.

They spent the morning making love, the afternoon exploring the town, and never made it to the ski slopes. That evening they returned to her room and watched a movie, cuddled together, before making love once more and falling asleep.

When Dillon woke Monday morning he knew she was gone before he even opened his eyes. The room was empty. Colder. He rolled over and stared at the note on hotel stationery, resting on the pillow that still bore the imprint from her hair. *Dearest Dillon. Thank you for the most wonderful weekend. I will never forget it, or you. I'm sorry I had to leave so early. I didn't want to wake you. All my best. Rosie.*

He crumpled the note and started to throw it away, throat tight with what he told himself was anger but he knew now had been grief. How many times that weekend had he started to ask for her number? But such practicalities had seemed out of place in the fantasy they were building.

He smoothed out the note and read it again. She said she would never forget him. But he needed to forget her. If she had really wanted to see him again, she would have offered her contact information. He turned the paper over to make sure nothing else was written there, but there was nothing but the hotel logo.

No, Rosie clearly meant for the weekend to be exactly what she said she needed—a break from real life. A life in which he had no place. He got up and dressed, and told himself it didn't matter. Long-distance relationships never worked out, and Chicago and Jasper were a long way apart.

But he kept the note, carefully folded and tucked into his bedside drawer at his house, where he took it out and reread it some nights when he couldn't sleep. He had started looking for her the next day, only to be frustrated by his inability to find any information about the mysterious Rosie Kenley.

And now she was here across from him. His mother, who believed in such things, would probably say the universe was bringing them together again. He didn't know about that, but he was happy to have a chance to build something between them, especially now that they had a child who would connect them forever.

Forever. A word that ought to fill him with fear but somehow didn't.

Chapter Ten

Roslyn and Dillon had coffee and protein bars for breakfast, while Bentley had the last of the kibble Dillon had packed. Not the most satisfying meal, but it would keep them going. While she repacked her belongings, he and Bentley walked down to the creek and refilled the water bottles with filtered water. He found a single boot print at the edge of the pool where he gathered water—maybe a size 10, with waffle soles. Probably made by whoever had tried to steal Roslyn's camera last night. The man in the photograph. Would he try to come after them again?

If Dillon were alone, he would show the boot print to Bentley, and order the dog to find the person who had made it. He was confident Bentley could follow the trail, barely eight hours old. But then what? The man might be armed. He might intend to harm them. Out of range of communication, with no backup and Roslyn and her unborn child to protect, Dillon couldn't risk a confrontation.

"Did you see any signs of last night's intruder?" Roslyn asked when he returned to the cave.

He hesitated, undecided how to answer her.

"I know you checked when you were out there." She slipped her daypack onto her back and shrugged to settle it on her shoulders. "You're always taking note of everything around you. I noticed it at the ski resort. I figured it was part of your law enforcement training—or did you do that even before you joined the police department?"

"I like to think I was pretty observant before." He handed her a water bottle and slipped the other into his pack. "But law enforcement training does make you hyper aware of everything that could be going on around you." Your life, and the lives of people you were sworn to protect, could depend on it.

"And you didn't answer my question," she said. "Did you see anything suspicious out there?"

"A single boot print," he admitted. "But not enough of a trail for me to follow." No need to mention Bentley. "My guess is the guy is long gone by now."

She searched his face, and he wondered if she knew he was holding back his real concern—that whoever had been tracking them since yesterday would keep following them. Or maybe he had already moved ahead of them on the trail, to find a spot where he could lie in wait to ambush them.

He glanced down at Bentley, who gazed up at him with trusting blue eyes. If the dog could talk, Dillon imagined he would say, *You can count on me to let you know if anyone is out there.* "Bentley will alert us if there's anything we need to worry about," Dillon told Roslyn. "If whoever it is is still following us, he won't know we have a secret weapon."

Her lips thinned as her mouth tightened, but no fear registered in her eyes. "I'm ready to leave when you are," she said.

"We'll take it slow," he said again, as much as a reminder to him as a reassurance for her. "And we'll rest whenever you need to. Just say the word."

"I'll be fine," she said. "I'm focusing on the prospect of a hot shower, a nap on a soft bed, and ice cream."

"Yeah. Those all sound good." Thoughts of those things would help him get through the rough stretches too—especially if he thought about enjoying them all with her.

CAMERA SHUTTERS CLICKED on all sides as Ava and Lacey passed through the crowd on the street around the police station. "Look! A police dog!" someone said.

"Isn't he gorgeous?" said someone else.

Ava resisted the urge to point out that "he" was a "she" and kept moving, though she watched the crowd out of the corner of her eye for any sign of trouble. The people filling the sidewalks and streets seemed to be a mix of tourists and media—the latter distinguished by bigger cameras, microphones and business casual clothing, while the tourists favored cell phones, shorts and T-shirts.

Lacey, as if aware of her admirers, practically pranced along the sidewalk, head up, mouth open in what Ava knew wasn't really a smile but sometimes looked like one.

"Officer, can you tell us anything about the search for Roslyn Kern?" A big man with a microphone blocked their path. Lacey sat as she had been trained, but kept her gaze fixed on the man. He noticed and took half a step back.

Ava tried for an expression that was pleasant, but stern. "I don't have any information on that," she said. "You're welcome to contact the police public information officer about that." That particular job rotated through the staff. Ava thought the current PIO was Captain Rutledge. Fitting, since he loved posing for the cameras. But

he wasn't going to be any more informative about Roslyn
Kern than Ava was.

"We understand one of your officers was part of the
initial search for Ms. Kern and that he is now also missing," the reporter continued. "Can you tell us about him?"

Ava fixed him with the cold look she reserved for people who especially annoyed her. Beside her, Lacey tensed.
Ava signaled the dog to stand down, but the reporter regarded the dog and took another step back. "Excuse me,
I have work to do," Ava said and moved around him.

They headed up West Main, passed the pink awnings
of the Pinup Girl Salon, then crossed over Elm. "Excuse
me, Officer." A gray-haired woman with a large canvas
tote stopped her. An older man in a large straw hat joined
them. "Can you tell us where to find a public restroom?"
the woman asked.

Ava gave them directions to the park in the center of
town and they thanked her and left. Half a block farther
on she helped a man with a laptop who was looking for
the public library. Shortly after that, a man pulled into a
no parking zone in front of Blaze's River Tours and Rafting, and Ava informed him that he would have to move
or his car would be towed. He wasn't happy, but he complied, and Ava and Lacey moved on. At the alley between
Millard's Diner and a T-shirt shop, Lacey began whining.

"What is it, girl?" Ava asked.

The dog looked down the alley, ears forward, forehead
creased in a way that made her look worried. Ava stared
down the alley, but saw nothing but the usual trash cans
and stacked pallets waiting to be picked up.

Lacey looked up at her, then back down the alley, and
let out a short bark. Something had the dog upset. Not
alert the way she would be if pursuing a suspect, but…

concerned. "Let's go see," Ava said and started cautiously down the alley, Lacey tugging at her lead.

The dog trotted straight to the set of trash cans at the diner's side door, and shoved her long snout between them. "Lacey, back!" Ava ordered, suddenly remembering that skunks sometimes raided restaurant trash cans. The last thing she wanted was to deal with a skunked dog.

Lacey obediently backed up, but she remained focused on the trash cans. She whined, and Ava was startled when a similar whine came in response. She unclipped her flashlight and crouched down to shine it into the gap between the two cans. A single brown eye stared back at her, soft and liquid. Then she glimpsed the tip of a floppy black ear.

"It's okay," she murmured, and carefully shifted one of the cans a few inches to the side.

The puppy cowered against the wall of the restaurant. Some kind of Lab-shepherd mix, Ava guessed, maybe a few months old. She squatted down and spoke softly to the dog, which looked to be in good shape, though it wore no collar. "Where did you come from, little one?" she asked.

The dog looked at her, trembling slightly.

She dug in her pocket for a treat and extended her hand, offering it. The puppy took it, wolfed it down, then moved toward her. The next thing she knew, it was pawing at her knee and licking her face. Lacey stepped forward to nudge the pup back, though very gently.

Ava picked up the dog and cradled it. Normal procedure with strays was to take them to the local animal shelter. But she knew from her work helping to evacuate families yesterday that the shelter was full up with cats, gerbils, ferrets and other non-canine pets at the moment. She looked down at the dog, whose brown eye-brows stood out against its black face. "I'm going to take you to a very nice lady," she said. "She'll know what to do with you."

THE MORNING WAS perfect for a hike. Though smoke lingered in the skies to the west, ahead of them all was clear and blue, sun warm on their skins, a pine-scented breeze moderating the temperature. Though Roslyn still carried the mask Dylan had given her, the air here was clear enough she felt safe foregoing it. She lifted her head and breathed in deeply. Even her ankle didn't hurt too badly, now that they were moving. She felt so alive and invigorated—happy in a way she had not been for a very long time.

Ahead of her, one of the reasons for her happiness strode, pack set on broad shoulders, sun glinting on his dark hair. The shadow of beard across his cheeks, visible when he turned to look back at her, only emphasized the handsome planes of his face—a face that had filled her dreams many nights since they had parted in February.

She had been desperate when she fled to Brundage Mountain. That was what the trip had felt like—not a relaxing vacation, but running away. Hiding. Valentine's was supposed to be a day for lovers, but every heart and cupid reminded her of how alone she was.

Then Dillon Diaz had slid onto the lift chair next to her and hit her with a dazzling smile and words that, if not flirtatious, definitely telegraphed his interest. She had been charmed, and relieved, too. Here was a chance to distract herself from misery. She decided to assume the role of the mysterious femme fatale. She flirted back, offering only teasing hints at her real identity. Instead of holding back against desire, she gave in and pursued him, though in truth he was never running away. She threw herself into enjoying every moment with him, whether it was skiing down the mountain, savoring a meal together or spending the night making love. She told herself that at the end of the weekend she would pop this fantasy bubble and it would all vanish, remaining only as a lovely dream she could look back on and smile.

Except that Dillon Diaz was no dreamy phantasm. He was a flesh-and-blood man who affected her much more than she wanted to admit. Back home in Chicago, he haunted her thoughts. The time they had spent together replayed in her dreams.

And the consequences of their weekend together had definitely not vanished. The day she had stared at the results of that first pregnancy test had felt like being pulled under by a tide she couldn't fight against. "Dillon." She had whispered his name. She had to get hold of him. She had to let him know.

But fear had won out over that thought. Fear and sheer inertia from having to deal with so much. She was ashamed that it had taken her five months to muster the courage to come to Jasper to find Dillon. And in the end, he had found her. Did the fact that they had come together again by chance mean anything, or was it just another odd coincidence?

Ahead of her, he stopped and called Bentley, who had been trotting down the trail before them. He turned to Roslyn. "How are you doing?" he asked.

"I'm great." She walked up to join him, then looked down toward her boots. "The ankle isn't hurting much at all today."

He nodded and scanned the area around them. Looking for the man who had followed them yesterday, she thought. "I wish I had gotten a better look at that guy," she said. At his questioning look, she added, "The one who was following us."

"I wish I knew why he wanted your camera," Dillon said. He pulled out his phone. "No signal."

"Let me check mine." She dug in her pocket and pulled out the phone, a newer model she had treated herself to when she started her new business—a tangible sign of the fresh start she was making with her life. No Signal warned a message on the screen. She tucked the phone away. "It doesn't matter," she said. "If we keep walking, we'll get to the trailhead before long, right?"

He nodded. "We should get a signal when we're closer to the parking area. I'll call ahead and have some people meet us there to check out your ankle."

"Or I could just go to a clinic in town," she said. "I really think I'm fine."

"Search and Rescue will want to declare the mission complete," he said.

The words brought her up short. "I'm a mission?"

He laughed. "That's why Bentley and I were out here in the first place, remember?"

Of course she remembered, but she hadn't thought about all the other people who were involved—a whole search and rescue team, apparently. "I'm really embarrassed now," she said. Then another thought ambushed her. "Do you think the media knows?"

"Are you worried the press followed you here to Jasper?"

"Oh, I'm sure they didn't." Interest in her had died down in recent weeks. "I guess I'm a little paranoid, after being in the spotlight so long."

"There's a lot going on in town this weekend," he said. He offered her one of the water bottles and she took it. "No one outside of Search and Rescue is going to pay much attention to us, I'm sure."

She drank, then returned the bottle to him. "I walked around a little bit downtown before I came hiking," she said. "The town is really cute. How long have you lived here?"

"My folks moved here when I was twelve."

"And you never wanted to move some place different—a big city?"

"Oh, I talked about it some, when I was a teenager. But when it came down to where I really wanted to live and work, this area was perfect for me. I like the outdoors and there's so much to do, any time of year. Hiking and fishing in summer and fall, skiing in winter and early spring. Rafting, climbing, golf if that's your thing. It's a short drive to McCall or Boise for live music. We have good restaurants and breweries."

She laughed at his enthusiasm. "You make it sound like paradise."

"I guess to me, it is." His expression sobered. "Maybe not so much for someone from the city."

"I live in the city for my work," she said.

"Do you think you'll go back to doing radio work?" he asked. "Do you miss it?"

She shook her head. "I don't miss getting up in the middle of the night to start work at six a.m. And I don't miss spending my weekends doing promotional events."

"You said you were ambitious. There's nothing wrong with that," he was quick to add.

She smiled down at the baby bump. "I guess now my ambitions lie elsewhere," she said. "I'm going to make a name for myself as an audiobook narrator and voice-over artist." She looked up and her eyes met his. "That's work I can do from anywhere."

The words hung between them, heavy with meaning—or no meaning at all. Was she really going to move hundreds of miles and change her life completely to be near a man who was still such a stranger to her? She could use the excuse that it would be easier for them to co-parent if they lived near each other. And Jasper looked like a wonderful place to raise children. But what happened if things didn't work out? Clearly, he was never going to leave his hometown, so she would have to pull up stakes and move again.

Was she being sensible to think this way, or a coward?

A low growl from Bentley distracted her from these whirling thoughts. Dillon was instantly alert. She stared at the dog, who was focused on something in the woods to their left. "What is it?" she whispered.

"I don't know." Dillon stepped forward, moving cautiously, his feet scarcely making a sound on the trail. "Get behind me."

It was more order than request, but she complied. This must be what he was like in cop mode, taking charge of the situation.

Bentley growled again, a low, fierce sound that seemed out of place coming from such a fluffy, normally friendly dog. Roslyn moved past Dillon to stand behind them, staring into the darkness amid the undergrowth. She held her breath as branches shifted and moved, even though there was no wind.

Bentley barked and started forward. "Bentley, come," Dillon commanded, and the dog returned to his side, though not without a last look over his shoulder. Dillon reached back beneath his shirt and drew out a pistol. She was sure he hadn't been wearing that yesterday, but the attempted theft of her camera must have unsettled him enough that he felt the need to be armed. "Who's there?" he shouted. "I'm a police officer. Come out with your hands where I can see them."

A crashing in the underbrush, and then a mule deer buck appeared between the trees. It stared at them a mesmerizing moment, then bounded off, away from them.

Roslyn let out the breath she had been holding and Dillon replaced the pistol in its holster at the small of his back. Bentley wagged his tail and grinned up at them both. "I should have realized he was barking at wildlife," Dillon said and bent to pat the dog. "I know his different barks by now."

"We're both a little on edge, I think." She rested a hand on his shoulder, calmed by the solid strength of him.

He nodded and straightened. "Are you ready to go on?" he asked.

"Yes. The sooner we get off this trail, the better." It was beautiful here, but for now she had enjoyed all the wildness she could handle.

Chapter Eleven

Brady told himself he should forget about Kent Anderson and let the US Marshals handle the search, but the knowledge that someone they couldn't identify was out there in the area where at least some people seemed to think Anderson might be nagged at him all during his morning patrol. When he returned to the station at lunchtime he sought out Margaret Avery. A tall woman with a sweep of long brown hair, the lieutenant was acknowledged as the force's best detective. "Do you have a minute to talk?" Brady asked.

"Sure." She swiveled her chair away from her computer to face him. "What's up?"

He sat in the visitor's chair in front of her desk and leaned closer. "What do you think of the marshal's theory that Kent Anderson is headed to Nevada?"

"I was just reading through the transcript of the interviews the McCall detectives did with Deena Marquette and Sean Tyson." She nodded at her computer screen. "I asked Eli to send them over."

"Did they say anything about Nevada?" Brady asked.

"No. They said Anderson asked for warm clothes and boots. Their impression was he intended to head north.

They claimed not to know where at first, then admitted Anderson had talked about going to Alaska."

"So that doesn't exactly contradict the guy who told the marshals Anderson was headed to Nevada. Anderson talked about Alaska, but maybe he decided on Nevada instead."

"No, but we also have the statement from the driver who dropped off the hitchhiker two blocks from the Williams Gap Trailhead," she said. "He was clear on his description of the man and identified Anderson from a photo lineup."

"That seems pretty definite," Brady said.

"But apparently the marshals discounted it," Margaret said.

"Deputy Rand said they thought Marquette and Tyson were lying, but they apparently believed the other guy they talked to. Do we know anything about him?"

She read from the notebook open in front of her. "Donald Aldeen, twenty-four, an auto mechanic in Yellow Pine. He and Kent Anderson apparently did attend the same elementary school. That's all I've been able to find out so far, but I think we'll be hearing more from Mr. Aldeen soon."

"Oh?" Brady sat up straighter. Margaret's expression, while not exactly smug, did hint that she knew something significant. "Why do you say that?"

"I got a call this morning from a reporter I know with the *Idaho Statesman*. She and I have known each other for years and she wanted to pick my brain about the hunt for Kent Anderson. I told her I couldn't tell her anything that hadn't already been in the news, but in the course of our conversation, she told me something interesting."

Brady waited. Margaret leaned toward him across the desk. "She said their newsroom got a call this morning from someone named Donald Aldeen who claimed to be Kent Anderson's best friend. He said he could give them the whole scoop on Anderson—for a hefty fee."

"He wanted to sell the story?"

"Exactly. The *Statesman* turned him down flat. They don't pay for news. But they also did a little research of their own and they couldn't find any indication that Anderson and this guy were all that close. None of the other people they talked to who knew Anderson remembered him hanging out with Aldeen. My friend said she's seen this before—people on the periphery of the story who claim a close relationship to the people involved, hoping to gain money or fame or just attention."

"And she thinks Aldeen falls into that category?"

"She does."

"So he made up the whole thing about Nevada?"

Margaret sat back. "I don't know. But he obviously convinced the marshals."

"He told them what they wanted to hear," Brady said.

"Could be," Margaret said. "In any case, my friend is going to dig some more into his background and her paper may run a story. At the very least, she agreed to share with me what she learns."

"What do we do in the meantime?"

"We ask the firefighters and others in the area to keep a lookout for Anderson and we try to get word to Dillon."

"He probably isn't in any danger," Brady said. "But still…"

"But still." Margaret nodded. "Dillon is one of ours, and we protect our own, no matter what the marshals say."

BY THE TIME Ava and the stray pup arrived, things were a little calmer at Daniels Canine Academy than they had been the day before. Or rather, the crowd of people milling about was smaller, and fewer cars clogged the driveway and parking area. But the air was filled with the sounds of dogs—barking, whining, yipping and howling. Emma raised her voice to be heard over the cacophony. "Hello, Ava." She bent to greet Lacey. "And hello, Lacey."

Lacey wagged her tail in greeting to one of her favorite people. Emma patted the dog, then straightened and zeroed in on the pup in Ava's arms. "Who is this?"

"I was hoping you'd know." Ava handed over the wriggling pup. Emma cuddled the pup—a male, Ava had determined—and stroked its fuzzy head.

"I don't recognize him," Emma said. She examined the dog, running her hands along its body and looking in its mouth. "He's about ten weeks old, I'd guess. He looks well cared for."

"I found him behind some garbage cans in the alley next to Millard's Diner," Ava said. "Or rather, Lacey found him."

"Good girl," Emma addressed Lacey, who thumped her tail in response.

"Can you keep him here while I search for his owners?" Ava said. "The regular animal shelter is full up with evacuees' pets."

"Of course," Emma said. "Even better, if you have time we can run him over to Tashya and have her check for a microchip. We have a scanner in our little on-site clinic."

"I have time. Do you think a pup this young would be chipped?"

"It depends. Most shelters chip them before they put them up for adoption, and some breeders, too, though I doubt this little guy is anything but a hundred percent mutt."

Ava scratched the pup's chin. "A really cute mutt," she said.

"Let's go see if Tashya can find anything." Emma, still cradling the puppy, led the way across the compound, Lacey and Ava in her wake. "Between random fireworks, houses full of strangers and the chaos of the fire, maybe he just escaped his backyard," Emma said as they walked.

She pushed open a door marked with a red cross. Tashya Pratt's attractive round face spread into a wide grin when she saw Ava. "Hey, there," she said. Her light brown eyes shifted to the pup in Emma's arms. "And who is this cutie?"

"I found him in the alley between the café and a T-shirt shop," Ava said. "I brought him here because the shelter is full."

"Let's check him with the scanner." Emma set the wriggling pup on the steel examination table.

"Sure thing." Tashya tucked a lock of shoulder-length, straightened black hair behind one ear, then rummaged in a deep drawer and pulled out a white plastic rectangle about the size of a cell phone. She switched it on and passed it over the dog's body, pausing at the neck. Her smile widened once again. "We're in luck." She read the information on the scanner's screen. "Looks like this little guy was adopted from McPaws shelter in McCall. We can call them, give them this code number, and they'll tell us who adopted the pup from them."

"Thanks, Tashya," Ava said.

"We can make the call for you," Emma said. "The owners can pick him up here. I know you've probably got your hands full, with everything going on in town this weekend."

"It is pretty busy," Ava said. She turned to Tashya. "And speaking of busy, how are the wedding preparations coming?"

"There's so much to do!" Tashya said. "Even for a simple wedding like ours. But it's kind of fun, too, picking out what I want. And Jason's been a big help."

"We're all looking forward to the wedding," Ava said. The resort in McCall that Tashya and her husband-to-be, rookie officer Jason Wright, had chosen was gorgeous, and had a reputation for good food.

"Jason did suggest we elope to Vegas or someplace," Tashya said. "But I told him I hadn't waited four years to marry him to do it without all the people who are important to me there." She sent a fond look to Emma, who had taken Tashya in when the girl was fourteen and very lost. Emma had recognized Tashya's love for animals and steered her into vet tech school and the career she loved, working with Emma at Daniels Canine Academy.

Ava rubbed the dog's ears and he rolled over on the table and gnawed at her fingers. "Somebody is probably missing you," Ava said.

"How are Eli and Bear?" Tashya asked.

"They're both great." Ava couldn't help but smile when she thought of her handsome boyfriend and his goofy Newfoundland who, despite weighing in at a hundred pounds, insisted on being a lapdog. "Eli stopped by the station this morning to give us an update on a missing fugitive."

Emma nodded. "I caught a news report last night. I remember when he killed all those people at ISU. Horrible. Why would he come to a place like Jasper?"

"He's familiar with the area. The US Marshals think he intends to hike cross-country to Nevada. But other people say he's headed to Alaska, starting from here. Local fire spotters saw a lone camper in the area around Williams Gap Trail last night—but you didn't hear that from me."

"Any word yet from Dillon?" Emma asked.

"He sent Brady a text saying he and Roslyn Kern were spending the night in those caves up above Cow Creek. They plan to walk out today."

"That's a relief," Emma said.

"How are the evacuees?" Ava asked. A particularly plaintive howl interrupted her. "It sounds like some of them aren't settling in so well."

"A bit of separation anxiety," Emma said. "Dogs are very sensitive and they pick up on stress in the people they care about. They'll be happier in a couple of days when they're back to their regular routines. Some people have already stopped by to reclaim their pets and take them to wherever they've found to stay until they're allowed back into their homes."

"I heard about the incident with Captain Rutledge and the poodle," Ava said.

Emma's expression grew fierce. "When he drew his weapon, I was so angry I was looking around for something to hit him over the head with," she said. "Though I doubt that would have knocked any sense into him."

"The captain just doesn't like dogs," Ava said.

"I think he's afraid of them," Tashya said.

Ava and Emma stared at her. Tashya shrugged. "You see it sometimes. People avoid dogs because they're afraid of them, sometimes because they've been bitten or had a frightening encounter, maybe when they were a kid. Sometimes it's because they haven't spent time around dogs and don't know how wonderful they can be."

"You could be right," Emma said. "But that's no excuse for violence."

"Of course not," Ava said. "Maybe teaching him how to interact with dogs will help."

"Word gets around fast, I see," Emma said. "Though I guess I'm not surprised."

"We all think the training program is a great idea," Ava said. "Let me know if you need any help."

"I might take you up on that," Emma said. "If I can get Arthur to really come to the training, I'm thinking about offering similar classes to other law enforcement people in the area. Fire departments, paramedics and EMTs, too. Knowing how to deal with an upset dog when they arrive at an emergency situation would make life easier and safer for everyone."

"That's a terrific idea," Tashya said.

"I will need help." Emma picked up the puppy once more and looked down at Lacey, who had settled onto her side on the floor. "Lacey could help, too," she said. "Police dogs like her can look really scary. She would be great for demonstrations."

"Count me in. Eli and Bear could help, too." Ava checked her watch. "It's been great talking to you, but I should go."

"It was good talking to you, too. And don't worry about this little fellow. I'll take care of him."

Ava and Lacey walked back out to the police cruiser, where they were hailed by a harried-looking woman with two small girls in tow. "Excuse me!" the woman called as Ava approached the cruiser. "Are you the officer who picked up the puppy in town? Someone told me they saw a police officer with a puppy."

"Are you missing your dog?" Ava asked.

"Where is Bruno?" one of the little girls wailed. Beside her, her sister burst into tears.

"He's mostly black, with brown eyebrows and two brown paws," the woman said. "We brought him to town with us because we were afraid if the fire shifted we might not be able to get back into our house, but when I opened the car door to help the girls out of their booster seats, he got out of the car and ran down the street. We've been looking all over for him and someone said they thought they saw a woman police officer with him. Then someone else told us you might have brought him here."

"Let's go see," Ava said.

The woman and her daughters followed Ava back to the clinic. Tashya looked up at their approach. "I think we've found the pup's owner," Ava said.

"Emma took him to her office," Tashya said.

Ava led the woman and her daughters to the office where Emma had placed the stray pup in a carrier next to her desk. She looked up when they entered, and set aside the phone she had been holding. "Do you have Bruno?" the woman asked, worry lines etched on her face.

"I think the pup I found belongs to this family," Ava said. "They've been searching for him."

Emma opened the kennel and the pup tumbled out. "Bruno!" the girls shrieked, and fell to their knees to wrestle with the puppy, who yipped joyously and licked their faces.

"Thank you for taking care of him," the woman said. She brushed at her eyes, then offered her hand. "I'm Kaitlyn Elwood," she said. "I was telling the officer that Bruno got out of our car when we came to town to run errands. We normally leave him at home in his crate, but we were afraid to do that in case the police decided to close off our neighborhood and not let us back in."

"Where do you live?" Ava asked.

"Off County Road 14. Our place backs up to the national forest. The last I heard, the fire wasn't threatening our area, but I've lived here long enough to know how quickly that can change."

"I know that neighborhood," Emma said. "You're not far from the Cow Creek Loop."

"That's right," Kaitlyn said. "We occasionally see hikers who have gotten off the trail. My husband is thinking about putting up some signposts to send them off our property and back in the right direction. I saw a guy this morning. I yelled at him that he was going the wrong way and he just glared at me." She shrugged. "There's no accounting for some people."

"There shouldn't be anyone on the trail right now," Ava said. "There's a big sign at the trailhead that says the trail is closed because of the fire."

"This guy was there," Kaitlyn said. "He had a big backpack and everything. Maybe he's one of those people who think the rules don't apply to them."

Maybe. But Ava's intuition told her there was something more. "What did he look like?" she asked.

"Average height and weight. He wore a cap so I couldn't tell much about his hair, but it was short. Khaki pants and a black T-shirt. A big backpack—that camo green."

Ava took out a notebook and wrote all this down. "Would you recognize him if you saw him again?" she asked.

The woman rubbed her mouth. "Well, I don't know. I only saw him for a few seconds." She lowered her hand and nodded. "But yeah, I think so, just because he stopped and gave me such a glare." She shuddered. "Why? Is something wrong?"

Ava didn't answer that question. "What's your phone number, in case we have more questions?" she asked.

The woman rattled off a number, glanced at her children, who were still wrestling with the puppy, then back at Ava. She lowered her voice. "Do I need to be worried about something?"

"No. But if you see the man again, don't interact with him at all. Call 911 and tell them I said to contact the police department." Ava took a business card from her wallet and handed it to the woman. "And call me if you have any questions or concerns."

The woman nodded and tucked the card away. "Come on, girls," she said. "We need to get Bruno home." She took a leash from her purse and snapped it onto the dog's collar. "And he's not going to get away this time."

Emma said nothing until the woman and her family were gone. "Do you think the man she saw is Kent Anderson?" she asked.

"I don't know," Ava said. She reread the man's description. It fit that of Kent Anderson and the clothes he had on the last time he was seen, but a lot of men probably matched those slim details. "I need to tell the chief."

"If it is him," Emma said, "he's not that far from the

caves, where Dillon and Roslyn Kern are supposed to
have spent the night."

Ava nodded. It was close. Too close for comfort.

Chapter Twelve

Roslyn did not want to think about her throbbing ankle, aching back, burning indigestion or sunburned nose. The energy and optimism of the morning had faded, and the miles were catching up with her. The pleasant breeze had died, the heat had intensified, and the thought of eating one more protein bar—the only food they had left—made her feel slightly nauseous. But she was determined to keep going. She wasn't going to complain, not when Dillon was marching on ahead of her and didn't appear the least bit tired or sore.

Why had she ever been worried about seeing him again? Clearly, she had stunned him with the news that she was carrying his baby, but he had recovered from the shock quickly enough. He seemed sincere about wanting to be involved in his future son or daughter's life. That was all good—right?

She wanted to believe so, but things had seldom worked out for her the way she hoped they would. What if they didn't agree about the best way to raise a child? What if he became interested in someone else and they married and he started another family? Last night in her arms she had believed they might have a future together, but they had had a wonderful weekend together before and said goodbye easily enough. At least, he had given no indication at the time that he wanted to see her again. Maybe he didn't think of her in terms of a long-term relationship, only someone he could enjoy in the moment. Would he abandon her and their child when someone better came along?

Why was she worrying about all this right now?

Maybe because as much as she liked Dillon, they still didn't know each other that well. He glanced back at her and stopped. "Are you okay?" he asked. "Do you need to stop?"

She opened her mouth to protest that she was fine, then decided to tell the truth. "I'm pretty tired," she said. "I could use a break."

He looked around, then led her to a grouping of boulders in the shade of a clump of aspen. It wasn't a cushioned easy chair, but she welcomed the chance to take a load off her aching feet and swollen ankle.

Dillon sat beside her and carefully lifted her injured foot into his lap. He massaged it gently. "I know it hurts," he said. "But I don't think you're doing any permanent damage."

"What you're doing right now feels great," she said. She closed her eyes and sighed. Every time he touched her felt great. Which made it difficult to think clearly when he was near. She wanted to lose herself in the moment, but she told herself she should be doing more to get to know him better.

"How did you get into search and rescue work?" she asked. "Was that before or after you became a cop?"

"After." He continued to massage her ankle, fingers strong but gentle. "I really did it to work with Bentley. I had friends with police dogs and it just seemed like working one-on-one with an animal like that would be really special. But I thought I'd prefer search and rescue. And I was right. Bentley has been great, and I've learned a lot."

"So I guess you're trained in first aid?"

He nodded. "And white water rescue and climbing and avalanche rescue—all the skills to address the kind of rescues we're called on to do here. Bentley doesn't even come with me on some calls, though neither one of us likes that much."

The dog sat beside Dillon and leaned against his leg. Dillon reached down to scratch his ears. "Do you have any pets?" he asked.

"No. I had a dog when I was a girl—Pepper. He was a little brown dog, maybe part Chihuahua." She smiled, remembering.

"You could get a dog now," he said. "Especially since you're working at home."

"Maybe after the baby is older," she said. "That might be nice." She searched for a way to direct the conversation back to him. There was so much she wanted to know—needed to know. "You said you moved to Jasper when you were twelve?" she asked. "Where did you live before that?"

"Denver. It was a big adjustment, coming from the big city, but it didn't take me long to make friends and settle in." His smile radiated the happiness behind those words.

She could believe that. Dillon was so charming and friendly he could easily be the most popular person in any room. "Does your family still live here?" she asked.

"Oh, yes. My dad owns a construction company. My mom manages his office—and she tries to manage me and my two brothers."

"Are you the youngest?"

"Oldest." He grinned. "And according to her, I am long overdue to get married and give her grandchildren." His gaze dropped to her abdomen. "She is going to be over the moon about this baby."

Roslyn's chest felt full of butterflies. "Is she going to be upset that we're not married?"

"A little disappointed, maybe, but my mom isn't judgmental."

"Do you think she'll like me?"

"She'll love you." He moved his hands from her ankle to her shoulders. "Don't worry. Mom can be a bit overwhelming at first—she has a big personality. But I know she's going to love you. How could she not?"

Lots of people in her life had managed not to love her, Roslyn thought. She could imagine a doting mother not being pleased to meet the woman who had ended up pregnant by her son as the result of a weekend fling.

"What about your parents?" Dillon asked. "Where do they live?"

"My mom is in Shreveport, Louisiana, and my dad is in Alaska. They divorced when I was three and they've both remarried a couple of times since then."

"Are they excited about the baby?"

Her mother's first words upon hearing the news were "I hope you're not counting on me for help with this kid." Her father had been kinder. "That's great, honey. You'll have to come up here so I can meet my newest grandchild after he's born." No offer to come see her—she hadn't laid eyes on her father in at least ten years. "My parents are really busy with their own lives," she said.

Dillon nodded, and she could practically see him processing this statement. Such a different response from what he expected from his own mother. It sounded like his family was still close. Would that make him a better dad? "My mom will do anything she can for you and that baby," he said. "She'll be thrilled, but if she gets too overbearing, don't be afraid to tell her to back off. She hears it from me all the time, and mostly, she's good about reining herself in."

You're her darling boy, Roslyn thought. *She would probably forgive you anything. I'm some stranger who dropped into her life unexpectedly.*

There she went, being pessimistic again. The last few months, since learning about the baby, she had been trying to nurture a more positive attitude. She couldn't control what happened in the future, only how she reacted. For her child's sake, she wanted to focus on the positive. "Where do you live?" she asked. "Do you have an apartment? A house?"

"I bought a house last year. I saw how real estate prices were soaring and figured I'd better get something while I could still afford it. I've done some remodeling to fix it up how I wanted it. It's nice, having a place of my own."

"What's it like?"

"Three bedrooms, two baths. Two acres with some trees. It's about three miles north of town."

"That's a big place for a single guy."

"I bought it with the future in mind."

The words sent a hot shiver through her. What was that supposed to mean? But she wasn't sure she was ready to hear the answer.

Instead, she turned her attention to the dog. Bentley wagged his tail at her, then resumed watching Dillon. "He seems very devoted," she said.

"Aussies are very loyal," he said. "But he likes pretty much everyone. It's a good quality in a rescue dog. You don't want a lost child running the other direction because a fierce-looking dog is coming after them. Bentley is so gentle he doesn't frighten people, though he can be protective when he needs to be."

"He chased off that intruder last night," she said.

"He'll let us know if anyone is out there," Dillon said.

"Or any deer." She laughed, remembering her relief at their earlier encounter.

"I've been watching him and he hasn't picked up on anyone or anything else," Dillon said. "Maybe the guy who was after your camera decided he'd be better off leaving."

"I hope so," she said. "Though I wish I knew who it was."

"I'd like to take another look at that photo you took," he said.

She fished the camera from her pack, switched it on and handed it to him. He studied the figure for a long time, then returned the camera to her. "Do you recognize him?" he asked.

"No."

"Take a good look. Does he look familiar at all?"

She focused on the photo, but nothing about the figure in it was familiar. "No." She shook her head. "Does he look familiar to you?"

He sat back. "No. I'm just trying to figure out who would be following us. Do you think someone in your life in Chicago would follow you to Jasper? Maybe a reporter trying to get a scoop? You said the media have been harassing you."

"They have, but like I said, a lot of that has died down in the last few weeks. And following me to another state is pretty extreme. It's not like anyone outside of Chicago even knows who I am. Really, I think the only reason the local press picked up the story and ran with it was because the station I worked for made such a big deal about my engagement to Matt."

"Rockin' Roz and Mad Matt." He scowled.

She sighed. "I wanted to keep my private life private, but the station manager and Matt both pushed for using the relationship to build ratings. The next thing I knew, there were billboards and ads in the paper. I was waiting to cross the street one afternoon and a city bus went by with my face plastered across the back." She shuddered at the memory.

"What happened after you broke off the engagement?" he asked.

"Oh, they tried to milk that, too. I had to hire a lawyer to prevent them from using my image in more ads. I think station management probably paid some reporters to keep my name in the paper and on local TV, though I could never prove it."

"Could Matt or the station have sent someone to follow you here?" Dillon asked.

She shook her head. "There's no need. Matt has a new girlfriend now. Her name is Dorothy, but on-air she's D-Licious. Matt didn't waste any time, making a move on her. I've been so tempted to call her up and tell her she's probably just another way for Matt to improve his chances of moving on to bigger and better things, but she probably wouldn't believe me. I wouldn't have if someone had tried to warn me."

"Does Matt know about the baby?" Dillon asked. "Would he wonder if it was his?"

She put a protective hand on her abdomen. "The baby isn't his. Definitely not."

"I believe you, but he might jump to the wrong conclusion, or not know how far along you are."

"No. Matt made it very clear he did not want children," she said. "I think that was real, not part of the publicity stunt."

As if knowing they were talking about it, the baby moved inside her. "I've always wanted children," she said.

"Me, too," he said.

"Really?"

"Really. Do you find that hard to believe?"

"Most men I've dated were ambivalent at best," she said. "They saw fatherhood as some far-off possibility, not a cherished reality."

"I bought my house with the idea that I'd have a family there," he said. "When I found the right partner."

He didn't touch her with his hands, but the look in his eyes was a caress. She swallowed the lump of emotion that rose in her throat. They had known each other such a short time. How could they know they were right for each other?

"I really don't think the person in that photo has anything to do with me," she said. "What about you? You're a cop. Maybe he's following you."

"I wasn't anywhere near here until I was sent to find you," he said.

"Maybe he saw you and recognized you," she said. "You might have made enemies."

"I probably have, but I don't know this man."

"Then maybe he's just another lost hiker," she said. "He's following us, hoping we'll lead him to safety."

Dillon shook his head. "If that's the case, why not say something? Why not ask for help, or to hike with us? Why try to steal your camera?"

"You're right." She stared at the man in the photo again. Just a blurred image, no features distinguishable. "I'm sure I don't know him," she said. "Maybe we'll never know why he's out there. I hope we never find out."

"I hope we do," Dillon said. "He's caused us enough trouble already. I'd just as soon arrest him for attempted theft and be done with him."

She supposed cops saw so many situations in terms of right and wrong, legal and illegal. They saw one correct way to deal with a situation. She rubbed her belly. So much of life was too complicated for those kinds of solutions. "How much farther to town?" she asked.

"Three more miles."

"How long will that take?"

He considered the question, either because he needed to calculate the time, or because he was trying to think of a diplomatic way to tell her they were traveling very slowly. But she already knew that. She had been a swift hiker before, but pregnancy and a sprained ankle slowed her down considerably.

"Not more than two hours," Dillon said.

Two hours didn't sound like so long. *And then what?* she wondered. How would she and Dillon work out how to parent a child together while remaining apart?

Don't obsess about the future, she reminded herself. *Focus on right now.* Right now, she needed to keep putting one foot in front of the other, walking her way out of one predicament, without angsting over problems that hadn't happened yet.

AT FIFTY, COLLEEN DIAZ still turned heads, especially among men of a certain age—though those familiar with her husband, Ramon, and her three sons, who included

Jasper Police Sergeant Dillon Diaz, didn't overtly stare, in case one of the men in her life took offense. Colleen was well aware of the effect she had on men, and dressed to impress in tasteful but stylish clothes that played up her generous curves and creamy skin. She wore her hair long, the red color still vibrant, and she held her head up high and looked people in the eye when she spoke to them.

Chief Doug Walters was the focus of Colleen's clear hazel gaze at the moment. "What are you doing to rescue my son?" she asked. She had cornered the chief in the squad room, where everyone who happened to be in the station pretended to be working. But Walters knew they were all avidly attuned to this conversation. Dillon's mother had a reputation as a woman who didn't take no for an answer. Her charm, beauty and refusal to back down had reportedly contributed to the fact that Diaz Construction had never had a client fail to pay them. If a payment was late, Colleen personally called upon the client and persuaded them to hand over the money.

But Walters had never expected to find himself the focus of Colleen's attention. "Dillon doesn't need rescuing, Mrs. Diaz," he said. "We expect him back sometime today."

"I'm sure Dillon would tell you that," Colleen said. "Never mind that he's trapped by a wildfire and there's an escaped killer running around out there."

Colleen had obviously been listening to the news accounts, which had half the town fearful of being killed in their beds by Kent Anderson, despite the fact that the marshals believed Anderson to be in Nevada and local law enforcement hadn't been able to gather evidence to prove otherwise. "Dillon texted yesterday that he's safe and he's in no danger from the fire or anything else."

Walters did his best to look stern, but Colleen's laser gaze made him feel several inches shorter.

"What do you know about this woman he's with?" Colleen asked.

"Roslyn Kern?" Walters furrowed his brow, trying to recall what he knew about the woman Dillon had rescued. "I believe she's from Chicago."

"Yes, and she's pregnant, and was on the radio. Who is the father of her baby and why isn't he here?"

Walters wanted to ask her why she was asking him if she knew so much about Roslyn Kern. But he didn't dare. "I don't know about the baby's father," he said. "But that's really none of my concern."

"I saw her picture. She's very pretty. Close to Dillon's age." She tilted her head, considering. "He's bound to make an impression on her—such a strong, handsome man, rescuing her from danger."

Walters stared. Was she imagining a romance between this woman and Sergeant Diaz? He remained silent, but Colleen wasn't having it. "What do you think?" she asked. "Would this woman be good for Dillon?"

"I've never met the woman," he said. "And I don't interfere in my officers' personal lives."

"None of the local women seem to suit him," she said. "But I know he's ready to settle down. He bought that big house that's perfect for a family."

Walters winced inwardly. Dillon's fellow officers were never going to let him live this down.

Colleen narrowed her eyes. "You say you've had a text from him? He hasn't answered any of my messages."

Walters wasn't even going to go there. "I'm sure you don't have anything to worry about, Mrs. Diaz," he said. "Your son is an experienced officer and a trained search and rescue team member. He's well equipped and prepared for any situation."

"You don't have any children, do you, Chief?" she asked.

"No, I don't."

"Then you can't understand a parent's worry." She leaned toward him and he fought not to lean away. "When you talk to Dillon, you tell him to call his mother."

"Yes, ma'am."

"Chief?" Teresa approached. "You have a call on line one. I forwarded it to your office."

"Excuse me, Mrs. Diaz." Walters nodded goodbye and moved past her, toward his office.

"Let me show you out," Teresa said, taking Colleen's arm.

He was holding the silent receiver in his hand when Teresa appeared in his doorway a few moments later. "There was no call," Walters said.

"There wasn't," she admitted. "But you looked like you needed rescuing."

He ought to be insulted by this, but could only return Teresa's grin. She had blue eyes, and they were less intimidating than Colleen's. "Thanks. I'd heard stories about Dillon's mom but never interacted with her one-on-one. She's definitely a force to be reckoned with."

Teresa moved further into the office. "Every organization in town knows if you need a job done, get Colleen Diaz on your committee. And she is a real mama bear when it comes to her boys. They're all three spoiled rotten, but it hasn't ruined them."

A knock on the doorframe turned their attention to the door, where Ava stood, Lacey at her side. "Excuse me,

Chief," she said. "I was out at DCA and learned something you should know."

"Come in, Ava," he said. Teresa nodded to Ava and slipped out the door as Ava moved to stand in front of Walters's desk. "What's on your mind?"

"I found a stray puppy and took it to Emma Daniels. The owner of the dog turned out to be Kaitlyn Elwood. She lives out County Road 14, on property that backs up to the national forest. She came to claim the dog and while we were talking she mentioned that she saw a man crossing her property this morning. She said something to him to direct him back to the Cow Creek Loop, which runs near there. She said he just glared at her." She pulled her notebook from her pocket and read from a page. "She described the man as average height and weight, his hair covered by a cap. He wore khaki pants, a black T-shirt, and had a camouflage backpack. That matches the description I saw for Kent Anderson."

Walters nodded. "That matches with the report from the fire spotter of someone camping in the vicinity."

"That isn't far at all from the caves where we think Dillon and Roslyn Kern spent the night," she said.

"Dillon and Ms. Kern should be hiking back toward town by now," he said. "Depending on how fast they're able to hike with Ms. Kern's injury, they should be here early afternoon, or sooner."

"I'd like permission to hike out with Lacey to meet them," Ava said. "That way he'd have backup if Kent Anderson is following him."

It wasn't a terrible idea, but it put an officer in uniform on the scene. Anderson probably didn't know Dillon was a law enforcement officer, but he wouldn't mistake Ava, in uniform and with a police K-9, for anything else.

Even out of uniform, someone alone on a closed trail might raise suspicion. "I can't spare you right now," Walters said. "The situation in town is too volatile, with the crowds of tourists and media, the fire and the news hyping the stories of both Roslyn Kern and Kent Anderson. I need every officer available to quell any problems that arise."

Ava pressed her lips together, clearly unhappy with this news, but too disciplined to argue.

Walters's phone beeped. He held up one finger to indicate she should wait while he answered the summons. "Walters," he said into the receiver.

"Jenny Dix from Dispatch, Captain," said a pleasant female voice. "We just had a 911 call about a fight at the corner of West Main and South Maple. That's practically in front of the police station."

"We'll get right on it. Thanks, Jenny." He hung up the phone and looked up at Ava. "Speaking of problems, we've got a report of a fight right outside." He heaved himself out of his chair. "Let's go see what we're dealing with."

Chapter Thirteen

The two combatants were young, fit and drunk, despite the fact that it wasn't yet noon. They grappled with each other in the middle of the sidewalk, staggering around and taking turns landing blows while onlookers shouted and cheered. A television news crew even filmed from the sidelines.

Ava and the chief dragged the men apart, Ava twisting one man's arm behind his back in a painful hold that rendered him helpless. She fastened cuffs on his wrists and pointed to the curb. "Sit!" she ordered.

"I don't want to sit," he said. "That guy made a move on my girlfriend and I want to knock his head off."

"Sit or my partner will make you sit."

The man looked toward the chief, who was cuffing the other combatant. "That old man?" he sneered.

"No. This partner." She signaled to Lacey, who stepped forward and uttered a low growl.

The man's face paled. "Don't let it bite me," he said.

"Then sit."

He sat, still focused on the dog. "Call it off," he said.

At a hand signal, Lacey sat, too. She was relaxed, but her gaze was fixed on the man. She would keep him out of the way while Ava helped disperse the crowd.

"…reporting live from Jasper, Idaho, where local police have just quelled an altercation on the street in front of the police department." A handsome man with a boyish face and broad shoulders in a tan sport coat moved into Ava's line of sight, a second man with a shoulder-mount camera tracking his movement. "Officer, can you tell me if this altercation had anything to do with either the disappearance of Roslyn Kern or the search for fugitive Kent Anderson?"

"No comment," Ava said. "And you need to shut off that camera and leave now."

"This is a public street," the man said. "We have a right to be here, reporting the news as it happens."

This last sounded to Ava like the tagline for the station he worked for. "This is a crime scene and you need to leave," she said. "Or I could arrest you for interfering with an officer in the performance of her duty."

The man stared, and for a moment he thought he was going to push his luck, but at the last moment, he turned to the cameraman. "Shut it off, Mike," he said. "Let's go see what we can find on the other side of the street."

Half an hour later, when the two combatants were safely locked in cells in the basement of the police department, Ava headed back upstairs to deal with the paperwork. She was sitting at her desk when Teresa called. "I have a couple here who say they need to talk to a police officer. Could you interview them?"

"Sure. Did they say what it's about?"

"No. But they look very nervous."

"I'll come out to meet them."

Margery and Michael Blake were one of those couples who resembled each other, with short white hair cut in no particular style, soft features and pale brown eyes. "Could we talk somewhere private?" Michael asked after Ava had introduced herself and gotten their names. "What I have to say is important, but kind of sensitive." He looked around him, shoulders hunched as if ready to ward off a beating.

"Sure. Come with me." Ava led them to one of the interview rooms—a small, square space with everything painted gray—gray industrial carpet, gray walls and gray table and chairs. She caught sight of Brady as she moved down the hall and motioned for him to come with her. "This is Lieutenant Nichols," she said. "He'll be sitting in on our interview."

She went through the formalities, notifying them that their statement was being recorded and reciting their names, address and the fact that they were here voluntarily for the tape. Then she settled across from them at the table, while Brady remained by the door. "What do you have to tell us?" she asked.

The couple exchanged looks. Michael cleared his throat, then said, "Kent Anderson is our nephew."

"By marriage," Margery added. "Not blood. He didn't grow up around us. He grew up in Ketchum and just visited sometimes in summer."

Ava glanced at Brady. They were both more alert now. "Do you know where your nephew is right now?" she asked.

"No." Michael shook his head. "If we did, we'd tell you. We think it's terrible what he did. We're here because we just found out his mother's people decided to help him."

"They were bragging about it," Margery said. "I know you already talked to Deena and Sean, but there are others involved."

"The whole clan is bad news," Michael said. "When our Joe married Kent's mother, Helen, I knew the family was trouble, but I never expected something like this."

"Was there something specific you wanted us to know?" Ava asked, wanting to derail this rant. It was no news to their department that Anderson's relatives didn't always respect the law, but you couldn't prosecute people for having a bad attitude.

Margery leaned across the table toward them. "We ran into some of Helen's relatives this morning while we were shopping and Michael asked them about Kent."

"We'd seen the news reports," Michael said. "One of them said Kent had family in the area who might have aided his escape. I came right out and asked them if they had helped that murderer and they said they had. Laughed about it." He twisted his face in a look of disgust.

"Thank you for letting us know," Ava said. "What are the names of the people you talked to?"

They gave her the names of four people, all known to them, all probably already questioned by federal authorities, but it didn't hurt to have someone else confirm their involvement with Anderson.

"Do you know a man named Donald Aldeen?" Brady asked.

Margery made a face of distaste. "We know who he is," she said. "But he's someone we try to avoid."

"He's been telling people he and Kent are best friends," Brady said.

Margery looked to her husband, who shook his head. "I don't think so," he said. "I mean, they may have played together some when they were kids, but I never heard Kent or anyone who knew him well mention anybody by that name."

"Donald Aldeen told the US Marshals Service that Kent was headed to Nevada."

"What would he want in Nevada?" Michael asked. "The only place anyone mentioned to us was Alaska. He figured he could change his name and get lost up there— all that empty land and people who mind their own business. That's what they told us."

"Maybe Kent has friends in Nevada," Ava said. "Or he's been there before?"

"I don't know," Margery said. "Like we said, we weren't close to him or anything."

"Is there anything else you want to tell us?" Ava asked.

"Yes," Michael said. "The whole reason we came here was to tell you that Kent told all his relatives that he wasn't going to go back to prison—that he would kill anybody who tried to stop him, and that included them if they said anything."

Ava nodded. "Are you worried about your own safety?"

Again, the two exchanged a long look. Margery spoke first. "We've lived a long time. We don't intend to die soon, but if we can save other people…" She shrugged.

"But you don't have to tell him we're the ones who came to you," Michael said. "He knows we don't have anything to do with the rest of that side of the family, so he probably wouldn't suspect us right off."

"We just thought you should know, in case you plan to go after him," Margery said. "People say things like that in movies and books, but I think Kent really means it."

"I knew there was something not right about him the first time I laid eyes on him," Michael said. "But nobody else would hear a word against him. They were all shocked when he shot all those people, but I wasn't."

"Is Kent armed?" Brady spoke up for the first time.

Michael swiveled to look back at him. "His cousin Jeff told me he had a Ruger 45 automatic pistol and a Beretta APX. And plenty of ammo."

"Mr. and Mrs. Blake, would you be willing to testify in court if Kent is apprehended?" Ava asked.

Michael Blake took his wife's hand. "Margery and I talked about this before we came here and we agreed we would testify if we had to. It's the right thing to do."

Ava nodded. "Thank you for coming forward," she said. "We appreciate it. Is there anything else?"

"That's it." Michael pushed back from the table. "Except we'd like it if we could go out the back way. We don't want anyone to see us leaving here."

"Of course," she said.

"I'll see them out," Brady said.

He left and Ava sat at the table, digesting what the Blakes had just told her. It wasn't news that Kent Anderson had long declared he would kill any law enforcement officers who crossed his path, but according to Margery and Michael, he had expanded that threat to anyone—which could include an off-duty cop and a lost former DJ from Chicago.

Brady returned to the room. "We have to get word to Dillon," he said, as soon as the door was closed behind him.

Ava looked toward the recording equipment. "I shut it off before I left," Brady said. He sat across from her, in the chair recently vacated by Michael. "One of us needs to hike out there and find Dillon and Roslyn."

"I tried to get the chief to let me do it," Ava said. "He said he couldn't spare anyone. Without Dillon we're already shorthanded."

Brady pulled out his phone and began scrolling. "Dillon hasn't answered any of my texts. There's a lot of places out there with no cell coverage."

"I heard the fire burned a cell tower, which could make things worse." She drummed her pen on the table, trying to think what to do. "We should talk to the chief again. With this new information he might see things our way."

"Let me check with Search and Rescue first," Brady said. "Maybe they know more about what's going on with Dillon and Roslyn." He punched a number into the phone and put the call on speaker while it rang.

"Hello, Brady." Mountaintop Search and Rescue Commander Andrea Wayne's voice sounded clearly in the still room.

"Hey, Andrea," Brady said. "Have you heard anything from Dillon?"

"No. And one of our repeaters is down, so we can't raise him on the radio." The repeater system that relayed emergency signals to more remote parts of the county was subject to the whims of weather.

"I had a message yesterday that he and Roslyn Kern planned to spend the night at the caves above Cow Creek," Brady said. "But if they did that, they should have hiked out by now."

"Depends on how badly injured Ms. Kern is," Andrea said. "They may be taking it slower because of that, and because of her pregnancy."

"Then she really is pregnant?" Brady asked. "That isn't just speculation from news media?"

"The friends who reported her missing confirmed that she's about five months along. Maybe one of them said something to the press."

"Ava and I were thinking of hiking out to meet them," Brady said.

"We're already on it," Andrea said. "I've got a team ready to head up the trail with a litter and first aid supplies. We're leaving for the trailhead now."

Ava shook her head vigorously. "Don't do that," Brady said. "It's too dangerous."

"The fire isn't anywhere near the trail now," Andrea said. "There's a little smoke, but there's no immediate danger."

"The fire may not be near there, but we have reason to believe Kent Anderson is," Brady said. "And you didn't hear that from me. But Anderson is armed and dangerous. He may not readily distinguish between uniformed search and rescue volunteers and uniformed law enforcement. And he's sworn to kill law enforcement."

"Does Dillon know about this?"

"No. That's another reason Ava and I intend to head out there."

"Roslyn Kern may need help getting out of there."

"Your people can stage at the trailhead and we'll call if we need them," Brady said. "But don't head out on your own. Give us time to get there first."

"Don't worry. We don't take unnecessary risks."

"I'll be in touch," Brady said. "For now, sit tight." He ended the call. "Let's go talk to the chief."

CHIEF WALTERS WAS at his desk when Captain Rutledge stepped in. "Diaz has done it this time," he said.

Walters regarded Rutledge calmly. He had learned long ago that his definition of something worth getting upset about and the captain's were very different. "Is Diaz back?" he asked. "Is Roslyn Kern all right?"

"No, he's not back. But when he gets back, he's in for it. Take a look at this." Rutledge dropped a printout onto Walters's desk. "That's a screenshot from the *Tattler* website."

"Since when do you read the *Tattler*—whatever that is?" Walters asked.

Rutledge's face turned a darker shade of red. "Since a search of Roslyn Kern's name brings this up as one of the most-viewed sites related to her."

"Why are you searching for Ms. Kern's name on a website?" Walters asked. "As far as we're aware, she hasn't broken any laws."

"As public information officer, it's my job to keep up with what people are saying about our department."

"But you weren't searching our department name. Or were you?"

"The press is roasting us for not having rescued Ms. Kern yet."

"There are always going to be people who criticize the way we do our jobs, Arthur," Walters said. "It doesn't matter what some website named the *Tattler* says. Nobody pays attention to that kind of thing."

Rutledge tapped the desk. "Read the printout."

Walters looked down at the paper and read out loud. "The hunky cop who raced to the rescue of Rockin' Roz Kern." This headline was followed by a picture of Dillon and his search dog, Bentley, from a fundraising calendar Search and Rescue had printed up last year. Dillon, in a muscle shirt and hiking pants, was flexing his biceps and grinning at the camera. Walters chuckled. "I guess they know what sells ads, or pulls in views, or however these sites make their money."

"Read the article," Rutledge said through clenched teeth.

Walters read, "Meet the man who is facing down wildfire and an escaped killer to bring radio sweetheart Roslyn 'Rockin' Roz' Kern to safety in the Idaho wilderness. Jasper Police Sergeant and local heartthrob Dillon Diaz loves dogs and kids and the ladies love him." Below this were photos of Dillon and Roslyn side by side, surrounded by heart emojis. Walters laughed. "Dillon is never going to live this down," he said.

"It makes us look like a bunch of lightweights," Rutledge said. "Playboys."

"Are you jealous, Arthur?" Rutledge was single, too, and bragged about his prowess with women. Seeing the twenty-years-younger Dillon lauded in the press probably got to him.

"I'm not jealous, I'm appalled. You never should have allowed him to pose for that cheesy calendar. And working for Search and Rescue is a conflict of interest."

"I don't see it that way," Walters said. "As for the calendar, it was for a good cause, and I don't control what my officers do on their own time, as long as it's not illegal, of course." He crumpled up the printout and tossed it into the trash can beside his desk. "Have we had any word from Dillon?"

"No," Rutledge said. "And I don't understand what's taking him so long. All he had to do was hike out of there on a marked trail."

"My understanding is Ms. Kern is pregnant and injured."

"Then why didn't he ask for more help when he still had a phone and radio signal?"

"Maybe we should send a couple of officers to look for them after all," Walters said. He had expected Dillon back by now. The fact that he wasn't pointed to trouble.

"You said it yourself. We don't have the manpower for that," Rutledge said. "We need every available body out there patrolling, with the town as packed as it is."

"Does that include you?"

"I'm too busy dealing with the press." Rutledge waved his hand toward the front of the building. "Have you seen the crowd of reporters out there? They're clamoring for information. I really think we should hold a press conference."

"To tell them what?" Walters asked. "We don't have an update on Roslyn Kern, and I'm not giving them any information about Kent Anderson." Not that they had much to go on about the fugitive, but the press would be sure to ask. They had latched on to the idea that Anderson intended to harm Roslyn and were running with it. "I'm not going to feed the media anything else they can blow out of proportion."

"You don't have to participate," Rutledge said. "I could reassure them we're doing everything in our power to rescue Ms. Kern and we're keeping a close eye on the situation."

Ah. Walters saw what was going on now. Rutledge wanted an excuse to preen before the cameras. "No," he said. "No press conference. Not until we have something to report."

A knock on the door made them turn. "Come in," Walters called.

Ava entered the room, followed by Brady. The small office was getting more crowded by the second. "Sir, we have some new information about Kent Anderson," Ava said.

"What new information?" Rutledge demanded. "Why haven't I heard about this?"

Ava didn't roll her eyes at him, but Walters could read the desire to do so clearly written on her face. "What do you have?" he asked.

"A couple came into the station a little earlier, wanting to speak to an officer," Ava said. "I took them into an interview room and talked to them. Turns out they're two of Kent Anderson's relatives who live here in Jasper. Margery and Michael Blake. I asked Brady to sit in on the interview with me."

"Why did you interview these people?" Rutledge asked. "You should have passed them to me or to the chief."

"You weren't here and the chief was on the phone," Ava said. She looked back to Walters. "The Blakes say they only just found out that some of Anderson's other relatives helped him to escape. He says they were bragging about it."

"Who did they say was helping Anderson?" Walters asked.

"They gave us the names of several relatives who claim to have abetted Anderson," Brady said. "And they said they weren't aware that Donald Aldeen and Kent Anderson were friends, and they were sure Kent was headed to Alaska, not Nevada. The Blakes were very cooperative and willing to testify."

Walters nodded. "Do you have signed statements from both of them?"

"Yes, sir," Ava said. "But that's not all they told us. They said Anderson is definitely armed—two automatic pistols, a Ruger 45 automatic pistol and a Beretta APX."

"And plenty of ammunition," Brady added.

"They also said Anderson swore he wouldn't be taken

back to jail alive," Ava said. "He intends to kill anyone who comes after him."

"He's sworn before to kill law enforcement officers," Brady said. "But this sounds like he'll shoot anyone he thinks is in his way. That could include Dillon and Ms. Kern, if he comes across them on the trail."

"I really think we need to send officers to warn and help Dillon," Ava said. "Brady and I are volunteering to go. And Lacey."

"I spoke with Andrea Wayne of Mountaintop SAR and she hasn't heard anything from Dillon," Brady said. "She was getting a team ready to go looking for them, but I persuaded her to wait until she heard back from us."

"We're afraid Anderson might see the SAR uniforms and mistake the rescue volunteers for cops," Ava said.

"Where are the Blakes now?" Rutledge asked. "Did you detain them?"

"They came in voluntarily and told us what they knew," Ava said. "We had no reason to detain them."

"They may know more they didn't tell you," Rutledge said. "Or they were setting us up for a trap."

"Shut up, Arthur." Walters focused his attention on his officers. "They were sure about the weapons?" he asked.

"Yes, sir," Ava said. "They were very definite."

"If I send you two out there, Anderson will make you as cops before you ever see him," Walters said.

"Not if we're not in uniform," Brady said. "We figured we'll just be a couple out for a walk with their dog."

"On a trail that's closed because of fire danger?" Rutledge scoffed.

"Anderson has been in the wilderness since before the trail was closed," Brady said. "Even if he knows the trail was shut down, we could just as easily have opened it up again now that the fire is moving away."

"If Anderson's goal is to escape, I doubt he'd be moving back toward town," Walters said.

"Unless he's following Dillon and Roslyn," Ava said. "That report from Kaitlyn Elwood about seeing a man who fit Anderson's description on her property this morning puts him a lot closer to Dillon and Roslyn than he should be if he's heading toward Alaska."

Walters considered this. He didn't like putting more officers at risk, but going in with SWAT or a bigger team would alarm Anderson and likely backfire. In the best-case scenario, Ava and Brady would find Dillon and Roslyn and help them get back to the trail safely. If not...he would have to trust his officers to be careful. "If you spot Anderson, don't approach him if you can avoid doing so," he said. "Call for backup, even if that means hiking back to the trailhead to do so. Don't take unnecessary risks."

"Yes, sir," Ava said.

"We'll be careful," Brady said.

"Then you can go," Walters said. "I want regular updates on your position."

"Yes, sir," Ava said. "Thank you."

"There's one more problem," Rutledge said.

They all turned toward him. "I've had word that there's a group of media at the Williams Gap Trailhead," Rutledge said. "They're anticipating Dillon and Roslyn Kern showing up there."

"How do we know some of them haven't already started down the trail?" Brady asked.

"I put one of our reserve officers—Castleberg—there to enforce the trail closure," Rutledge said. "I checked with him less than half an hour ago and he says so far everyone is being compliant."

"So we'll need to sneak past the media to get onto the trail," Brady said.

"We can start from the Elwoods' house," Ava said. "Kaitlyn said her property backs up to the trail."

"Do that," Walters agreed. "Now go change and get going."

They left the office. "Do you really think that was a good idea?" Rutledge asked.

"If I didn't send them and Dillon ended up having to face off against Anderson alone, they'd never forgive themselves," Walters said. He'd carry that guilt with him, too, added to the burden of all the regrets he'd accumulated during a long command. You couldn't always do the right thing in every situation. But he considered it a point of honor to keep trying. Once he stopped trying, it truly would be time to hang up his badge.

"There's still the problem of the media gathered at the trailhead," Rutledge said. "One reserve officer probably isn't going to be able to stop someone who's determined to head down the trail to meet Roslyn and Dillon and get the scoop."

"We don't have the personnel to put more officers on the scene," Walters said. "Unless you're suggesting you go."

"I've got a better idea," Rutledge said.

"What is that?"

"Let me hold a press conference here. I'll send word to the reporters at the trailhead that we have big news. None of them will want to miss that."

"And what big news do you plan to share with them?"

Rutledge waved his hand. "I'll think of something to

get their attention, without revealing anything critical to the search for Anderson."

He probably would, too. Say what you would about Arthur, but he had a knack for giving the media what they wanted. "All right," Walters said. "But get busy. We don't have time to waste."

Chapter Fourteen

Roslyn remembered a time not that many months ago, when walking three miles would have been no challenge to her, but these last three miles to Jasper were taking forever. She was reduced to hobbling along on her swollen ankle, doing anything she could to distract herself from the discomfort. Dillon kept her going, encouraging her, waiting for her and urging her to rest. And thinking about him was a good way to avoid focusing on the pain. Dillon as he was now, and Dillon as he had been when they had met on Brundage Mountain.

"I've never been to McCall," she'd told him as they strolled down the town's main street the Sunday after Valentine's Day. They had forsaken the slopes for sightseeing, with Dillon eager to show her a place he knew well.

"What made you decide to come to Brundage?" he'd asked. "It's not exactly well-known."

"I was looking for someplace smaller and off the beaten path." She'd glanced at him. He was so gorgeous, giving off a lumberjack vibe that day in a buffalo plaid jacket and a sheepskin-lined cap with ear flaps.

"I get it," he said. "Hiding from the paparazzi." He laughed at what he had probably meant as a joke, but he didn't know how close to the truth he was.

"Something like that," she said. She hooked her arm in his. "Like I said, it's a really cute town." They passed a candy store, the front window filled with displays of truffles, decorated gingerbread and candy apples.

"You should come back in the summer," he said. "There's boating and swimming on Paiute Lake and a great beach area. And there's tons of hiking. I'd love to show it to you."

Her first impulse had been to declare that yes, she would love to come back and spend more time with him, but she'd pushed that away. That weekend hadn't been about building a relationship for the future. It was about nurturing the fantasy of now. It was an interval of passion, between two people who would never argue over whose turn it was to do the dishes, or who was going to call and deal with the apartment super. And she was a woman of mystery enjoying an assignation with a sexy lover. So she'd only smiled enigmatically and said, "Maybe I'll see it one day."

And now one day had come, and not only was she no longer a sexy woman of mystery, but she was a limping, pregnant female who hadn't had the sense to stay with her hiking group, necessitating a search and rescue mission. Dillon was seeing her with messy hair and no makeup, and right this minute she couldn't think of a time when she had felt less sexy.

He looked back at her now and smiled. "How are you doing?"

"I'm hanging in there." She tried to stand up straighter and not think about how her back was aching almost as badly as her ankle. "Have you ever done anything like this before?"

"Like what?"

"Have to hike out of the wilderness with someone you've rescued?"

"No," he said. "Usually there's a whole team working a rescue. If not for the fire cutting off the trail, we would have carried you out on a litter, and you would have probably been back at your rooms by nightfall."

And he would have been in his house—the house he bought for a family he didn't yet have. "If you hadn't been stuck with me for the last twenty-four hours, what do you think would have happened?" she asked. "When you found out about the baby, what would you have done?"

He considered the question for a long moment. She listened to her heart pounding, knowing how much the answer meant to her. "I would have stayed with you," he said. "I would have tried to figure out what you wanted from me, and how I could help with the baby."

"I didn't come here looking for money." The thought horrified her. Though legally he might be obligated to support her, she was making a good living and didn't want him to think this was all about finances. "I just thought you'd want to know."

"I'll support my child," he said, a little stiffly. "And I'll try to be a good father." His expression softened a little. "And I want us to be good friends, too. However we end up handling the parenting."

"It's terrifying sometimes, thinking of being responsible for a life," she said. "What if we mess things up?"

"I think you'll be a wonderful mom," he said.

She was mortified to find she was crying, but she couldn't stop herself. She hadn't even realized until now how much she had longed for someone to say that—to reassure her that at some point instinct would take over and she would know how to care for this child. That it would be him—the one person who would have the most right to question her decisions and choices—undid her.

She stood in the middle of the path, blubbering, until he came and gathered her into his arms. "You're tired and hurting, and probably hungry and thirsty, too," he said. "But you're doing great. This will all be over soon. Just a little farther."

"Are you going to tell me that when I'm in labor, too?" She blushed as soon as she said the words, but the image of him by her side while she brought their child into the world was a powerful one. He had been her rock through this ordeal, so why not depend on him for an even greater trial?

"If you want me to, I will," he said, with all the solemnity of an oath.

She closed her eyes and rested her head on his chest, listening to the steady beat of his heart, feeling the strength in his arms as he held her. All these months she had been telling herself she was strong enough to carry this baby alone. She was strong enough to give birth alone and to raise a child by herself.

But she didn't have to be that strong now. Dillon wanted to share the burden, and finally, standing here in the middle of nowhere, as worn down as she had ever been, she was ready to believe him.

She didn't know what kind of future they would have together, but right now, she would hold on to the promise that he would be there for her and for their child. It was far more than she had ever expected.

DILLON WALKED SLOWER and slower, but still Roslyn struggled to keep up. She had recovered her spirits somewhat but was still limping badly, and she stopped frequently to arch her back and knead at her spine, her brow furrowed in pain. "Is something wrong?" he asked, alarmed.

She shook her head. "The baby is fine," she said. "And I'm fine. I promise." She started walking again, doing her best to increase her pace, but he could see what the effort cost her.

"Let's stop and rest," he said.

"We just stopped not long ago."

Yes, when she had been crying, as if something he said had upset her. She seemed so fragile right now he was hesitant to say anything, but more rest was something he could be sure about. "We can stop again," he said. "We've got hours of daylight left."

She nodded. "All right. But I feel terrible that I'm going so slowly. You would have been out of here hours ago if it wasn't for me."

It was true they were moving at a crawl. He estimated they had come barely half a mile in the last hour. "I'm not going anywhere without you," he said. He moved in beside her and put his arm around her waist, supporting some of her weight. He searched for somewhere comfortable to sit, but there was really nowhere in this open area. He guided her to the side of the trail and lowered her to a patch of grass. "Let's see your ankle again."

He unlaced her boot and drew it off, aware of her wincing as he did so. "It's more swollen, isn't it?" she asked, leaning over to look as he peeled off her sock.

He nodded. The standard treatment for a sprain was rest, ice, compression and gentle exercise. Roslyn was getting none of that right now and her ankle was protesting. "Let's see if a cool compress helps," he said. He took out a water bottle and a square of gauze and applied the damp gauze around the ankle. "We'll leave that there for a while." Then he took out his phone.

"Any signal?" she asked.

"No." He stared at the No Service message on his screen. His radio also produced nothing but static. He wanted to get in touch with Search and Rescue and ask them to send a team with a litter for Roslyn.

"Guess we're going to have to tough it out and keep going," she said.

He liked her attitude, but he hated seeing her in pain. "Maybe I could carry you," he said.

She snorted. "Please! You'd ruin your back. Or you'd trip and drop me."

"Hey, I'm not that clumsy."

Her smile was so tender it moved him. "You're not," she said. "You've been great."

He touched a finger to the side of her mouth. "I was attracted to you from the very first by this smile. It stopped me cold in that lift line and I told myself I had to meet a woman with a smile like that."

"And we ended up on the chair together," she said.

"Oh, I made sure that happened," he said. "I let the couple in front of me go ahead so you and I would be sure to match up."

She laughed. "I was watching you and wondered."

"So you noticed me, too?" he asked.

"Oh, yeah. I thought you were hot."

He laughed, a big, joyous laugh. "And then we got on the lift together and started talking and you were so charming," she said. "And funny. You made me laugh and I hadn't laughed in so long."

Some of the mirth went out of him. "I'm sorry you had to go through so much heartache," he said. She hadn't said much at the time, only that she had recently broken up with someone. They hadn't been into talking about their histories or the future, only focused on the present.

"Thanks." She brushed her hair back from her eyes. "It didn't feel like it at the time, but I can see how much better off I am now."

"That's good. You seem happy."

"I have a lot to be happy about." She smiled down at her baby bump.

He settled in to sit beside her. Columns of smoke were visible in the distance, but directly overhead the sky was deep blue, and everything was peaceful. "Do you think you'll stay in Chicago?" he asked. When she had said earlier that she could work anywhere, he had hoped she was hinting that she might want to move closer to him.

"I don't know," she said. "I have friends there, and a nice apartment, but there's nothing to really anchor me there. We moved around a lot when I was a kid, so no one place has ever felt like home." She glanced at him. "Not like you."

"You already know I love it here, but I think you'd like it here, too."

"Why do you think that?" She was genuinely curious. Did he see something in her that she didn't?

"You like photography, right?"

She nodded.

"The scenery here draws photographers from around the world. In every season of the year there's natural beauty to capture with a camera. And you like the outdoors, at least judging by your hiking boots. You've put a few miles on those."

"I do enjoy hiking," she said.

"And skiing," he added. "You're a lot closer to Brundage Mountain here than you are in Chicago, not to mention Jackson Hole."

"I've always wanted to ski Jackson," she said.

"And there's peace and quiet. You need that for recording, right? There's plenty of peace and quiet here." Was he pouring it on too thick?

She laughed. "You're doing your best to convince me."

"I'm not trying to pressure you," he said. "But I could be a lot more help to you and the baby if you were closer."

"I'll seriously consider it," she said. "And it would be good for the baby to have his or her father close by." She frowned, a momentary wrinkling of her brow.

"What's wrong?" he asked.

She shook her head. "Nothing, really. It's just…your job. Isn't it dangerous?"

She really was giving this serious thought. He told himself that was a good sign. "It can be," he said. "But there's less crime here than in a city like Chicago. Probably because there are fewer people. There's still danger, but it's not a constant. We have some officers who come from a big city environment and they all agree working in Jasper is a lot less stressful."

"I've never lived in a town so small," she said. "But I can see how it could be nice. Especially with a family. What brought your parents here?"

"Like I said, they moved from Denver. My dad had been fishing in the area and fell in love, and my mom wanted a bigger place. The two of them are usually on the same page about decisions like that."

"That's a good thing for a marriage."

"It is. It's funny, though—they only knew each other six weeks when they got married."

"You're kidding."

"I'm not." He shook his head. "I asked them about it and my dad said he fell hard for her right away and didn't want to waste any more time. My mom said she just knew Dad was the man she needed to spend the rest of her life with." He thought about how hard he had fallen for Roslyn, from that very first day in the lift line. He risked looking at her. Her eyes were misty.

"That's so romantic," she said.

Their eyes met and he felt again the pull of desire, of needing to be closer to her. He reached for her and she leaned toward him. Their lips met, and the emotion of the moment overwhelmed him—tenderness, protectiveness, longing, fear that what he felt was too fragile to last. The sensation was unsettling. He had never hesitated when it came to relationships. He went after what he wanted, and the women he had been with had all reciprocated his feelings, brief though they might have been at times.

But no woman had mattered to him the way Roslyn did. Was this what his dad had felt for his mom—this sensation that life without Roslyn in it would be a little dimmer, a little less complete?

She broke the kiss, her eyes looking deep into his, as if trying to read his thoughts. "Dillon, I—"

"Arf! Arf! Arf!" At their feet, Bentley erupted into fierce barking. He ran forward, leash trailing, the hair of his ruff standing on end, his whole body tense.

Dillon tensed also. He gently pushed Roslyn away from him and stood. "What is it, boy?" he asked, following the dog's gaze to the border of woodland to their far left. Had something moved within the shadows there?

"Arf! Arf! Arf!" Bentley took off running toward the dim figure, Dillon right behind him.

EMMA HAD ONLY come downtown for a few minutes to pick up tidbits to entice some of the evacuees who were too upset to eat properly. She could have sent Barbara or one of her other helpers, but she thought it would be a good idea to take a break from the chaos at DCA. Barking dogs didn't really bother her after so long, but add in a steady stream of people looking to drop off or retrieve pets and it got to be a little much.

She was on her way back to her car when she noticed a crowd gathering near the police station. "What's going on?" she asked a well-dressed man who was walking briskly in that direction.

"The local police have called a press conference to release information about the hunt for Kent Anderson," the man said.

Emma followed him toward what turned out to be a portable stage that looked suspiciously like the one the parks department used for summer concerts in the park. Directly in front of the police department, East Main had been closed off with barricades. Emma spotted Tashya's fiancé, Jason, at one of the barricades. "What's happening?" she asked, hoping for more specifics.

"Captain Rutledge is holding a press conference," Jason said. He stood straight and tall in his uniform and tried to look stern, but couldn't hold the expression when he asked, "Is Tashya with you?"

"Sorry, just me." Emma held up the bag from the local pet boutique, Chow. "I had to run a few errands. Why is Rutledge holding the conference instead of Chief Walters?"

Jason shrugged.

"Probably because the chief has better ways to spend his time than put on a show for the media." Emma leaned past Jason and squinted at Rutledge, who had just stepped onto the stage, sharp in dress blues, his hair carefully gelled. "Is he wearing makeup?"

Jason turned to look and his eyes widened. "I'm not sure he normally has that much color in his cheeks. Or his lips."

"I guess he figures if it's good enough for actors, it's good enough for him," Emma said.

A squawk from the sound system made her wince. Rutledge cleared his throat. "All right, everyone. Let's get started," he said.

The assembled media shifted and murmured. Rutledge cleared his throat again, consulted his notes, then began. "I'm Captain Arthur Rutledge with the Jasper Police Department. I know you have a lot of questions about the hunt for convicted mass murderer Kent Anderson, as well as the search for Roslyn Kern, but I want to assure you we have the situation in hand and expect to have Anderson back in custody and Ms. Kern restored to safety within a matter of hours."

"We do?" murmured Jason.

No one but Emma heard him in the uproar that followed these claims. "Does this mean you know Anderson's whereabouts?" someone called.

"Are the federal authorities who are leading the manhunt aware of this information?" someone else asked. "I thought they were looked for Anderson in Nevada."

"What about Ms. Kern?" a woman called. "Do you know where she is? Is she all right?"

"When will you be bringing Anderson into custody?"

"Are Roslyn Kern and Kent Anderson together?"

"How were you able to locate the two of them?"

Rutledge held up both hands, gesturing for calm. "We

have one of our best officers with Ms. Kern now, escorting her back to safety," he said.

"What about Anderson?" a man directly in front of the stage asked.

"We are closing in on him," Rutledge said. "We have been tracking his progress for some time now and it's only a matter of time before we have him in custody."

Emma felt Jason tense beside her, but he said nothing.

"What about the federal marshals who are pursuing Anderson?" a woman Emma recognized as a news reporter from a Boise television station asked.

Rutledge scowled. "Anderson is in our jurisdiction," he said. "Jasper PD is better equipped to apprehend a fugitive here than people who are unfamiliar with the area."

"Did he just say we're better equipped than the Feds?" Jason whispered to Emma.

"That's what it sounded like to me," Emma said. The media would no doubt take that statement and run with it. Chief Walters would stroke out when he found out.

Rutledge ignored other questions fired his way, and droned on for several minutes about his experience with the department and plans for the future. "You're going to see a whole new era of policing in Jasper soon," he said.

"Are you saying Chief Walters intends to take the department in a new direction?" The reporter for the local paper, Pam Xavier, asked this question.

"Chief Walters will be retiring soon and his successor will focus on updating the department with the latest policing methods," Rutledge said.

"Who is Chief Walters's successor?" a woman asked.

"There's nothing official yet, but as the most senior officer on the force, I'm the most logical candidate for the position." Rutledge struck a pose as cameras flashed—

chin up, steely glint in his eyes, Hollywood's perfect portrayal of a dedicated law enforcement officer.

"If he's made chief, the first thing he'll do is get rid of the canine program," Emma said. She kept her voice low but could barely contain her rage. She hoped her proposed training would help the captain deal with dogs in a less confrontational manner, but she had little faith she could turn him into a dog lover, or make him see the worth of Chief Walters's efforts to pair dogs and officers as a vital part of the public safety community here in Jasper.

"A lot of the officers won't like that." Jason looked at her, sadness in his eyes. "I was hoping to work with my own dog one day soon. Tashya and I had talked about it. When I'm ready."

"You'll do great with a dog," Emma said and squeezed his arm.

"That's all the questions we have time for," Rutledge said. "Thank you for coming."

"Wait! You haven't told us how you tracked down Anderson."

"When will Ms. Kern be returning to Jasper? Is she all right?"

"What were Anderson's intentions when he escaped? Why did he come to Jasper?"

Rutledge ignored the questions and turned away.

"Wait! I have something to say!"

Rutledge's eyes widened and he held up one hand, as if trying to stop traffic, as a woman climbed the steps onto the stage. Colleen Diaz, her red hair caught up in a rhinestone clasp and her sapphire blue wrap dress accentuating a mature but curvaceous figure, strode to the microphone as if she was accustomed to addressing a crowd.

"My name is Colleen Diaz and my son, Dillon, is the officer who is rescuing poor Ms. Kern," she announced.

Cameras flashed and a new energy surged through the crowd of media. "I hope they run those photos on a lot of front pages," Emma said, smiling. "Rutledge might burst into flames with envy."

Jason chuckled but quickly resumed a straight face.

"Have you spoken with your son today?" someone asked. "Is Roslyn all right?"

"How did he find her?"

"Have they seen Kent Anderson? Has he threatened him?"

"Dillon is very good at his job," Colleen said. "So of course he was able to locate Ms. Kern. I haven't spoken to him this morning, but this young woman, Roslyn Kern, is in very good hands now. Dillon is not only an excellent police officer and a wonderful son, he's also very good-looking."

Laughter rippled through the crowd. Colleen's smile broadened. "I know a mother is always biased, but you ladies out there have seen his photo and you know, right?"

More laughter. Someone else in this situation might have come across looking ridiculous, but Colleen was charming them all—a talent she had passed on to her oldest son.

"Is Dillon single?" someone asked.

"He is! And so is Ms. Kern." Colleen winked. "It's a very romantic scenario, don't you think? A young woman in need of assistance, and a handsome, dedicated young man in need of the right woman in his life."

"Are you saying your son and Roslyn Kern are romantically involved?"

Colleen gave an elegant shrug. "There are worse ways to begin a relationship."

Emma couldn't keep back her laughter. "Dillon is never going to hear the end of this," she said.

"Who knows?" Jason said. "She could be right."

"What?" Emma stared at him. "You think Dillon and this stranger from Chicago could really end up together?"

"They'll have had plenty of time to get to know each other by the time this is all over."

"How long did you date Tashya before you proposed?" Emma asked, though she already knew the answer.

He flushed. "Three years. But we were teenagers when we met. And I don't know—a few things Dillon has said make me think he's ready to settle down."

Was he? Emma wondered. Dillon had always struck her as the type who liked to play the field. He never had to work to attract women, so why commit to one? Though supposedly he had fallen pretty hard for someone he met while skiing this past winter. But she'd heard that hadn't worked out.

"That's all we have time for." Rutledge stepped in front of Colleen and took the microphone from its stand. "You can all leave now. This press conference is over."

Colleen leaned close to Rutledge to speak into the mic. "Thank you, Captain Rutledge," she said. "It was so nice to hear you acknowledge my son as one of your best officers. It makes me so proud."

Faced with the full force of both Colleen's personality and her physical presence, Rutledge could only looked stunned. Only when she had sashayed away did he find his voice once more. "What are you doing just standing there?" he barked at Jason. "Get that street reopened, then return to patrol."

"Yes, sir." Jason hefted one of the barricades.

"I'll leave you to it," Emma said. She smiled and waved at the scowling Rutledge and headed back toward her car. He seemed confident that he would soon be in charge of Jasper PD, but she wasn't so sure about that. Not if his plans meant getting rid of the dogs.

Chapter Fifteen

Ava and Brady, with Lacey between them, drove slowly past the Williams Gap Trailhead. Search and Rescue was there, with an ambulance and the Jeep used to transport personnel. Andrea and several other SAR members stood around the back of the ambulance, all wearing bright yellow search and rescue vests. The yellow caution tape that had previously blocked the entrance fluttered loosely from one of the posts marking the entrance. A couple of cars with Idaho plates sat on the far side of the parking area. The bright yellow warning sign Ava had posted yesterday was still in place at the entrance to the trail.

"Those two on the edge are rental cars," Brady said as he eased his truck past. "Probably reporters."

"I see two people standing by the trail map, talking," Ava said. "That's probably them."

"Everyone else must have taken Captain Rutledge's bait and gone to the press conference," Brady said.

"What should we do?" Ava asked. "If we park at the trailhead, they'll have questions, and they might make us for cops."

"We can head to the Elwoods' house and cut across from there to the trail," Brady said. "But I'm afraid if we do that, we'll miss Dillon and Roz. We don't know how fast they're traveling, and it's possible they're closer to the trail's end by now."

Ava nodded. "So, do you have a plan C?"

"We could park down the road," he said. "There's a gate to a hayfield. There's a path that runs from there and hits the trail a few hundred yards past the start."

They left the truck at the gate, climbed over a stile and followed a faint trail through tall grass to the more defined trail. "This leads up to Cow Creek," Brady said, checking the GPS on his phone. "This should be the path Dillon and Roslyn take."

The plan was for them to hike until they met Dillon, keeping an eye out for Kent Anderson or any sign of trouble. They set out with Lacey in the lead, loping along at a steady, brisk pace. "I'm a little freaked out, crossing this open section," Ava said. "What if Anderson is watching us?"

"What if he's not out here at all?" Brady said. He scanned their surroundings—tall grass beginning to yellow at the tips, and stands of dark evergreens and lighter aspen to their left. Not a single wisp of cloud marred the perfect blue of the sky, and the only sounds were their footsteps crunching on the trail and the jingle of Lacey's tags.

"It's too quiet," Ava said. "Where are the birds?"

"I thought you were a city girl," Brady said.

"I've been doing a lot of hiking lately," she said. "With Eli and by myself. I've discovered I like the outdoors."

"Next thing you know, we'll have you rafting rivers and climbing cliffs," Brady said.

"I'd like to do those things and more," she said. "And I'd do them better than you."

"You could try," he said.

"Shh!" She held up a hand to silence him and nodded toward the dog. Lacey stood frozen in the middle of the trail, tail low, ears forward, staring intently into the trees.

"Can you tell what she's alerting on?" Brady asked. He slid his Glock from its holster and held it loose at his side.

Ava shook her head. The three of them stood there for a long moment, the two people watching the dog. Brady tried to slow his breathing, eyes straining into the woods, trying to see what the dog saw. Or smelled. Or felt with that sixth sense some dogs seemed to have.

"Lacey, seek!" Ava commanded.

The dog glanced back at her.

"Seek!" Ava said again.

Lacey trotted off the trail and into the woods, the two humans jogging to keep up.

HEART POUNDING, ROSLYN stared as Dillon headed after Bentley. "What is it?" she called. "Why is he barking like that?" This was definitely a different sound than when Bentley had alerted them to the presence of the deer earlier.

"I don't know," Dillon called back. "But stay here."

She glanced down at her bare foot, the ankle still wrapped in wet gauze. It wasn't as if she could go anywhere like this. But just in case, she decided she'd better put her sock and boot back on.

She finished lacing up her boot and stood, trying out the ankle. It still hurt, but she was determined to keep going. They were so close to safety and rest. She had never wanted a hot shower so much in her life. And after that…after that, she and Dillon needed to have a serious talk about the future. She had to tell him she wanted them to be more than two people with only a child in common.

She would never have believed she could have such intense feelings for a man she had known for only a short time, but she wanted the chance to nurture those feelings.

When he had talked about his home, and his desire to raise a family there, it had been all she could do not to shout, *I want to be part of that family, too. I want that to be us in that house, raising our child together.*

She glanced toward the woods, where Dillon and Bentley had disappeared among the trees. She felt shaky—and afraid. Had the man who had tried to steal her camera returned? Would Bentley frighten him away? Or would he hurt the dog—or hurt Dillon? She put a hand over her heart, trying to quell the fear that welled inside her.

"Stand right there and don't move."

The man's voice was deep and hoarse, and she let out a squeak of surprise at his words and started to turn around.

"I told you not to move!" he shouted.

She froze, and clenched her jaw to keep from crying out again.

"Where's the camera?" he asked.

"The camera?"

"You were taking pictures. You had a camera."

This was the man who had tried to steal her camera earlier! The knowledge made her shake. She took a deep breath. *Stay strong,* she told herself. *Your only chance is to be smarter than he is.* And hope that Dillon returned soon. "It's in my pack." She gestured toward the pack, which rested on the ground.

"Get it and toss it over here," he said. "The whole pack."

Moving slowly, she sidestepped toward the pack, imagining the man pointing a gun at her. But she didn't know that, did she? What if he was bluffing? She reached the pack and bent to pick it up by the straps, but as she did so, she looked back, and started shaking again.

Yes, he had a gun pointed at her. She didn't know anything about guns, but this looked like a big pistol. And he was close. Maybe ten feet from her. Even a little gun could probably kill her from that distance.

"Throw it over here!" he ordered.

She did as he asked, though her toss was weak. The pack landed halfway between them. If the man wanted it, he'd have to move closer. Which would bring the gun closer. "Why do you want my camera?" she asked. She didn't care about his answer, but she wanted to buy time for Dillon to return to her.

Then what? He was a cop. He was armed. And he had Bentley with him. But what if the man shot them? Maybe she should be doing everything she could to keep them from returning to her. "There's just a bunch of pictures of wildflowers on there," she said.

"I saw you aiming the camera at me," the man said. She had been so focused on the gun that she hadn't noticed much about him, but she had the impression of blandness—bland clothes and hair and very ordinary looks. Only the gun made him sinister, and the way he had it trained on her.

"Is that why you've been following us?" she asked. "Because you don't like your picture being taken?"

"Shut up. You ask too many questions."

She heard a shuffling sound in the grass, and sensed him moving toward her. She tensed, imagining the bullet striking her at any moment. But as she waited, movement ahead of her caught her eye. Dillon and Bentley appeared at the edge of the woods, moving toward her. *Stay back!* She wanted to shout to them. And *help me!*

She risked a look back, and the man moved closer to her. Maybe she could distract him so he wouldn't see Dillon.

"Turn back around!" he barked.

"Why should I?" she asked. "If I took your picture, I already know what you look like. And what does that matter anyway? Who are you?"

"You don't know who I am?" He had reached the back-pack now. He picked it up and slung it over his shoulder.

"No." She squinted, as if trying to bring him into better focus. There was nothing remarkable about the man. "Are you famous?"

His laughter at this comment startled her. "Are you really as dumb as you sound?" he asked. "Or are you only pretending?"

She glared at him. "I might be ignorant, but I'm not stupid," she said.

"Stop right there! Don't move!"

Dillon's voice rang across the clearing. Roslyn turned toward him and her heart leaped to see him standing there, a pistol aimed at the man who had accosted her.

"You shoot me and I'll kill her," the man shouted. "This close, I won't miss." A sharp click of his weapon being cocked, and Roslyn forgot how to breathe.

Chapter Sixteen

Dillon froze, paralyzed by the sight of the gun trained on Roslyn. "Drop the gun!" Anderson ordered. Dillon opened his hand and let the gun fall. It seemed to take forever to hit the ground, time slowed down by the cold fear that gripped him. Beside him, Bentley quivered, a low growl rising from deep in the dog's chest. Dillon told himself he should signal the dog to stay, but he was unable to move. *Breathe*, he reminded himself, and did so. *Think*.

"Don't be a fool, Kent," he said.

"How do you know my name?"

"Every law officer in the state is looking for you," Dillon said. "There's a SWAT team on its way here right now."

"You're a liar," Anderson said. "But even if you aren't, I'll be gone before they get here. I'm not going back to prison. Never."

Dillon had seen images of Anderson on television right after he was captured. He had looked small and weak then, the kind of person whose only power is in the weapon they wield, not in their own character. Up close, he didn't look so small, but ordinary. If they had passed on the trail, Dillon would have taken him for just another hiker out enjoying the day.

"Get over here, by the woman." Anderson motioned with the gun. Moving to where Roslyn sat meant getting closer to Anderson, but not close enough to disarm him. One wrong move and Anderson would kill him. Then he'd be free to kill Roslyn, too. Dillon had to stay alive. As long as he was alive, they had a chance to get away, though he couldn't see a clear way to make that happen, yet.

He moved slowly, hands out at his sides in clear view. "Sit down next to her," Anderson ordered.

He sat, and Roslyn gave him a shaky smile. He looked into her eyes, trying to reassure her somehow, but she was clearly terrified, pupils wide, arms folded protectively across the swell of her abdomen. He focused on Anderson. The fugitive had turned to face them, holding the pistol in both hands, aimed at them. Dillon studied the gun—a 45, a Ruger, he thought, not that the make mattered. Anderson had plenty of firepower to kill them at this range.

Dillon kept his gaze fixed on Anderson but noticed out of the corner of his eye that Bentley hadn't followed him. Instead, the dog lay flat on his belly in the tall grass, scarcely visible except for the tips of his ears. Was the dog hiding because he was frightened?

"Why don't you just go and leave us alone?" Roslyn said. "It's not as if we can do anything to stop you."

"You'll tell the cops you saw me, and which direction I'm headed," Anderson said. "Right now, because of the fire, no one knows I'm out here. I'm going to make sure it stays that way."

"Law enforcement knows you're here," Dillon said.

Anderson glared at him. Dillon thought the fugitive was going to accuse him of lying again. Instead, Anderson took a step closer. "You're a cop, aren't you?" he asked, his face flushed. "I should have known. You look like a cop. You've been following me, haven't you?"

"No! He came out here to find me," Roslyn said. "I hurt my ankle and—"

"Shut up!" Anderson took better aim with the pistol. Dillon stared, bracing for the bullet's impact. He reached for Roslyn, wanting his last sensation to be of touching her.

He didn't see Bentley explode from his hiding place in the grass, but he saw the dog leap, his jaws latching on to Anderson's outstretched arm. Anderson shouted and flailed. Dillon jumped up as the gun went off, but the bullet didn't strike him. He rushed forward and grabbed Anderson's other arm and twisted it behind his back. Bentley held on to the other arm, even as Anderson struggled to free himself.

Dillon pulled Anderson to the ground and subdued him. "Bentley, leave it!" he ordered.

The dog released his hold and backed up, panting, gaze fixed on Dillon. Dillon pulled flex-cuffs from his pack and secured Anderson's hands behind his back. "Good boy," he told Bentley.

But the dog had already moved away, to Roslyn. The dog whined and pawed at the woman, who lay on her side, moaning. "Roslyn!" Dillon abandoned Anderson and raced to her side.

Roslyn stared up at him, her cheeks streaked with tears. "He shot me," she said.

"Where? Where did he shoot you?" Fighting panic, Dillon knelt beside her.

"My arm." She rolled onto her back and he saw blood welling from a wound in her biceps.

"It's going to be okay," he said, to himself as well as to her. "I'm going to stop the bleeding and we're going to get you to the hospital and everything is going to be okay." How he was going to do that, he had no clear idea, but if he had to carry her on his back all the way to town, he would do it.

AVA AND BRADY heard the gunshots and someone screaming. Lacey barked and launched herself toward the sound, leaping through the underbrush until Ava lost sight of her. Someone was shouting now, and another dog barking. Was that Bentley? Ava pushed herself to run harder, feet pounding on the leaf mold, ducking to dodge branches, her pack bouncing against her back. Her ballistics vest dug into her bottom rib, but she ignored the pain and pushed on. Who had screamed? Was that Anderson shooting? Or Dillon? Was someone hurt? Were they running to rescue, or into an ambush?

DILLON PULLED A stack of gauze pads from his pack and pressed them to Roslyn's shoulder. She cried out at the pressure. "I know it hurts," he said. "But we have to stop the bleeding." He looked around them, hoping to see help approaching. Anderson lay on the ground glaring at him. How long before he made a move to run, or to attack?

At first Dillon thought he might be hallucinating. A large, dark dog burst from the trees and raced toward them, followed by two running humans. Bentley barked, tail wagging, and Anderson let out a string of curses as the other dog skidded to a stop in front of the prisoner and sat. He recognized Ava's partner, Lacey.

Dillon raised one arm to wave. "Over here!" he shouted to the people, who had slowed and were looking around, weapons drawn. "We need help!"

"Who is it?" Roslyn asked. She lay with her back to the trail now, eyes closed, her breathing shallow.

"Ava Callan and Brady Nichols, with the Jasper Police," Dillon said, as the two raced toward them.

"What happened?" Ava looked from the prone figure of Anderson to the gentle mound of Roslyn's belly.

"This is Kent Anderson," Dillon said. "He shot Roslyn Kern." He looked down to where he still pressed gauze to Roslyn's arm. "She's lost some blood but she's going to be all right. But we need a litter team to carry her out, and an ambulance waiting at the trailhead."

"I'll run back for help," Ava said. "Lacey can stay here and help with Anderson." The dog sat by Anderson's head, and let out a low rumble when the fugitive raised his head.

"Good idea," Brady said.

Ava took off running. Things happened quickly after that. Brady took charge of Anderson while Dillon finished bandaging Roslyn. "How did you know to come looking for us?" Dillon asked.

"We were pretty sure Anderson was in the area and worried you might cross paths," Brady said. "He had sworn to kill anyone who interfered with his escape." He relieved Anderson of another gun, a knife and his pack, ignoring the fugitive's cursing and complaining as he worked. He turned to Roslyn, who stared up at him. "I'm Brady Nichols, by the way," he said.

"Hello. I'm Roslyn Kern."

"Oh, we all know who you are," Brady said. He tagged and bagged Anderson's weapons as he spoke. "Jasper is full of media right now, all covering the story of Rockin' Roz lost in the wilderness."

Roslyn moaned and closed her eyes. "I can't believe they followed me here."

"I don't think they followed you," Brady said. "I think they were in town because of the fire, and because Kent Anderson escaped from prison. Apparently, he had relatives in the area who helped him get away and he planned to head to Alaska. But once you went missing, that was one more story to add to the news cycle." He turned to Dillon. "How did the two of you meet up with Anderson?"

"He's been following us since I found Roslyn." Dillon rested his hand on Roslyn's. "While she was photographing wildflowers, she inadvertently caught Anderson in one of her shots. He realized it and thought when she showed the photo around, law enforcement would know where he was and come after him."

"Law enforcement has known where he was practically from the beginning," Brady said. "The man who gave him a ride to near the trailhead identified him in a photo lineup."

Anderson started swearing. Lacey growled again and he fell silent. Brady looked at Roslyn again. She lay with her eyes closed, her breathing shallow. "How's she doing?"

"She's going to be okay." Dillon squeezed her hand.

"Just to warn you, there are a lot of reporters in town who are going to be excited to see her," Brady said. "We don't get celebrities in Jasper all that often."

"She's not just a celebrity," Dillon said. He smiled down at Roslyn. "Brady, meet Rosie Kenley, aka Roslyn Kern."

Brady stopped what he was doing and stared. "So you finally found Rosie," he said. He eyed the baby bump again. Dillon could almost see him doing the math in his head.

Roslyn, who had fallen quiet while they talked, opened her eyes and said, "Yes, the baby is Dillon's. Now could I have some water, please?"

Both men hurried to offer water, but Dillon won out. He held her head while she drank and watched blood seep through the bandage he had wrapped around her upper arm. How long was it going to take Ava to get to help, and how long after that for help to get to them?

"Search and Rescue is staged at the trailhead," Brady said. "Once they get the word, it won't take them long to get here."

"That's good," Dillon said.

"There's going to be a circus once word gets out you've been found," Brady said. "And Anderson. The media have really been playing up the idea of the beautiful DJ being pursued through the wilderness by a wildfire and an escaped killer. That is, those reporters who haven't decided that Roz and Kent are in this together." He pointed to Dillon. "And they've latched onto you as the hunky knight in shining armor who set out to rescue her."

"Welcome to my world," Roslyn said. Her eyes met Dillon's. "Sorry."

He squeezed her hand. "I can handle it."

"He thinks so," Brady said to Roslyn. "But wait until he sees the grief everyone back at the station is going to give him."

Bentley's barking interrupted the rude reply Dillon had in mind. Brady stood. "Looks like the cavalry is here," he said, and walked out to greet the EMTs and law enforcement headed toward them up the trail.

Dillon looked down at Roslyn. "How are you doing?" he asked.

"I'm hanging in there," she said. "How about you?"

"As long as you're good, I'm good." He laced his fingers with hers. "You're stuck with me now."

Her smile burned through him, like a brand on his heart. "I like the sound of that."

"You're doing great," Charla, the paramedic, said when she had finished checking Roslyn over. "The baby is doing fine, too."

Roslyn managed a smile. "That's good to know." She had been such a trouper through this whole ordeal—so brave and steady. She found Dillon and smiled a little wider at him. "Did you hear that? The baby is okay."

"I heard." He took her hand and held it all the way up the trail to the waiting ambulance. Though he saw Andrea and the other SAR members exchange questioning looks, no one said anything. Jason Wright and Cal Hoover arrived to take Kent Anderson into custody, and a crime scene team arrived to process the site of the shooting. Ava and Brady trailed Dillon and the SAR team to the ambulance, where Dillon finally released Roslyn's hand so she could be loaded into the ambulance.

"Do you want a ride to the hospital?" Brady asked as they watched the ambulance pull away, siren wailing.

Dillon shook his head. "Thanks, but Roslyn will go straight into surgery and I'll drive myself crazy waiting for word from her. Better to go into the station and deal with all the paperwork."

"Then Anderson is all yours. You're the one who captured him. You deserve the glory."

"Right. You just don't want to deal with the press."

Brady clapped him on the back. "Hey, you're already a celebrity. Might as well run with it. And I guess congratulations are in order."

"Congratulations?" Ava asked. "For capturing Anderson?"

"Oh, you missed the big news," Brady said. He punched Dillon's arm—hard enough that he felt a sting, though he tried not to show it. "Dillon here is going to be a father."

"A father?" Ava looked confused, then her eyes widened. "You don't mean Roslyn Kern?"

"Roslyn is actually Rosie, the woman Dillon met over Valentine's weekend and has been searching for ever since."

Ava shook her head. "Okay. Well, congratulations!"

Dillon couldn't keep back a foolish grin. "Yeah. I'm still getting used to the idea."

They spent the ride to the station hearing a recap of Dillon's reunion with Roslyn. "So, what happens now?" Ava asked. "Do you all live happily ever after?"

"That's my goal," Dillon said. "Though I don't know what that looks like." He wanted Roslyn to move to Jasper, to move in with him, even, and the two of them to raise their child together as husband and wife. But he realized that was a lot of change at once, and might be too much for her to handle.

At the station the three of them walked in to applause. "Congratulations on stopping Kent Anderson before he injured more people," Chief Walters said.

"Thank you, sir," Dillon said.

"How is Ms. Kern?" Walters asked.

"She's been taken to the hospital for surgery to remove a bullet from her shoulder," Dillon said. "But the paramedic said she and her baby are doing well." He shot Brady a look. While word would spread soon enough that he was the father of Roslyn's child, he wasn't ready to repeat the story to the whole station. Not until he had at least told his family.

"The US Marshals Service isn't going to be happy you made them look bad," Captain Rutledge said. "They've been hunting for Anderson in Nevada."

"That's not on us," Walters said. "Come into my office, Dillon, and give me your verbal report. Then you can go home and get some rest. I imagine you need it."

Dillon followed the chief to his office and gave a recap of the past day and a half, including that he and Roslyn had had a previous relationship and he was the father of her child. "I would say that's a remarkable coincidence," Walters said. "But I've been in law enforcement long enough to wonder if there really is such a thing as blind chance. It sounds like you did a good job of keeping you both safe."

"Bentley deserves the most credit," Dillon said. He looked down at the dog, who lay stretched out on the floor beside him, snoring softly. "He attacked Anderson when he fired at Roslyn and threw off his aim, and also distracted him long enough that I was able to overpower him. I'm also grateful Ava and Brady showed up when they did. I would have had my hands full trying to get both Roslyn and Anderson to the trailhead."

A knock on the door interrupted them. "Come in," Walters called.

Captain Rutledge stepped in. "The press is asking

for a statement," he said. "I think Dillon should speak
to them."

"It's your call," the chief said to Dillon.

"You'd only have to make a brief statement, maybe
answer a few questions," Rutledge said.

He thought of Roslyn, dealing with the press on her
own for so long. Maybe he could say something that
would help her. "I can do it," he said.

From the chief's office he returned to the squad room,
intending to start work on his report, but he was greeted
again by both applause and hoots of laughter. "It's local
heartthrob Dillon Diaz!" Jason sang out.

"The man on the US Marshals' Most Wanted list,"
Ava said.

"Our own Hunk of the Month," Cal said.

"What are you people talking about?" Dillon asked.

"According to the press you're a cross between a Chip-
pendales dancer and a superhero," Brady said.

More hoots of laughter. Brady rested his hand on Dillon's shoulder. "Seriously, we're glad you're okay."

"We weren't really worried," Cal said. "I mean, who
messes with the knight in shining armor who's rescued
the damsel in distress?"

Dillon tried to smile, but all he could think of was that
in a few minutes he was going to have to go out and face
the people who'd written such preposterous things about
him. He sympathized with Roslyn more and more. No
wonder she hadn't wanted to reveal her real name when
they first met.

Teresa hurried into the room. "There's someone here
to see you, Dillon."

Before he could ask who, his mom and dad burst into
the room. Or rather, Colleen burst—his dad followed at

He took Dillon's arm and hustled him into the conference room upstairs from the squad room. The chief was already there, along with more than a dozen men and women with notebooks and cameras and microphones. Chief Walters, in full uniform, stepped up to the microphone. "Thank you all for coming this afternoon," he said. "I wanted to announce that Kent Anderson is in custody. Roslyn Kern is at Cascade Medical Center, where she is expected to a make a full recovery from a gunshot wound to the shoulder, a wound inflicted by Anderson before Sergeant Dillon Diaz of the Jasper Police Department, aided by his search and rescue canine, Bentley, subdued and arrested Anderson. And now I'd like to introduce you to Sergeant Diaz."

Dillon moved to the podium and gripped the sides, hoping no one would notice how nervous he suddenly was. "Hello," he said.

"Can you describe what happened out there today, Sergeant Diaz?" A woman in the front row of reporters asked.

Dillon looked toward the chief, who nodded. He took a deep breath. "Search and Rescue received a call about a missing hiker and my search dog, Bentley, and I responded." But really, the story had begun five months ago, when he decided to go skiing on Valentine's Day.

He summed up the events of the past two days as briefly as possible, then brought Bentley in to pose for pictures. The dog was happy to pose both with and without Dillon as long as Dillon kept feeding him treats. And Dillon was relieved to have some of the focus taken off himself.

"That's all the questions we have time for this evening," Chief Walters finally said. "Sergeant Diaz has been through a lot and deserves a rest."

He ushered Dillon and Bentley out of the room. "You should go home now," Walters said. "And I'm taking you off the schedule tomorrow."

"Thank you, sir," Dillon said. "I will go home, but then I plan to go to the hospital." He needed to see Roslyn. He needed it more than he needed a shower or a meal, though he would take care of both those things at home, if only so he could spend more time with her.

Chapter Seventeen

Roslyn awoke with a feeling of panic in her chest. She must have cried out, because someone laid gentle hands on her and a woman's soft voice said, "It's all right. You're safe and well."

"The baby?" Roslyn tried to feel for her belly, but medical equipment attached to her hands shortened her reach.

"The baby is fine," the woman said.

Roslyn's vision was clearing now, and she could make out a hospital room painted a soft blue. She turned to stare at the woman—a beautiful older woman with long red hair and bright hazel green eyes. "I'm Colleen Diaz," the woman said. "I'm Dillon's mom. I've spoken with the doctors and you're going to be just fine. The surgery went well. You'll be sore for a while but you should recover completely. In about four and half months you'll have no trouble holding your baby."

"They told you all that?"

"I told them you were the mother of my future grandchild." Colleen sat back. "They balked a bit at first, but I persuaded them to see it my way." She took Roslyn's hand in hers. "Since your own mother isn't here, I thought you wouldn't mind if I stepped in. No one should be in the hospital without an advocate."

Roslyn had to blink back tears. "Thank you," she said.

"Dillon will be here soon," Colleen said. "He was still busy at the station, but I know he wants to see you."

"You have a wonderful son," Roslyn said.

"I have three wonderful sons, but yes, Dillon is very special. And you must be special too, if you've captured his heart."

Had she captured his heart?

"I can see in his eyes how much he loves you," Colleen said. "You might think I'm imagining things, but a mother knows these things. One day you'll know them, too."

The door to the room opened and Roslyn's heart climbed into her throat as she looked toward it, expecting Dillon. But it was only a nurse, who checked her vitals and showed her how to operate the bed. The nurse nodded to Colleen. "I can see you're in good hands," she told Roslyn. "But if you need anything, press the call button and someone will come."

As the nurse was leaving someone else appeared in the doorway. Someone tall and broad-shouldered, whose face shone with a light when he looked at her. Roslyn's heart stuttered when she saw that light. Colleen was right—she knew. Did he see the same light in her eyes?

Dillon moved to the bed and kissed her forehead. "How are you feeling?" he asked.

"Groggy. A little sore." She tried to move her bandaged shoulder and winced.

"She's doing great." Colleen stood on the other side of the bed. "The doctor says she and the baby are in excellent health."

"Thanks, Mom, but I can take over now," Dillon said.

"You see how it is," Colleen said to Roslyn. "He wants to be alone with you." She waved goodbye and swept from the room. That really was the only way to describe it. Colleen Diaz obviously had a flare for the dramatic.

"I see you've met my mother," Dillon said.

"She's very nice."

"I'm not sure 'nice' is the word most people use to describe Mom, but she is a good person, if a little forceful at times."

"I think she and I will get along fine." *Because they both loved him.*

He leaned down to kiss her again, on the lips this time. "It's good to see you again," he said. "You frightened me for a little bit."

He had frightened her, too, when he launched himself at Kent Anderson. "Where is Anderson?"

"In jail, where he will stay for a long time," Dillon said.

"And Bentley! He saved my life."

"They don't allow dogs in the hospital. Not even heroes like him. He's home having a good nap." He settled onto the edge of the bed and gently held her hand, positioning around the IV.

He had obviously showered, shaved and changed clothes. "You smell good," she said.

"You look good. Not as pale." He traced her cheek with the back of his free hand and she fought the urge to lean into his touch, like a cat being petted. "I know you're tired," he said. "I won't stay too long."

She wet her dry lips. "I've been thinking."

"What about?"

"Maybe I could move to Jasper. I mean, I already

know I like the town, and I'd like to be closer to you."
She hurried to get the words out before she lost her nerve.

He didn't answer for so long that she was afraid she had misread everything. She felt panic rising. "I've got a better idea," he finally said.

"What's that? You don't want to move to Chicago, do you?"

"You remember I have a house. With three bedrooms and a big yard."

"Perfect for a family."

"We could make that family—you and me and our baby."

She swallowed hard. "It's a big step. Are we ready?"

"I think so." He moved their clasped hands to cover his heart. "I love you. I knew I loved you after our first day together. I don't want to lose you again."

She nodded. It was a big leap. But one she was ready to take. "I love you, too. And I want us to be together. So yes. Let's make that family. You and me and the baby. And Bentley."

He laughed. "And Bentley." And he kissed her again, their hands clasped now on the mound of the baby, a promise for the future. For forever.

* * * * *

MILLS & BOON

THE HEART OF ROMANCE

A ROMANCE FOR EVERY READER

MODERN

Prepare to be swept off your feet by sophisticated, sexy and seductive heroes, in some of the world's most glamourous and romantic locations, where power and passion collide.

HISTORICAL

Escape with historical heroes from time gone by. Whether your passion is for wicked Regency Rakes, muscled Vikings or rugged Highlanders, awake the romance of the past.

MEDICAL

Set your pulse racing with dedicated, delectable doctors in the high-pressure world of medicine, where emotions run high and passion, comfort and love are the best medicine.

True Love

Celebrate true love with tender stories of heartfelt romance, from the rush of falling in love to the joy a new baby can bring, and a focus on the emotional heart of a relationship.

Desire

Indulge in secrets and scandal, intense drama and plenty of sizzling hot action with powerful and passionate heroes who have it all: wealth, status, good looks...everything but the right woman.

HEROES

Experience all the excitement of a gripping thriller, with an intense romance at its heart. Resourceful, true-to-life women and strong, fearless men face danger and desire - a killer combination!

To see which titles are coming soon, please visit

millsandboon.co.uk/nextmonth

LET'S TALK

Romance

For exclusive extracts, competitions
and special offers, find us online:

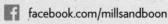 facebook.com/millsandboon

@MillsandBoon

@MillsandBoonUK

Get in touch on 01413 063232

For all the latest titles coming soon, visit
millsandboon.co.uk/nextmonth

MILLS & BOON
Desire

Indulge in secrets and scandal, intense drama and plenty of sizzling hot action with powerful and passionate heroes who have it all: wealth, status, good looks…everything but the right woman.

MILLS & BOON

MODERN

Power and Passion

Prepare to be swept off your feet by sophisticated, sexy and seductive heroes, in some of the world's most glamourous and romantic locations, where power and passion collide.

MILLS & BOON
MEDICAL
Pulse-Racing Passion

Set your pulse racing with dedicated, delectable doctors in the high-pressure world of medicine, where emotions run high and passion, comfort and love are the best medicine.